RECEIVED

JUL 0 / 2022

D0179635

NO LONGER PROPERTY OF
SEATTLE PUBLIC LIBRARY

In
SEARCH
OF A
PRINCE

IN
SEARCH
OF A
PRINCE

TONI SHILOH

BETHANYHOUSE

a division of Baker Publishing Group
Minneapolis, Minnesota

© 2022 by Toni Shiloh

Published by Bethany House Publishers
11400 Hampshire Avenue South
Minneapolis, Minnesota 55438
www.bethanyhouse.com

Bethany House Publishers is a division of
Baker Publishing Group, Grand Rapids, Michigan

Printed in the United States of America

All rights reserved. No part of this publication may be reproduced, stored in a retrieval system, or transmitted in any form or by any means—for example, electronic, photocopy, recording—without the prior written permission of the publisher. The only exception is brief quotations in printed reviews.

Library of Congress Cataloging-in-Publication Data
Names: Shiloh, Toni, author.
Title: In search of a prince / Toni Shiloh.
Description: Minneapolis, Minnesota : Bethany House Publishers, a division of
    Baker Publishing Group, [2022]
Identifiers: LCCN 2021040497 | ISBN 9780764239847 (casebound) | ISBN
    9780764238956 (trade paperback) | ISBN 9781493436033 (ebook)
Subjects: LCGFT: Christian fiction. | Romance fiction. | Novels.
Classification: LCC PS3619.H548 I5 2022 | DDC 813/.6—dc23
LC record available at https://lccn.loc.gov/2021040497

Scripture quotations are from the New King James Version®. Copyright © 1982 by Thomas Nelson. Used by permission. All rights reserved.

This is a work of fiction. Names, characters, incidents, and dialogues are products of the author's imagination and are not to be construed as real. Any resemblance to actual events or persons, living or dead, is entirely coincidental.

Cover design by Kelly L. Howard

Author is represented by the William K. Jensen Literary Agency.

Baker Publishing Group publications use paper produced from sustainable forestry practices and post-consumer waste whenever possible.

22 23 24 25 26 27 28   7 6 5 4 3 2 1

To the Author and Finisher of my faith.

Prologue

Your Majesty, I am afraid the news is not good."

Tiwa Jimoh Adebayo, king of Ọlọrọ Ilé Ijọba of Africa, closed his eyes and lowered his chin to his chest. But even that slight movement was enough to bring a cough to his lips. His shoulders shook with the effort to expel the phlegm that did not seem to move from his lungs. He wiped his mouth, using a handkerchief embroidered with the kingdom's crest, as his chest ached from the exertion.

"How bad is it?" he rasped.

The doctor sighed, lines furrowing his brow. "I am afraid there is nothing more that we can do, my king. The chemotherapy has been too taxing on your body and ineffective against the cancer." He shifted on his feet. "All we can do now is make you as comfortable as possible." His pause stretched heavy in the room, the only sound the king's struggled breathing. "Dare I suggest, Your Majesty, that you present an heir to our great country?"

Yes. Of course. The time had come for the nation to know his heir—*heiress*. The granddaughter Tiwa had never met. He had wanted to remedy the situation, but regrets and pride had lengthened the time since his gross mistake and expanded the distance.

Tiwa wiped his mouth again. "You are right, Dr. Falade." He

rose unsteadily to his feet. "Rest assured, the kingdom will continue to thrive after I am gone."

Dr. Falade bowed. "You have my direct number, my king. Please
call if I can be of service."

Mobo, Tiwa's royal assistant, stepped out of the shadows and
offered his aid, ensuring the king did not stumble as they left the
hospital. A black SUV waited outside the hospital's private royal
entrance. Tiwa had traveled to the hospital for each past visit, but
with Dr. Falade's pronouncement, Mobo would be tasked to move
his care to the palace for the future.

"It is time," the king declared as lush tropical vegetation flew
past the vehicle's tinted window.

"You will call her mother?" Mobo asked.

"Yes." Tiwa sighed. He could only hope his daughter-in-law
would accept his call. He would not blame her if she didn't.

"I will await further instructions."

"Please do." Tiwa nodded at his most loyal friend. Entrusting
the secret of his heir had been a wise decision. "I am not sure how
much my granddaughter knows about her future."

Mobo nodded, his face devoid of all emotion. Tiwa had once
joked that his assistant did not know how to feel, to which Mobo
had replied, *"I feel what my king tells me to feel."* Tiwa smiled at
the memory. Mobo's stoicism covered a mind constantly thinking
and mapping out possible outcomes.

As the driver transported them back to the palace, Tiwa imagined the words he would say to his daughter-in-law. How could he
convince her to bring his granddaughter to Ọlọrọ Ilé? He feared
the number of years that had passed between them would rule
against his wishes. He had not talked to Marie since the time he
begged for her forgiveness—which she had denied. As a result, he
had never once set eyes on his grandchild, now a grown woman of
twenty-five. He had much to atone for before the Lord took him.

Forgive me, Father God. May I make wise use of my remain-
ing days.

Palace guards saluted the car as it passed through the iron gate.
Palm trees lined the driveway as the white sandstone mansion

beckoned up the hill. Tiwa watched his home grow larger. The three-story structure held many memories. Images of his son playing guardsman morphed into those of his funeral. Despite the heavy memory, Tiwa had peace that his son had lived well. Had time not cut Tayo's life short, he would have stepped into his royal duties with dedication and honor.

Tiwa squinted against the sun's light as Mobo helped him from the car. The guards stood sentry as he made his way into the palace and along the corridors, then up the elevator until he arrived at his personal hallway. He leaned against the wall, struggling for breath. Thankfully, no one other than Mobo was around to see his weakness.

Mobo reached for the ring on the African blackwood door leading to Tiwa's personal chamber. The carvings in the wood depicted the coast of Ọlọrọ Ilé with the kingdom's crest in the top arch. The shield depicted a picture of the coastline, and four banner flags fanned out around the shield.

Tiwa nodded his thanks and trudged into his bedroom. His canopy bed beckoned him, but he needed to place the call to the States before he could rest. Perspiration beaded along his hairline as he sank into the wingback chair behind the blackwood desk. After gathering his breath, Tiwa pulled his personal mobile phone from his suit pocket and selected his daughter-in-law's number from the contact list. Although he had not spoken to her in years, Mobo had kept tabs on her and updated Tiwa when necessary.

After four rings, a voice answered. "Hello?"

"Hello, Marie."

"Who—"

"It is I. Tiwa." Silence met his ears. Had she hung up?

"Your Majesty."

He winced at her icy tone. "You are well?"

"I'm fine," she snapped.

She was still sore with him. *And she has every right to be.* If he had not tried to denounce her relationship with Tayo—

But no, the insult of offering her money to disappear had sealed his fate. It did not matter that grief had clouded his judgment. He had harmed an innocent.

Tiwa licked his lips, trying to keep a cough at bay. "My time is coming to an end, Marie. I would like to see my granddaughter."

"What's happened?"

He exhaled, wincing at the ache in his lungs. "I am sick." He grimaced at hearing the admission aloud.

"How sick?" she asked cautiously.

"My doctor told me to get my affairs in order."

There was a pause. "I'm sorry."

"The price I pay for smoking my pipe." He glanced at the empty piece carved from okoume wood resting on his desk. A reminder of what the vice had cost him.

"It's cancer then?"

"Yes. It is . . . extensive." He muted the phone and let loose the cough that had been building. He dabbed at his upper lip and pressed the button again. "Chemotherapy is no longer an option."

"And you want me to bring her there for what purpose?"

He could not tell which emotion lurked in Marie's tone. Was she concerned for him? Herself? His granddaughter—*the princess*?

"She is my heir apparent, Marie. I must ensure the people have someone to lead them and look out for their best interests." Though that was not the only reason he wished to meet her.

"Who will look out for hers?"

Tiwa wished he could say he would, but time was not on his side. "When I am no longer here, the royal council will." They would not be happy to find out he'd kept the princess a secret, but their sworn oath would ensure they came to her aid.

Marie sighed. "She knows nothing."

"I am sorry." He had feared as much. "But it is time to tell her everything."

"*Everything?*"

He grimaced, knowing Marie would not paint him in a good light when telling his granddaughter what had transpired all those years ago. Not that any of what Marie would say would be lies. He had tried to annul her marriage to his son, stopping only at

10

the confirmation of her pregnancy. Then he had signed a check and washed his hands of them.

His head drooped. "Yes, everything."

A long pause filled the air. "I will talk to her."

"*Mo dúpẹ.*" He blinked. "I am grateful, Marie."

"Hold your gratitude. You may not feel that way after I talk to her."

His lips twitched at her dry humor. "Whenever she is ready, I will see to your travel arrangements."

"If we come—and I do mean *if*—we will pay our own way."

"As you wish. Do know that both of you will have rooms waiting for you here at the palace." He would have Mobo see to everything and maybe even appoint a secretary for his granddaughter. She would need one in the upcoming days.

"How long?" Marie asked softly.

He closed his eyes, his heart still reeling from the verdict. "Six months at the most."

"I will tell her soon. Good-bye."

Before he could express his thanks, the call ended.

Tiwa set his phone on the desk. God willing, he would see his granddaughter for the first time very soon.

ONE

Ah, summertime in New York City. Could there be anything better? The greenery of the trees made me smile.
Unlike others, I was a fan of the heat and thrived under
the warmth beaming on me. I wanted to take a moment to soak
it all in, but my mother expected punctuality, and I was already
ten minutes late. I glanced down at my Apple watch. Okay, fifteen
minutes.

As one of NYC's top pediatric surgeons, my mom had to
squeeze me into her fully packed calendar. But when she could, I
considered it a win. I bumped into a man in a suit arguing on his
Bluetooth and sidestepped a mom pushing her kid in a stroller.
Finally, I broke free of the crowd and lengthened my strides.

Nonna's came into view, and I sighed in relief. The Italian
restaurant would most likely be packed at this hour, everyone
attempting to grab lunch before heading back to their offices. Fortunately, it was a school holiday, and I didn't have to worry about
rushing. I bounded up the steps of the stone-marble building and
through the automatic doors. An air-conditioned breeze welcomed
me with a *whoosh*, and my arms pebbled with goosebumps as I
headed for the hostess podium.

"Do you have a reservation?" The cool disdain on the hostess's
face would have put a damper on my mood if it weren't for the
fact that most hostesses in the city had that practiced bored look.

"Yes. It should be under Marie Bayo." I smiled, hoping kindness would chip away at her bad mood.

She scanned the readout before her. "This way." She pivoted on her heels and strolled through the busy dining room. As if Moses led her way, the other waitstaff moved, making the aisle clear for her procession. The restaurant was filled with families, businessmen, and couples bonding over Italian dishes.

A nervous energy filled my gut as I followed the hostess to the second dining area. Mom only ate here when she wanted to share important news. No matter how hard I'd tried to think of what she could possibly want to talk about, my ideas fizzled.

The hostess came to a stop and motioned toward a table for two, then made her way back up to the front of the restaurant.

My mother stood, a grin covering her face. "Brielle, I'm so happy to see you." She wrapped her arms around me.

"Me too." I returned the hug, resting my chin on her shoulder, and soaked up the contact. Two months had passed since I'd last seen her, but the time seemed to span further. She pulled back and kissed my cheek before breaking the hug altogether.

We stood the same height—five feet five inches—though my mother's flats put her at a disadvantage to my wedges. Our thin eyebrows (courtesy of great threading), pert noses, and full lips resembled each other's. But my mother had a great chestnut color to her skin, and mine resembled a lovely shade of espresso. Our long hair did hold the same wave, though mine was black and hers dyed a light brown shade she spent hundreds on in the salon.

I lowered myself into my chair and spread a maroon cloth napkin across my lap. "So what's the big news?"

My mother's dark brown eyes flashed before she gave me a *no-no* signal with her pointer finger. "First, tell me how the end of the year is going. How are your students?" She smiled, the crow's feet around her eyes crinkling.

I shook my head at her diversion tactics but complied. I loved talking about teaching—the joys and pitfalls of eighth grade civics. "They're antsy, ready for school to end. Hopefully the Memorial

Day holiday will ease some of their jitters." I sighed. "I can't wait for our summer vacation."

Mom laughed. "You just like the beach."

Understatement of the year. The ocean was my happy place, and our yearly vacation to Martha's Vineyard centered me. I couldn't wait to return.

"You do too." I rested my elbow on the table, propping my chin on my hand. "Have we done enough small talk now? We could have discussed our vacation over the phone." Not that I didn't appreciate seeing her face-to-face, but I wanted to know her big news.

A grimace stole across Mom's face, lines framing her mouth. Her brow wrinkled, marring her smooth skin.

Unease churned my stomach. "What is it?" The words seemed to stick on the unexpected lump in my throat. Was she ill? Her features held no signs of sickness. No pallor. No jaundice. But who was I kidding? I wasn't the doctor, she was.

"I have a story to tell you, Bri, and I need you to listen without interruption." Mom licked her lips. "I promise to answer all the questions you have at the end. Can you do that for me?"

I nodded, my heart knocking against a wall of fear. Was it worse than being sick? Was she . . . *dying*?

"After graduating high school in Jersey, I came to New York to get a college education. To become a doctor. I'd dreamt of being a doctor since I was a child. I used to pretend to heal my dolls and stuffed animals."

Where was she going with this? I'd heard this tale more times than I could count. My mother enjoyed retelling the story as an example of the importance of perseverance and hard work. It was why she'd encouraged me to be so passionate in my studies growing up. It turned out I didn't have the fortitude to work around blood like she did, but teaching fit me.

Before she could continue, our server appeared with two glasses of water and their complimentary bread-and-oil platter. He took our drink and entrée orders, then moved on to the next table.

My mother's gaze met mine. "My studies were all I thought about until I met your father. He didn't see my dedication to my degree as an obstacle but a challenge." She paused and reached for the bread plate in the center of the table, dipping a breadstick into the small saucer of herb-infused olive oil.

Her languid movements got under my skin. I wanted her to jump to the point, but no one could rush Marie Bayo.

"Your father believed we could be together and still have enough time to devote to our courses." A wistful smile curled her lips. "He passed me notes in the classes we shared, took his meals with me, and studied in the library simply because I was there." She blinked. "Before I knew it, I had fallen in love with Tayo Bayo."

Her nostalgia and the rhyming of my father's name brought a smile to my lips. I used to wish my mother had carried on the tradition with me instead of naming me Brielle, but once she told me it meant *God is my strength*, I'd fallen in love with my name.

My father came from a small island off the coast of West Africa and passed away before I was born. My mother didn't share many details about him with me. It was as if everything about him was too painful to repeat, too unbearable to relive. Which made her words now all the more captivating. I leaned in, eager to hear more about my father.

"As you know, we married one weekend." She swallowed. "Pure spontaneity, and an occasion I still marvel at. It was totally unlike me. We got a license one day and said *I do* the next." Mom exhaled. "I was so happy, Bri. Until—"

"Until he died," I said, breaking my silence. I knew how the rest of the story went.

What would life have been like if I had known him? Growing up, I'd make up reasons he was away, preferring imagined dreams to the truth of his death. I'd pretend he was a spy who needed to save the world from imminent doom. Even an astronaut studying the heavens. Or simply away on a visit to his native country, unable to come to us for whatever reason my mind could conceive. My mother had never taken me to see his birth country, and the desire to visit remained a constant one, but a teacher's salary wasn't conducive to world travel.

"Actually, no."

I blinked. "What?"

"I was happy until he sat me down in our five-hundred-square-foot apartment to tell me there was something important that I didn't know about him."

My breath hitched. What did that mean? Why hadn't I heard this part of the story before?

"His full name was Naade Tayo Adebayo." My mother took a sip of ice water. Then her eyes met mine, piercing me with their sorrow. "And he was the crown prince of Ọlọrọ Ilé."

My breath whooshed out of my body. Time slowed as my pulse pounded in my ears. I stared at her, trying to gather my wits. "Are you saying . . . my dad was a prince? Like, an heir-to-a-throne type prince?" I forced a laugh. Surely she was joking.

Instead of the mirth I wished for, she simply nodded, gaze somber.

"That can't be right. You wouldn't have kept a secret this big from me." Would she? I swallowed. "Did he even really *die*?"

Tears sprang to her eyes. "Yes, baby. But let me back up to that moment in our apartment." She shook her head, her brown hair swaying against her shoulders. "I was livid when I managed to move from disbelief to realizing he was telling me the truth." She pressed a hand against her forehead.

I gripped the napkin in my lap. This was insane.

"I told your father to get out. To leave. And after weeks of me ignoring every form of contact . . . he did just that. He left the country and returned to his homeland without me." Mom's lower lip trembled. "I found out about his departure from a college friend and realized the cost of my pride. I called the phone number your father had left for me, hoping we could work things out, only his father, the king, answered. After I explained who I was, he told me Tayo had died two days before my call." Her voice broke, and tears spilled down her cheeks.

My heart ached, torn between wanting to comfort my mother and fury that she had kept a secret of this magnitude.

She took a sip of water, then dabbed the napkin against her cheeks. "I went to the funeral and was permitted an introduction to the king." Her jaw tightened. "He informed me that he would arrange to have the marriage annulled. Apparently, I should never have been permitted to marry Tayo."

I gasped. How many more twists could there be? I wanted to run away, hands over my ears. But the trembling in my stomach told me to keep listening. To hear the *whole* truth.

"What your grandfather didn't expect was you." Mom traced the condensation on her water glass as a soft smile covered her lips. "When I told him I was pregnant, it changed everything. He agreed to keep the marriage intact and filed paperwork to make our union legal in Ọlọrọ Ilé as well. Although, from my understanding, he kept all that information secret. He then wrote me a check to cover any expenses you could ever possibly have." She paused. "And told me never to contact him again."

I blinked, thoughts whirring faster than a blender. Which controversial subject did I dissect first? "He didn't want to know me?"

"He blamed me for your father's death. Accused me of driving his son to a depression."

"I thought he died in a boating accident," I accused.

"He did, but your grandfather said he was an excellent swimmer and should never have drowned."

I covered my mouth at the image my mind immediately conjured. Could all this really be true? I'd had no reason to doubt my mom before today, but now . . .

"When you were five, your grandfather called to apologize, only I . . ." Mom looked away, sorrow etched into every line on her face.

"You said no, didn't you?"

She nodded.

"And the money? Are we talking about enough to cover clothing expenses?"

"Whatever you needed, Brielle. I tried not to spend it, but . . ." She shrugged.

Certain things began to click into place. "Is that why you pressed me to do cotillion and debutante balls? Language lessons?" She'd known I would need to move in a world I'd never imagined was a possibility.

She nodded. "I used the money to pay for all of those things." She swallowed. "Plus your college education. The rest I placed in an account for you."

Disbelief filled me. "Why?" I whispered. "Why tell me all of this now?"

"The king is dying." Her gaze met mine. "And you are the heir to the throne."

TWO

White noise filled my ears. Heat flushed through my body, quickly replaced by a chill. Surely this was a dream. It couldn't be real. Could it?

My shoulders jerked back, the chair supporting my still form. Judging from Mom's downcast expression, she was serious. I opened my mouth but quickly shut it. What could I possibly say when I couldn't even process my own feelings?

"I know this is a shock—"

"You think?" I blew out a breath, squeezing my eyes shut. How? *How* could she have kept this a secret? For twenty-five years, no less!

"I'm so sorry, Bri."

Seconds ticked by, punctuating the silence and rolling into minutes. Every dream I'd fantasized as a child about my father's life shattered before my eyes. Pieces of who I thought I was, where I thought I'd come from, lay scattered around me. How could I sweep up the debris of my mother's secret and glue myself together again?

A princess?

Mom's concerned gaze snagged mine, and the last fragment of my composure snapped.

I pushed away from the table and grabbed my clutch as I stood. "You don't get to be sorry." My words cracked like a whip in the silence between us. "You should have told me *years* ago." I clenched my teeth as I attempted to remain calm.

"Brielle—"

I slashed a hand through the air. "Don't." I swallowed back more words. "You know what? I'll talk to you . . ." When? I couldn't imagine I'd wake up tomorrow and suddenly have the urge to reach for the phone after the confession my mother had just made. "When I *feel* like it."

"I completely understand that, but the king requested your presence," she rushed out, holding out her hands to stay me. "He has cancer, Bri, and has been given six more months to live."

I struggled for air. This was too much. I couldn't listen anymore.

I threaded my way through the tables, pushing past patrons as tears blurred my vision. My mother called out to me, but I ignored her. Muscle memory propelled me through the streets and down the stairs to the subway. Crowds swarmed into the car, and I resignedly grabbed a pole, trying to keep from falling apart in front of strangers.

I managed to keep myself together until I made it home, but as soon as my feet crossed the threshold, the tears came. Hours later, when my throat ached along with my heart, the waterworks finally ceased. I tucked my hair behind my ears and pushed myself up to a sitting position on my sofa. The streaming show I'd selected had done its job of drowning out my tears, but now the screen asked *Are you still watching?* I clicked *yes*, then shuffled across the living room and straight to the kitchen space lining the wall. Just because I lived alone didn't mean I needed silence to remind me of the fact.

My freezer stayed stocked with ice cream for emergency purposes. After a short perusal of the variety of pints lining the freezer door, I picked one and popped open the lid to scoop out a generous portion. The first taste of salted caramel woke me from my stupor and set my mind to thinking.

Mom had said the king wanted to see me. Since he was dying, the last thing I wanted to be was heartless. But . . . where had he been all my life? Had he really wanted to get to know me when I was five, or was that all about duty?

What about the times when *I'd* needed *him*? Did no one believe I deserved to know the truth? A chance to know my own grand-father and whatever family I had left on my father's side?

I snorted. Mom had the nerve to be mad at my father for keep-ing a secret for a couple of months. I guess she one-upped him by keeping one from me for twenty-five years.

The ice cream curdled in my stomach, and I stuffed the pint back into its spot. *Lord, what am I going to do? How is this even possible?*

My mother *had* to be mistaken. *I can't be a princess.* I walked back to the sofa and grabbed my cell phone off the end table. A quick internet search pulled up the Wikipedia page for Ọlọrọ Ilé. Mom had never said the country's name before, and I had chosen to respect her silence in the immense grief she suffered. Only now I knew why she'd kept the name from me.

I read in amazement as the site listed the reigning king.

King Tiwa Jimoh Adebayo
Age: 78
Born: Àlàáfíà, Ọlọrọ Ilé Ijọba, Africa

He certainly didn't look like a man in his seventies. His bald head shone without blemish, but his mustache and beard were salt-and-pepper. His skin shone the color of deepest mahogany. Perhaps this was an old picture? Maybe I could find a current one showing lines of age.

"Grandfather?" I whispered.

I traced the lines of his face, the jutted jaw that reminded me of the picture of my dad Mom had given me at the age of ten. I scrolled down, searching for a mention of my father. My fingers paused on the screen when I saw his name.

Prince Naade Tayo Adebayo, Deceased

It *was* him. Although, he looked younger in this photo than in the one I had of him. This had probably been taken before he'd even met my mother. He wore a black uniform jacket, and a patterned blue, white, and purple sash adorned with gold medals crossed his chest. Perhaps their royal dress or military uniform?

The Wikipedia page, in a matter-of-fact manner, reported the details of the tragic boating accident that had taken his life, thanks to a bad storm. Was that why Mom had insisted on swimming lessons? No, she'd said my father could swim.

I squeezed my eyes shut. The mere thought of her brought back a sense of betrayal. How could she have done this to me? Tell me I was related to a king and think I would . . . what? Cheer? Give a royal wave while joyful tears ran down my cheeks? I wasn't a beauty queen.

No, but I would be one day. Queen, that was. *Right?*

My head swam, and my eyes fluttered closed. For the first time ever, I couldn't talk out my problem with Mom. Couldn't get her advice and know that everything would be all right. She was the one to put me in this predicament.

Lord, what do I do?

My apartment intercom buzzed. "Brielle, can I come up?"

I took the few steps to the door of my small studio apartment and pressed the button to let my mother in. I should have known she wouldn't leave well enough alone. She liked to externally process and make amends as quickly as possible. I did not.

After unlocking both deadbolts, I returned to the couch, grabbing the accent pillow from the corner of the sofa to hold in front of me like a shield. Two beats later, Mom opened the front door. She stood there for a moment, then closed it before locking the deadbolts.

She set her purse on the end table and pulled the chair from my desk closer to me. "I'm so very sorry, my Brielle." Her words broke the haunting silence and brought tears to my eyes.

I stared straight ahead, trying not to break and run into her arms. *She'd* hurt *me*, not the other way around.

"Please, Bri, talk to me."

"How could you keep this a secret?" I gaped at her. "Especially considering how you must have felt when Dad did the same thing to you."

"I know. I'm so sorry. But I was angry that the king dismissed me. And when he wanted to make amends, I let my anger rule. I told myself we were better off without him."

So not a good enough excuse. "Who *am* I? Is Bayo even our real last name?" It didn't match the Wikipedia page. Then again, anyone could edit the site.

My mother tucked her chin, eyes trained on my pale pink rug. "It's the name your father and I married under. The name I kept over the years." She fixed her gaze on my face. "Your father came to the U.S. under diplomatic status. He enrolled at NYU with Bayo as his surname, and it's legally recognized in the States, although in Ọlọrọ Ilé it's Adebayo."

That news did nothing to erase the bitterness churning my stomach. "So I *am* Brielle Bayo?"

"You are Brielle Eden Adebayo, daughter of Prince Naade Tayo Adebayo and heir to the throne of Ọlọrọ Ilé." Her fingers twitched as if she wanted to reach out and touch my hand. "And you are, as you've always been, Brielle Bayo. All these years you have been *my* daughter. Mine alone to raise and make decisions for. You can't understand the magnitude of that until you become a mom yourself. The weight of knowing that your choices will impact your child's future. Every time I made a choice, I did it as a single mother, a widow. *Alone,*" she stressed.

My heart thumped in my ears. The sacrifices my mother had made for me over the years hadn't gone unnoticed. She'd finished her medical degree through night school while I went to different home daycares. I loved her for her dedication to providing us with a better life.

But that didn't negate the fact that she'd lied to me my whole life. Lied about who my father was. Even about not having family on his side. She'd made them seem like a nonentity, and I'd foolishly thought they didn't exist. Now, knowing that the king had reached out—whatever his reasons—soured the contents of my stomach. She'd *chosen* to be alone.

Mom reached out to squeeze my knee.

I scooted away from her touch. "I can't absolve your guilt right now."

"I'm not expecting you to." She sniffed. "But, Bri, you do need to make a decision for your grandfather's sake."

"Did he not want to meet me before now?"

She licked her lips. "When he called all those years ago, he left the choice up to me."

My stomach spasmed as if I'd been punched. Hearing her confirm my thoughts hurt more than I'd expected.

Mom regarded me, her stare steady, but pain etched into every line that showed her forty-six years. She was right. My dad's father was alive, if only for a little while longer. I now had a very real link to the Bayo—*Adebayo*—side. Someone who could provide the missing pieces of Dad's life and maybe even, by extension, mine. A grandfather to regale me with tales from his youth and answer the questions I'd always had.

And I only had six months to get to know him. To squeeze out the lifetime of memories my mother had denied me.

"Fine," I whispered. I tore my gaze from hers and studied the front door. For my own sake, for the unanswered questions plaguing me, I'd do this. "I'll meet him."

Could I dare hope he wanted an actual relationship with me and not just a warm body to sit on a throne?

"I'll make our travel arrangements."

My eyes darted back to hers. "I need to make arrangements for a long-term substitute teacher first." I swallowed. "And I'm going *alone*."

"Brielle . . ." she breathed out. "You can't do this by yourself."

I didn't want to be thrust into a world—a *royal* world—without someone by my side. But I also couldn't deal with whatever awaited me in Africa along with my crippling feelings of betrayal thanks to Mom's dishonesty.

"I'll ask Iris to go." My best friend could be my anchor.

My mother's lips turned downward, but she nodded. "Then I'll get everything taken care of for you two."

I swallowed back my automatic thanks.

"I'll call you with the info." She took the few steps toward the door and paused. "I love you, my Brielle." Then she walked out of the apartment.

I squeezed the pillow tighter, and my tears resumed. Was I doing the right thing, going to Ọlọrọ Ilé without my mother?

Lord, what am I going to do? How do I go forward?

Did the country's citizens know about me? I hadn't seen any mention of me on Wikipedia, so maybe my identity had been kept a secret from more people than just me. Would this be some *Princess Diaries*–type nonsense where the king's council would do everything in their power to thwart my succession? Did I even *want* to step into my role as heir apparent?

My head flopped back onto the couch cushion. There was too much to think about. Too much weighing on my heart. This morning when I'd awoken, my biggest worry had been wondering what special news my mom had to share. Now I just wanted to close my eyes, go to sleep, and request a do-over. God willing, tomorrow wouldn't hold any more life-altering revelations.

Please, let it be so.

THREE

Iris agreed to meet me for lunch, so I showed up at our favorite spot in Central Park with two lamb gyros dressed to perfection with tzatziki sauce, onions, and tomatoes. The potted plants across from the park bench bloomed a gorgeous lavender color. I set down the takeout bag and scanned the area.

People were out enjoying the mild June temps and sunny skies. Two guys tossed a Frisbee back and forth. A family attempted to fly a kite. A couple lay on a blanket, sunbathing. I shook my head. A cold front had blown in last night, leaving the temperature in the low seventies. Not hot enough to wear a bathing suit, in my opinion.

"You beat me!"

At Iris's exclamation, I rose to my feet. "Slowpoke."

"Maybe I should keep these?" She held a cardboard drink carrier close to her chest.

"I'm glad you're here, Iris."

She set down the drinks, and we hugged before sitting.

"Ha, you just want the Frappuccino." She offered me one of the two drinks.

I took a sip and sighed with pleasure as the mocha flavor cooled my insides. "Thank you so much. I needed this."

"Thank you for the gyro." She saluted me and then took a huge bite, moaning with pleasure. The toppings threatened to spill over as she munched on her food.

So much for sharing my secret right away. Iris would probably choke on her lunch if I told her my news this second.

We ate in silence while the sounds of chattering people and squealing kids surrounded us. Yet each bite I took might as well have been of moldy bread. The secret inside me threatened to upset my lunch.

Finally, Iris stood and gathered our trash to dispose of in the nearest bin.

"You excited for your trip to Martha's Vineyard?" She settled back onto the bench. Her black eyes watched me, and her curly mane dwarfed her face, stealing the limelight from her other features, as her black spiral curls hung past her shoulders. Iris's mom was Caucasian, and Iris had inherited a lot of her mom's delicate features but with a tanned tone to her skin, a nod to her dad's Black ancestry.

"That's actually why I wanted to meet up." I bit my tongue, searching for the right words.

"Oh no! Did your mom back out?" Iris's bottom lip poked out as if a cancelled vacation were the saddest thing that could happen to me.

Twenty-four hours ago, that might have been true.

"Actually . . ." I faced her. "I'm going somewhere else and was hoping you'd come with me." A thought struck. "Oh no, do you even have a passport?"

Iris's eyes widened. "I do, and now I'm curious. Where are we going?"

"Ọlọrọ Ilé."

"Where?"

I chuckled at the befuddled expression on her face. "It's an island off the coast of West Africa."

"Oooh." She clasped her hands together and rubbed them with glee. "Tell me more. Did you win tickets or something?"

Ha! Didn't I wish. I smoothed a hand down my skirt. "Well, it turns out I'm a long-lost princess, and my dying grandfather— AKA the king—wants me to come and take my place in the family." I bit my lip and watched Iris's face.

"Shut up!" She smacked my arm and looked around. "Where are the cameras? Does Ashton still punk people?"

"I wish it was a joke," I muttered.

"Bri, what are you talking about? I didn't even know Africa *had* royalty. Aren't all their countries democratic? I mean, they have presidents, don't they?"

"Apparently not all of them." Five countries belonged to the African Kings Alliance, and Ọlọrọ Ilé was one of them.

Iris studied me. I'd probably worn that same expression when my mom dropped this bombshell. "So you're saying you're really a princess?"

I nodded slowly. "My mom told me yesterday." Bitterness ran rancid in my mouth.

"Girl, tell me everything. Don't leave a single thing out."

I leaned back against the bench and shared all that had happened from the moment I stepped foot in Nonna's. I even showed Iris the many articles that came up when searching the royal side of my family. When my tale was over, I blew out a breath and stared unseeingly into the distance.

"So your last name is Adebayo?"

"No, it's pronounced Aa-DEH-baa-yow."

"Not much different than Bayo."

"It's not. Apparently, Bayo was my dad's diplomatic name. I'm not really sure how that works." I smiled at a dog playing fetch, wishing my life were that simple right now. "I just can't believe she kept this a secret for the past twenty-five years, Iris."

"I know you're angry, and I'm sure that's making everything seem worse." Iris's chin trembled, and tears welled in her eyes. "I'm sure your mother had her reasons. You have to fix this with her, Bri. You'll regret it if you don't." She squeezed my arm.

Iris was a sweetheart and incredibly empathetic. But right now I really wanted someone who would side with me. "Wouldn't you be angry?"

"Of course, but I don't want you to let this fester and ruin your relationship with her."

"Maybe tomorrow I'll try to talk to her. Just not today."

She nodded. "This is really tough, Bri. I'll be praying for you. It all seems so . . . so overwhelming, doesn't it?"

My shoulders sagged. She understood. "Yes!" I groaned. "I mean, do I have any allegiance to a kingdom I just learned about? Would it be selfish to abdicate the throne? Or what if I actually love the place and stay?" Just a few of the questions that had plagued my sleep last night.

"Then please give me a job!" Iris fake-begged, hands fisted under her chin. "I can be your personal assistant."

I laughed, thankful for her friendship and the lighthearted moment. "You don't even know if you'll like it there."

"Well, when will we find out? I'm definitely coming with you."

"Thanks, Iris." My phone chimed, and I saw a text notification from my mother. "My mom said she'd make all the arrangements. That's why I asked about your passport."

"Oh, I have one." She grinned, clapping her hands together.

I unlocked my phone and pulled up my mother's text.

Mom

There are no direct flights. Contacted your grandfather, and he will have a plane ready to pick you and Iris up Friday.

"Friday." I gulped. Suddenly, this seemed way too real. Was I really going to my father's country? Was I really a princess?

"What?"

I stared at Iris. "My mom says our flight is Friday. We'll meet my grandfather then." My hands shook.

Lord, what if he doesn't like me? What if he doesn't think I'm fit to be a princess or . . .

My thoughts trailed off. I wasn't even sure I wanted to be a princess.

"It'll be okay, Bri. We'll get you through this." Iris squeezed my hand. "I'll let my boss know. He owes me some vacation time." Iris worked in the fashion industry, procuring fabrics for James Frederick's company.

30

"Thanks." My heart thumped in my throat, and I held on to Iris's hand.

"That's what friends are for, right?"

I drew in a ragged breath. "If you break out into song, I'm out."

She chuckled, and my tension ebbed away.

"I guess all that's left to do is pack."

"Eek!" She clapped her hands together. "Let's go shopping."

I smiled. "Okay."

We got up and headed for the nearest subway entrance.

Would this be my last time shopping in the city? What kind of clothes would I need to pack? I had so many questions running through my mind and no answers to go with them. At least the weather in Ọlọrọ Ilé could be answered with a quick search on my phone.

"It says the average temps in the summer are in the eighties. Tropical climate."

"This is going to be so much fun." Iris raised her eyebrows. "Do you have to dress fancy since you're a princess?"

"I have no idea."

She waved a hand. "We won't worry about that. If you don't pack the right things, I'm sure there will be shops there. It'll give us a chance to do more shopping."

True. I kept reading about Ọlọrọ Ilé's climate. "We should pack loose-fitting clothes, umbrellas just in case, and light sweaters for the evening."

"Sounds like we're going to have a wonderful time. Don't forget to add swimsuits to the list."

"Right."

We chatted quietly on the subway as we made our way to Iris's favorite boutique. Jolie had a lot of cute clothes along with accessories to dress an outfit up or down and was one of the best shops in SoHo.

Iris always chose some sort of patterned apparel to wear. She had a face that looked good in prints, no matter what. I preferred solid colors because, honestly, patterns scared me. Solids brought out my confidence.

When we arrived, a few other women were shopping and perusing the racks of clothing. I stopped in front of a stand of blue blouses and contemplated the choices. Would any item in this boutique really be a right fit for Ọlọrọ Ilé? I was just a middle school teacher. How could I go from dressing for young teens to dressing for an entire country? Then again, teenagers had strong opinions on what was in and what was out.

"Oh, Bri, look at this." Iris held up a black pencil skirt. "This would be a perfect purchase for you."

My hands trembled. "I can't do this, Iris. I can't be a . . ." I glanced around for prying ears and leaned closer to her. "Princess," I whispered.

"Of course you can. You manage people for a living."

I shook my head. "I manage kids. A whole country is different."

Iris pursed her lips, brow aiming high. "Please. We both know that working with adults is just like working with teens. Don't show any fear, and they won't walk all over you. If they try, you reprimand them as their princess. I'm sure you'll find out what you can and cannot legally do there." She smiled. "In the meantime, you need some smart business wear to show them that you can be who they need. Plus, it'll boost your confidence."

"What would I do without you?"

"Eat ice cream?"

I chuckled. "I was so upset last night that I only had one bite of salted caramel."

"That was your first mistake. You should have gone for the mocha marshmallow."

"Now you tell me."

Iris passed the skirt to me in both black and purple options, grinning. "I'll find some blouses for you."

"How much stuff do you want me to buy?" I started to object, then stopped. Mother had transferred money from the secret account she'd neglected to tell me about into my personal checking account this morning. The money she hadn't spent after I graduated college. I'd been stunned by the amount. "Wait. Don't you need clothes too?"

"Sure, but I don't want my choices to look as nice as yours. You're royalty, not me."

I shook my head and waltzed toward the dressing room. Iris handed me skirt after skirt, blouse after blouse. She even flung an evening gown over the door.

"You'll probably need that for something," she called out.

I peered in the full-length mirror on the dressing room wall. The boatneck top of the gown had been beaded, but the rest of the garment was chiffon, flaring out in an A-line style. This was so far removed from just a little black dress. Could I pull off formal wear?

"Bri, come out already."

"I'm coming, I'm coming." I opened the door and held out my arms. "Ta-da."

Iris gasped, fingers covering her mouth. "Oh, Bri," she whispered. Her hands dropped to her sides. "This dress is gorgeous. You're gorgeous. You *have* to get it."

"What if I don't have a reason to be this dressed up?"

She rolled her eyes. "You're going to be a"—she glanced around—"you-know-what. Of course you'll have a chance to wear it. You'll perfectly slay in that gown."

"Okay," I breathed. "I'll get it and a few of the others."

Iris clapped. "Fabulous. My turn!" She wiggled her hips, then grabbed a pile of clothes from the nearest chair.

I changed out of the gown, and by the time I'd put my own clothes back on and grabbed the items I was purchasing, Iris was ready to do her own version of a fashion show. She got a bunch of dresses that she could accessorize for a day or evening look. I managed to convince her to get her own evening gown—sweetening the deal by offering to pay for it. She went with an over-the-shoulder emerald-green number. The color did wonders for her complexion and added a softness to her features.

Satisfied with our choices, I paid for them all—ignoring Iris's protests—and we left the boutique.

I gave Iris a hug. "Thank you so much. I really needed this."

"Of course. And thank you again for the clothes. I can't believe you did that."

I smiled. "You're my best friend."

"Olọrọ Ilé won't know what hit it when we arrive."

I laughed and hugged her once more. "See you Friday?"

"I'll be there. Make sure you pack that gown in a garment bag," she said as she hailed a cab.

"Yes, Mother." I hailed my own cab and waved good-bye as she left.

FOUR

My stomach burned, threatening to expel my nonexistent dinner. The Uber we'd hired rolled to a stop near the private hangar where Iris and I would say good-bye to New York. The Bombardier Global jet awaiting us on the tarmac would guarantee us a nonstop flight. Despite the lack of stops, the flight was still ridiculously long. It would take about twelve hours to fly to Ọlọrọ Ilé.

I pulled my purse strap over my shoulder and stepped out of the car into the evening heat. My mother claimed flying overnight would be better, considering the six-hour time difference that would be added to our travel.

"Dang, girl, do we really get to travel in that?" The awestruck tone of Iris's voice matched my thoughts exactly. It probably cost my whole teaching salary to maintain a plane like this.

"I know, right?"

"You really are well-to-do now," she said in an upper-crust accent.

Laughter shook my frame.

The driver placed our luggage next to us, and we thanked him. He dipped his head, then got back into his car. I pulled up the app to add a tip. Would we be his most interesting drop-off of the day? Maybe if he knew who I was, not that *I* was even all that clear on my identity any longer.

A tall woman appeared in the aircraft's doorway, and Iris and I walked toward her. Her features were striking. Gorgeous ebony skin, high cheekbones, and a cropped haircut that showcased her petite head. She descended the steps in a regal manner and walked right up to me. She bowed, hands clasped as if praying. "Greetings, Your Highness."

My mouth dropped, and Iris elbowed me.

The woman straightened, a soft smile accenting her cheekbones.

"Um, thank you," I stuttered.

"I am Dayo Layeni, your royal secretary. If you have any questions at all, please let me know, Your Highness."

Your Highness? I was so not ready for this. I studied Ms. Layeni, apparently my very own personal assistant—no, *royal secretary*. "Nice to meet you?"

"I'm Iris Blakely, Bri's best friend." Iris stuck out her hand. "Nice to meet you."

Oops. Nerves had me blanking on my manners.

Ms. Layeni winced but shook Iris's hand. "Nice to meet you, Ms. Blakely." She looked between Iris and me. "Your Highness, I will be instructing you both on our country's protocol on the way to our capital."

Uh-oh. I swallowed down a bout of anxiety as I stood there, feeling all sorts of awkward and nothing close to resembling a princess.

"Is that all you have brought with you?" Ms. Layeni pointed to our bags.

"Yes," I said.

She snapped her fingers, and a tall gentleman who had been lurking at the foot of the airstairs hurried forward. He wore a black uniform with gold buttons down the front. He bowed before me, and as he straightened, our eyes locked.

My breath caught as his dark eyes poured into me. He exuded such a sense of calm that my shoulders relaxed instinctively. I attempted a smile, but the skittering of my pulse had rendered me mute. Something about this man made me want to catalogue his every feature. From the dark beard gleaming against his chocolate skin to the bump on his nose that hinted at a past fight.

"You can do this, Your Highness," he murmured, then took my suitcase before reaching for Iris's.

"Thank you," I murmured.

"It is my pleasure, Your Highness." His deep voice surprised me almost as much as the use of the title. I watched his tall form stroll away.

Iris elbowed me again, squealing quietly under her breath. Good to know I wasn't the only one tripping over the pomp and circumstance. Or had she been captured by the man's looks as well? Had she seen the intensity in his gaze, or had that look been solely for me?

"If you will follow me, Your Highness, we have a long flight ahead of us." Ms. Layeni gestured toward the steps.

"Of course."

I followed her up the airstairs, my mouth dropping as I crossed the threshold and came face-to-face with the interior of the jet.

Lush white carpet contrasted with stark black furnishings. There was a sitting area and a couch, and who knew what lay beyond the hallway near the back. The jet screamed opulence and high-class living.

"Look at this place," Iris whispered.

"I can't wrap my mind around it," I murmured.

Ms. Layeni motioned toward a group of reclining seats in the center of the plane. "You may have a seat anywhere you wish, Your Highness. There is also a private suite when you are ready to sleep."

A bedroom? "Thank you."

"What am I? Chopped liver?" Iris asked under her breath.

I tried not to laugh, thankful her low tone stayed out of the protocol instructor's hearing.

Ms. Layeni turned her gaze to Iris. "Some of these recliners pull into a bed. We reserve the bedroom for the royal family."

"Understandable," Iris said.

I wondered if Ms. Layeni had heard Iris's comment, after all.

My friend and I sat next to each other as Ms. Layeni took a seat opposite me. She pulled a binder from a hidden compartment in the plane's wall and handed it to me. Her mouth curved upward, showing white teeth that had me wishing for whitening strips.

"I took the liberty of putting all of our protocols in one location." She crossed her feet at the ankles, hands resting on her knees. "You can read through them, and then, if we have time, I will go over any questions you have. We should arrive at the capital around ten o'clock Saturday morning Ọlọrọ Ilé time, weather permitting."

She spoke with a lilt to her words. It almost sounded like a French accent, but maybe not. I loved the way she pronounced the country's name. I repeated it in my mind, hoping I'd sound more authentic the next time I said it. *Oh-low-ROW ill-LAY.*

"If reading is not your preferred method of learning, I recorded the protocols on audio as well." She handed me a small electronic device with earbuds attached.

Guilt pricked me. "You didn't have to go through all of that trouble. Reading is just fine."

"I'll listen." Iris took the electronic device from me.

"Your Highness, it is my job to see to any need you may have. I will keep you well informed because there are those . . ." She trailed off, studying me as if she couldn't decide whether to continue or not.

I leaned forward. "'There are those'?"

"There are those who wish to see you fail, Your Highness. I pray you do not take offense at my honesty."

"No, please. Honesty is very important to me." More so, considering the secrets my mother had kept. But how could I trust that Ms. Layeni acted out of integrity? I knew nothing about her.

"Some were not happy to hear of your existence. There is still the old way of thinking, that women should not lead. That they are better suited as wives and mothers."

Iris gasped.

"I see." But I didn't. I could mentally process the words, but how could I comprehend how deep that belief went? Was the society heavily misogynistic, or did only a few men hold those views? Did it stem from the government and flow all the way down to the citizens?

"Why should she trust you?" Iris asked.

"Besides my sworn oath to the throne?" Ms. Layeni arched an eyebrow.

I broke out in a grin. Okay, it was official. I liked her.

"Besides that," Iris said.

Apparently, Iris wasn't swayed. I studied Ms. Layeni, waiting to hear what else she had to offer as assurance.

She gave Iris an assessing look before meeting my gaze. "I have worked for the royal family in some capacity since I was a child. My mother was head housekeeper and groomed me for the position, but I wanted to make a bigger difference." She inhaled, then exhaled slowly. "Your Highness, you are to succeed our king, making you the first woman to rule in our country's history. I will assist you every step of the way to see a woman on the throne and bring our country into the twenty-first century."

"I can get behind girl power," Iris said.

I shook my head. "Hush, Iris." I needed to think about what Ms. Layeni had said. Did she just want me to be a trailblazer, or did she really have my best interests at heart? "How long have you known about me?"

"Since our king had me ready your chambers at the palace and secure your travel arrangements."

What did my existence mean to the kingdom? Had I ruined someone else's chance to reign?

"I appreciate your honesty, Ms. Layeni."

"Please, Your Highness, call me Dayo."

"And you can call me Brielle."

She was shaking her head before I even finished. "Oh no, I will address you as Your Highness."

"What about Princess?" Iris asked. "Am I allowed to call her Princess and still uphold protocol?"

"You can, Ms. Blakely, but I am not her friend. I am a loyal citizen of the kingdom."

"But I could use another friend," I offered. It would ease my arrival, knowing I had an ally on my side.

Ms. Layeni's head dropped, but not before I saw a brief smile.

She may not be able to break protocol, but I was beginning to believe she would stand by me.

"I'll be sure to finish reading the protocols before we land." I'd have to rely on college study habits. Thankfully, my experience as a teacher helped me know how to be a good student.

"I will be here with any questions you have, but first, I must let the pilot know we are ready to take off."

"Thank you, Ms. Layeni."

Dayo nodded and strode toward the front of the plane.

Iris peered over her shoulder, then turned to me, shaking my arm. "Can you believe this, girl? Her calling you *Your Highness*"— she air-quoted—"and instructing you on all you need to know." She held up the electronic device. "Bri, she recorded all those notes. You're legit, girl."

"It's mind-boggling, right?" I paused. "But not everyone will want to recognize me as heir, it seems."

Iris waved a hand. "We won't even worry about that. Between me and Dayo, we'll have you ready to step into your calling like the princess you are." She clapped a hand over her mouth and squealed.

I laughed. "I'm so glad you're coming along."

"So am I. I was so tempted to give my two weeks' notice at work instead of a two-week leave request." She shook her head, tendrils falling from the hair clip trying to contain her massive curls.

"Whatever. You love your job. Besides, you don't even know if you'll like Ọlọrọ Ilé." I gave myself a secret pat on the back as the name rolled off my tongue.

"I looked up photos on Instagram. It's gorgeous. If I can find me a cute guy, I'll trade in my passport if necessary."

My shoulders shook as I suppressed laughter. The plane moved, and I glanced out the window. This was happening. We were really flying to an African island, one near the equator in the Gulf of Guinea. A country I was supposed to learn how to rule.

Lord, please keep my brain from exploding from all of this new information. I have no idea if I'm even capable of this. This isn't a middle school classroom.

I exhaled, trying to push the worry away, and inhaled as I searched my mind for a scripture on peace.

Peace I leave with you, My peace I give to you; not as the world gives do I give to you. Let not your heart be troubled, neither let it be afraid.

I couldn't let the unknown trouble me or make me afraid. I just had to take everything one step at a time. And that first step was seeing this plane land at the capital, Àlàáfíà. Would my grandfather be waiting, or would he see me at the palace?

I supposed I could ask Dayo, but first I needed to read some of the etiquettes of the culture. A twelve-hour flight should give me ample time to dip my toes into my new world. I could only pray the people would welcome me as their princess and not treat me like an unwanted outsider.

Let not your heart be troubled. . .

It was a promise I would have to keep at the forefront to prevent my mind from stressing. I opened the book and began reading.

FIVE

I finished brushing my teeth and put the toothbrush back into my quilted toiletry bag. Despite the nerves eating the inside of my stomach, I'd slept well last night. It could be because the mattress on the plane felt like sleeping on air, while my Murphy bed back home was more princess-and-the-pea style. Now that I knew we were due to land in twenty minutes, anxiety had swallowed the effects of a peaceful rest.

I left the plane's bathroom and walked down the short corridor to the main seating area.

"Good morning, Your Highness," Ms. Layeni's warm voice greeted me. How long had she been awake? She sounded a little on the chipper side.

"Morning." I sat next to Iris's sleeping form, her chair in full recline mode.

"Did you sleep well?"

"I did. How about yourself?"

"I as well. Thank you for asking."

I smiled. "I'm a little nervous. Can you walk me through meeting my grandfather again?"

"Certainly." Ms. Layeni leaned forward. "Our driver will take us to the palace, where the king awaits us for a private greeting. A public ceremony will be scheduled for some time in the future."

That made sense. From what she'd told me, no one knew the king had an heir except for the royal council and appropriate royal staff members. Information about the council had filled quite a few pages in the huge binder Dayo had given me.

"When we arrive at the palace, I will escort you to the king's royal sitting room. You will kneel before him as a sign of respect. Then I will leave to give the two of you privacy."

"Okay." I held back a sigh.

Tiwa Jimoh Adebayo wasn't simply my grandfather. He was my elder and now my king—despite my American citizenship. Dayo's protocol binder explained that kneeling before elders was a tradition I couldn't overlook, even being a foreigner. Still, would it be outrageous to hope for a hug? He *was* my grandfather, after all. Surely, meeting him for the first time warranted a greeting that went beyond royal customs.

I turned to wake Iris, nudging her shoulder.

"Make him go away," Iris mumbled in her sleep.

I chuckled. "Iris, we're almost there."

She opened one eyelid, saw my face, and shot upright. "We're there?"

"Not yet."

"About ten more minutes, Ms. Blakely," Ms. Layeni said.

"How come you look so fresh-faced?" Iris asked, her features puckered with irritation.

"I brushed my teeth and changed my clothes." Not to mention touched up my makeup.

"We haven't even landed, and you're already receiving the royal treatment," she groused as she stood. "Can I borrow your toothpaste?"

"Sure." I slipped it from my bag and passed the tube to her.

"I'll be right back."

"Hurry, before we make our descent," Ms. Layeni warned.

"Oh, can we see Ọlọrọ already?" I moved to a window seat and lifted the shade.

Azure waters spread out below us. An island covered with tropical greenery appeared in the gulf's midst. Certain areas seemed to change the landscape. I assumed those were towns.

"It's so beautiful."

Dayo moved next to me, peering out the square window. "Ọlọrọ typically experiences a tropical climate. The landscape consists of rolling hills, a great lake, a couple of rivers, and plentiful trees. Plus, we have the best beaches in Africa."

I grinned at her. "I love the water. The beach is my happy place."

"Then I suspect you will be very happy here, Your Highness."

I really hoped so. Yet a future of unknowns tugged at me and threatened to weigh me down. Surely the Lord would make some kind of sense out of it for me. *Please, Lord.*

Looking down at the serene waters, I wondered where my father's accident had occurred. Had he been alone? Terrified of the end? A weight pressed upon my chest. I sniffed, pushing the dark thoughts away.

The pilot's voice came over the intercom, interrupting my musings as he asked us to fasten our seat belts. Iris came out of the bathroom and quickly righted her recliner. She *oohed* and *aahed* as the scenery drew closer and a runway finally appeared.

"Is this the public airport?" Iris asked.

"No, ma'am," Ms. Layeni said. "We always use the royal airstrip when traveling by jet."

I couldn't believe how different my grandfather's life was compared to mine. Royal jet. Palace. Royal secretaries.

My stomach lurched as the wheels touched the ground. This was it. I was in Ọlọrọ Ilé. I would meet my grandfather and discover what he expected of me.

Lord God, please, please *let everything work out for good.*

Iris reached over and squeezed my hand. "Are you scared?" she murmured.

"Out of my mind terrified."

"You've got this, and I haven't stopped praying yet."

"Thanks, Iris."

She smiled.

We all stood when the plane came to a stop. I grabbed my carry-on bag and followed Ms. Layeni down the aisle and airstairs. Warm air caressed my skin, chasing the chill bumps away and welcoming me to Africa. I inhaled the scent of salt water and something else I couldn't quite identify but loved all the same.

I scanned the horizon, and my gaze caught on the same tall man who had stashed my luggage on the plane. He held open the rear passenger door of a black limo that waited by the airstrip.

He bowed as I neared and murmured, "Your Highness."

The deep timbre of his voice drew goosebumps along my arms. His dark walnut skin shone in the sunlight, but it was his obsidian eyes that captivated me.

Iris nudged me in the back. "Thank you," I murmured. I wished he had a name tag on so I knew what to call him.

He rose to his full height, dipping his head in acknowledgment.

I slid onto the leather seat of the limo, and Iris and Dayo followed. As the car sped toward our destination, my pulse beat erratically in the base of my neck. I couldn't do this. What was I even doing here?

My gaze darted to my new secretary. All of a sudden, the protocol procedures I'd pored over left me. "I'll go straight to his sitting area?"

"Yes, Your Highness." Ms. Layeni smiled. "You will be fine. You will see."

I nodded, rubbing my hands up and down my pant legs.

"Perhaps you want to gaze at the scenery?" Ms. Layeni gestured toward the tinted windows.

"You're right." I had plenty of time to freak out before seeing my grandfather. Right now, I wanted to take in the sights of Ọlọrọ Ilé. Lush green trees filled the landscape as we traveled down a solitary, one-lane road. "Is this a private road?" I should have been paying attention from the moment we entered the limo.

"Yes. It leads directly to the palace from the airport."

"Where's the palace?" Iris asked, checking my window, then peeking out of hers.

"It is up ahead." Ms. Layeni pressed the Bluetooth in her ear. "Tomori, lower the partition please."

The window separating the front of the limo from the back descended, and I gasped at the sight of the building in front of me.

"Is that it?"

"Yes."

A white sandstone palace with a red tiled roof stood on top of a hill, shining against a forested background. As we drew closer, I noticed the arched windows on the second and third floors of the building. Staircases curved from the left and right, but in the center a majestic staircase led to the ground floor of the palace.

"It's amazing." The fortress was no King-Arthur type of castle, but one that gave a tropical feel and made me think of beaches and warm summer nights.

"Oh, Bri, this is going to be the best vacation ever," Iris proclaimed.

Before I could reply, the car came to a stop. I watched as the guards at the gate checked the ID of our driver, and then the black iron gate parted, letting us through.

I bit my lip as the palace came closer and my journey to meet my grandfather came to a head.

"Please wait for Tomori to open your door, and then I will escort you to His Majesty," Ms. Layeni said.

"And Iris?" I glanced at her.

"Tomori will take her to her room. All will be well, Your Highness."

I nodded. *Right.* Somehow, someway, this would all work out, and one day I'd laugh at how nervous I'd been. I hoped.

The gentleman who'd carried our luggage—Tomori, Dayo called him—opened the door with a bow, and I exited with Ms. Layeni behind me. She assumed her position as lead, strolling through the open palace doors two guards held open. The wooden doors had intricate carvings etched into them, and more carved doors lined the hallways. I wanted to explore, stop and take in the images the etchings depicted, but Dayo Layeni was on a mission.

I followed, thankful for the quiet. Were there no people? No palace employees? Did the palace have secret passageways?

Dayo stopped before an elevator that had been hiding in a nook. "This elevator goes to the royal suites on the third floor. We are almost there, Your Highness."

I blew out a breath. *Lord God, please be there in the midst of us. Amen.*

We stepped out of the elevator, turned right, and headed for the door on the left. Ms. Layeni knocked, and a man wearing a suit opened the door. He had a commanding presence about him that surprised me, considering his short stature. Our eyes met at the same level, his widening as he stared at me.

He bowed, clasping his hands together. "*E k'aabọ,* Your Highness."

Dayo turned to me. "He says, 'welcome.'"

His eyebrows rose. "Your mother did not hire a tutor for you? You speak no Onina?"

"I'm sorry, sir. I don't . . . *yet.* I've been watching some videos on YouTube to learn." My cheeks heated at my admission. How would the people of Olọrọ Ilé see me as a leader when I couldn't even talk to them in their own language? Not very royal.

He nodded, but his expression gave no clue as to what he thought of me.

"Your Highness," Layeni said, "this is Mobo Owusu, the king's most trusted servant."

"Nice to meet you."

"And you, Your Highness." He turned to Ms. Layeni. "He is ready for her." He stepped aside and motioned for us to enter.

The interior walls were a rich cream color with dark, almost black wood used for the baseboards and crown molding. My gaze briefly catalogued the leather sofa and bookshelves lining the wall.

Ms. Layeni caught my gaze. "I will go see that Ms. Blakely is settling in."

My mouth dried out, and I nodded. She was leaving me alone. I stared at the door—the one I assumed led to my grandfather.

"I will let His Majesty know you are here," Mobo stated.

The door opened, and an imposing figure filled the doorway. "He is quite aware."

Although the voice sounded weak, the authority present could not be denied. The royal secretary took one look, then left me alone with the man who had been listed as king on the Ọlọrọ Ilé Wikipedia page.

SIX

The man before me appeared a few years older than the picture I'd seen on Wikipedia. His bald head shone, and there were deep grooves in his forehead, as if he often furrowed his brow while contemplating a royal problem. Vertical lines ran down his cheeks, while a mustache and short beard framed his mouth. His mahogany skin held a sickly pallor that gave away the secret of the cancer invading his body.

"You have your father's eyes." The raspy timbre of his voice shattered the stillness that had enveloped the room.

My breath suspended in my lungs. My mother had said the same thing, but hearing the words from my grandfather brought tears to my eyes. "Thank you." Then, remembering my etiquette lesson from Ms. Layeni, I lowered myself to my knees, tucking my chin to my chest.

"Please. Stand." He stepped forward, his large hand on my upper arm encouraging me to rise. "We are family." His ragged breathing filled the air as his hand rose to cup my face. "*Ọmọ ọmọ*. Grandchild, how I have longed to meet you. To find how much of my Tayo I would see in you." He licked his lips. "And to know you as well."

My head tilted as I leaned into his hands, thankful he mourned the years we'd lost as much as I did. "I have so many questions."

He gave a heavy sigh. "I am quite sure you do. Come." He motioned for me to enter his personal room.

A huge ebony four-poster bed stood off to the left, and a black-and-tan geometric mat covered the cherrywood floors under the bed. Two potted palms flanking the window brought warmth to the room.

Grandfather shuffled to the right, where another sitting area had been arranged next to an office setup. He sank into a woven-backed chair. "No one but Mobo usually comes in here, but we are family." His brow furrowed, and a cough rent the air as his shoulders heaved up and down with exertion.

I glanced around, searching for a glass of water or . . . *something*. Spotting a tray, I rushed to his nightstand, grabbed a tumbler, and filled a glass with ice cold water from the pitcher sitting there. I made my way back to him.

"Drink slowly." I placed the rim to his lips.

My heart shattered as he struggled to still the coughs. I'd hoped the report from my mom had been wrong, but there was no denying the truth. He really *was* sick. My insides twisted, bringing acid to my throat. I placed the tumbler on the nearest end table.

Grandfather leaned back against the cushions, a weary sigh falling from his lips. He dabbed at his mouth with a white handkerchief. "My apologies."

I sank into the seat across from him, swallowing back tears. "Please don't apologize."

"Brielle, I am afraid I cannot blame this on old age. My love for the pipe and cigar has hastened my time." He mopped at the beads of sweat dotting his head. "I am sorry for how we have come to meet. I did not wish you to find out about your destiny this way."

"Then you did intend to tell me?" I leaned forward.

"Of course." He struggled to straighten in his seat. I rose, only for him to wave me back down. "I had plans to contact you in the next couple of years." His mouth tugged downward, deep grooves appearing in his cheeks. "My timetable has been sped up, you see."

"Why didn't you contact me when I turned eighteen? I would have legally been an adult, able to form my own opinion and make my own decisions." My mother wouldn't have been able to keep him from me or me from him.

"Truly?" He stroked the thin beard that connected to his mustache. "When children become adults, they often adopt a sense of invincibility. Maybe even feel they are wise beyond their years. Superior to their elders." He studied me. "Unfortunately, time shows us how young eighteen truly is." He coughed, dabbing his mouth. "I did not want to do that to you, Brielle Adebayo."

His deep tenor settled my hurt, and I couldn't help but agree with the wisdom of his words. Most likely I wouldn't have handled the news any better than I was now. Probably worse.

"Now what?" I asked softly.

"We get to know each other."

"Is that all?" I paused, gathering my thoughts. Maybe I didn't have to dive into the princess issue right now. "What should I call you? King? Your Majesty?"

He waved a hand. "*Bàbá àgbà* or *Grandfather* is just fine. You are a citizen of Olorò Ilé, since you are my son's daughter, but until you decide if you will take the throne, there is no need to refer to me as *King* or *Your Majesty*."

Would I take the throne? Obviously someone needed to. Grandfather wouldn't be around much longer. What would happen to the country if he passed before someone assumed the throne?

I gulped. "Do you want me to be your heir?" How could my words sound so strong while my insides quaked?

Grandfather met my gaze. "I have thought long and hard about this. Prayed to the Lord. Olorò Ilé needs to move forward, and I believe having you on the throne will help them succeed in this endeavor."

Move forward in what way? I didn't ask, because asking such a question when we'd just met felt awkward. Still, I needed some answers. "What happens if I decide not to accept my place on the throne?"

Sadness filled his eyes. "The council will vote either to have my brother succeed or to become a free democracy and dissolve our monarchy."

"Is there a reason you don't want your brother to follow you?"

His mouth drew down. "Yes."

I wanted to ask more questions, but tension had seeped into his frame. Instead, my thoughts turned to the monarchy. How long had Ọlọrọ Ilé been ruled by a monarch? How many years of legacy would I be throwing away if I said no? I needed to know the country's history in order to make an informed decision.

"Has the island always been a monarchy? If not, why that type of government?" I prayed he didn't see my questions as impertinent.

"Those are good questions." He rubbed his chin. "Our ancestors were the ruling tribe on the island before the French and British invasions. Their colonization did not change tribal rule or entirely erase the customs of the Ọlọran people, though their stamp on our country can still be seen today. The council of old was made up of tribal elders, and when we received our independence, they voted on a monarchy to honor our ancestors. The Adebayo family became the ruling tribe, and Ọlọrọ Ilé has operated as a hereditary monarchy ever since."

I let his words seep in. "And if I abdicate the throne, the Adebayo legacy ends with you?"

"If the council does not want Sijuwola, my brother, to continue the monarchy."

Oy. I blew out a breath.

"Granddaughter, I do not expect you to make a decision your first day here. I want you to know this country and its people. To know in your heart that this is the right choice for you."

"But the doctors say you only have six months left. . . ." My voice trailed off as tears clogged my throat.

"Do not let the clock push you into a decision you are uncomfortable with. God's will will be done no matter what."

Gratitude filled me at his proclamation. God had us in the palm of His hand. I didn't need to worry unnecessarily. "Then I will take my time."

"Good."

I ran my hand down my pant leg. "Ms. Layeni said you would

introduce me to the people at a later time. Is that only if I decide to rule?"

Because how easy would it be for me to walk the halls as a mere guest? My grandfather could get to know me, I could see the country as a foreigner, and no one would be the wiser. Right?

"What are you thinking?"

I shared my thoughts.

"Hmm. The idea does have merit. If you do choose to rule, the countrymen will know you did not come here to rule in ignorance." Grandfather nodded slowly. "There are those in the palace who already know who you are but have been sworn to secrecy. If we keep it quiet from the public, then you can move about the country as a tourist." He paused to cough and take a sip of water. "I will have Mobo plan a party for a month from now. If at that time you feel you want to lead our people, everything will be set in motion. If not, then the gathering will just be a party. No pressure, I promise."

"All right." Surely I would know how I felt after a month in the country.

Grandfather rose to his feet. "Come, ómọ ọmọ. We will see if Dayo has your room ready."

"Can you do that?"

"Do what?"

I tugged on my thumb. "I mean, is my room very far away? Can you handle the walk?" Would the excursion cause his lungs to labor too hard?

"I may be dying, Brielle Adebayo, but I am not dead yet."

If the thought didn't chip at my fragile emotions, I would have laughed at the twinkle in his eye and the humor curving his lips into a half smile.

"Come. It will be okay." He extended his elbow.

I slipped my arm in his as we walked out of his suite. Silence settled around us as I tried to come up with something to say. "What's your favorite color?"

"Are we making small talk?" He chuckled.

I smiled. "Is that so bad?"

"No. You tell me first."

"I actually don't have a favorite color. I like them all."

"I am a fan of green."

"Really? Why?"

"To me, the color represents growth. I have never wanted to stay the same person." He peered down at me. "And I hope meeting you will bring about my greatest growth yet."

Tears filled my eyes, and my thoughts turned to my mother. Her bitterness and hurt had kept me from my grandfather—a man who seemed wise and understanding, humble and caring. I could only imagine the many lessons he could have taught me over the years. Now I'd have to cram every last moment into memories and pray they would last me the rest of my life as he said good-bye to his.

It was so unfair.

How could Mom have kept me from this life? Were the words of a man grieving his son so unforgiveable? Not that I was ready to talk to her. I had texted her to tell her we'd arrived and then completely ignored her plea for a heart-to-heart.

Lord, forgive me and help me forgive. Because today, all I could see were the years lost to me.

We walked the halls, sometimes stopping to give him a rest, all the while telling each other of our favorite things. He loved the ocean as much as I did but thought snow an abomination. That drew a full laugh from me as I imagined him in New York, looking horrified at our winters. I didn't hate the snow, but winter couldn't compare to spring. We both had a love for God's creation, and our peaceful place could be found outdoors. Grandfather promised to take me on a tour through the palace gardens.

Finally, we arrived at my chambers. He'd put me in the guest corridor for now, explaining that the suite that used to be my grandmother's was not habitable yet. He hadn't put away her things after her passing three years ago.

Grandfather patted my hand. "I will see you later. For now, I must rest."

I nodded. "Do you need help walking back?"

His breathing had worsened, and I hated to think of how he'd sound by the time he returned to his room.

"I am going to my office. It is closer than my room, but on the second floor."

"All right." *I am so glad I met you. I think I love you already.*

But instead of voicing these thoughts, I smiled a good-bye and walked into the suite that would be mine for at least the next month.

SEVEN

S taff had unpacked my suitcase, placed my clothes in an espresso-finished dresser drawer, and hung others in the walk-in closet. There was an espresso-colored wardrobe in the closet, which held my evening gown. Although Ọlọrọ Ilé was thousands of miles from England, I still checked the back of it for portals leading to other worlds.

Sadly, there was no gateway.

The white linens gave an airy feeling to the room and added to the wonderful light coming from the French doors. I walked out onto the balcony. Gorgeous waters greeted me as I viewed the Àlàáfíà beach. Dayo had said that Ọlọrọ had some of the best beaches, and the view from the third floor confirmed her claim. Sandy coastline beckoned me to come out, soak up the sunshine, and marvel at the beauty before me.

First, I needed to find out where Iris was and tell her about my conversation with Grandfather. I walked back to the main door and glanced in the hallway. Indecision rooted me to the doorway. I couldn't just go knocking on random doors. I didn't know if the staff that worked in this part of the palace knew I was the princess or not. Grandfather had said certain people had been informed and sworn to secrecy, but I'd forgotten to ask just who knew.

I closed the door and pulled out my cell. My cell phone company didn't have a data plan available here but had informed me that I'd still be able to text and call people.

Me

What room are you in?

Iris

Bri! Are you done talking to the king? Dayo showed me your room so I can come by if you're there.

Me

I'm done. In my room now.

A knock sounded on a door that I'd originally assumed led to a closet. I opened it, and Iris stood in the doorway that apparently led to a connecting room.

"We're neighbors," she squealed.

"Thank goodness." I moved back to let her in.

Iris scanned the room and with an *oh!* headed straight for the balcony. "You have a view of the beach! That's amazing. We should go down there."

"What time is it?"

She glanced at her phone. "Noon. Dayo said lunch would be sent to our sitting area." She pointed to the door next to the one connecting our rooms. "That leads to it. She said to let her know afterward if we want to explore the area. She can have a driver waiting for us anytime we need one."

"Oh, but I'm kind of going incognito. Won't a driver be suspicious?"

Iris tilted her head. "What?"

I sank onto the bed—wow, was it soft—and told her my plan not to announce who I was so that I could explore the island as a tourist and get to know the people. If the citizens didn't know who I was, maybe I could get a genuine understanding of what it was like to live here.

"That's a great idea. Sort of like that secret boss show."

I nodded.

"Then how about we just relax today? We can sit on the beach and then tomorrow go out and about. Start exploring and discovering what makes this country unique."

"Sounds perfect. Even though I slept on the plane, I still feel tired." I threw a hand over my eyes. "I could actually fall asleep right now. You know it's about six a.m. in New York."

"Oh, my body knows." Iris groaned and flopped backward on the bed. "I can't believe how soft these beds are. This is going to be the best vacation ever."

I chuckled.

"Bri?"

"Hmm?"

"Did you call your mom?"

I stared at the wall in front of me, noting the art portrait of an African woman. Was she someone important to the Adebayo family or simply a stunning painting found to decorate the room?

"You going to answer me?" Iris pressed.

"I texted her."

"Still angry?"

"Yep."

Iris sat up. "Don't let bitterness take root." She squeezed my arm, then stood. "Let's see if lunch has arrived. Or do you want to change into our bathing suits first?"

"I have to figure out which drawer mine is in." I stared at the blackwood dresser in front of my bed.

"They unpacked for you?" Iris's eyebrows shot up.

"They did."

She grinned. "Love it." She headed for the connecting door. "I, on the other hand, have not finished unpacking, so I know exactly where my suit is."

"I'll find mine and be out for lunch soon."

"'Kay, girl."

Fifteen minutes later, we sat in the sitting area, snacking on mini sandwiches. Unlike Grandfather's room, this one had wicker chairs and couches with plush cushions. I picked up a mini sandwich with cucumber in it. Was this how the people here ate regularly, or had the staff made a special meal just for us? Regardless, my famished self was thankful. I ate more sandwiches than I probably should have.

Iris told me that pressing one on the room phone would connect me to Dayo. I called, asking if there was any special protocol to go to the beach. She came by my room within minutes.

"The palace has direct access to the beach," Dayo informed us as she led the way to the beach exit. "We have asked one of our guards to tail you. He will not sit with you, but he will keep an eye on you. I will introduce you before you two leave."

She turned down a hall. The corridor looked like all the rest of the palace hallways except for the man standing by a door, watching our movement.

When we got closer, he straightened, and a huge grin covered his ebony face. "Ẹ káàsán, Your Highness."

A greeting I knew! "Good afternoon."

The man placed a hand on his chest. "I am Chidi. I will be your bodyguard and driver while you are in our great country. Today I will make sure no harm comes to you and your guest." He dipped his head toward Iris.

"Ẹ seun, Chidi. I appreciate that." I smiled, pulse ticking up in tempo as I attempted to thank him in Onina.

"Enjoy the beach," Ms. Layeni said.

Chidi opened the door before us, and I gasped. I hadn't expected it to lead directly outside. The beach was straight ahead.

"Can anyone come this way, or is this strictly for palace use?" I asked.

"This is a private place for the royal family and guests, but the king still wants you guarded." He motioned us forward. "Go. Enjoy the rest. It is hard switching time zones."

"Thank you."

Iris and I headed down a gentle slope away from the palace and, hopefully, prying eyes. Not that the palace was crawling with people who stared. So far everyone we'd met knew who I was. I guess tomorrow would really show how well the palace staff could keep a secret.

I tipped my chin up and let the sun's rays caress my face as we got closer to the shore. "The sun feels so wonderful," I murmured.

"Isn't it glorious?" Iris stretched out her arms. "Summers really are the best." Her bathing-suit wrap fluttered in the wind.

"I can imagine any day of the year in Ọlọrọ will be amazing with the beach right here."

"Good point."

We found some lounge chairs and took a seat. The warmth of the seat seeped into my bare legs as I exhaled.

"What do you think of the place so far?" Iris asked.

My eyes went from the stunningly blue waters to the dark green palm trees providing shade a few yards away. "I think if I can come out here every night, I can handle whatever comes my way."

Iris laughed. "You and your water."

"But I also have so many questions." I stared into the gulf. "Do you think I'm staring at the place where my father died?"

"Oh, Bri."

Iris's silence was answer in itself. Not that I really expected her to answer.

"I can't imagine what you're going through," she murmured. "Maybe being here will give you the answers you've sought for so long. I mean, your mom never really talked about your dad, but maybe the king will be willing to."

"I hope so. He said I had my dad's eyes." And it was a treasure I would hold dear. "I think he really does want to get to know me. He even told me not to worry about making a decision yet on whether I would be his heir or not."

"You did just arrive," Iris countered.

"That's what he said."

"Good. We'll pray each day that God gives you clarity. Until then, let's explore the island and enjoy ourselves like we would on any vacation."

"I can do that," I murmured. I *had* to do that. If I spent every day agonizing over my decision to ascend the throne after my grandfather's passing, I'd be a ball of anxiety and no use to anyone, especially Grandfather.

I wasn't sure how everything would play out, but a daily reminder that God's will would be done would hopefully keep me focused.

Please make it so, Lord.

EIGHT

Light hit my eyes, and I groaned, turning away to snuggle deeper into the down pillow that cradled my head.

"Bri, wake up."

The whispered plea broke through the fog in my brain. Why was someone in my room?

I sat up when the memory of the past day hit me. I was in Àlàáfíà, Olorọ Ilé, sleeping in the king's palace. My grandfather's palace.

I blinked, and Iris came into focus. She wore a black halter top and burnt-orange joggers. She clapped her hands in childish glee when my gaze met hers.

"Get up so we can go explore, Bri!"

"What time is it?" I winced at the crack in my voice. My mouth held no moisture whatsoever.

"Ten. Dayo already came and left. There's a breakfast tray waiting for you in the sitting room. The king will be busy until dinner, which is at six. So get up, get dressed, and let's go."

"Yeah, yeah. Please tell me there's coffee."

"The coffee here is out of this world. The smell is divine, and the taste brings you that much closer to heaven."

The earnest expression on her face pulled laughter from my chest before my brain could even catch up. I sank into the mattress. "Iris, we are definitely not in New York anymore."

She flopped onto the bed, lying next to me. "We aren't, which is why we need to go explore."

I exhaled. "After coffee."

"And a shower." Iris laughed. "Wash that jet lag off."

"I did that last night. That showerhead is life."

Iris snickered. "You're going to get spoiled while you're here. If you decide not to stay, going back to your place in the city will be another culture shock." She moaned. "Dang, *I* have to go back to New York. Two weeks will be over before I know it."

"Maybe you can extend your vacation to a month? I promised my grandfather I'd stay at least that long before making any major decisions."

Iris bit her lip. "Let me call my boss and see what he says. Go eat some breakfast." She shooed me like a pesky fly.

"Fine, fine."

I got up and headed for the sitting area as Iris left my room through the connecting door. The smell of coffee greeted me, and I made a cup with one sugar cube—they had *real* cubes—and a dollop of cream. With the first sip, my taste buds danced with delight. It was so delicious I followed with a bigger gulp. The drink tasted like liquid gold, and I could feel my brain coming to life.

The breakfast spread caught my eye as I sat on the sofa. Scrambled eggs, a medley of fresh fruit, and some fried bread balls had been neatly arranged on the coffee table. The aroma encouraged me to grab a plate as my stomach made loud demands.

I grabbed a dough ball and took a bite. *Yum.* A hint of spices mixed with some type of bean greeted my tongue. I added another bread ball to my plate along with scrambled eggs and fruit. A few minutes later, Iris walked in and sat on the sofa across from me.

She beamed. "I'm good for a whole month!"

"He was awake?" It had to be o'dark thirty back in the city.

"That man never sleeps," Iris muttered.

"Well, that's excellent." I let out a sigh. Knowing Iris would be here so long calmed my nerves. "I can't believe James gave you the whole month. Who's going to pick out all the fabric for his designs now?"

Iris loved being near all the best fabric warehouses in New York. Mood was one of her favorite hangouts. She also sewed in her spare time and dreamt of being a leader in the fashion industry.

"Well, I still have to do some of the work, but he said I could do it remotely. Since I'm now in a similar time zone to some of our distributors, I can make those phone calls before the other New York companies are open. I figure I'll just wake up a little early and work for a few hours. Then we can explore and enjoy the island, and before I go to sleep, I can do anything else I missed during the day."

It wasn't a perfect vacation, but at least James was letting her stay. "Is he going to hire someone else to go to the shops in your stead?"

"No. We do most of our purchasing ahead of time, so all the current projects are covered. I'll actually be working on next year's fabric purchases."

Phew. "Sounds like we need to celebrate."

"No kidding. Plus, by the time I leave, we'll make sure you know what to do about the whole princess thing." Iris made a crown motion around her head.

"How do we do that?"

"Prayer. And the rest"—she shrugged—"we leave up to God."

Right. I'd spent time last night praying and asking Him to help me forgive my mother, figure out what to do in Ọlọrọ, and make a ton of memories with my grandfather in the limited time we had left together. I still had no clue what to call him. In English, *Grandfather* sounded too formal, but I couldn't remember the Oninan word.

I needed to add *take Onina language lessons* to my to-do list.

"I'm going to get dressed," I announced as I put down my plate.

"Good. The forecast calls for a high of twenty-seven degrees Celsius." Iris scrunched her nose. "I had to look it up. That's about eighty-one degrees Fahrenheit."

"Thanks." I walked back into the bedroom, headed for the wardrobe, and leafed through the items. I chose a maxi dress with a halter neckline. The red-and-blue print dress had a geometric pattern reminiscent of the West African prints I'd seen when doing research online. I'd made the last-minute purchase at a boutique in the city. The dress seemed like the right choice for my first day of exploring. Hopefully I could pull off the pattern with a faux confidence I didn't possess.

After pulling my hair into a high ponytail, adding some earrings, and completing my makeup, I was ready to explore the capital city.

When I walked into the sitting room, Ms. Layeni sat on the sofa, talking to Iris. She rose to bow, dipping her head in respect. "Good morning, Your Highness."

"Good morning, Dayo."

"Ms. Blakely tells me you are going to explore Àlàáfìà." The capital's name rolled off her tongue. *Uh-LAH-fee-ah.*

I repeated her pronunciation in my mind. If I chose to accept my princess responsibilities, I would need to make sure everything was above reproach, including my accent. "Is it okay for us to go sightseeing?"

"Absolutely, Your Highness. One of our bodyguards will drive you where you wish to go. He will ensure no harm comes to you."

"Do I really need a bodyguard when the people don't know about me?"

A small smile tilted the corners of her mouth. "Yes, Your Highness. The king will take no risk with your safety."

I bit back a sigh. "Ms. Layeni . . ."

"Dayo, please, Your Highness."

I could do that, but could she? "Dayo, is there something else you can call me besides *Your Highness*?"

Her eyes widened. "Princess Brielle Adebayo, but only when referring to you to another."

Then I guess I'd simply need to get used to *Your Highness.* Perhaps I could ask her to tone them down.

"If you will follow me, I will escort you to your driver."

"Is Tomori a bodyguard?" I asked. My heart rate sped up as I asked the question. Not that I was nervous, but I couldn't get his dark eyes out of my mind.

"No, Your Highness. He is not."

I wanted to ask more questions but stopped myself when Iris raised her eyebrows.

As we walked down the palace halls, flecks of gold in the marble tiles danced in the sunlight that streamed through the windows. The click of Dayo's heels against the floor reverberated in the long, narrow corridor.

I peeked down a second hallway but didn't see a soul. "Dayo, where is everyone?"

She glanced over her shoulder. "This is the royal wing. Only those who have business on this floor may enter." She stopped at the elevator and pressed the down button. "The elevator has a code that you must know to get onto the floor. I will tell you once we are inside."

The doors slid open, and we entered. She hit 1 and then typed a set of numbers into the security system near the floor buttons. "The code is five-nine-zero-two."

I quickly added the numbers as a note on my phone. Iris had her phone out as well, probably doing the same thing.

When we exited the elevator, the main floor was alive with people moving about. I even spotted what looked to be a tour group and asked Dayo about it.

"Yes, Your Highness," Dayo murmured softly. She then spoke at a normal level. "They give tours every Tuesday to schools. Public tours are held on Fridays."

Dayo led us down so many halls, turning left and right, that there would be little chance of me finding my way back on my own. Finally, we exited the palace to find a white Mercedes sedan idling. Music thumped from the speakers, muffled by the closed doors. Chidi leaned against the passenger side. His hands rested behind his head, and his feet were crossed at the ankles. He shot to attention when he spotted us.

His gaze settled on me. "It is an honor to escort you today, Your Highness."

"It's good to see you again, Chidi."

He grinned and opened the door. "Your chariot awaits, Your Highness."

Iris giggled and nudged me in the back. I slid all the way over and buckled myself in as Iris got in after me.

When Chidi settled in the driver's seat, he turned to us. "Where can I take you? A restaurant to eat lunch? The mall? I can drive you anywhere, Your Highness."

"How about a market?" Iris asked.

Chidi looked at me. "Is that acceptable, Your Highness?"

"Yes. That sounds like fun."

"*D'accord.* Then I will take you to the Àlàáfíà day mart. It is the best."

I blinked at his use of French. "Is French an official language of Olọrọ, Chidi?"

"Yes, Your Highness. We speak French, English, Onina, and some use a Creole of Onina and French. Do you speak another language besides English, Your Highness?"

"I took French in high school." And would now brush up on my vocabulary so I wouldn't feel lost if someone spoke it. "I've been looking at YouTube videos of Onina lessons."

"Oh, I love YouTube. It is how I visited New York. They have walking tours you can watch."

I had no idea. I didn't spend much time on the site. I was more of a picture person. "Have you always lived in Àlàáfíà?"

"No, Your Highness. I am from Bulu. It is on the southern coast. We have magnificent beaches and the best seafood. You should visit soon."

"Thank you. I'll have to add that to my sightseeing list."

"Stick with Chidi, Your Highness. I will show you all the best places of Olọrọ."

Iris squeezed my hand to get my attention, then mimed internal screaming. I peered down into my lap, trying to keep the laughter at bay. The night before we left New York, Iris and I had talked about how different it would be in a foreign country, but the added fact that I was royalty kind of elevated me to celebrity status. Not that I was famous.

I blew out a breath. *Yet.*

I stared out the window. Chidi had rolled his down, and the breeze caressed my skin. Mopeds weaved in and out of traffic. All the vehicles were older by a couple of decades. Or maybe it was simply the design of the vehicles that made them appear aged. Their square silhouettes reminded me of the cars in '90s movies.

Chidi turned off the main highway and onto a dirt road. People strolled along the grass shoulders. A few families had small children with them. A group of women carried baskets of goods on their heads as they all headed in the same direction. I shifted to get a better view and looked through the front windshield. A sea of canopied tents spread before us in a rainbow of colors.

Chidi slowed the car. "Your Highness, cars are not allowed within the mart." He pointed to the right. "I will pull over and park there, but I can let you out now so you will not have to walk in the mud. I promise I will not let you out of my sight."

"Thank you."

"You too, Ms. Blakely."

Iris smiled her thanks as we got out of the vehicle and waited while Chidi maneuvered the car and parked at the end of the row.

"I'm going to start calling you *Your Highness* at the palace," Iris stated.

I raised an eyebrow. "Please don't. Someone has to keep me humble."

She snorted and nudged me with her arm. "Like you would ever get a big head. You're too grounded."

"Whatever. Having people treat you like you're better than everyone else would make anyone's head blow up."

"Not you, Bri. No matter what happens, I know you'll let God remain your king."

I wrapped an arm around Iris. "I love you, girl."

"Love you too. Now, let's follow Chidi and go exploring."

NINE

The Àlàáfíà Mart consisted of wooden booths with cloth canopies. Each owner called out to customers, and my ears registered multiple dialects. Somewhere here was a food booth, because my stomach danced at the tantalizing smell of candied goods. My gaze couldn't settle on just one thing as it jumped from booth to booth to booth. They were filled with food, blankets, dresses, and more.

Iris squealed when she spotted some colorful headwraps. "I *have* to get one. Or two." She smirked.

I laughed. "I want to look at the food." More accurately, the chocolate booth I'd spied.

"Split up?" Iris asked.

"And meet right back here?"

She nodded. "Thirty minutes?"

I agreed.

Iris turned to Chidi. "You'll watch over Bri?"

"Of course, Ms. Blakely."

Iris beamed and dashed toward the beautiful scarves. I headed for the cocoa booth, noting that Chidi stayed a few paces behind me. Each step brought me closer to the tantalizing scent coming from the booth. But then I saw a stand selling flowers tucked into a corner.

I changed directions and smiled at the lady.

"Ẹ káàárò, *omidan.*"

"Ẹ káàárò." I didn't repeat the second word, not recognizing it. The woman tilted her head. "*Parlez vous français ou anglais?*"

My brain perked at the switch to French. Obviously, my Oninan pronunciation gave me away as a foreigner. "*Je parle anglais.*"

"Sorry, miss. Good afternoon."

My shoulders righted at the familiarity of the English words. "Good afternoon. These flowers are beautiful." I couldn't identify most of the blooms, but that didn't stop me from admiring the gorgeous variety and array of bright colors.

"Thank you, miss. Do you see anything you like? A favorite flower, perhaps?"

"I do love orchids." So much so that I'd toyed with the idea of a small tattoo of the elegant flower on my right shoulder. The only thing that stopped me was a fear of needles.

"Ah, miss, I have the perfect one for you." She reached across the stand and picked up a beautiful violet orchid. "Elegant just like you." She smiled, her cheeks bunching with the movement. "It requires a spritz of water about once a week."

A new voice joined our conversation. "Let me get that for you, Your—"

I whirled around. "Brielle," I interrupted.

The voice didn't belong to Chidi. I'd been so enchanted by the flowers, I'd missed another person joining me at the stall. Someone who knew my identity.

Tomori.

He tilted his head in question, and I gave a slight shake of mine.

"Okay. Miss . . . Brielle, let me buy you the orchid as a welcome to Ọlọrọ."

My pulse fluttered at his direct gaze. Those gorgeous dark eyes had invaded my sleep and were making my cheeks heat. How had I missed the long eyelashes framing his eyes before?

"Please?" he asked.

I blinked. "Thank you, but that's not really necessary."

"It is a gift. Just to brighten your days while here."

I studied him. "All right."

He handed over a couple of Ọlọran francs and passed the potted plant to me. I inhaled the scent of the orchids. This moment felt like a hug from the Lord. A reminder that He saw me in the midst of the turmoil of discovering who I was and the betrayal of my mother. Despite it all, there was still something to be grateful for, and I had a God who cared.

I peered up at Tomori, who had to be a few inches over six feet tall. "This means a lot to me." I held up the flower. "Thank you."

"You are welcome, Your—Brielle." His brow furrowed, and he lowered his voice. "Do you have no escort?"

"I do." I matched his tone. "Chidi is a few paces that way." I flicked my eyes to the right.

"But you have come as . . . yourself?" The extra lilt he added turned the statement into a question.

I gestured for us to walk, hoping that looked a little less conspicuous and wouldn't draw unnecessary attention. "I need a chance to learn about the island, the people. I can't do that as . . . you know. I have to be Brielle." I shrugged. Did that sound as vague and confusing to him as it sounded to my ears?

Tomori nodded slowly. "That is very wise. I think you will learn a lot."

"Really?" I bit my lip. "I admit I'm a little overwhelmed." Why was I admitting this to him? But sharing my worries eased my burden, and I had a strong sense that Tomori was trustworthy.

"Yes. If you are just Brielle, then you will be treated as such. You may learn secrets the"—he looked around—"king might not learn."

Peace filtered into my heart. I might not know what I would do at the end of the month, but I was moving in the right direction. "Good. Then that means you can call me Bri."

His eyes widened. "I am not sure that is wise. What if I see you elsewhere? I cannot call you Bri *there*."

"I think you can handle it."

He rubbed his beard. "I will try." He extended his hand. "I am Tomori Eesuola."

Tuh-MOOR-ee EE-soh-la.

"Or you can call me Mori, if it is easier."

"No, I like Tomori." But knowing I could call him a nickname made me want to grin.

"And Brielle is nice. It is French, right?"

I nodded, but the joy I normally felt at sharing my name's origins wilted. Had my mother picked a French name because of my father? I could no longer trust the story behind her choice infallibly.

"Do you know what it means?"

"Yes. It means 'God is my strength.'"

Tomori studied me. "Do you believe in the Lord, Brielle?" He placed emphasis on my name, stretching it into two words like the French instead of making me sound like a Brillo pad.

"I do."

The corner of his lips ticked north. "Then I am sure He will make your time here a success."

"Do you think so?"

"I do. He will not waste your efforts."

I hadn't thought of it like that. "But how do I know if I will be a good leader? Of an entire country, no less?"

"I am not sure that is a conscious decision a lot of monarchs get to make. They are born into their role and learn to accept it. Then their choice becomes whether or not they will leave a legacy to be proud of or one of shame."

Born into their role. When my mother told me my dad was a prince, being born into the royal line had been a simplistic thought. Tomori's words gave me pause. What kind of legacy could I leave behind?

"Did I overstep?" he asked.

"No." I smiled. "You made me think, actually." I sighed. "I have a feeling I'll be doing that constantly."

"Then make sure you save time for pleasure too, Your—I mean, Brielle."

I regarded him. "What do you do for fun?"

"I like to fish."

Àlàáfíà sat on the western shore of Ọlọrọ. Did he fish there or maybe in Bulu, where Chidi was from? "Do you fish along the coast?"

He shook his head. "Lake Opolopo. It is about an hour from the city, up near the hills."

"Near the Fadaka River?" I had spent some time studying a map of the country. Granted, I didn't have every city, hill, or river memorized. Fadaka had stuck in my mind because it emptied into the lake.

"Yes."

"Maybe you could teach me how to fish." My lips quirked in a smile, and I quickly schooled my features. I didn't want to come across as a flirt. That probably wasn't princess behavior and definitely not my normal behavior. Still, I couldn't deny Tomori was a ten on my personal good-looks meter. His beard and mustache only enhanced the line of his jaw and the curves of his lips. Usually I found a clean-cut look more attractive, but the facial hair suited him. Plus, there was something about him that made me feel distinctly feminine.

Tomori stopped walking and peered into my face. "That could be arranged."

"Then I look forward to it." I motioned for us to continue. "What brings you to the market?"

"I am going to visit my mother soon and wanted to bring her a gift."

"That's sweet." *He brings his mom gifts!* The urge to swoon had me wanting to fan my cheeks. *You're only here for a month, remember?* I cleared my throat. "Tomori, what do you do at the palace?"

"Bri!"

I whirled around at the shout of my name. Iris jogged toward me, a huge grin on her face.

"I thought I'd lost you, but then I found Chidi, and he said you went this way and—oh, girl!" Iris inhaled, then let out another stream of words. "I found a booth that had the *cutest clothes.* They sell jumpsuits, skirts, and dresses. We have to go back and add some items to our wardrobes, especially you. Oh!" She stopped, eyes finally settling on Tomori, who stood next to me. Iris blinked. "I know you."

Tomori inclined his head. "Nice to see you again, Ms. Blakely."

"Yes! It is." Her eyes found mine. The slight widening and flickering toward Tomori was code for *What is going on between you two?*

I smiled and gave a slight shake of my head to let her know absolutely nothing was going on. Nothing could. I was either just visiting the island of my father or would take a crown that would prevent me from having an ordinary life where boy meets girl.

Iris pursed her lips, then continued talking as if we hadn't finished a silent conversation. "So do you want to see the booth?"

"Yes, please." I turned toward Tomori, holding up the orchid. "Thank you again."

He dipped his head. "My pleasure. Until next time."

A shiver went down my spine at the promise of his words.

Nothing can happen. Just keep saying that until it sinks in. I waved good-bye and followed Iris, wishing my walk with Tomori could have lasted a bit longer.

TEN

Chidi kept the windows down as he drove us back to the palace. Floral scents mingled with that of the coconuts hanging heavy on the trees. I couldn't get over the vast sky or the quiet of the city. Island life was worlds different from New York, where you had to go to Central Park in order to get away from the crowds and find shade not provided by a skyscraper. Àlàáfíà wasn't a city with a garden in the middle but a tropical paradise with a city in it.

If the smells riding on the wind weren't enough to convince me how far from home I'd come, then the colorful homes dotting the lush green foliage would. There were no doormen, no brownstones, no high-rises. The houses were brilliant in shades of yellow, blue, green, and coral.

I wanted to take in every sight, catalogue every memory in case I decided not to stay, but my mind constantly circled back to my conversation with Tomori. Could I accept my birthright and the fact that I was born to be a princess? Would that lead me to step willingly into a role where I could leave a legacy to be proud of? To take up the mantle of the Adebayo name and people?

Never had I been one to shirk my duties. I was always the kid cheerfully sitting in the front row, hand in air, asking the teacher all sorts of questions, eager to dive into a world of learning. I was

Hermione without the wand. Yet the thought of accepting my royal heritage and saying yes to life in Ọlọrọ made my stomach swirl faster than an ice cream churner.

Not for the first time, I wanted to call my mother and get her opinion. Except an overwhelming bitterness clawed at me and made tears spring to my eyes just thinking of her. If she had been honest with me and told me about my father's family, this would be so much easier to bear. I could have grown up knowing what was expected of me and simply stepped into my inheritance or abdicated if I believed myself to be unfit. Mom had taken the choice from me and thrust me into chaos, complete with a dying grandfather.

If he died before the month was up, the country would be in turmoil. Who knew how it would affect their government and the common man? I sighed.

"You're thinking awfully loud over there," Iris stated quietly.

"I can't get my brain to stop overanalyzing."

"I imagine it'll be in overdrive for a while, Bri."

I looked at Iris, glanced at Chidi happily singing along with the radio, then met her gaze once more. "What do I do? If I say yes, will my inexperience be worse than if I abdicate?"

Iris's brow furrowed. "But you can always learn. I'm sure Dayo and whoever else could teach you all you need to know. Inexperience isn't necessarily a problem. Are there others who are smarter and know how to handle everything better? Yes. But you also have to remember that everyone has a starting point. Yours just happens to be in your twenties."

I worried my lip. "And if I abdicate?"

"Talk to the king. You're going to be dining with him tonight. Maybe that's the next step to take. Weigh the pros and cons."

Iris made sense, but my insides continued to contort like the best Cirque du Soleil performer.

"Want me to say a prayer?" Iris asked.

"Please."

"Dear Lord, I come to You on behalf of my bestie, Brielle. Lord, You know her thoughts, her wishes, and desires. And most of all,

You know what her future holds. Nothing is outside of Your sovereignty or greatness. Please make Your will plainly known to Bri so she can take the necessary steps going forward. If Your will is for her to remain here, then may she step on the path with a boldness that can only be attributed to You. If she needs to return to New York, give her peace and bless her time here with her grandfather. Whatever Your will may be, please bring a measure of peace to Bri. In Jesus's name, amen."

"Amen." I wiped my eyes. "Thanks, Iris."

"Anytime."

My shoulders still held tension, but a calm had begun to filter through the tightness in my chest. God had this. Whatever He called me to, He would equip me and be with me every step of the way. I just had to keep reminding myself of that instead of counting the numerous troubles that could occur. Focusing on *what-if* would sink me faster than Peter walking on water.

The palace guards waved Chidi through the gate, and he drove to the same spot where he'd picked us up. He turned in his seat. "It has been a pleasure driving you, Your Highness." He turned to Iris. "Ms. Blakely."

"Thank you," we chorused.

"My pleasure. Please let Ms. Layeni know if you need a ride anytime, night or day." He got out and opened the car door for us.

"I will. Have a good day."

"You too."

We ambled up the walkway to enter the side of the palace. The guards gave us nods and opened the door. Did these guys know I was the princess? Their stoic expressions didn't give anything away. Perhaps I should ask my grandfather who in the palace knew of our familial tie.

"I got a message from work," Iris said, thumbs flying across the screen of her cell phone.

"Are you reading email on your phone?" Maybe I should buy a phone with a local carrier so I could get full data features. I should probably ask Dayo about that.

"No, texting. I can't get email on my cell. When I spoke to James this morning, I let him know I could only call and text. He's been messaging me like a madman ever since."

"Well, you did leave during your buying season."

Iris nodded, deep in the throes of texting her boss.

"He wants me to broker a deal here. Apparently, he's been trying to break into the West African textile trade."

"Huh." I had nothing else to add. An overwhelming sense of inadequacy flooded me. How could I run a country if I didn't even know about trade items? I was pretty sure that issue was high on the list to know.

Breathe, Bri. You can learn.

We took the elevator to our quarters and parted ways in the hallway. Jet lag weighted my eyelids, and the welcoming white comforter beckoned to me. I opened the French doors to let in a cool breeze, then pulled the netting around the canopy bed closed and lay down for a nap.

A text notification chimed, waking me from a labored rest thanks to an awful dream that didn't require a psychologist to decipher. I held a tiara in my hands, putting it on and taking it off. Even in my dreams, I couldn't decide what to do.

I looked at my cell.

Iris
Ready to eat?

Me
Give me five.

Iris
K

I went into the black mosaic-tiled bathroom and redid my makeup after checking to ensure my hair looked okay. I hadn't wrapped it for the nap, though I probably should have. A quick brush smoothed the flyaway strands. Thank goodness my locks were maintaining their sleekness in the tropical air.

A moment later, Iris and I followed Dayo down the corridor as she explained how there was a formal royal dining room used to host dignitaries and other political figures, and then one for the family's casual use.

Family. Why hadn't I thought of anyone outside of my grandfather? I hadn't asked about his brother, who would be my great-uncle. But did I have cousins? Aunts and uncles? He had briefly mentioned my grandmother's passing, but who else was still alive? I placed a hand on my stomach. Would they like me, or had my arrival shaken up the hierarchy of power?

Lord, please . . . I didn't know what to pray. Maybe that it all went well and I could add some family to the small circle of me and my mother.

Before I could continue my thought, Dayo stopped in front of a pair of blue carved double doors. Depictions of a family eating had been etched into the wood grain.

"These doors are beautiful," Iris said.

"They are as old as the monarchy." Dayo smiled and opened the door. "Enjoy your meal, Your Highness, Ms. Blakely."

"Are you not joining us?" I asked.

"No, I do not eat in the family quarters. I will be eating with the rest of the staff."

"Oh. Thank you for showing us the way."

"My pleasure."

I walked into the dining room, and my stomach dropped to my toes. There were five other people in the room besides my grandfather, all dressed in suits and dresses. Were they other members of my family? I was glad I'd been instructed to wear my pencil skirt and blouse, or I would have been severely underdressed.

"Whoa," Iris murmured at my side. "Not what I was expecting."

Same.

"Brielle, welcome." My grandfather rose from his seat at the head of the table. The exquisite rectangular piece held about ten black chairs, four on each side and one on each end. Underneath the place settings, I spotted a geometric design painted on the black wood.

The men and women—my *family!*—turned at my grandfather's

greeting. Conversation stopped as Iris and I were openly scrutinized. A young woman, maybe even teenaged, gave me a small smile. The others looked very somber.

"Come, ómǫ ǫmǫ, come." The king reached out his arm, motioning forward with his hand.

I walked past the onlookers and came to stand beside him. My stomach heaved up and down as I fought to breathe steadily.

"Ah, Iris. You too. Come, let me introduce you both."

Iris smiled at him once she stood next to me. I should have smiled too, but I was too busy trying to prevent a *Who are these people?* look.

"Everyone, please welcome Brielle to the family. As I told you earlier, she is Tayo's daughter." My grandfather rested an arm around my shoulders and squeezed. "I am so very happy she has joined us." His eyes teared up, and he looked away before coughing into his handkerchief.

I grabbed his port glass and handed it to him as he dabbed at his mouth.

"Thank you," he whispered. He straightened his shoulders. "Brielle is here to visit and get to know us all a little better. Her friend, Iris Blakely, will be staying with us as well. Please stand and introduce yourselves." My grandfather sank into his chair and motioned for Iris and me to take the two empty seats to his right.

We sat, and the man across from me rose and bowed slightly. "Ẹ kúròlé, Brielle. I am Sijuwola, your great-uncle. Allow me to introduce the others."

His manner was cordial, but there was an undercurrent I couldn't quite put my finger on. Maybe my great-uncle was one of the people Dayo had warned me about.

"This is my son, Maseso."

Sijuwola laid a hand on the shoulder of the gentleman next to him, who was in his forties. He dipped his head, his lips thinned with . . . irritation, perhaps?

"His wife, Fade."

The woman sitting next to my cousin—would he be a second cousin or one of those removed ones?—pursed her lips, giving me a little head tilt.

"Their daughter and my precious granddaughter, Ola."

"Digi," the young woman proclaimed, arching an eyebrow. She met my gaze. "I'm Digiola, but I prefer Digi, *not* Ola."

"Watch your tone," Fade ordered.

My uncle sat, and I turned to the man sitting next to Iris. Why hadn't Sijuwola introduced him?

"Ah yes." The man in question rose. "I suppose it's my turn." He peered down at me. "I am also your great-uncle. Perhaps a little illegitimate, but an uncle nevertheless."

"Lanre," Sijuwola censured.

Lanre smirked at his . . . brother?

"I am Olanrewaju, but everyone calls me Lanre." He sat down.

What had I stepped into? Yet Grandfather acted like nothing was amiss. He wiggled his pointer finger, and staff members stepped forward from their places along the walls.

A server wearing a purple tunic stepped to my side, bending to lower a large covered plate onto the table. He lifted the bell-shaped dome to reveal spiced boiled shrimp layered in a circle. I inhaled the wonderful aroma.

Plates were set along the length of the table, one after the other, containing a brown spiced rice, bread, and other exotic items I couldn't identify. The aroma of peppered spices filled the air, and my stomach rumbled in anticipation.

"Everything smells so good," I told Grandfather.

"Yes, but it may taste a bit spicy for you, my dear. Ọlọran food has a kick." He winked.

"My king," Maseso said, "may I bless the food?"

"Please do."

We bowed our heads.

"Father God, we thank You for the abundant blessing of this bounty. We pray that it nourishes our bodies and souls and strengthens us for the work You have called us to. Amen."

"Amen," everyone chorused.

"Brielle," Grandfather said, "try the catfish. We have the best seafood in West Africa." He grinned with pride.

I loved most seafood, but fish turned my stomach and made me wish for mouthwash. Instead of sharing this, I took a small piece, grateful I didn't have to grab a piece with the eyes still hanging on. I put the glistening white meat onto my plate. Iris's slight gasp reached my ears.

"Shh," I whispered, gathering up the nerve to take a bite.

Her slight snicker was the only response I got. She probably already had a comedic reel going through her head of my impending downfall. I could only pray my gag reflex wouldn't kick in.

"Try it, try it," Grandfather urged.

I cut a slice and placed it in my mouth. My taste buds curled up into a fetal position as the back of my tongue tried to eject the offender. The food didn't even make it near my throat. Hoping to swallow quickly to end the torture, I forced it backward—

And choked.

I reached for my neck, forced a cough and then another, then sighed in relief when I could take a full breath. The fish no longer blocked my windpipe.

A soft *thwap* echoed from the other side of the table, and my eyes widened in horror when they landed on the piece of fish that had been in my mouth. I watched, stunned, as it slid down Uncle Sijuwola's face.

"Oh no!" I shot to my feet. "I'm so sorry."

He wiped his face, one eye squinted shut. He opened his mouth and—

"No harm was done, right?" Grandfather asked, a twinkle lighting his eyes.

Sijuwola looked at Grandfather for a moment, then back to me. "Right," he said through gritted teeth.

Was he lying because Grandfather was his king or because of who I was? "Are you sure you're okay?" I asked.

"I may have gotten a piece of fish in my eye, young lady, but it takes a stronger attack to waylay me. Now, if you would excuse me." He stalked out of the dining room.

I sat back down slowly, trying to ignore the gaze of everyone else in the room. Was this how my future would be, full of people waiting to see what I would do? That wasn't even throwing social media and world news into the mix. I'd be a pariah.

I leaned close to Grandfather. "Maybe I should go back to my room."

"Nonsense. Besides, I want to talk to you after dinner."

"And I you."

"Then eat."

Iris squeezed my arm in comfort. How I wished I could bury my face in her shoulder. Maybe we would laugh about it later, but for now, humiliation burned my cheeks.

ELEVEN

Silence greeted me as I sat on the couch in my grandfather's sitting room. I took a sip of decaffeinated coffee, trying to block the mortification of the fish fiasco.

"I am sorry, Brielle. Perhaps I should have introduced you to the rest of the family slowly." Grandfather heaved a sigh.

"It's okay. That was everyone, right?"

"Everyone of consequence. I did not bring other cousins and their children into the mix. I am sure there is a time for you to meet them if you so desire."

"What do you mean 'of consequence'?"

"Well, it has been assumed that I would turn over the reign of Ọlọrọ Ilé to Sijuwola. He has a son, and Maseso already has a daughter. But Sijuwola wants to stay in the old ways. He is very traditional, and I think it is time for Ọlọrọ to come into the twenty-first century. And I could not introduce you to him without also giving you a chance to meet Lanre. He does not have an official capacity because of his illegitimacy, but he does work for the kingdom."

My head spun, and I blew out a breath. "At least the major introductions are over with." And hopefully fish would not be on the menu in the future. That, or I'd learn how to choke it down.

He chuckled. "Rip off the bandage, eh?"

"Exactly." I smiled, watching him.

Whenever we were together, I couldn't keep my eyes off him.

It was like I had to memorize every feature for future reference when time and his passing widened the gap between then and now. Like the lines that furrowed his forehead with every expression. They tilted up when he smiled, deepened when he thought, and wrinkled when he frowned.

"Your father was the same way. He did not want to prolong the waiting, as he would say."

My breath caught. "Tell me about him."

"Tayo?"

I nodded.

He studied me. "Does your mother not speak of him?"

"It's too painful." At least that was what she'd always said. Now I wondered if she'd lied to avoid telling me who he really was. Not just her husband or my father but the crown prince to the kingdom of Ọlọrọ Ilé.

"I understand the agony of loss. It strikes deep and hits each person differently. She lost a spouse, something I have experienced as well. But losing Tayo, a child . . ." He coughed into his handkerchief. "Children should not pass before their parents."

I stared into my coffee cup. I'd lost a father before I'd ever known him, a loss that I equated to phantom pain. My heart grieved because the world told me I should have two parents. But having never shared a life with him, I wasn't exactly sure *who* I was missing.

"I can never decide if I've been saved from a deeper grief by my father dying before my birth or missed out on the greatest relationship." Did God spare me, or did death cheat me?

"Oh, ómọ ọmọ, you have been cheated and maybe, in God's wisdom, spared as well. Tayo was my delight and joy. Your grandmother and I had been married for ten years and had given up all hope that we would ever have a child." He rubbed his knees. "You can only imagine your uncle's joy at the thought that the throne would revert to his line because of my inadequacies."

"How does that work? The line of succession?"

"It is a direct inheritance going to the first child regardless of gender. Hence why you are allowed to rule. Some of the council members were not happy when I informed them of you *and* your gender. Not to mention that you have been brought up as an American and know nothing about our ways." He waved a hand. "But if there is no successor, then the line can revert to a sibling or the council can vote to move to a more democratic type of government." He took a sip of water.

Dayo had already hinted at the discontentment of the council, and now Grandfather had explained my great-uncle's problem with me. Should I add this to the cons side of my list? Sijuwola probably already had plans in place for when he became king.

"Tayo was born a month before my wife's and my eleventh anniversary," Grandfather said.

I focused on him, eager to hear something new about my father.

"He was an absolute joy, which was why we called him Tayo. It means *joy*. Although we also had to give him a royal name, hence Naade."

Grandfather stared at something over my shoulder, a slight crook to his smile. "He got into everything. Took apart everything he could find. He was very curious."

I smiled, imagining my father as a child. "Did he play outside a lot?"

"Oh yes." His chuckle quickly turned into a cough, and silence descended as he drank water.

Like the flip of a switch, an awful realization hit me. I was going to be a spectator to my grandfather's death. Every passing moment was like sand in an hourglass. How could I return to the States while he still lived and squander any remaining time with him? Would he let me stay even if I decided to abdicate?

I swallowed. "I think I should let you get some rest."

"I am okay, ómọ ọmọ," he rasped. "I simply had a tickle in my throat."

"Are you sure?" I didn't want to tire him.

"Positive. Plus, I know you must have questions for me. We have so much to discuss."

Yes, but where to start? I tried the Oninan form of address, hoping it would aid me in picking a question. "Bàbá àgbà . . . do you think I have what it takes to lead this country as well as you do?"

Tears sprang to his eyes, and he patted his chest. "Hearing you speak Onina does my heart good."

I smiled, glad I'd taken a chance and spoken in his native tongue.

His lips twisted as the lines in his forehead deepened. "You are not me, but I do think you will come to love the people as I do, if not more."

"How could I possibly love them more?" I wasn't raised here and knew nothing about the culture.

"Because you have been without us for so long. You will treasure the time you have in Ọlọrọ, knowing life is short and you must make the most of it. Plus, you are an Adebayo. Caring for others is in our blood."

His words stayed with me all the way back to my room, while I went through my nightly makeup removal routine, and in the quiet moments as I stood on my balcony, listening to the ocean's waves. The curtains danced in the soft breeze.

Staring at the water made me realize just how far away I was from home. I couldn't walk out the door and find a halal cart on every corner. Couldn't hop on the subway and meet my friends in a matter of minutes. I also couldn't help but feel at peace as I peered into the vastness of the gulf.

"Lord, what do You want me to do?" I sighed and settled into one of the balcony chairs, propping my feet on the ottoman. Waiting, praying He'd answer me and make the decision crystal clear.

My thoughts switched to Iris and her advice to take life one step at a time. I felt like a major step needed to be taken soon. She'd tried to cheer me up about the fish incident, casting a few jokes my way. But like the fish, they'd fallen flat.

I had no idea which direction to go. How could I say no to the Adebayo legacy?

I did care for people. My mother had always lauded my kindness as a strength. But what did I know about being a princess? I couldn't even say I was from Africa or Ọlọrọ. My father had been born here, and my mother was of African descent, but I was very much a Black American, which held its own contradictions.

I closed my eyes, letting the waves lull me into what I hoped

would be a state of quiet. One that ceased the hundred unanswer-
able questions in my mind. Maybe I just needed to spend more
time exploring the island and meeting the people. Perhaps then
I'd find the love Grandfather spoke of. Maybe that would point
me in the way I should go.

For now, I would continue to pray and seek answers and *try* to
have fun. After all, I was in a tropical paradise.

TWELVE

Fort Battre stood sentry high on the hill before us. The sand-stone brick structure blended with the shoreline of the coast, looking forbidding and somewhat medieval. I could picture it outfitted with cannons at the top to secure the northern shores from enemies.

Tomori moved to stand beside me, and the soft breeze accompanying the movement made me shiver. I'd done a little digging and discovered he was a palace runner. With a few questions here and there, I'd gotten Dayo to task him to be our tour guide for the day.

Iris had teased me that I blushed when he was around. Of course, I denied all her claims even though my heart was pretty much beating in my throat.

"Fort Battre was built after the arrival of the French in 1725," Tomori stated as we all stood there. "The French believed the northwest coast of the country needed to be guarded. After we gained independence, the council converted the fort to a museum."

"How many times have you been here?" Iris asked.

"A few. Once in primary school and a couple of times as a tour guide."

"Is it awful to see?" I asked. Knowing the French had used the fort to enslave the natives made my stomach tangle tighter than a bug in a web. Who knew what atrocities the Ọlọrans had endured while forced to labor in the fields and build up the towns and cities of today?

My hands shook as we walked up the sandy path leading to the entry. Chidi had promised to keep his distance for anonymity but stay close enough to guard me if needed. I peered up at Tomori's tall, lean frame. He was quite imposing himself. I figured we'd be fine if someone tried to bother us.

Tourists mingled outside the gate, some stopping at the booths where locals peddled their wares. The line at the walk-in ticket counter was short, but it didn't matter. Dayo had secured tickets for us online. All we had to do was go to the pick-up window.

I gave my name, and the woman working slid four tickets to me.

"Do you like working here?" I asked quietly.

She paused, searching my face. Probably to see if I was like every other tourist—here for the fascinating history or to learn about slavery but having no real heart or hurt in the matter.

"It is a job that feeds my family, madam." She paused. "Though perhaps someone will walk down the halls of Fort Battre and see that we are people. Then maybe it will have been worth it."

"I see you." I didn't know why I said it out loud, but I battled back tears of understanding.

She gave a small smile. "And I see you. We are kin, yes?"

I nodded. She didn't know how close to the truth that was.

Silence weighed heavy as we walked up the stone steps of the fort.

"Do you ever wonder what they felt? Being ripped from their homes and taken to a strange place?" Iris asked.

"Honestly, I've tried not to think about it," I admitted. "Slavery and the oppression of Blacks in various countries has always hurt my heart and stirred an anger I don't know what to do with. And knowing that my father was African made me feel even closer to the plight. But being raised in New York, seeing past protests . . ." I sighed, feeling like I was just rambling and not making sense.

"It awakened something in you, yes?" Tomori asked softly.

It was like he could see straight into my soul. "It did. I'm still not sure what to do about all these feelings."

"Well, if you choose to be princess, you'll have some very real, tangible power," Iris said. "You could change lives here. I'm not sure what needs to be improved in Ọlọrọ, but I'm sure God will put some cause on your heart."

"And what about you?" I asked. Tomori pointed to himself, and I chuckled. "Both of you."

"I am not sure what God has in store for me," he said. "For now, I try to do everything to the best of my ability in the hope it glorifies Him."

Heart sigh. A perfect answer that held genuineness and sincerity. "What about you, Iris?"

Iris looked at me. "I get a sense He's preparing me."

"For what?"

"I don't know. I've asked and haven't received a response. There's just this awareness in my spirit, you know? Like I need to pay close attention to my surroundings. To soak up information for when He calls me to step into whatever He's preparing."

"I'll be praying for you, then. It sounds like something big will happen."

"I don't know. I just know I want to be able to say 'yes, Lord' and not falter."

"I agree," Tomori interjected. "I do not know if He will call me to something big one day, but I hope I have the faith to respond as Ms. Blakely said."

"You guys are right," I said. "Sometimes, I feel my battle with constant doubts will prevent me from saying yes so readily."

"I do not think doubt goes away," Tomori said. "If it did, would we ever choose to lean on Him and His understanding?"

Iris snorted. "Probably not. Thank goodness everything serves a purpose, even our doubt."

I squeezed her arm. "When did you get so wise?"

"When my friend found out she was a princess," she replied. "I can't have her leaving me behind. I need to prove my worth."

I stopped short. "No, you don't. You *never* have to prove anything to me. We're friends for life, sisters of the heart and soul, and that means I love all of you."

"Thanks, Bri."

I peeked at Tomori as I tugged Iris forward. What did he think about us? Our friendship? And why was I so consumed with his thoughts about me and my best friend?

"I even love that annoying part of you that bounces awake at the crack of dawn, ready to greet the day with joy," I teased Iris. "How *do* you do that without coffee?"

"I'm happy to greet a new day, I guess. Thankful for the breath in my body, and that joy just bubbles out. Besides, I drink coffee in the afternoon."

"Amen, Iris," Tomori said.

"Ugh. You're a morning person?" I asked Tomori.

His lips twitched. "I love all hours of the day."

"Well, I need a couple of cups of coffee before my brain feels any gratitude for being awakened."

Iris laughed. "You're definitely not a morning person. Remember how you used to growl at me when we shared that apartment? I called my mom, convinced I was living with some postapocalyptic being."

"You're so dramatic."

"But you love me," she singsonged.

I did. I wouldn't have made it through college without Iris's zeal to help me. Not that I was cynical by any stretch of the imagination, but I was more introverted. Making the step to teach and put myself in front of an audience—even a young one—had required a lot of effort to bring me out of my shell. Plus, I loved having a person who understood me and all the things that made me tick—and still wanted to be my friend.

We quieted down when we entered the old fort. Tomori went into tour guide mode, explaining the various displays that detailed the history of the Ọlọran people and the tribal groups within the country. He answered our questions about the French colonization and the rise to freedom.

I squinted at the bright sunshine when we exited the fort an hour later.

"What did you think?" Tomori asked.

"I think their independence is something to celebrate, considering the tragedies they overcame. Unfortunately, I imagine all the countries in Africa have a similar history. It reminded me of one of the Smithsonian museums, the African-American one," I said. Iris and I had taken a trip to D.C. one spring break, hitting all the museums and other cultural offerings.

"I totally agree," she said. "Does seeing that help you any? Sway your decision?"

"Decision?" Tomori asked.

His eyes captivated me. I cleared my throat. "Uh, I need to decide if I want to be Grandfather's heir or abdicate," I murmured. Thankfully no one was around, and Chidi still trailed behind us.

"I see. Does hearing about our history help or just further overwhelm you?"

Did I look overwhelmed? I thought I'd done a good job of acting like a tourist. "Honestly, I don't know." I shrugged. "I'm taking it all in, but I'm unsure what I need to know or how to connect with the people."

Iris made a noncommittal noise but reached out to hook my arm with hers. Judging from that sound, she'd have more to say when we were alone. We strolled down the hill and toward the car.

Chidi lengthened his strides to catch up to us, then opened the door for me. "Where to next, Your Highness?"

I wanted to go to a local restaurant and enjoy the food and just soak in the people. "Can you take us somewhere local for lunch?"

"Of course."

As he drove, lush greenery soon gave way to houses with dilapidated roofs. The homes—more shacks than anything—were built nearly on top of one another, with no space in between.

"Chidi?"

"Yes, Your Highness?"

"Why is there such a disparity between wealth out here?" I turned, meeting his gaze in the rearview mirror. "Àlàáfíà is so rich, and the homes around the capital are more modern. Why is Òkè so poor?" Did it have anything to do with the proximity to Fort Battre?

93

"That is a good question, Your Highness. This is where most of the fishing industry is conducted."

"Oh. Do they do that in Opolopo too?" Was the lake good for just recreational fishing, or could it provide sustenance for an entire country?

"No, Opolopo has more recreational fishing," Tomori stated. "They even have a couple of resorts there and a golf course. However, our seafood comes from the Òkè region, which Fort Battre is part of. Unfortunately, in the last few years, production has lowered. Now the people are trying to find other trades to secure their income. Also, during the fight for independence, this portion of the island was hit the hardest because of the fort. The people have battled ever since to leave the life of poverty."

I sat back, stunned. Not by the knowledge but by the destruction their fight for independence had wrought. Ọlọrọ Ilé had been free for over a hundred years, and still the people struggled.

"What's the electricity infrastructure like? Do they depend on solar and hydropower here?"

"No, Your Highness," Chidi answered. "There is one hydro plant here, but Opolopo has a market on that. They have a dam at the height of the lake. Òkè leaches power from other regions when possible."

"But why?" My forehead puckered, and I took a deep breath, telling myself to relax. "Why don't they have their own source?"

"The *alàgbà*—that is, the elders who sit on the royal council but also represent a region of Ọlọrọ—well, the elder for Òkè does not want to advance the region in those areas. He is intent on rebuilding our fishing industry." Chidi's mouth turned downward. "Forgive me, Your Highness. I hope it did not sound disrespectful against the council member."

"No, not at all. Thank you both for your insight."

Chidi dipped his head. Tomori gave me a soft smile, his full lips slightly curved. I looked at Iris, who met me with a wide-eyed stare, telegraphing her eagerness to delve into this topic. But we'd have to wait until we were back at the palace.

Soon Chidi stopped at a roadside stand. He turned, crooking

his elbow onto the headrest of his seat. "Your Highness, this stand sells the best meat pies. The *paiis* can be made from livestock, fish, or other seafood. This stand has some good fish and shrimp options."

My stomach revolted as I remembered my last fish experience. "Is fish in all of the paiis?"

Iris snickered under her breath.

"No, Your Highness. There are some without fish. Do you know how to read Onina? If not, you can stay in the car, and I will order."

"Actually, Chidi," Tomori interrupted, "I can walk her."

Iris poked me in the side.

"What do you want me to get you?" I asked her, ignoring her teasing expression.

"Whatever you think I'd like," she replied.

I got out of the car. Tomori shortened his strides as we walked to the end of the line. The chalkboard next to the stand had the options written out in French.

"Do you know French?" I asked him.

"*Oui, mademoiselle.*" He winked, and my heart fluttered. He pointed toward the board. "You have the options of beef, fish, shrimp, or crab."

"I bet the crab is decadent."

"You like crab?"

My stomach already rumbled with anticipation. "I love it. What about you?"

"They are all good. I suggest you get more than one. Maybe try the shrimp."

"I'll do that, then."

I took in the fragrance his cologne emitted and swayed. Something about this man made me want to take up Iris's suggestion of an island romance. *If wishes were real, right?*

"Thank you for today, Your Highness."

I blinked at him. "For what?"

"I have enjoyed showing you what a great place Ọlọrọ is. I hope you"—his Adam's apple bobbed—"and Ms. Blakely have had a good day."

95

"You've been the perfect tour guide."

"I am glad you think so."

We stepped forward and ordered our paiis. I ordered two—one shrimp and one crab—and got Iris a beef and a crab paii.

"Aren't you going to order?" I asked Tomori.

"I am working."

"Please order. I'm paying. Oh, and get two for Chidi too."

He studied me for a moment, gaze searching mine, before nodding. I handed over some Ọlọran francs.

When we got back to the car, Tomori passed the food to Chidi. "Her Highness bought us lunch."

Chidi dropped his gaze. "You should not have."

"You haven't eaten, have you?"

"No." His eyes flew up. "I just meant that you should not think of me. I would have eaten upon returning to Àlàáfíà."

"And have to smell us eating these? Please. You can eat and drive, or we can just sit here a moment and enjoy our lunch."

"Ẹ seun, Your Highness."

"My pleasure, Chidi."

I bit into the pie and moaned in delight. The pastry was buttery, and an explosion of crab and vegetables hit my tongue. "So good," I murmured when I had finished the first bite.

"The beef one is to die for," Iris mumbled.

"Wait until you taste the crab."

I went back and forth between each paii until I had eaten the very last bite. A quick wipe with the napkin I'd taken at the booth and I was ready to go. I buckled up, then noticed Chidi and Tomori doing the same. Chidi set his food aside and put the car in gear. I wasn't sure if he was done eating, but maybe it was like a queen-of-England situation. Once royalty was finished, the others must be too.

Was this what my life would be like if I stepped into my grandfather's shoes? Just another item to pray over.

THIRTEEN

The past week had been amazing. Iris and I had explored the rural area of Lake Opolopo, taking a raft tour down the Fadaka River. Actually, we'd been to every region in Ọlọrọ Ilé, experiencing the food, the culture, and the general splendor of the island. Ọlọrọ didn't feel like home, but the possibility of it becoming that one day no longer seemed ridiculous. Which was why Iris and I had chosen to take a palace tour, despite our residence in the guest quarters.

I listened to the whispers of the other tourists as we walked along the marble floors. Our tour guide's voice had a beautiful lilt to it—like Dayo's—and she beamed with pleasure as she ushered us into the ballroom.

A ballroom! I couldn't imagine living in this place on a daily basis. Granted, the third floor was completely secure and away from the noise of the tours. But to call the palace my home—could I do it?

The tour guide pointed out the opulent chandeliers and the tapestries hanging from the walls. "The tapestries get changed regularly. The royal family likes to hang ones that match the purpose of the event. Every time there is a tour, the independence tapestries are hung."

I squinted, trying to see what was on them, but I was too far from the closest one.

"That's so neat," Iris whispered. "We should come back tonight and get a closer look."

"You just want to see what they're made of."

"May-be," she drawled.

We left the ballroom and headed down the corridor to the next open public space—the library. I bit my lip in anticipation but slowed when my eyes caught those of Tomori. What was he doing down here? I hadn't seen him since our trip to the fort, so he could have been roaming the palace halls ever since. I slowed my pace until I was the only one left in the hall, having nudged Iris to proceed into the library without me.

"Tomori," I whispered.

He dipped his head, then peeked into the library. "Are you taking a tour, Your—Brielle?"

I couldn't keep my lips from smiling. "I thought it would be fun."

"Has it been?"

"So far, yes. There's so much I've learned that I didn't know already."

"You should take the tour they give to students one day. Although, it is in Onina, so you might want to wait until you understand the language better."

"Or you could translate for me?"

Tomori's lips quirked. "That could be arranged."

Were we flirting, or was he simply being kind? Was there any harm in flirting? It could be seen as innocuous, but I was afraid my heart would get entrenched.

Before I could retreat into the library, words flew from me. "My orchid looks wonderful in my room."

A small smile touched his lips. "I am glad. Have you been back to the market?"

"No. We've been visiting other places." I'd been sad to have a different palace runner as our tour guide. I guess Tomori had been otherwise occupied. Maybe he'd been on a different shift when we went rafting?

"Did you go fishing?"

I grinned. "I'm still waiting for you to teach me."

"One day."

"I'll put it in my calendar."

A soft chuckle fell from his lips. Then a noise that sounded like a walkie-talkie echoed in the hall.

"Excuse me." He lifted the device from his back pocket and listened in. "I am sorry, but I must go."

"Of course. I should get back to the tour."

"Have a good day, Brielle."

"You too, Tomori."

I walked into the library, intending to scan the sea of faces for Iris, but got distracted by the light streaming in and the bookshelves centered in the middle of the room. Tables lined the outer walls, a tropical lamp at each one.

"Although the royal family has access to this library, it is most often used by the public." The tour guide smiled. "Besides, I hear they have their own fabulous library."

Was that true? Apparently, I needed to explore the third floor. Would Grandfather grant me access to all the rooms?

"Bri." Iris grabbed my arm. "Girl, do you have a crush?"

"What?" I whisper-shouted.

"I see how you are every time Tomori is around. You light up."

"I can't have a crush. I'm just here for the summer."

"But that's so dreamy. Summer crushes can turn into longtime romances."

"But if I chose to . . . you know, then I probably can't have a relationship with someone who works here."

Iris pursed her lips. "That may be true." She sighed. "I guess you can add that to your list of considerations. What will your love life look like if you say yes?"

That was a good question. I'd always figured I had time to get into a serious relationship with the hope of leading to marriage, but if I accepted my role as a princess and ascended the throne after Grandfather's passing, what *would* my personal life look like? Did they arrange marriages out here? Have expectations of who you could marry?

I rubbed my forehead. So much to think about.

The tour ended just outside the palace, and we made our way to the entrance that we'd been using all week. The guards let us in without a second thought, and we made our way to the elevators and then to the third floor. I opened my text messages and sent a question to Dayo.

Me

Is my grandfather available?

Despite his health, he was still running the country. I wished he would relax more, but he didn't want the world to know he was ill yet.

Dayo

His schedule is wide open at the moment, Your Highness. He is in his room if you would like to speak to him.

Me

Thank you!

A few minutes later, I knocked on his sitting room door.

Mobo answered and bowed before me. "Your Highness, the king is expecting you."

"Thank you, Mr. Owusu."

After rapping my knuckles on the door, I entered Grandfather's private room.

He sat behind his desk and smiled at me. "Good afternoon, ómọ ọmọ. How was the tour?"

"Amazing. I didn't realize just how big the palace was."

"Ah yes. It is a great workout to walk the halls and take the stairs to every floor."

"Do you do that?"

"In the past. Now . . ."

Now he couldn't walk more than a few steps without sucking in air or coughing. My heart twisted. "Maybe I'll do it for you."

"Yes, you can be my eyes."

I smiled. "Grandfather, I was wondering if I could get some lessons on the history of Ọlọrọ and the monarchy to help me make an informed decision."

He relaxed into his chair. "That is a wise request. I would be happy to have Mobo instruct you. He can tell you the history and what the council expects of a king—well, queen, in your case."

"That would be great."

"You know our Independence Day celebration is coming up."

"June twenty-eighth, right?"

"Yes. It will be wonderful to have you there. Maybe by then you will have made a decision?"

"I'm not sure." I bit my lip. "I hope you know I'm praying every day. I'm soaking in all I can from my excursions. I'm not just having fun."

He leaned forward. "Oh, do not worry. I was not making a slight or trying to rush you. Please, take your time, ọmọ ọmọ. I just thought it would make the Independence Day celebration more special if you knew by then." He waved a hand. "Please ignore the babblings of an old man."

"Bàbá àgbà," I started slowly, "would it be okay with you if I remain here the rest of the summer? Regardless if I inherit the throne?" I couldn't imagine leaving him while I had a chance to make lasting memories. To learn more about my father and the other half of me. I wouldn't even mind getting to know the rest of the Adebayos. Well, maybe not Uncle Sijuwola.

"Brielle, you can stay as long as you want. Even if you decide that being princess is not for you, you will always have a place in Ọlọrọ."

Would my uncle feel the same way? He had skipped the second family dinner Grandfather hosted a couple of days ago. I wasn't sure if Sijuwola was afraid of another fish incident, or if he objected to my presence. Everyone else, including Sijuwola's own son, had shown up. The conversation had been a little stilted, but we'd asked questions of one another. Thankfully, Digi appeared to like me. She'd reached out and wanted to take Iris and me shopping.

"Thank you. I really appreciate it. I don't have to return to work until August." The next school year wouldn't start until after Labor Day. Maybe I could get my boss to give me an extension on returning later than teacher workdays. Then again, I could always end up changing my mind and sending them my resignation in order to become Princess Brielle Adebayo.

I blew out a breath.

"We will enjoy our time together regardless."

"Yes." I smiled.

"I will let Mobo know to start instructing you. He will either contact you directly or set everything up through Dayo."

"Thank you."

"My pleasure, ómǫ ǫmǫ. Please know that I am praying for you as well, that the Lord God will bless you with the wisdom needed to make this decision. It is one for life and one that cannot be made lightly. I know He will give you the insight you need."

Relief flooded me. I was so grateful for the prayers. From Iris, my mom—though she hadn't said so, I knew she was praying too—and now Grandfather. Their comfort was immeasurable. The more people praying, the better.

"I'll let you finish your day." I stood.

"Before you go, there is something I want to tell you."

I nodded.

"Some of the lower staff have heard rumors of your existence. I have put measures in place to ensure no one else learns of your stay."

Who told? "Did you fire them?"

"No. I am not sure who started the rumors yet. If I find out who leaked the information and it is a staff member, they will be fired for breach of the NDA they signed."

"Am I still okay to explore the island? Will I need more than Chidi to guard me?"

"At this time, I do not think so."

I nodded. "Okay, then. I'll see you at dinner?"

"Yes. And we will not have any fish dishes." His eyes twinkled.

I covered my face. "What an impression," I said through my fingers.

"It is okay. It happens to us all."

My hands dropped as my eyebrows rose. "Really, Grandfather?"

"Ha, no. But I wanted you to feel better."

I chuckled all the way out the room.

FOURTEEN

his will be your temporary office." Dayo stopped in front of a blue door situated halfway down the hall. "The red door on the right leads to the conference room. There is an adjoining entryway to your office, so you do not have to come back into the hall to access the room if you ever need it."

Grandfather had decided I needed an office for lessons from Mr. Owusu. It would look more professional than going to various sitting rooms. That, and I think Grandfather wanted to entice me to say yes to the crown.

Dayo pointed down the hall toward a green door. "That is the king's office."

She pulled down the gold handle on the blue door and pushed it open to reveal my new office. A simple desk and chair sat in the middle of the room. Beyond that, another door led to yet another room.

"This is where I will sit to accept your visitors or turn them away. Your suite is through there." She gestured to the second door.

We went through it, and a very masculine office greeted me. Brown beams blocked in squares covered the wood-paneled ceiling. A huge black desk sat in the corner with a matching chair behind it. In front, two leather chairs rimmed in gold beckoned guests. The one window in the room was hung with heavy gold drapery. Overall, the room was kind of dreary.

"This room was decorated by your father before he went off to college," Dayo said.

I gasped, feeling like I'd been punched in the gut. My eyes took in each furnishing again, imagining what my father must have thought when choosing the style for the room.

"Everything in here is so dark but the door." I pointed behind me. "Why is it white?"

Dayo's mouth turned down. "When we lose someone, we go through a three-month mourning period. After that, the doors to their chambers and office are painted white as a symbol that they are ready for the next occupant. His Majesty has not changed a thing since then."

I gulped. Then my grandfather's door would soon be painted white. I pressed a hand to my stomach, trying to still the dodgeballs hurtling in my insides. *Don't think like that. Stay in the moment and today's troubles.*

I walked toward the desk, ensuring my inhales and exhales were slow and steady.

"Mobo will be by in a few minutes to begin your lessons."

"Thank you, Dayo."

"My pleasure."

When Dayo ushered Mobo into my office a few minutes later, I rose. He bowed at the waist, his hands in petition. "Ẹ káàárò, Your Highness."

"Ẹ káàárò, Mr. Owusu. Please be seated."

He held a portfolio in his arms as he sat in one of the leather chairs. "I am honored to assist you. The king told me you wish to learn more about our history. Once you have a deep understanding and appreciation for our rich past, I believe you will not only be able to make an informed decision but be a better leader for it."

I blinked rapidly, surprised by the desire to cry. "Thank you. I really appreciate you saying that." I pulled my chair closer to the desk and reached for a pen. A legal notepad was all I needed to take notes. Writing with a pen and paper always ingrained the lessons into my head better than taking notes on some electronic device.

"Let us start with the basics, Your Highness."

"I'm ready."

He nodded. "The land has been here for centuries. There were a few tribes here when the French invaded and decided to cultivate the island for its resources. They also enslaved many people from mainland Africa and brought them here. It is why the Onina language is so similar to theirs. Our people were forced to farm cocoa and yams and to mine minerals. We will delve deeper into those items at a later time."

"Okay." My pen raced across the page. "And the French arrived in 1725, right?"

"Yes, Your Highness. They established Fort Battre to be a barrier to other countries and a port to move slaves. You have visited the museum, yes?"

I looked up. "I have." I sighed. "It was tough to see, but not unbelievable."

"Yes. I know you can understand the turmoil of slavery."

I nodded, blinking back tears as I thought of different stages of racial unrest in the States. "Mr. Owusu, why don't I see you and Ms. Layeni with iPads or other tablet devices? I mean, you're using a notepad."

A ghost of a smile appeared on his serious face. "I appreciate you calling me Mr. Owusu, but I promise, Mobo is just fine, Your Highness."

I nodded.

"The reason for the notepads is because of the frequent outages we experience. Our cell phone towers are sparse, so there are many gaps in coverage, and our internet cables are undersea. When fault lines shift, we lose connectivity. There are currently deals in the works to improve our network, but until then, we use paper as a fail-safe."

"What about in the palace? Is there a gap in cell coverage?"

"No, Your Highness. If you prefer electronic devices to paper, we can get your office equipped with all you desire."

I wanted to ask more but needed to remember that we were focusing on the history of the country, not its current state. I made a note to ask more questions later. "Sorry. Please continue."

"Because of slavery, the different tribes bonded and began to develop their own traditions. Of course, Ọlọrọ is heavily influenced by its French colonization as well. Around the 1800s, the many tribes of Ọlọrọ came together as one and adopted the Onina name and language to show unity despite our oppression. Therefore, you will often hear people referred to as Oninan or Ọlọran. *Onina* means volcano."

My eyes widened. "Was the island made by volcanoes?" I knew the Hawaiian Islands were, but how many other islands were formed through the same process?

"No, Your Highness. The people wanted to make a statement and show how resilient we are and that we were ready to erupt with independence."

"And the language? Did each tribe have their own? Is Onina a mix of them all?"

"Some of the tribes had their own language, but much of that has been eradicated. They did not hold onto it as Onina became more prevalent. With the French enslavement, our language became even more blended, which is why we have the Creole dialect today." Mobo rubbed his forehead. "I hope I am making sense. Know this: the majority of us who travel to the mainland can converse with those who speak a similar dialect to Onina, English, or French."

"How many countries does the kingdom have dealings with?"

"Quite a few. But that lesson will wait for another day, Your Highness."

"All right. Please go on."

"Our independence came earlier than that of many countries on the mainland. That is primarily because France pulled their forces out of the country sooner. The country became unstable as we sought leadership, and when France sent an ambassador, the people rebelled. The Adebayo elder banded the people together and got them to discuss their issues with the ambassador. France then made a decision to give us our independence. The king's grandfather was alive at that time—1912—and was chosen to be our king by the newly formed royal council."

So I would be the fourth Adebayo to lead if I said yes.

"The Ọlọrọ Ilé Royal Council is made up of one tribal elder from each region. An elder from each *tribu*—tribe—is selected based on the people's recommendations. There were three members at the onset, with the king residing as the fourth member. Later, when the Muslim population grew in Ọlọrọ, they earned a seat at the table as well. When a sitting councilman passes, the vacated spot is open for vote amongst that tribe's elders."

"Is there a cabinet or a prime minister?" I hadn't seen anything in my readings, but I wanted to make sure.

"No cabinet. I suppose you could consider the council your cabinet. We do not have a prime minister. When there are heads of state meetings, the king goes."

Mobo continued my lesson on the history of the island, with me taking copious notes. I could already tell there were more areas I would need to explore in the future. Like why we used hydro- and solar power. Or why we had a high poverty situation outside the capital, but an influx of tourists within Àlàáfíà. Òkè was near the northern beach—shouldn't that bring in tourists?

After an hour of history, I needed a break. "Mr. Owusu, can we please pause for a moment?"

"Certainly, Your Highness. Maybe you should take a walk in the gardens and clear your head. Have you visited them yet?"

"I haven't." I wanted to explore them with Grandfather. At the same time, I was worried the walk would be too taxing.

He stood. "I will call an escort for you if you wish to go."

I bit my lip, then nodded. "Please."

He disappeared into Dayo's small receiving room.

I stood, stretching my arms to the left then the right. I couldn't believe I had been sitting for an hour without moving. My hand cramped from all the note taking. I walked around the office, opening drawers and peering into containers for any last traces of my father, but everything had been wiped clean. No dust, no remnants of life. I grimaced at the thought.

A rap of knuckles sounded on the doorjamb.

"Come in."

Dayo walked in, Tomori following her. I stopped the gasp that had risen halfway up my throat, grasping for a poker face and calm. *Where did he come from?* He wore the same uniform he had at the airport, the same one he'd worn the day I took the palace tour.

"Your Highness, Tomori will lead you to the gardens."

"Thank you."

He bowed.

Dayo stepped close to me and dipped her head. "Your grandfather wishes to see you afterward."

"In his office?" I whispered, matching her tone.

"Yes."

"Should I skip the walk to the gardens?"

"No. He is eager for your report but is in a meeting and cannot take you himself."

"Thank you, Dayo."

She walked out, leaving the door wide open. I wondered if that was for propriety's sake or something else.

"This way, Your Highness," Tomori said, extending a hand.

I dipped my head in acknowledgment, all the while telling myself that those flutters in my middle weren't attraction but excitement for the excursion.

Yet when I passed him to exit my office, the hint of cedar greeting my nose made a liar out of me.

FIFTEEN

Silence pervaded the hallway as Tomori led the way to the first floor. I wanted to break the quiet, but the slight undercurrent pulsating between us muted me. Could Tomori feel the hum of attraction? Even if he did, would either of us pursue the other? I didn't know the expectations of a princess's love life, but I was pretty sure my life would belong to the people if I said yes to the throne.

Tomori opened a brown wooden door, and fresh air greeted me, carrying the tropical scent of a garden. I gasped at the lush greenery before me and looked up. We were outside but still on palace grounds.

"People often take off their shoes because the feel of the grass is like nothing else," Tomori said.

I smiled shyly. "Will you tell if I do?"

He made a zipping motion over his mouth. I didn't stare at his full lips . . . or not for very long, at least.

I slipped off my flats and sighed. I'd thought the grass would tickle, but the thickness cushioned my soles. "This is amazing." I stared down at his sandals. "Are you going to take yours off too?"

Tomori's lips twitched. "Will you tell if I do?"

I mimed sealing my lips, and a soft chuckle escaped from him. The low vibration of his laughter made my stomach dance with delight. I swallowed, pushing the emotions away, and looked around. "It's pretty out here."

"They have a variety of orchids."

My eyes widened. "They do?"

"Yes. I could ask for some fresh ones to be sent to your new office if you would like."

A frisson of pleasure raised the hairs on my arms. This tiny crush on Tomori could further complicate my days, but I couldn't stop the satisfaction from coursing through me. He remembered my favorite flower.

"No, you don't have to do that." They'd probably just make me think of him more than I already did. I started walking. "This is all beautiful, but I have no idea what I'm looking at." Emerald-green leaves along the path fanned out wide but were stout. Were these trees? Shrubs? I fingered the waxy fronds. "Who cares for all the plants in here?"

"There is a team of landscape workers. They come early in the morning to prune and cultivate."

"It's immaculate."

"They would be pleased to hear you say that."

"You think so?"

"Yes. They take great pride in their work."

"Speaking of work . . ." I turned toward him. "How many palace runners are there?"

"There are twenty of us, and we rotate shifts. We do not always do the same job because we can be called to fulfill any need of the palace."

"That explains why you were at the airport and took us on tours."

He dipped his head, and as his chin lifted, his gaze captured mine. "Do you think the job unnecessary?" He frowned, and the space between his eyebrows scrunched like an accordion. "I do not think that is the right word."

"Unnecessary?"

"That means unneeded, right?"

"Right."

He shook his head. "I am looking for, um . . ."

I took a guess. "Beneath me?" I asked softly, praying that wasn't what he meant.

He snapped his fingers. "Yes. That is it."

"No. Of course not. We all have a part to play, and we all have talents. I believe the Bible when it says no one is better than another."

"Even though you were born a princess?"

"I didn't know that until recently. I was raised as a doctor's daughter."

His eyes widened. "That is very prestigious in Ọlọrọ too."

"Well, in America it is as well, but I'm just a schoolteacher."

We continued walking, and I inhaled the scents. Something floral tickled my nose, and I had to fight a sneeze.

"What subject do you teach?" Tomori asked.

"Middle school civics."

"Do you like it?"

"I love it. I teach eighth grade, and they're a great age group. Not young like elementary kids, but not yet jaded like high school students."

"I can see you as a teacher. You have a calm way about you, but you are authoritative too."

I wasn't sure what to think about that. Probably because a part of me wanted him to see me in a romantic light. Once more I reminded myself that it could *not* happen.

"Are you learning the palace ropes?" Tomori asked, motioning to a teak bench. I sat at one end and he the other.

"Trying to. I'm learning about the country's history right now."

"Are they teaching you Onina as well?"

"I actually haven't brought it up. I've been too focused on making an informed decision." I shrugged. "But YouTube has been useful, even though I can't seem to make the lessons stick."

"I would be happy to teach you."

More time with Tomori? The teenage girl in me squealed with excitement while the adult me made shushing motions. Still, I did want to learn. . . .

I swallowed. "I need to check my schedule." I shook my head. "That sounds crazy to say, but I'm not sure what Dayo has placed on it."

"Ask her to schedule lessons every day this week at three o'clock. My shift ends at two thirty, so that will give me time to eat before I come up and teach."

I almost told him we could share a late lunch, but that seemed to cross the line of whatever was between us. "I'll do that. Thank you."

He stood. "Good. I will show you the way back. I am sure your grandfather has much to tell you."

I had completely forgotten about that. My mind considered possible scenarios. Hopefully the news was nothing terrible.

I peered up at Tomori. "Will you be able to celebrate the Ọlọran Independence Day, or do you have to work?" I wasn't sure how the day was observed in Ọlọrọ or how Tomori's shift schedule worked.

"The whole palace staff—well, except security—will have the day off, unless they are directly helping the king. He prefers us to celebrate and not cater to the family." He held up his hands. "His words, not mine."

I laughed. "I'm enjoying getting to know him." I mentally stopped. Did everyone know he was dying? That was something I needed to ask before I spilled my secrets to Tomori.

"See you tomorrow, Your Highness." He bowed, then turned, leaving me in front of Grandfather's office.

As I watched him stride confidently down the hall, a part of me longed to join him. To see what his day was like and just be near him. His presence brought such a calm to my spirit, and I always felt a little more assured after talking with him.

Instead, I knocked on Grandfather's door, then pushed it open at his summons.

His eyes lit as he spotted me. "Ọmọ ọmọ, come in, come in."

"Hi, Bàbá àgbà."

His grin widened. "You have seen the gardens?"

"They're magnificent."

"I quite agree. Your grandmother and I spent many a day walking the paths or sitting and talking. Now, I am afraid the activity literally takes my breath away."

I wanted to laugh, but the stark reminder only brought sadness. "Maybe use of a wheelchair would help you get around without taxing you so much?"

He shook his head. "It would not be fitting for Ọlọrans to see their king disabled."

I bit my lip, moving forward to take the chair in front of his desk. "Grandfather, do the citizens know you're sick?"

"The council does. I have not told anyone else."

"Shouldn't you?"

"I had not dared until I met you and knew your choice. The council was making plans, but now . . ." He waved his hand.

"I've interrupted them."

"They may consider you an interruption, but I have found that is when God reveals Himself in the details, giving us an opportunity to step onto the path He has paved for us."

My heart quickened. "Do you truly believe that?"

"I do."

Relief flooded me. "I don't feel ready to be a princess right now, but what you just said really forces me to think. To ask the hard question of what path He has paved for me."

"As long as you keep Him in the forefront, He will reveal His will. Then you will be able to face anything that comes your way."

Words to write on my heart.

"I'm afraid that whatever choice I make, I could fail you," I whispered. I wanted to make him proud, even after his death.

"Ah, ómọ ọmọ, I know you will not."

He rose and came around the desk, arms extended, and I went into them willingly. I laid my head against his chest and sniffed back the tears.

"Whatever happens, Brielle," he said, emphasizing the two syllables, "God will be glorified."

A tear slipped free and onto the cotton of his shirt. I squeezed my arms around him and mumbled into his chest. "I love you."

SIXTEEN

Digi had mastered the art of disguise. Gone were her mini dreadlocks, and in their place was a silken black wig. She'd added light gray contacts and a beauty mole to the top left of her mouth. Of course, she also dressed like a stereotypical seventeen-year-old girl going to the mall instead of one belonging to the royal family. No one spared her a glance.

Iris and I didn't have to worry about being noticed, but we were dressed casually as well. Chidi walked with Digi's bodyguard right behind us, and the men carried our purchases. I wasn't sure if others assumed they were our boyfriends or that we were well-to-do. All I knew was I was having fun.

For once my mind wasn't focused on the looming decision ahead. Instead, I studied the menus above me, trying to figure out what to buy from the food court.

"I still can't believe they have KFC," Iris said.

"We like fast food too," Digi exclaimed.

"I know that," Iris said. "I just didn't expect to see it in an Ọloran mall. I thought you'd have your own chains."

"Right over there, Miss Iris." Digi pointed to the other side of the court, where restaurants advertising African cuisine served lunch.

My nose twitched at all the scents. Unlike Iris, the KFC hadn't shocked me, but the Cold Stone Creamery had. I hadn't realized they were international. Still, I didn't plan to buy anything from someplace I could go to back in the States. I wanted to dive into the culture, and I couldn't do that eating food I'd had before. Maybe if I lived here long enough to get homesick, I'd change my mind.

After we ordered our food, we picked a table big enough for five. Chidi and Digi's bodyguard—whose name I couldn't remember—sat at separate ends of the table.

"So, Brielle, will you step into your duties?" Digi asked softly, careful to ensure our conversation couldn't be overheard.

"I haven't decided." I eyed her. "How do you feel about it?"

She grinned and leaned forward. "I think it is fantastic. A woman who can rise to be queen? We have not seen that in Ọlọrọ. I would love to see a woman in power and bringing about real change." Her lips turned downward. "But Grandpa is pretty misogynistic. I cannot see him letting you take over without a fight. And Dad will do whatever he says."

What kind of fight? Was she insinuating a battle of wills, or one where I should be thankful Chidi guarded me? Would Maseso do Sijuwola's bidding? Maybe I was overreacting.

"What would he do?" Iris asked.

I shifted in my seat, waiting for Digi's answer.

"I am not sure." Digi spoke carefully. "All I know is he flew into a rage when the king told him of your existence. My father did not seem so bothered, but Mother . . ." She blew out a breath. "Our family has believed that we would succeed the king since Uncle's death."

I blinked, realizing she meant my father.

"Just be careful, Brielle. Know that if you do step into your birthright, there will be opposition." Digi reached a hand across the table and gently squeezed mine. "But there will also be those rooting for you to blaze a trail for the rest of us."

"Thank you, Digi."

My anxiety was back like a wrecking ball. I'd thought learning about the country's history from Mobo and touring the island would give me the understanding I needed to make a decision. Hearing what I was up against and receiving warnings from both Dayo and Digi made me nervous. My decision had bigger ramifications than where I would live. I would be in charge of a kingdom—

a monarch—and the face of good or bad in Ọlọrọ. Who knew how many ripples my actions could cause? Even deciding to abdicate had ramifications I couldn't project.

But, as Digi said, I could be seen as a trailblazer and a hope to women in the country who wanted more in their lives. Yet how could I fight years of patriarchal society when America had barely made more strides in that area? Women still fought for equality in many countries around the world. No one had *made it*. I could understand the Ọlọran woman's plight, but I hadn't lived in her shoes.

I rubbed my forehead. I wished Mom had bridged the gap with Grandfather when I was young. If I'd had an opportunity to visit or grow up with the expectation of being an heir, how much easier would this choice be? I took a bite of my food, but there was no flavor. Every cell in my body was attuned to my thoughts and not what my lunch tasted like. I needed to go back to the freedom I'd felt before and have fun with my best friend and new cousin.

My phone chimed with a notification, so I pulled up my messages.

Shondra

Bri! How's Africa? Where are the pics? Your IG is silent. How's your grandfather?

I chuckled. Shondra taught world history for seventh graders and was usually my lunch buddy since our school schedule was similar. I'd let her and one other friend know that Grandfather was ill. Shondra and Tami were close enough friends that I'd shared my mom's deception. I left out the whole princess dilemma, though. I wasn't ready to share that just yet.

Me

It's gorgeous here, but my grandfather is really sick. I'm thinking of staying the whole summer until . . .

Shondra

I'm sorry, girl. That's gotta be so hard.

Me

It is, but we're also making great memories.

"Who are you texting?"

I glanced at Iris. "Shondra. She's wondering why I haven't been posting on social media."

"You do not have a mobile data plan here?" Digi asked. "The king puts all of us on his. It ensures our cell is secure and gives you data."

"Thanks. But if I return to the States . . ." My voice trailed off.

"Yes, but you are here for at least a month. Why not get on his plan, even temporarily?"

"I'll think about it."

"It is okay to enjoy the perks of our family, Brielle," Digi said seriously.

"Maybe I don't feel like part of the family yet."

I wanted to slap a hand over my mouth and crawl under the table. Digi had been nothing but kind and didn't deserve my bad mood or feelings of guilt.

"Go to a few more family dinners and you will. When they start making suggestions on how to live your life, you will fit right in." Digi grinned.

I peered at her. "And what do you want to do with your life?"

"I want to be a scientist." A dreamy look crossed her face. "Unfortunately, *Bàbá* wants me to marry. He does not believe I should go to university."

"But won't you work for the family in some way? Won't a degree help you?"

"I am a girl, cousin. Bàbá will marry me off to some tribal elder or his son and call it 'for the good of the country,'" she air-quoted.

I sighed. Maybe taking up the Adebayo mantle didn't have to be about what I would lose but what I and women everywhere would gain.

We left the food court and continued perusing the stores in the Àlàáfíàn mall. There were stores that sold groceries and spices, clothing stores, shoe stores, and ones providing all sorts of accessories. Iris bought a bunch of earrings and a few jumpsuits. I bought trinkets for Tami and Shondra, then paused when I saw a perfect gift for my mom in one of the tourist shops.

The vase was a swirl of color: purples, blues, and a dark brown blended in harmony. Mom loved the abstract look when it came to art.

"What's wrong?" Iris came to stand beside me.

"I'm wondering if I should get this for my mom."

"Have you guys talked yet?"

"No." I bit my lip. "I don't know what to say. I respond when she texts, but I'm just not ready to go further than surface level."

"Well, maybe if you send this to her, it'll be a peace offering. I'm sure someone in the palace could ship it for you."

I nodded, indecision tearing me in two. I wasn't sure how to get over the betrayal from my mother, but letting it fester wasn't an option either. I grabbed the vase and paid for it, not letting my mind settle on the emotions or the thought behind the action.

I'd ask Dayo to have it shipped to her. Maybe I could write a letter to accompany it, getting all my feelings out in the open. Then, just maybe, I could move past this intense hurt that gripped my chest and threatened to make me erupt in tears. I missed the easy relationship I'd had with my mom, and being apart wasn't healing my wounds. The gap had only been widened and the hurt deepened.

SEVENTEEN

I stared at my office door as I mindlessly adjusted the items on my desk. Any moment Dayo would knock and announce Tomori's arrival for my first Onina lesson. To say I was nervous would be a gross understatement. I probably shouldn't have had that last cup of coffee, because now I'd become a jittery mess.

A rap sounded, and I jumped. *Breathe, Brielle.* I exhaled, then called, "Come in."

Dayo bowed before me. "Your Highness, Mr. Eesuola is here for your language lessons."

I rose. "Thank you, Dayo."

Tomori stepped through the doorway and stopped next to my secretary. She gave him such a perfect side-eye that I bit the inside of my cheek to hold in my laughter. Ọlọran customs were still so new to me that I wasn't sure if I'd overstepped some bounds of propriety. The way Dayo looked at Tomori, like a mother sizing up her daughter's first date, made me wonder if our private lessons could be construed as more than they really were.

"Your Highness." Dayo dipped her head in respect and closed the door behind her.

Despite the tingle of awareness humming up my spine as I inhaled Tomori's cedar smell, I was very aware of who I was. I may not have accepted the role of future queen, but by birth, I was royalty. Grandfather had been giving me tips on what it meant to be a good ruler in case I decided to stay. Right now, all I could think of was Adebayo rule number one.

"If you choose to step into your destiny, remember rule number one. Always be aware of who you are: Princess Brielle Eden Adebayo, the granddaughter of King Tiwa Jimoh Adebayo, the daughter of Naade Tayo Adebayo. No matter where you are, no matter who you are with, remember you are responsible for our country and must represent yourself accordingly."

Being around Tomori made me want to be simply Brielle. Acknowledging the royal side of my life meant I couldn't afford to be swayed by his good looks and charm. Suddenly the thousand-square-foot room seemed entirely too small for the two of us.

Remember who you are.

I straightened my spine and gestured to the seat in front of me. "Have a seat."

Tomori bowed deeply. "Ẹ káàsán, Ọmọba Brielle Adebayo."

A thrill shot straight through me at the low tenor of his voice as he wished me a good afternoon.

"Ẹ káàsán, Tomori." I switched to English. "Thank you for offering to help me."

"Mais bien sûr." He winked as he sat down, crossing his ankle over his knee. I wasn't sure if the wink was a happy-to-see-you greeting or a sign of mischievousness at the switch from Onina to French. *Mischievousness, of course.*

I sank into my wingback chair. "Do you use French often in the palace?"

"When necessary. Being knowledgeable in multiple subjects makes me an asset as a palace runner."

"Is that so?"

He nodded.

I cocked my head to the side, picturing him as a child. "I bet you kept your mother on her toes."

His head fell back as a belly laugh erupted. Pure delight filtered through me, like receiving a gold star from a teacher.

"I am the youngest. I could not get away with anything. My brothers before me ruined all the tricks."

"How many brothers do you have? Do you have any sisters?"

Tomori smiled. "I have two sisters. The rest of the six are boys."

My mouth dropped open. "Your mother is a saint."

"That she is." His lips curved in a soft smile.

Suddenly I wanted to meet her. To see how Tomori would act around her. See him in his own environment.

I swallowed. *Think business. Don't entertain this crush.*

"I didn't know what I needed," I said, motioning to the notepad and index cards before me, "so I have a bit of everything."

"Perfect. Do you know any French?"

"I do. I studied it in high school, then brushed up on some vocabulary when I saw it listed as a language here." I wouldn't call myself fluent, but hopefully I could hold my own.

"Good. Because the citizens who speak Creole will mix the two. If you know Onina and French, you should be able to converse with them as well."

"Does everyone know all the languages?"

Tomori shook his head. "No. There is kind of a class system in Ọlọrọ. Those with the most education and money know all the languages, though a lot will deny knowing any Creole. Those who haven't had the same opportunities as the wealthier citizens speak Creole or strictly Onina. Naturally there are those who will take the time to learn on their own."

"Who uses French?"

"Mostly businessmen and -women. Ọlọrọ conducts a lot of business on the mainland and with France. It is essential to know the language if they wish to be successful."

"That makes sense."

"Since you are versed in English and French, I will dive into the Onina lessons."

I nodded.

"Do you know the greetings?"

"Yes." Onina didn't have a word that translated to *hello*. Only phrases of well wishes that differed depending on the time of day.

"What are they?"

"Ẹ *ku idaji*, ẹ káàárò, ẹ káàsán." The last was how Tomori had greeted me when he walked in. "Ẹ kúròlé, ẹ *káalé*, and *o d'àáró*."

He grinned, flashing his pearly whites. "Very good. Your pronunciation is spot on."

My cheeks warmed at the compliment. "Mo dúpẹ, Tomori."

"*Kò tópé*. I am here to help."

We went through a few more phrases, ones I had been practicing in my head since I arrived. After twenty minutes, Tomori leaned forward and grabbed a few index cards.

"I am going to write down some words. These will be your homework, and I will see how well you do tomorrow."

"Okay. What are they?"

"They are vocabulary relating to the government."

Definitely something I'd need to know. "Oh, that will be helpful." Especially if I stayed.

"Has Mr. Owusu given you a lesson on the council yet?"

I met his gaze, and stillness entered my heart. How were his eyes so dark but full of such light? I cleared my throat. "Uh, no, he hasn't."

"I am sure he will, and when he does, you will be able to refer to everyone by their proper title." Tomori put down the black marker and handed me the stack of cards. "There you go. I will see you tomorrow?"

I nodded. "Yes. Thank you again for doing this. I really appreciate it."

"It is my pleasure. Truly."

We stood, and Tomori started to bow. Before I could think through my emotions, I stopped him. "Please don't, Tomori. Don't bow before me."

My heart pounded. I shouldn't have said that. Shouldn't have forgotten Grandfather's first rule.

But being around Tomori made me long for the simple life of Bri.

Tomori froze, his eyes rising to meet mine, then he slowly straightened. "Your Highness, I can be your friend, but please, you cannot ever forget you are the heir to the Ọlọran throne."

I felt chastened but not rebuked. How could I, when respect dripped from every word he spoke? And the soft way he addressed me, as if he wished for more and knew it could never be.

Or maybe that was me projecting my wishful thinking.

"And if I said no to the crown?"

A sad smile touched his lips. "I do not believe you will."

I had no words, but I was sorry for overstepping and asking Tomori not to be who he was: a respectful man who loved his country and its traditions.

"I'm sorry," I whispered.

"There is nothing to be sorry for." He bowed. "Until next time, Your Highness."

"*Ó dàbọ̀*, Tomori."

"Good-bye, Brielle."

He strode out of my office, and I sank into my seat.

Why couldn't I keep my composure around him? Why did I have to fall apart and seek a deeper connection? He was right. I was an Adebayo and couldn't forget it. No matter how much I longed for someone to remind me that I was still me. Brielle Bayo.

Maybe my wrestling with the crown was really about my identity. I'd been brought up as a Bayo only to discover I was truly an Adebayo, an heir to a kingdom I'd never heard of until my mother decided to be honest. I blew out a breath.

Maybe if I could reconcile the two, I could make a decision. Then again, perhaps Grandfather would make a full recovery and all this worry would be for naught. Until then, I needed to heed the advice of those who knew more.

Heavenly Father, I pray that I remember all that Mobo, Tomori, and Grandfather are trying to teach me. May I soak up the information. May I keep my heart attuned to Your will so that I'll please You in all that I do.

And thank You, Lord, for being a God who would allow me to pour out my heart before You and for caring about my worries.

Amen.

EIGHTEEN

Dayo interrupted my musings, a harried expression on her face. "Your Highness, the king needs to see you now."

I jumped to my feet. "Is he . . ."

"He is fine. It is not health-related."

I blinked back the tears that had sprung to life at the thought of his decline. Dayo set a brisk pace as we set out for Grandfather's chambers. When we entered the waiting room of his office, Mobo stood, then bowed before me.

"He is waiting for you, Your Highness." Mobo knocked on the door, then let me in.

"Are you okay, Grandfather?"

I stopped short. A graveness furrowed his brow, tugging his mouth downward and telling me all I needed to know. I sank into the chair across from his desk. "What happened?"

"Sijuwola has demanded a meeting with the council. He has claimed you are unfit to reign and wants to be named successor."

My heart pounded in my chest.

"I am sorry to pressure you, granddaughter, but I need an answer from you tomorrow. If you wish to abdicate, I will inform the council, and they will then make a decision on how to handle Sijuwola. But . . . if you decide to succeed me, they will need to meet you and determine if you are fit to rule."

I gulped. "When tomorrow?"

"At breakfast you can give me your answer. I will handle everything from there."

Why had Sijuwola pressed the issue? He knew I was taking my time. It was a topic of every family dinner. Surely Maseso and his wife had reported back to him, since Uncle had failed to attend them.

"I understand. I'll have an answer for you then."

Grandfather dipped his head. "If you need to go and think, please do."

"All right." I stood. "I will see you at dinner."

He winced. "Sijuwola is in a mood. I am sure he plans to show up for dinner tonight. Perhaps it is best you take dinner in your room with Iris or go out."

"I think staying in sounds like a good option." I offered a smile. "I'll see you tomorrow at breakfast."

"I love you, granddaughter. No matter what you choose."

"I love you too."

My mind was in a daze as I headed to my room. What path was God's will? Which path would give me the most peace?

Oof. I stumbled back as I bounced off the body I'd bumped into. My gaze ran up the tunic before me and stopped at my uncle's cold black eyes.

"Brielle." The frost in his voice raised goosebumps along my arms.

I steeled my spine. "Uncle Sijuwola, how are you today?"

He arched an eyebrow. "Small talk, Your Highness?"

"Manners, Uncle." I wouldn't let him make me feel weak for trying to be respectful.

He smirked. "Did Tiwa tell you the good news?"

"He did. Thank you so much for making my trip here memorable. It was a surprise to learn I had extended family, and now, to know your character . . ."

"Are you insinuating something?" He took a step closer. "Be careful, *niece*."

"I'm simply making an observation." I paused. "Now, if you'll excuse me, it appears I have a decision to make." I stepped aside and strolled away, hoping I looked cool and collected.

Too bad my mouth had lost all moisture and the sweat glands in my hands had apparently gained it. My throat ached with unshed tears. I thought I'd have more time to make a decision. But to have someone from my family *force* the issue in such a nasty way . . . What else would I have to endure in order to be crowned?

Once in my room, I called Dayo to request a dinner tray, then texted Iris. She offered to eat with me, but I just wanted to be alone. I didn't want any more advice but desired clarity and peace to make the right decision.

As the night wore on, I moved from my bed to the balcony, allowing the sound of the waves to soothe the pounding in my head. After a few deep breaths, some of my tension ebbed. I sank onto a chaise, leaning back against the headrest to close my eyes. The splash of water was peaceful white noise that I hoped would help me be still. *Lord, please don't let this be one of those times You let me choose my own path. I need to hear from You.*

I desperately wanted to remain in His will, and this felt too big for me to go *eenie meenie miney mo.* I practiced slow breathing until my eyes shuttered closed.

"Brielle Adebayo."

A quiet voice pricks the edges of my consciousness. "Hmm?" *I mumble.*

"Brielle Adebayo."

I sit up, then raise my hands in the air to work out the kinks in my back. How long have I been sitting out here? Wait, someone is calling me.

"Brielle Adebayo."

"Yes?" *I stare in astonishment at the scene before me.*

The waves of the ocean splash onto the shore. Palm trees line the wooded area to my left. I wiggle my toes in the damp sand. I had only closed my eyes for a brief second. Surely I didn't sleepwalk onto the shores of Àlááfià.

"Brielle Adebayo."

The voice is coming from ahead. I peer above the waves to

match my sight line with the horizon. An apparition shimmers above the water. My feet move forward as my spirit quickens. I stop at the edge of the beach, waves lapping my feet.

"Lord, is that You?" I whisper.

I squint to get a better view, but the Spirit remains transparent—a light shimmering above the dark waves. I recall the story of Samuel, and my heart leaps.

"Speak, Lord. I'm listening."

The apparition—no, the Lord—walks to me and holds out His hands.

I stare at the space between us. The night sky has fallen, and I can't see where the beach ends and the deep starts, for that's where He hovers.

"My child, your focus is not where it ought to be."

My eyes shoot upward, and for a brief moment, I see a face. One my heart knows but my eyes do not recognize. "But the water . . ." *How deep did I have to tread?*

"Come to me."

I reach for Him. My fingers tremble as I realize I'll have to take more steps to close the gap between us. Without looking down, I place one foot forward. The waves caress my ankles as my heart thuds in my ears. I move the other foot, thankful the gap is closing. Still my heart pounds, wondering how many steps my feet will need to take to bring us together.

The unyielding kindness in His eyes bores into my soul and eases the many questions clamoring for attention. My breath evens out as I take another step. He has me. He's always had me. No matter what I've gone through, no matter what has surprised me, none of it was out of God's purview.

He wants my full trust despite the unknowns, or maybe because of them.

I barely notice the mounting water as I slip my hand into His. Every fear ceases. A peace floods my heart, and tears spring to my eyes.

"Are you listening, Brielle Adebayo?"

"Yes, Lord."

"You are exactly where you need to be. Do not look back unless you want to count how far you've come."

"Yes, Lord." My bottom lip trembles.

"I will lead you, if you but keep your eyes on Me."

"I will." Even now, I can look nowhere else.

I sense His pleasure, and then He's gone.

———

I jolted upright, pulse throbbing, looking left then right, an eerie sense of déjà vu hitting me. When had a dream ever felt so real? I peered down at my feet, bare but not covered in sand. I still sat in the chaise on my balcony.

Yet there was a definite awakening in my spirit. A certainty that the Lord had spoken and that my life was now in Ọlọrọ Ilé not New York.

"Is that right?" I whispered, wondering if the Lord was still with me.

Of *course* He was. He promised to never leave me, and His Spirit dwelled within me. I had *never* experienced anything like that dream. As if I had been in His very presence.

I headed inside and closed the balcony doors behind me. Grabbing my journal from the nightstand, I sat on the bed and wrote everything down before it slipped away. I had a feeling I would need a written reminder of this moment for the days of doubt that surely loomed ahead.

Uncle Sijuwola would not be happy with my decision, but I was not saying yes to show him up. God had called me to something greater, and Grandfather was asking me to continue the Adebayo legacy in a way he no longer could.

I could only pray that God would continue to guide me and that the people around me would help equip me to be a leader worthy of the people.

NINETEEN

"Did you decide?"

Iris and I sat in our sitting room, chatting until it was time to meet Grandfather for breakfast.

"I was praying all yesterday," she said.

"I'm going to stay." Saying the words out loud made everything final, but the peace from last night lingered. I hadn't known if the morning light would bring me a host of doubts, but the moment I'd experienced in my dream prevailed.

"How do you feel about the decision?" Iris's eyes scrutinized me as if trying to decide if she should be happy for me or not.

"I'm so relieved because I *know* God wants me to stay."

"Oh good!" She wrapped her arms around me. "I'm so happy for you. I know you've been agonizing over this. Did you tell your grandfather yet?"

I shook my head. "I will at breakfast. You're the first to know."

"You're going to make a great queen, Bri."

Queen? I gulped. I'd barely wrapped my thoughts around the title of princess, let alone—

Iris dipped her head, her gaze boring into mine. "Breathe. You've made the decision. Now just wait for the next step."

"Right." I exhaled. "Who knows, my grandfather could beat the odds." My prayers had been asking for that since I'd first met him, because I didn't want to say good-bye.

"Exactly. Six months could be years for all we know."

"You're right. I still can't believe I'm Princess Brielle Adebayo." The title and full last name still sounded strange to my ears, despite my time in Ọlọrọ Ilé.

"Oh, girl, this is so exciting." Tears filled Iris's eyes.

"I think the excitement for me will come . . . later?"

Part of me wondered what Tomori would say about it all. My next language lesson couldn't get here soon enough.

"What are you thinking about?" Iris asked.

Heat filled my face. "Just all the lessons."

"Hmm, maybe the language ones specifically?" she singsonged.

I dropped my head into my hands. "It was a totally platonic thought. It's just that Tomori's so easy to talk to."

"And dreamy."

My stomach dipped in agreement. A perfect picture of his chiseled features and steadfast calm settled in my mind.

"You're thinking about him again, aren't you?"

I blinked. "What? No. No." I smoothed my hand over my knee.

"Yeah, you are. You bite your lip and stare into the distance as if you can picture him perfectly and you two are in some romantic tale made for the big screen."

I sighed. "Nothing can happen, though."

"Why not?"

"I'm a twenty-five-year-old princess. My life is in upheaval. And frankly, adding relationship drama to the mix seems a bit foolish."

Iris groaned. "But you could have an island romance. We're in a beautiful country. The people are friendly." She shook her head. "But I understand your hesitation. I'd love a summer romance, though. It's like all the men are missing my neon sign that says *Here for fun, won't take life too seriously.*"

I rolled my eyes. "Please, you want a romance more than I do. You're the poster child for committed relationships."

"But unlike you, I'm not staying. James would die if I didn't return."

"Nothing says you can't change your mind. I'm sure he's quite capable of hiring a replacement."

"I can't imagine what would make me leave my life back in the city."

True. Iris loved her job. I couldn't think of anything that would make her give up her career and stay in Ọlọrọ. But wouldn't it be nice to have my best friend nearby?

"You ready for breakfast?" Iris asked.

"Yes. Thank goodness they don't serve fish for breakfast."

We headed for the family dining room, making the right twists and turns until we came to the blue dining room door. I grabbed the ringed handle and tugged. The smell of fresh bread and tropical fruits greeted us, and I sighed with pleasure. Breakfast was my favorite meal here. They always had those *akara* balls—the yummy bean bread balls I'd had the very first day.

The dining table also held platters of chocolate pastries, fresh fruit, and a frittata, as well as carafes filled with coffee and juice. Grandfather sat next to Mobo.

"Ẹ káàárò, ómọ ọmọ, Ms. Blakely." Grandfather dipped his head in acknowledgment.

"Ẹ káàárò, Bàbá àgbà."

"Good morning, Your Majesty," Iris stated.

He grinned and motioned for Mobo to leave. "Sit, sit, ladies. Did you have a good rest?"

"I did." The best sleep since we'd landed. It could have been the peace brought by last night's dream or the relief of making a decision. *Or both.*

"So did I. Everything looks so good." Iris practically vibrated in her seat. She'd been up working for a few hours already and hadn't eaten yet. She was existing on coffee alone right now.

"Fill your plates. Then I will say grace so we may start the day off right."

"Do you go to church, Grandfather?" He'd mentioned his faith a few times, but I had yet to delve into the specifics of his beliefs. I started filling my plate.

"Yes. I go to the eight o'clock service. It is done in Onina, but we have a French and English service as well."

"And it's . . . a Christian service?"

"Yes. Ọlọrọ is predominantly a Christian nation. We have a Catholic church in the city, and the eastern part of the country has a small Muslim population. They have two mosques in the area."

"Are you required to attend the service as the king, or do you go by choice?"

"Good question. Are you simply curious about my faith or wondering about all the monarch duties?"

This was it. Time to tell him my decision. I took a deep breath for fortification. "I've decided to assume my duties as your heir."

"Praise the Father." He brought his hands together in benediction. "You have made me so happy, ómọ ọmọ. So happy," he rasped, then started coughing.

It was a stark reminder of why my decision held so much weight.

After Grandfather collected himself, he met my gaze. "I cannot wait to tell the council. Your uncle will be upset, but that is not my main concern."

"You said I might need to go before the council, right?"

"Yes. I am sure they will determine when once I notify them of your decision."

"Is there anything I can do to prepare?"

"Yes. I will alert Mobo so he can walk you through everything. He will teach you how to present yourself to the royal council." He dabbed at his mouth. "Then we need to introduce you to the country."

I gulped. "At the party you mentioned, right?" I wasn't ready for anything else right now. I twisted my cloth napkin in my lap.

"Yes. We will have it the night of Independence Day. We can announce your position as the heir that day so the country can meet you during the throne parade."

"Do they use the one that sits in the throne room now?" Iris asked.

"Oh no." Grandfather's breathing punctuated his words. "Craftsmen make a new one each year, and then it is added to the throne museum after the procession is complete."

"Seriously?" I asked. *Amazing!*

"Yes. It is a wonderful event. I will make a speech and have you sit on the throne instead of me. It will be symbolic, and the people will understand you are my successor."

A host of bats took flight in my stomach. "So I have until the twenty-eighth to prepare myself?"

"You will be fine." Grandfather squeezed my hand. "If you can meet the council and pass muster, everything else will be as it should be."

Would it really? Digi and Dayo had me thinking otherwise. I turned to Iris, widening my eyes in a plea. But for what, I wasn't sure. Help? Reassurance?

"You've got the crazy eyes," she whispered.

And just like that, I laughed, letting the tension go.

"I will text Mobo to let him know to prepare you for a council meeting. After I talk with them myself, I will let Dayo know what day you will see them."

A few minutes later, Mobo walked into the room and bowed before Grandfather. "Yes, Your Majesty?"

"My granddaughter is ready."

Mobo's gaze flickered to mine, then back to Grandfather's. "I will prepare her."

"I know you will. Please meet with her right after breakfast."

"I will let Ms. Layeni know as well."

"Ẹ seun, Mobo."

He bowed and disappeared once more.

My heart did a strange tango of palpitations as reality sank in. I would lead a country. *A whole country!* Then the memory of waves lapping at the shore pushed my panic aside, and peace wrapped around me like a warm hug.

After breakfast I said good-bye to Iris. She was going to explore the island with Chidi. I proceeded down the hallway to my office so I could discuss the rules of the council with Mobo. Once he arrived, we jumped right into business.

"The most important thing to know is the council members. The king also sits on the council. He is the tiebreaker. He can make suggestions and implement decisions, but as a last resort or at a council member's request. He is there to ensure the council does not act untowardly and adheres to the rules we have. However, he usually wants them to work without his input if possible."

"That makes sense. Kind of like watching over kids. You hope they follow rules and work to solve problems without coming to the teacher."

Mobo nodded, his face devoid of expression. It was hard to get to know him. He was helpful and very knowledgeable, but I couldn't figure out if he liked me or merely tolerated me for the king's sake.

I licked my lips. "And the council members?"

"Each tribe in Ọlọrọ is represented in the council. There is a head council member who opens the meeting for business and closes it when done. Jomi Oladele is the elder from the Etikun tribe."

"The alàgbà, correct?" I asked.

Mobo blinked. "You have studied the words for the council already?"

"Tomori thought it would be best to start with vocabulary for the government."

"He was right." Mobo adjusted his black tie. "The other three members are Adeyemi Ladipo of the Òkè tribe, Oyinlola Keita of the Opolopo tribe, and Jamal Ibrahim of the Musulumi tribe. Ms. Keita is the only female council member."

My eyebrows shot up. "I thought women in power were frowned upon." Wasn't that the explanation given by Dayo and Digi?

Mobo swallowed. "Ọlọrọ has a long way to go in terms of women's equality. However, the Opolopo tribu has always embraced their women in leadership roles. Although, overall, Ọlọrans may have a difficult time accepting your rule."

Did he? But the question remained behind my lips. I didn't need Mobo's approval, though I wanted his respect.

I took notes as he continued describing the council, praying they would not be a roadblock but a support system in the transition of my life from Brielle to Princess.

Later that evening, Dayo led Iris and me to the royal fitting room. I shouldn't have been surprised that the palace had a room exclusively for dressing purposes, but I was. My five-hundred-square-foot apartment in the city hadn't prepared me for the many laps of luxury befitting a title, especially the sight behind the double doors.

White-and-tan marble tile covered the floor, while gold-rimmed ivory crown molding framed the room. Floor-to-ceiling mirrors covered two of the four walls, making the room seem bigger and brighter. Brown leather tufted ottomans were situated to provide seating around a raised dais in the center of the room.

"Wow," I murmured.

"I'll say," Iris concurred.

Dayo studied me. "Your Highness, Ms. Blakely, I have an idea."

"Okay."

"Since we are not telling everyone who you are just yet, I thought it would be wise to ask Ms. Blakely to create a dress for you to wear to the Independence Day celebration."

"I would love to!" Iris shrieked.

I laughed at Dayo's wide eyes. She clearly hadn't expected Iris to squeal as if Michael Jackson had been raised from the dead and moonwalked into the room.

"I have so many ideas! What are my fabric options? Color choices?"

"The dress must be the royal colors, but you can use whatever fabric you need."

"Yowzers. You may regret that."

"No, you won't," I interjected before Dayo ran away, petrified by Iris's exuberance.

Dayo walked over to a wall full of drawers. "We have fabric samples from the vendors we deal with the most. If you find something you like, tell me, and I will order it."

"Yes, ma'am."

Dayo peered down at her calendar. "Your Highness, do not forget your afternoon appointment with Mr. Eesuola."

"Thank you."

"Do you need me to escort you back to your office?"

I shook my head.

"Then I will be in the office."

"Thank you again, Dayo."

As soon as Dayo left, Iris turned to me. "Girl, how can you see that fine man every day and not swoon?"

I threw my hands in the air. "Iris, *nothing* can happen."

"Yeah, tell me that after a few more days of seeing his pretty face."

"You're incorrigible."

"Or so prophetic that I'll be saying *I told you so* in a couple of weeks."

I shook my head, but deep down I wondered.

TWENTY

I slipped on a navy long-sleeved silk blouse, tucking it into the matching pencil skirt covered in green medallions. Today I would stand before the royal council to gain their approval to be named an official heir to the throne. Grandfather assured me it was a mere formality, that the council members would meet me, express any concerns they might have—which I could refute—and then vote.

As such, I needed to look my best. Iris had chosen this outfit as professional and stylish as well. I wasn't sure if the council cared whether or not my clothing could trend on the latest social media sites, but the ensemble made me feel elegant and capable. The pattern wasn't as overwhelming as I'd imagined.

Lord God, please empower me with Your words, and may Your will be done in the council meeting. Thank You.

I remembered Tomori's excitement at my news. How he believed I would be a great queen. To commemorate the occasion, he'd brought me another pot of orchids. This time they were black with pink centers. Every part of my heart that ached for a love like my parents' had come alive at the gift. Our eyes had locked until his walkie-talkie squawked an assignment for him. His shift had changed, and now he worked after our lessons were complete.

I snapped out of the memory and moved forward, my heels echoing in the corridor. The royal council gathered on the second floor near the royal offices. Grandfather had said we'd walk in together to make an entrance. Whether he meant literally or figuratively had yet to be determined. In my nervous state, I hadn't bothered asking for clarification.

"Brielle, you look wonderful," Grandfather exclaimed as I walked toward him. He met me partway, leaning forward to kiss my cheek. He stepped back, holding out my arm to take in my appearance.

I smiled and did a twirl. "Ta-da."

He chuckled softly. His face looked a little wan.

"Are you feeling okay?"

"Just a little tired today, but that cannot be helped. It is hard to get a good night's rest when one cannot stop coughing."

My heart turned over. "Can the doctor give you something to ensure a better rest?" I could email my mother. She wasn't an oncologist, but surely she knew a good one. Maybe then I'd finally have an excuse to bridge the gap I'd been avoiding. I'd failed to respond to her call when she received her vase. I felt too guilty for not including a note with it like I'd intended.

"Dr. Falade offered something, but I do not like how the medicine makes me feel. I need my wits about me for the meeting."

"Grandfather," I gently admonished.

"I know, I know. Maybe after Independence Day." He offered his arm. "Come, let us show the council you are the right fit."

"Yes, sir."

We strolled toward the room at a sedate pace. I could hear Grandfather's labored breathing, the noise breaking something inside of me. At this moment, a miraculous healing seemed impossible. *Lord, help my unbelief. Please bring healing to his body. I need more time with him.*

"Brielle, do you remember all the council members' names?"

"Yes." After the lesson from Mobo and the Oninan vocabulary from Tomori, I believed I was ready to meet everyone. "Will Uncle be there?"

"No, Sijuwola has had his moment before the council. Now it is your turn."

Grandfather stopped before a door guarded by a man in a royal uniform.

The man bowed. "Welcome, Your Majesty. I will announce you both to the council." He slipped into the room.

I gulped around the lump in my throat as my palms grew sweaty. "He knows who I am?"

"He does not know your station." Grandfather patted my hand. "You will be fine, ómọ ọmọ. You will see."

"I hope so," I murmured.

The double doors opened, and Grandfather stepped forward. I straightened my spine and kept pace as he headed straight for the center of the room. We faced the half-moon table occupied by the alàgbà from the different Ọlọran tribes.

Grandfather spoke in Onina, greeting each one by name before he introduced me.

I stepped forward and bowed to each council member. "Ẹ káàárò, alàgbà tribu."

Jomi Oladele, the elder of the Etikun tribe, smiled. I recognized him from the pictures Mobo had shown me and the many articles that had come up when I searched the internet one night. His cheekbones were dotted with moles, and his afro was a wiry gray color.

"Ẹ káàárò, Brielle Adebayo. The council acknowledges your presence on this day. You are here for a formal vote accepting your succession to rule Ọlọrọ Ilé upon the passing of King Tiwa Jimoh Adebayo. Do you believe you are fit to rule?"

My stomach tossed and turned as Mr. Oladele spoke, but when he asked the last question, it heaved upward. I swallowed down the contents of my stomach. God had called me to do this. *He* thought I was fit.

"Yes." My voice came out steady, and I wanted to cheer.

"Before we have an official vote, the council members have a right to state any objections and give you an opportunity to refute or correct any problems they find. I will go first."

His eyes roamed me from head to toe in an appraising manner. I prayed that I exuded confidence and respect at the same time.

"Why would you, an American, one who did not step foot into our country until a couple of weeks ago, be *fit* to rule our great nation? Especially considering Sijuwola Adebayo doubts your credentials?"

Why indeed? "I believe that it is God's will. But I am also taking steps to ensure I know the history of the country and understand the heart of its people."

Adeyemi Ladipo scoffed, his bushy eyebrows tilted into a V. Yet he made no comment.

"And after two weeks, you think you understand it all?"

That wasn't what I'd said. Still, I tempered my expression and answered Mr. Oladele's objections. "I do not, alàgbà. I am making and will continue to make efforts to understand so that the people get the ruler they deserve."

"Hmm." He rubbed his chin. "King Adebayo, do you agree that your granddaughter is fit to rule?"

"I do," Grandfather stated. "My trusted assistant, Mobo Owusu, has worked tirelessly to make her knowledgeable. She is also taking lessons in Onina."

"Oh, really?" Mr. Ladipo crooned in Onina. "Can she speak it fluently?"

"*Rárá.*" No. "However, I will continue taking lessons until I am proficient," I added in English. And didn't that just send butterflies to my stomach, imagining seeing Tomori so often.

"Wait your turn, Mr. Ladipo," Mr. Oladele objected. "I am not finished."

"Carry on."

Mr. Oladele peered at me, his gaze scrutinizing. "When was Ọlọrọ granted its independence?"

"June 28, 1912."

"And its official name?"

"The Kingdom of Ọlọrọ Ilé or Ọlọrọ Ilé Ijọba."

Mr. Oladele asked me a few more questions, which I answered correctly. Finally, quiet descended as he stared at me. "I, Jomi Oladele, alàgbà for the Etikun tribu, have no more questions or objections."

The lone female council member was next. Her black locs fell shoulder-length and were woven with gray here and there. Black glasses with circular lenses covered most of her face. She cleared her throat and spoke.

"I, Oyinlola Keita, alàgbà for the Opolopo tribu, have one question."

"Please speak, alàgbà," I prompted, following the formalities of the council.

"Do you feel any allegiance to the people of Ọlọrọ?"

I paused to gather my thoughts. "I do. I have spent time exploring the island and talking to the people. From the moment I stepped off the plane, I have felt a connection to this place. One I cannot explain but know is very real nonetheless." I stopped myself before I began babbling. Had I said too much or just the right amount?

"Does the answer satisfy the questioner?" Mr. Oladele asked.

"It does," Ms. Keita replied. "I, Oyinlola Keita, alàgbà for the Opolopo tribu, have no objections."

"Then I believe it is my turn." Mr. Ladipo smirked. I wasn't surprised to see the smarm coating his features. Studying his picture over the past few days had been enough to make me uneasy. Had no one ever asked him to dial down the condescension a bit? Perhaps I was being judgmental.

"I, Yemi Ladipo, alàgbà for the Òkè tribu, have an objection."

Ms. Keita pursed her lips, as if his objection was something that happened at every council meeting.

"Please speak, alàgbà," I requested.

"Are you married?"

Uh . . . "No, alàgbà."

"That is what I thought."

Something foreboding slithered down my spine.

"According to Ọlọran Royal Decree fourteen twenty," Mr. Ladipo continued, "a female heir can only secure her succession if she is married." His lips curved into a Grinch-like grin as he formed his fingers into a triangle.

"Grandfather?" I whispered.

"Let me handle this," he murmured, then raised his voice so all could hear. "Gentlemen, that decree was written over a hundred years ago. I think we can all agree that we have progressed into a modern-day society. After all, Ms. Keita was able to fill her role as alàgbà with no complications."

That was Grandfather handling this? Judging from the side-eye glances of the councilmen, his answer would not appease the objection.

"Your Majesty, we need to confer before we can continue," Mr. Oladele stated.

"If I may," interjected Jamal Ibrahim, elder of the Musulumi tribu, "I would like to state my lack of objection before we confer. She is Prince Naade's child and as such should be allowed to be the king's heir."

"So noted," Jomi stated. "Your Majesty, if you and the princess would give us a few minutes to confer, we would be grateful."

As soon as the doors closed behind us, Grandfather began pacing back and forth.

"What does this mean?" I asked.

He coughed and held up a finger. I waited to see if the coughing fit would stop or if I would need to have the guard grab a glass of water.

After a few seconds, he wiped his mouth with his handkerchief. "It means they will require you to rectify the objection, or they will decide the decree is outdated and no longer necessary. If they choose the latter, they will vote for an amendment."

"Can you amend the law without their approval?"

"No."

God, help. They wouldn't really expect me to marry just to become the next ruler, would they? Talk about archaic. I had male acquaintances from school and church, but none of them were someone I'd feel comfortable posing the question of marriage to.

An image of Tomori came to mind, and I pushed it away. No way would that fly. Besides, the marriage issue could end up being moot if the council voted to amend the decree.

Please, please, please.

Grandfather soon tired, and the guard provided a chair for him to sit in while I stood nearby. An hour later, *finally*, the council was ready for our return.

Mr. Oladele adjusted his purple tie. "The royal council has searched for any reason modifications should be made to the decree after discussing the reasoning for its origins. After conferring about the ramifications of an amendment, we have decided that the decree shall stand. In order for Princess Brielle Eden Adebayo to succeed King Tiwa Jimoh Adebayo upon his death, she will need to be married. Female rule is nonexistent, and the majority of the council would feel better knowing she is married."

I gulped as the words rang in my head like a clanging cymbal. If I had to guess, Ms. Keita had probably been the only one on my side. My gaze shifted to hers, and she gave me a commiserating nod.

"Are there any restrictions on who she must marry? A time frame the vows must be spoken by? Any extra stipulations?" Grandfather asked in a tired voice.

"Whoever she chooses *must* meet council approval. If we have no objections, she is free to marry such man. We all agree she should be married before your death, Your Majesty. It does not matter how long before your passing, as long as the ceremony is performed by a minister. We would also prefer that her future husband be an Ọlọran."

"If I may, Jomi?" Mr. Ladipo asked with a sneer.

"The floor is yours, Yemi." Mr. Oladele waved a hand for him to proceed.

"We have created a list of appropriate eligible men from Ọlọrọ. Each of us has chosen a respectable man from our tribe. Mr. Ibrahim has declined a recommendation due to religious differences." He pushed a sheet of paper forward. "We strongly suggest you give consideration to the men here when proceeding."

A runner retrieved the paper and handed it to me. I stared down at the list of strangers.

"You must choose your future prince if you wish to become our future queen. Do you agree to this undertaking?" Mr. Ladipo stared me down, daring me to object. To fold. To say I couldn't handle it.

Which I couldn't. I wanted to curl into a ball and cry for my mother. Instead I remembered the deep waters I had walked through to get to the Lord and His will. I pressed my shoulders back and met Mr. Ladipo's gaze head on.

"I agree. I will choose my prince."

"Then the council formally recognizes you as the king's heir. If you do not marry according to the agreed-upon terms, then the heirship will be revoked. Council is adjourned." Mr. Oladele cleared his throat. "We will convene again when the princess presents her choice of husband."

The council stood, bowed before Grandfather and me, then left the room.

TWENTY-ONE

"You have to what?" Iris's mouth dropped open.

I paced blindly back and forth, my limbs heavy and an ache so intense in my being that I couldn't even tell where it originated. "They said I have to get married before Grandfather dies in order to ascend the throne." My eyes heated at the threat of tears.

Knowing opposition would come was completely different from living through it. It was bad enough I had to give up a career I loved. Teaching civics to my students, sharing my passion for how to be a good citizen and the knowledge needed for that was what I'd built my whole adult life around. The desire to be in God's will was my greater wish, but how could I lose one more part of myself?

There would be no romance in my future. No movie-worthy story where boy meets girl and they fall madly in love with one another. Instead, the council had given me a "choice" that really wasn't one at all. And who were these men on their list?

"That's craziness, Bri. They can't expect you to find someone to marry in that kind of time frame."

"Oh, but they do. Stupid, *stupid* decree," I muttered as a tear slipped down my cheek.

Iris took my hand, halting me in my tracks. Her big brown eyes met mine, water filling their depths. "What are you going to do?"

"I want to wallow in the unfairness of it all. My grandfather is dying. I can't be a teacher anymore. And now I have to marry some man I don't know? For the good of the country? I knew I'd have to give up part of myself, but this?"

Iris drew me into a hug, and I barely recognized the tears dampening her shirt. I sobbed until I couldn't cry any longer. Iris reached for a tissue from the end table and passed it my way.

"I can't believe they're doing this," she said. "Are you sure? Are you really sure you want to stay? To be their future queen?"

Did I truly have a choice? God wanted me here, that much was clear. If He placed me here for a greater purpose, what faith would I show if I ran at the first sign of trouble? How would choosing my wants in this moment show my love to Him? Because right now I wanted to run faster than Usain Bolt and hop on the next flight back to my quiet life of teaching.

But deep down in the recesses of my soul, I knew I couldn't. *Wouldn't.* I believed that God was good, and though the council's orders seemed anything but, I chose to hold on to my faith.

"I have to do what I must, Iris." I wiped the last of my tears away. "I *know* God wants me to be queen. I can't just turn my back on that knowledge and pretend like I'm still searching for answers."

"Then you're just going to marry some *stranger?*"

"I don't want to." I groaned. "But what else *can* I do?" I flopped onto the couch, and Iris followed suit.

She audibly gulped. "Asking something of this magnitude seems so wrong."

"They gave me the option of saying no." Maybe refusing would have kept me from feeling like I'd been in a hit-and-run. But I'd also have to bear Grandfather's disappointment.

"Then what would happen to Ọlọrọ?" Iris threw her hands in the air. "They put you in an impossible situation."

"Mr. Ladipo found that decree. Is it their fault for upholding it?"

"Uh, yes! They could have amended it."

"There was only one person for that."

"Misogynistic . . . chauvinistic . . . *ugh!*" Iris flopped back against the cushion. "It's like we're going back in time."

"Yep." I stared down at my hands, not seeing anything but my own hurt, my own losses.

Silence filled the room. My head felt too heavy to contemplate the whys. Instead, I blew out a breath and looked up at the ceiling. Maybe I could find strength to take the next step if I could visualize the Lord hovering over the waters.

"You said they gave you a list of men?" Iris asked.

I reached for the piece of paper I'd crumpled during my pacing. Smoothing out the sheet, I passed it to Iris. She studied the names.

"Chimnoya Sule, Kambili Udo, and Ekon Diallo. What do you know about these men?"

"Nothing." Wasn't that another fiery dart. "I'm sure Grandfather, Dayo, or Mobo could give me the inside scoop."

"True." She tapped her chin. "What if you turn the search into an adventure? Kind of like *The Bachelorette*? Go on a date with each of them, and if you catch any bad vibes, eliminate the man from the list. But if you *do* feel a connection, go out with them again."

"It's official." A forced chuckle fell from my lips. "I've entered an alternate universe. Some portal I had no intention of stepping through. I knew I shouldn't have checked the wardrobes when we arrived."

A peal of laughter filled the air. Iris wiped her tears as she continued to laugh and then laugh some more. My lips twitched, and soon I joined in. It was that or continue shedding tears.

"Bri," Iris gasped, "if you went down a rabbit hole, you sure did drag me with you."

I snorted. "You have a return ticket, but if I click my heels three times, I'll probably just change outfits."

She laughed. "At least you'll stay fashionable in this mess."

"Ugh."

"Bri?"

Nervous energy filled the air. "Yes?"

"Are you going to tell your mom?"

I blew out a breath. "When they told me their verdict, she was the first person I wanted to talk to."

"Then you'll call her?"

I closed my eyes, remembering that piercing need for her wisdom and comfort. "I will."

"Good." Iris squeezed my hand. "I'm going to leave you to it and find Dayo. Maybe she can give me the inside edition on these bachelors. I'll report back."

"Thanks, Iris."

"Anytime." She left the room.

I picked up the Ọlọran cell phone Dayo had handed over last week. Unlocking the screen and clicking on my contacts, I pulled up my mother's info. *Lord God, please give me the words. Please be in the midst of our conversation. Amen.* I hit DIAL and waited for her to pick up.

After four rings, I looked at the clock in the room. *Yikes.* It was only five in the morning her time. I went to end the conversation, but her groggy greeting halted my fingers.

"Brielle?"

"Hi, Mom."

"Hi, sweetie. How are you?"

That question seemed simple, but the emotions pushing for release proved the complexity of my life. Tears welled once more, as if my mind knew she'd make everything better.

"Bri?"

"I'm here." I wiped away an errant tear.

"What's wrong?"

"I told Grandfather I'd be his heir."

"I knew you would." Pride rang in every word.

"How?"

"You were made to lead, Bri. You've been the steady presence behind so many ventures. Think of how you led your Model UN students. Think of the ways you helped during election years, the clubs you joined in college and high school. You've always had a natural ability to gather a group and guide them to a purpose bigger than themselves. I don't think you ever fully utilized your skills because you were always trying to be behind the scenes."

I sighed. She wasn't wrong. I found comfort in being in the

background. The limelight had never appealed to me, but I had often been frustrated at the roles I had been placed in, always yearning for something just out of reach. Maybe everything in my life hadn't been orchestrated by her to groom me for a role she kept secret. "I suppose you're right."

She chuckled. "I get the feeling that's not the real reason you called. Although I am glad you shared it with me. It's a huge decision."

I bit my lip. Shouldn't we talk about the elephant in the room? Her betrayal? My reaction? Because that *was* part of the reason I'd called. "I met the royal council this morning." I told her about Sijuwola and everything that had led up to the events of the morning. "Mom, they won't let me succeed Grandfather unless I'm married."

"What? Is there no way around that?"

"No." I sniffed. "The council won't change the decree because I'm American and a woman." I rubbed my forehead.

"Did you agree to get married?" Shock echoed in the aftermath of her question.

"Yes," I squeaked, my throat raw from suppressing the urge to bawl my eyes out.

"To whom? You don't know anyone there!"

Knowing my mom was as upset as me wasn't helping. "They gave me a list of acceptable candidates. Iris thinks I should treat the husband hunt like a game show and date them all, then eliminate the ones I don't have a connection with." I forced out a chuckle, but a tear fell as well.

"That's so Iris." Her sigh filled the line. "I don't know if I should applaud her for trying to make the best of a situation or pull this blanket over my head and hope this is a dream."

"Right?" I shook my head, then pinched myself. Nope, this was my life.

"How do you feel about this, sweetie?"

"Lost. Angry. Resigned. Basically all the emotions. I don't know how I can marry a stranger."

"Brielle, would you like me to come there?"

Flutters erupted in my stomach. I wanted my mom here more than anything, but the hurt she'd inflicted kept me mute.

"I know you're still upset with me. And if you say yes, I know that doesn't mean you've forgiven me. But, Bri, if you let me come, you'll have one more person rooting for you. One more brain there to help you figure things out."

"But your work . . . how can you just take time off?"

"I'm not the only doctor at the hospital." I could hear the amusement in her voice. "Plus, being in a senior position gives me leeway. With our Martha's Vineyard vacation canceled, I'm still owed some time off."

I closed my eyes. I needed to do this—forgive my mother so our relationship could be restored. Not only that, God would want me to take this step. But I'd wait to tell her in person.

"Please come."

"I'll find a flight, then."

"Don't. I'll let Dayo know. She'll arrange everything."

"Who's that?"

"My secretary." I grimaced. That sounded so pretentious, but that was my world now.

"Okay. Then I'll wait to hear from her."

"Thank you, Mom." The burden I'd felt since the council had given me my options weighed less. My mother couldn't stop the decree, but maybe she could help me choose the right man.

"Anytime, sweetie."

We ended the call, and I walked over to the bathroom mirror. I needed to fix my face before finding out what Iris had discovered. What would the men think about this? Had the council already alerted them? Would they treat me with respect or like a possession?

I finished touching up my makeup, then made my way to my office, where I assumed Dayo could be found. Fortunately, I was correct. Iris was there as well, her fingers flying across her phone, probably taking notes as Dayo talked.

As soon as she saw me, Dayo shot to her feet and bowed. "Your Highness, we were just discussing the council's choices for your husband."

I gulped at the word *husband*. Would I really be married before the year's end? Most likely even by the summer's end? The end of June was already looming. "Could you catch me up, please?"

"Of course, Your Highness." Dayo sat and held up her phone, which displayed a picture of an older gentleman. His face was completely devoid of any facial hair, and he was bald as well. His almond-shaped eyes held a glimmer that was either mischievousness or a shade past sinister. He looked old enough to be my father.

"Who is he?"

"This is Prince Chimnoya Sule of the Òkè tribe."

"He's a prince?" I asked.

"That's exactly what I asked." Iris's nose wrinkled. "Apparently some of the other tribes have princes. However, since the Adebayo line is the one that inherits the crown, they do not rule. They're just well-respected within their tribe."

Huh. I'd have to talk to Mobo about that and ask for an increase in lessons. I needed to cram as much knowledge as possible before I stood in front of the council again. Who knew what they would ask of me next time.

I turned my attention back to the matter at hand. "So he's a prince but not a ruling one?"

"Yes, Your Highness."

I licked my lips. "He also looks quite a bit older than me." I was no Monica, and he was no Tom Selleck.

Dayo grimaced. "He is twice your age."

My stomach revolted. *I can't marry a fifty-year-old!* "How serious do you think the council is regarding these choices?"

Iris frowned. "You can just eliminate him from your list. No one says you have to meet him."

"Oh, but she does," Dayo stated. "The council will expect you to give these men serious consideration. You will *have* to meet them and go out with them for the council to believe you are working to correct your unmarried state."

Why? This was ridiculous. What world did I live in that I had to date a man twice my age in order to be seen as respectful and adherent?

Ugh. I needed the council to respect me. It was vital for my future and the kingdom's.

"Fine. I suppose I should have you reach out to him for me?" I asked Dayo.

"Most certainly, Your Highness." Dayo made a notation on her notepad.

"The next one is younger," Iris said.

"Oh yes," Dayo agreed. "Kambili Udo is not a prince, but he is a respected elder in the Opolopo tribe."

I wondered how much thought the council members had put into their choices. Did they just pick an elder from a hat or one they thought would make a fit husband? Were my options elders only? "How old is he?"

"He is thirty-five."

Ten years wasn't terrible. "How is he an elder already?"

"His father passed away, and he was voted into the spot."

"Okay, then please contact him as well."

"Yes, Your Highness. I will reach out to them after the Independence Day parade. I doubt the council has exposed your royal status yet."

That made sense.

"The last guy is Ekon Diallo," Iris said. Her cheeks flushed. "Um, I don't remember what tribe he's from, but he's twenty-eight."

Dayo held up her phone to show another picture. This man had classically handsome features and looked much closer to my age. Finally, a decent choice, if I based it on looks alone.

"What can you tell me about him?"

"I have heard many great things about him," Dayo said. "If you want my opinion, Your Highness, he would be the best pick. He comes from the Etikun tribe and is also a nonruling prince."

I tilted my head. "When I marry, if the man is untitled, does he become a prince? Does his title change after I become queen?" The queen of England wouldn't make her husband a king, but I wasn't sure how the law worked in Ọlọrọ.

"Yes. If he is not already a prince, he will become one upon your nuptials. Ọlọrọ Ilé does not allow the ruling couple to be unequally yoked in title. When you become queen, he will become king. However, you will be the ruling monarch. If you were to pass before him, only then could he ascend the throne. Following that, if you do not have a child together and he remarries, his line now becomes the ruling one, and any children he has thereafter would be his heirs."

"Will my kids have the Adebayo surname, or would I take his last name and my children as well?"

"Not exactly." Dayo straightened. "You will always be Princess Brielle Adebayo. When you marry him, you may add his name to yours, but Adebayo will be the ruling name, and any children you have will be Adebayos." Her brow furrowed. "You should know these things, Your Highness."

Ouch. But she wasn't wrong. "Is there anything else I need to know?" Though, how much more could my spinning brain handle?

"No, but do not forget about your Onina lesson this afternoon. Also, Mobo would like to do lessons all day if you are not scheduled for anything else."

Oh, good. "Please tell him that would be great."

Dayo dipped her head in acknowledgment.

I pointed toward my door. "I'm going inside to study." I headed for my office, then stopped. "Oh, Dayo, could you make arrangements for my mother to fly over on the private jet? She'll be coming for a visit."

"Certainly."

Iris beamed at me. *We'll talk later,* she mouthed.

I nodded and closed myself into my office. *Lord, please help me get through the rest of the day.*

I wasn't sure I could handle any more shocking news.

TWENTY-TWO

Tomori and I had been going through Oninan vocabulary for twenty minutes before I interrupted the lesson. "I have news."

He dipped his head. "Please share."

Great. I should have thought more about how to drop this hand grenade the council had lobbed at me.

"Your Highness?"

"Brielle . . . *please*."

Tomori nodded. "Sorry, Brielle."

I shivered at the sound of my name on his lips. Maybe I shouldn't have asked him to use my first name.

"Please tell me your news. Is it good? Is it about the council?"

"Sort of." I could feel my face twisting up like my knotted insides.

"What happened? Did it not go as planned? Did you forget to address them by their honorary titles?" He sat forward, brow furrowed.

I blew out a breath. It was now or never. "I remembered how to greet them and how to answer them. You and Mobo prepared me well." I smoothed a hand over my hair. "Mr. Ladipo just had one *slight* objection." I held my pointer and thumb a smidge apart, indicating the size of the objection. Perhaps I should have opened my arms wide to be more accurate.

"He objects to you being a woman?"

I guessed that was it in its simplest terms. "He never stated outright if my gender was an issue. Instead, he dug up an old decree that states I need to be married in order to rule." I pasted on a false smile, cheeks threatening to crack from the absurdity of it all.

Tomori blinked. Blinked again. Then shook his head before slumping against his chair. "I . . . uh . . ." He licked his lips. "What does that mean, exactly? Will they not let you succeed the king?"

"It means if I'm not married before he dies, they won't recognize me as the rightful heir." The hairs on my arms rose as I took in Tomori's inscrutable expression. What was he thinking?

"Did they give you an exact deadline?" His voice came out measured and raspy.

"No. Just before he d-dies." I stumbled over my words. No matter how many times I repeated the pronouncement, the acrid taste never left my mouth.

His lips twisted. "I am sorry, but at least you have time."

I shook my head. "I don't, though." I stared at the door, then at Tomori. "You cannot tell anyone what I am about to tell you."

"You can trust me."

My heart warmed. "Grandfather is sick. He doesn't have much time."

"No," Tomori rasped. "How long?"

"Maybe six months."

He rubbed at his beard, his gaze staring through me. "Then that means you have to marry soon."

I nodded.

"Do they have someone in mind, or will they allow you to . . . to choose?"

"They gave me a list of prospects but did say I could choose." My gaze roamed his features. Was he upset for me? For . . . us? "I think they want me to pick from their suggestions, and considering that I know no one else who would meet their approval . . ." My voice trailed off as Tomori's gaze caught mine.

How I wished something more could happen. It was one thing to entertain a crush and daydream about *what-if*. It was an entirely different matter to consider marrying him. Because if the council barely approved of me, how much more disdain would they feel for a palace runner? I needed to ignore how my pulse sped up whenever Tomori was in my presence.

"Tomori?" I whispered. *Say something!*

"Do you remember any of the men's names?"

There was a note in his voice that I couldn't place—maybe a finality of sorts. My heart sank, and I repeated the names that had somehow stuck in my consciousness in so short a time.

Tomori sighed. "Your best option is Prince Ekon. He is around your age and treats everyone with respect."

Two votes for a man I had never met. "The other two do not respect everyone?"

His lips thinned. "I do not want to speak badly of anyone. Yet I do not want you to be surprised or go into a situation without proper knowledge either."

"I appreciate that and promise not to repeat what you say." Which meant I couldn't discuss it with Iris or my mom. But I wanted Tomori to be assured of my discretion.

"Chimnoya has a reputation for being a . . . what is the phrase in English? . . . a lady's man."

"But he's old." I shuddered.

The sound of Tomori's laughter washed over me, bringing lightness and a comfort to the craziness of the day.

"Well, he is. He's *twice* my age." Just *no*.

"When you reach his age, you will not think him old but just starting life."

I raised an eyebrow. "Are you trying to school me, Tomori?"

Delight lit his obsidian eyes. "Just advice, Brielle, just advice. Besides, when you meet him, you will quickly realize how ill-suited he would be for a husband."

"And Mr. Udo?"

Tomori lifted a shoulder. "He is okay, but he does not like leaving Lake Opolopo. His concern is only for that region. I do not think he would shoulder the burdens of the entire kingdom nor want to live in the palace."

"How do you know this?"

"We fish together. I have gained a reputation of knowing the best spots, and ever since I met him, we have made an effort to meet up once a month."

A laugh escaped. Of course it would be about fish. "Would you recommend anyone who isn't on this list?" *You?*

Don't be silly! Still, my heart double-timed, waiting for his answer.

Tomori rubbed his bearded chin. "I will have to think about that."

"Thank you."

He nodded. "How are you dealing?"

My heart melted at his concern. "In some respects, I feel too young to marry. Not because I'm opposed to marriage, but because I haven't found my perfect someone. I always thought I'd have plenty of time to do so."

He raised an eyebrow. "How old *are* you?"

"Twenty-five."

"I have three years on you."

"I wondered. You seem older and wiser but still look young."

He laughed. "You should see me around my family. They accuse me of being immature and without drive."

"I can't imagine."

"That is what happens when one is born the youngest. My older siblings believe my life is too easy. They would love for me to apply myself."

"Tell them you're teaching the princess how to speak Onina. Surely that has to carry some weight." Gah! There I went with the pretentiousness.

"Maybe after Independence Day, Your Highness."

My smile faltered at the gentle reminder of my station. "Right. After."

"Let us continue with our lesson, then, so you can impress the country, and I can impress my family." He winked, and my cheeks heated. "A few more days until the parade and your debut."

"Right." I forced my lips to curve upward, then began repeating the vocab of the day.

Hours later I found myself back in the royal dressing room for a fitting for my Independence Day dress. Iris stepped in front of me and placed her hands on my shoulders, studying me intently.

"You're scaring me," I said.

"Promise me if you hate the dress, you'll tell me. Then again, you could love it and the rest of the country could hate it." She bit her lip.

"Did you go traditional?" I asked.

"You'll see."

I rolled my eyes. "Just show me already."

"Promise you'll still love me."

"I always will, Iris. Come on."

She huffed and walked to the royal wardrobe outlined in ivory. "Close your eyes," she called over her shoulder.

I complied, listening to the sounds. I heard a zipper then a swish of fabric. "Can I open them yet?"

"Almost."

"Now?"

"Now." She held the dress before me.

I opened my eyes . . . and gasped. The gown had purple cap sleeves and a square neckline. The bodice was blue, with purple-and-white stripes wrapping along the sides. It flowed at the waist, ball-gown style, in a pattern of blue, white, and purple, with a diamond-shaped medallion at the center.

I fingered the material of the dress. "This is amazing, Iris. I can't believe you made this."

"Bri, they have fabulous fabric, and the sewing machine Dayo got me was off the charts."

"So, basically, you were in your happy place?" I asked.

"Uh, yeah."

I motioned to the dress. "Can I try it on?"

"Please. I want to make sure everything is perfect."

I went behind the dressing screen.

"There's a long zipper in the back so you can step in and not have to worry about messing up your hair," Iris called out.

"Oh, I didn't think about my hair. How should I wear it?"

"You'll wear their traditional headdress for a princess. I already talked to the king about it." Iris squealed.

I peeked around the screen. "What's the scream about?"

"Do you realize I rub elbows with royalty every day? It's unreal!"

"Amen," I mumbled.

"Has it sunk in that you're a princess and will be queen one day?"

"Not at all. But when I stand before thousands of people, it just might."

"Hey, at least Ọlọrọ's population isn't over a million people."

"Way to bring perspective into it, Iris."

She giggled.

"I'm going to need your help zipping it," I said.

I came around the screen and presented my back to Iris. Soon she had me zipped and standing on the dais.

She pointed to the mirrors. "Take a look."

"Wow. This is amazing."

"How do you feel? Does it constrict anywhere?"

I stared at my reflection, looking at the beautiful combination of colors. The purple *amure*—the thick sash that showed I was part of the royal household—fell across my left shoulder. The cap sleeves bent toward modesty but wouldn't make me overheat in the June sun.

"It fits perfectly." I smoothed a hand over my stomach.

"Great. I have the headwrap. It looks wonderful, if you don't mind me tooting my own horn."

I chuckled as Iris went to grab it. She handed me a hair tie, asking me to put my hair into a bun so she could pull on the turban-like headdress. A moss agate jewel—the family's official gemstone—dangled from a gold chain and stopped at the center of my forehead. The headdress was made out of the same material as the gown.

"This is beautiful."

160

"Does it feel real?" Iris asked reverently.

"Almost."

I wasn't sure what would make me feel like a princess. Maybe it was simply a matter of time. If that was the case, then the longer I lived here, the more I would feel worthy of such a calling.

I hoped.

TWENTY-THREE

I searched the sky from the back seat of the Mercedes SUV, looking for the private jet. Dayo had flown with the aircrew to pick up my mother, and they were due to touch down in Àlàáfíà soon. I'd received a text about five minutes ago saying they were close, which was why my nose practically pressed against the window.

Azuka, my new bodyguard and driver, didn't want me to roll down the window to get a better view. Chidi had been fired due to his lack of discretion. Apparently, he was the one who'd informed other palace staff of my status. Azuka and Merrick would be protecting me going forward.

"Your Highness, please sit back. You will see the plane when it draws near. I promise."

I peeked at Azuka. "Sorry." Nerves had prevented me from eating this morning, and even my cup of coffee hadn't perked me up. Mom was so close to being in Ọlọrọ.

"No apologies necessary, Your Highness. I am only concerned with your safety."

I nodded. When I first met Azuka, relief had coursed through me. My thankfulness was purely based off his appearance and a gut instinct that he would keep me safe. Hopefully his well-defined muscles and intimidating stare would deter any person intent on harm.

"There it is, Your Highness."

My nose hit the glass as I squinted at the horizon. My breath quickened. I could see the plane and its landing gear. My mother was truly here. What was I supposed to say to her? Would the resentment rise once more when I faced her? I wanted to get out and greet her, but Azuka would probably have a fit.

I sat back and concentrated on my breathing as the plane's wheels hit the runway. I pulled on each finger, popping my knuckles as I waited for the door to open and the airstairs to fall. I should have asked if Tomori would be on the crew. A funny feeling entered my heart as I thought of him meeting Mom. Would he like her? Would she like him?

"Your Highness, please stay in the car. Merrick will open the door for her."

I barely heard Azuka's instructions as Mom walked toward the car, her gaze intent before her. Was she trying to see through the tinted windows? Merrick led her to the right side of the car and opened the door.

"Bri," she exclaimed as she slid onto the seat and wrapped me in a hug.

My arms came around her as I buried my face in her neck. The smell of her gardenia perfume greeted me, causing a familiar tickle in my nose. I always teased her about smelling like a garden on her days off. Since she didn't wear scents while working, she always made up for it when on vacation.

"Hi, Mom," I whispered.

She squeezed me. "Are you okay?"

"I am now."

I pulled back while she grabbed a tissue from her purse and dabbed at her eyes.

The car jerked as Azuka drove away from the tarmac. I peeked behind us and saw a second armored vehicle. I had forgotten to see if Tomori was driving it and hadn't even noticed if Dayo exited the plane. Oh well, I would catch up with both of them later.

We kept our conversation to superficial topics as we rode to the palace. I was very aware of the bodyguards' presence. Even though

I could raise the partition between us, having a heart-to-heart was best left for another time and place.

Soon we pulled up to the palace gate. The guards checked the bodyguards' identification and then waved us through. Once inside, we kept quiet as we walked the halls to the guest suites. Grandfather had informed me I'd be able to redecorate Grandmother's rooms and move in there. Until then, I'd remain in the guest corridor with Iris and my mother. I showed Mom to her room, and soon Tomori arrived with her luggage.

I couldn't keep the smile from my face or ignore the flutters in my heart. "Ẹ seun, Tomori."

"My pleasure, Your Highness." He bowed, then left the room.

"Oh my goodness. I can't believe this," Mom said.

"Believe what?" How handsome Tomori was? I sat on the edge of the bed, remembering his soft smile.

"Seeing everyone bow to you. It's kind of mind-blowing, Bri."

Truth. I still wasn't used to it and said as much.

She frowned. "Are you not happy?"

"I'm not *unhappy*." I sighed. "I just . . . some days it's a little hard to take everything in. I'm supposed to rule a country, but before I can do that, I have to get married." I shook my head. "And tomorrow's the Independence Day parade, then the ball." I sighed.

"Have you met any of the men yet?" The bed dipped as she sat near me.

"No. I'll meet the council's three choices early next week."

"And?"

"And there's not much else to say right now. Grandfather agrees with Iris that I should just start meeting them one-on-one and cross them off the list until I get to the right one."

"And they said you have to marry before he dies?"

I nodded.

"I'm so sorry, sweetie. I can't imagine the burden you're carrying."

Tears welled in my eyes, and I leaned my head against her shoulder, begging the sobs to hold themselves at bay. Just because my mother was here didn't mean I would give myself permission to fall apart. Plus, I was so very tired of crying.

"What am I going to do?" I whispered.

"If you really believe this is the right course of action, then pray every day until you find the most acceptable man."

"I never imagined settling for a husband. I always thought I'd have this great romance like you and Dad."

"Oh, sweetie. I've prayed that for you as well. With a happier ending than mine."

"I guess now we should pray I can fall in love with him."

She rubbed my back and let the silence speak.

"I'm glad you're here, Mom."

"Are you really?" she asked softly.

I straightened and met her gaze. "I am. I know how I left things." I sighed. "I know it was ugly, and I'm sorry for that."

"Please don't apologize." She smoothed the hair back from my face.

"I need to. I can't imagine the position you found yourself in. Now that I'm here, I can see that not everything is cut-and-dried or as black-and-white as I'd like to believe. I don't want to have to tell my kids that I didn't love their father but married for the sake of the country. But that doesn't mean I won't come to love whomever I marry." I stopped. I was rambling. "Anyway, I realize now that I don't know how I'd respond in the same situation you found yourself in." I shrugged. "So maybe I should stop acting like a brat about it."

She chuckled and laid a hand on my cheek. "I could never think of you as a brat, Bri."

I snorted. "I don't remember you saying that when I hit thirteen."

She shuddered. "Too true. Apology accepted."

"Thanks, Mom."

"And, Bri." She paused. "I'm sorry for not telling you sooner. For not giving you a chance to acclimate to the news and what it meant for your future. I feel awful that you didn't get a chance to know this side of your family."

I thought back to the first family dinner here. Despite the animosity from Uncle Sijuwola, Digi was wonderful to talk to. I didn't think I'd be best friends with her parents, but I could be cordial. And Uncle Lanre brought a levity to most family dinners. He had never been in the running for heir, and I think that helped us forge the beginnings of a friendship or whatever you called it when getting to know long-lost family.

Thankfully, Uncle Sijuwola didn't live in the palace. He, Maseso, and Lanre all had their own homes in Àlàáfià.

"I'm not sure I missed out on much. I mean, I do regret not knowing Grandfather." Then again, maybe Sijuwola wouldn't be so antagonistic if he'd known about me from the get-go. I blew out a breath. All water under the bridge, right? I couldn't change the past.

"Did I tell you we're reading Narnia together?" I could hear the excitement in my voice as I told my mother how it had been Dad's favorite series as well.

She sniffed, dabbing at her eyes once more. "That makes so much sense. I'm so glad you know that now."

"It's been nice finding out who Dad was from Grandfather's perspective. A few of the museums out here have pictures of him that I've never seen before." I snapped my fingers. "Oh, and Grandfather has a photo album of Dad when he was young. He said you're more than welcome to take a look at it."

Her head bobbed, too overcome with emotion to say or do much else. At least, that was what I assumed the tears coursing down her face meant. I wrapped an arm around her shoulders and squeezed.

"I love you, Mom."

"I love you too, Bri." A beat of silence weighed between us before she spoke once more. "Are we okay?"

"We're perfect."

TWENTY-FOUR

I swayed back and forth, my body punctuating the rhythm of the *dundun* drums played by the musicians gathered in the street. The people of Ọlọrọ crowded around, answering the call and response of the singer. His voice held a grit reminiscent of some rockers. The drummers around him kept up the rhythm as the singer led the crowd in what to say.

Or rather, he led Iris and me. The Ọlọrans knew the song, as evidenced by their jubilant singing. The music had that island feel that made my hips automatically sway, and my hands shook along with the maracas one musician held in the air.

Azuka and Merrick were with us as undercover bodyguards. Grandfather believed I would be safe until the royal procession. I had another hour until that happened, with orders to be dressed and ready on time. Whenever I thought of the throne ascension, flutters erupted in my stomach and acid rose to my throat. To say I was nervous would be a gross understatement.

I was petrified. Terrified the country would consider me a fraud and boo me until I returned to America.

Last night I had fallen to my knees, begging the Lord for more of His peace. I wanted to be flooded with calm like I had in my ocean dream. I'd uttered scripture after scripture. Replayed the dream of God speaking to me at the beach and tugged at the memory of the assurance I'd felt. None of those things stilled the tumult in my middle or kept me from the intense nausea.

I'd fallen into a fitful sleep and awakened only to start the sorry business of worrying all over again. That was, until Mom had forced me to eat. Now we all danced in the streets with the rest of the Ọlọrans and praised God they'd found their independence.

Maybe the real reason I could relax was Tomori's presence as our guide. I wanted to look like a tourist until the last possible moment, and he had accomplished that. He'd taken us to different events, directed us toward goods to buy and food to eat.

As Iris clapped beside me, I peeked to my left, studying him out of the corner of my eye. We hadn't talked much today. At yesterday's lesson, he'd helped me put together a speech to give to the people. Writing the oration had been painstaking in its slowness, as I didn't know enough Onina to be fluent and had relied on Tomori's constant help.

I didn't know why I'd thought two weeks of lessons would make me proficient. Yet when I'd finished reciting the heartfelt message from memory for the third time, I couldn't help but feel a sense of pride. I might not be native to the country, but I would work hard for the land and its people. Both already held a special place in my heart.

Part of me wanted to say something—*anything*—to Tomori before I was introduced as the princess. I opened my mouth, then promptly shut it as a woman squeezed her way through the crowd and threw her arms around him.

My gut clenched.

"Mori, I have been looking everywhere for you," she shouted in Onina. At least, that's what I thought she said.

She stepped back and smiled at him. She was beautiful, lithe, and had a riot of curls framing her upturned face. Not as impressive as Iris's mane, but just as striking in their own right. I started to turn away, but Tomori caught my gaze. He dipped his head before turning to the woman—who now watched us like a hawk.

"Nika, this is my friend Brielle," Tomori introduced in English. "Brielle, meet my sister."

A breath blew from my lips as my shoulders sagged in relief. How utterly ridiculous that I had been jealous—but so undeniable.

"Hi, nice to meet you," she said. Her words held a nice inflection, and she spoke steadily, like Tomori.

"Nice to meet you too."

"How do you two know each other?" She pointed between us.

"Oh, Tomori is teaching me Onina." I smiled up at him.

A wide grin split his face, and my heart swooned.

"I did not know you tutored, Mori. How enterprising of you." Shock showed in her gaze as she appraised him.

"He's an excellent teacher." His family needed to know how wonderful he was.

"Hmm." She peered up at her brother. "*Màmá* wants you to come for dinner tonight. Can you?"

"Yes. I will be there."

"Good." She eyed me. "Would you like to come as well, Brielle?"

I held my breath. I would *love* to meet his family, but an hour from now I would not be allowed to move about freely. "I'm not sure what my plans are. It depends on my grandfather."

"Of course." She waved. "See you later, Mori. Nice to meet you, Brielle."

"Bri," I said.

"Bye, Bri."

We watched her go, an odd tension settling between us. Had I been wrong in not declining the invitation? "I'm sorry." I leaned close so Tomori could hear. I breathed in, my eyes shuttering at the scent of cedar.

"No apologies necessary. I know my family would be honored to have you."

I fidgeted. "It won't make your mother panic if I show up?"

He shook his head. "She has eight children. Panic is not in her nature."

I chuckled, then frowned. The ball was tonight. "Maybe another time? I have that event, you know?"

Tomori caught my meaning. "Ah yes. I remember." He eyed his wristwatch. "You need to get ready."

Immediately my nerve endings came alive. "Okay."

"You will be fine. Trust in God."

Right. He'd put me here for a reason. "Thank you for that reminder."

Tomori spoke to Azuka, then they motioned for us to follow. We moved through the crowd, the sound of drums pulsing more quietly with each step away from the celebration. Soon we navigated to where Azuka had parked, then climbed into the SUV.

Iris and I worked quickly in the royal changing room. She zipped me up in the ceremonial gown she'd created and settled the *gèlè* on my head. Dainty gold chains dangled across my forehead between the parts of the turban that came to a point where my hairline met my forehead. The last chain held the pear-shaped moss agate gemstone that symbolized prosperity.

"It's beautiful, Iris."

"You're beautiful, girl. Now, go do your royal wave and wow them."

I gave Iris a hug, then left to find Grandfather. He'd said he'd be waiting near the cars. Dayo stood outside the royal fitting room.

"Oh, hi."

She bowed before me. "Your Highness, I am to escort you to the king."

I had to break the silence as we walked down the halls. My nerves were ramping up, and my stomach rolled like a boat in stormy weather. "Any last words for me, Dayo?"

"Do not take any opposition personally."

Great. Would the citizens boo me or, worse, throw produce in my face? Then again, I was royalty, so maybe that was against the law. Still, I wanted to be well received by the people. I repeated my speech in my head as Dayo pressed the down button on the elevator panel.

Before I knew it, we were exiting the palace, and a guard opened the back door of the armored Mercedes SUV. I slid inside.

Grandfather smiled. "Ah, Brielle, you look magnificent."

"Thank you, Bàbá àgbà. How are you feeling?"

"Like an old man."

I snorted. "You certainly do not look old."

"The Adebayo gene is strong. We do not wither easily. If you keep away from vices, unlike me, you will live a long and victorious life."

I took his hand in mine. "You have lived a long and victorious life as well."

"You are right." He peered into my eyes. "I count it victorious because I have been blessed to know you. You are a wonderful woman, Brielle Adebayo."

Tears filled my eyes. "I feel the same about you, Grandfather. I'm so glad I came here. That you even wanted me to."

"How could I not? You are my blood and part of my heart."

This man! How I would miss him when he passed. I didn't want to think like that, but his death faced me every time I looked at him. I tried telling myself to stay in the moment, but death shrouded each instant.

"Thank goodness we still have time with each other."

A shadow filled his eyes. "Do not expect a miracle, ómọ ọmọ. God will not add more years."

"How do you know? If we ask, He will answer. Look at Hezekiah. He was blessed with more time."

"He was, but I am an old man. I have a successor and know the country will be left in good hands. There is no need for more time on this earth when I could be with my Maker."

"What about me?" My voice cracked. "I need you."

"Aw, Brielle, I will treasure the days I have with you. But I know you will be just fine." He brushed his lips against my cheek and squeezed my hand before settling back into his seat. "Let us get ready to walk proudly through the streets. Now is not the time for heartache and the shedding of tears. Okay?"

I nodded, drawing in a slow breath before exhaling. *Lord God, please bless me with a huge helping of composure.*

"It is time."

I thanked the guard who opened the door for me. The crowd on my side hushed as they eyed me in the traditional garb, noting the gèlè on my head and the royal colors. Whispers spread like wildfire as I rounded the front of the car and joined my grandfather. He hooked his elbow out to me, and I slipped my arm through as we walked down the street. A path had been created, and the crowds obeyed the invisible lines on each side.

"Can you handle this walk?" I murmured as I stared straight ahead, a lift to my chin.

"As long as you do not sprint to the end."

I suppressed a chuckle. Trust him to make a joke out of something serious. But I loved him for bringing a lightness to the present situation.

A stage came into view, and I could see a throne at the center. We were still too far away to see the details, but anticipation thrummed through me. As we neared, I noted a cape covering the back of the chair in panels of blue, white, and purple. Gold rimmed the purple throne that seemed to be made from velvet.

I visualized the instructions Grandfather and I had gone over and over these past couple of days. In a few moments, we would be on the stage, and the country—plus those watching via the media—would know who I was.

Mobo appeared on the stage and bowed before the king, who then took up a spot to the right of the chair. I took the spot to the left of the chair.

Mobo would be the official master of ceremonies, speaking as herald per the Ọlọran tradition. The crowd hushed as he took the microphone and began speaking. He shared the story of the uprisings that had run rampant across the nation, the withdrawal of French citizens, and the formation of the royal council.

"As we do every year, we pay homage to our king as we celebrate another year of freedom. I will now share the king's words," Mobo said.

Grandfather stepped forward, and I remained frozen, looking out into the vast crowd. If my heart pounded any harder, there'd be an imprint on my clothing like a dead body outlined on the ground.

"Good afternoon, people of Ọlọrọ Ilé. I am thankful for your patronage and presence in our capital on this day as we celebrate our independence. My sincere thanks and gratitude go to all who contributed their skills to build the throne for this year's celebration. Like years before, an Adebayo will continue to rule our great kingdom."

Mobo paused, and I peeked at Grandfather, who'd begun coughing. He dabbed at his mouth and motioned for Mobo to continue. Mobo read from a script, but Grandfather mouthed the words he'd written.

"Today I come forward to tell you that I am sick, and my life will come to an earlier end than I had anticipated. But do not fear—"

Rumbles moved through the crowd. Some cried out, distraught at the news. Others lifted their hands in benediction. Grandfather held up a hand to quiet them all.

"Do not fear," Mobo continued. "I leave an heir, your future queen."

Grandfather motioned for me to hold his hand, and I slid my palm against his.

"I introduce to you Her Royal Highness, Princess Brielle Eden Adebayo, daughter of our beloved Prince Naade Tayo Adebayo and future queen of Ọlọrọ Ilé."

Grandfather raised our hands in the air, then gave me an encouraging smile. I moved to stand before the throne. Then, while the crowd watched, I sat down as successor and held my breath.

Silence weighed heavy, but then, when my heart felt like it would crack in two from the shame, I heard a cry. A feminine shout rent the air with jubilation. I searched the crowd for my mother and Iris. Relief coursed through me as I spotted them clapping. The applause was subdued, but I didn't know if it was shock at my existence or Grandfather's illness. Still, I sat there as the future queen, my body a quivering mess.

I tried not to fidget as Mobo waited for the applause to die down so he could introduce me as the future heir. Then I would give my speech. Only I couldn't remember a single word of it at the moment.

Grandfather held up his hand, and the crowd quieted. Mobo spoke into the microphone.

"Her Royal Highness will now share a few words."

I stood and took the microphone. I'd been given the option of having Mobo translate for me, but it was important to make this first step on my own and with the strength of God. *Please give me the words.*

"Greetings, my countrymen," I said in Onina. "I came to Ọlọrọ Ilé as a woman searching for her family, and I stand before you now as a princess who has found the other half of myself. It is my greatest wish to honor the Adebayos before me and continue a legacy that will enrich this country and its people. I ask for your grace through this transition and covet your support. Thank you."

There was no pause between my thanks and the applause. The crowd cheered with approval, and I waved, praying they could see how much their encouragement meant to me.

Perhaps everything really would work out just fine.

TWENTY-FIVE

It was official. I was now Princess Brielle Eden Adebayo. My days of going through Ọlọrọ incognito were over.

Now I had to put on a happy face and rub elbows with the important people of Ọlọrọ Ilé at the grand ball my grandfather was hosting. At last, that gorgeous black dress I'd found in New York City would be worn.

Iris and my mom had dressed and were ready to go. Fortunately, Mom had had the foresight to pack a gown as well. She had plenty to choose from because of the various fundraising dinners she'd attended in the past. The navy sheath dress had a lace overlay and fell to the floor. She looked stunning with her brown curls falling loose to her shoulders.

Mom and Iris would enter the ballroom using the guest entrance, and apparently Grandfather and I would be using the royal entrance. My arm rested on Grandfather's bent elbow as he escorted us through the ballroom.

His steps were labored, and his breathing held a slight wheeze. The Independence Day celebrations were wearing on him, but he refused to go rest. He'd promised to leave after an hour, but I wanted to convince him to go after half that time. Surely I could stand here, look regal, and let Grandfather rest.

"When I have introduced you to everyone important, then perhaps I will leave for the evening," Grandfather said.

"Promise me?"

"Do not worry about me, Brielle. Tonight is for you."

I nodded, barely registering a voice introducing us to the crowd and the applause that came in response. I scanned the premises, looking for a certain palace runner. My heart sank as I remembered his plans with his family.

"What are you thinking, ómọ ọmọ?" Grandfather asked.

"Just wondering who all is here."

He nodded to the right. "There is your mother and Iris."

I smiled at them. There was a strained tension between my grandfather and my mom. Considering their history, it wasn't surprising. However, I wanted them to make up before it was too late. Perhaps tomorrow I'd bridge the subject instead of putting it off.

Grandfather walked me around the room, as was custom, and then we stood off to the side as people began to dance.

"Do we dance tonight?" I asked.

"If you wish to, please do, only let me introduce you to some people first."

"All right."

Grandfather motioned for Mobo to come forward, then leaned to whisper in his ear. I couldn't hear what was said, but Mobo nodded, then walked away.

"He will come by with the men on the council's list."

"Wait, what?" My stomach tensed. "I thought I had time to reach out to them."

"I am running out of time, my dear Brielle. We cannot leave this country ungoverned. That would send us into a chaos you may not be able to recover from."

I gulped, searching the room for Mobo. "You're still here, though. You're alive, not—" I clammed up.

Grandfather squeezed my hand. "Granddaughter, I need you to hear me. Really listen."

"I'm listening."

"I will *not* survive this cancer. It will be my demise."

"You can't see the future." Sure, the doctor had given him a death sentence, but we didn't actually *know* it would kill him until he drew his last breath. My eyes watered.

"No, but I know that death is coming. I have seen it, have survived it, and now it hovers in the air, waiting. Perhaps it is biding time until you are settled, but it *is* coming, Brielle. You cannot expect a miracle."

I gulped. "But God can do the impossible."

"Amen. He can. He is surely able. But that does not mean it is in His will to add more years to my life."

"Grandfather," I whispered, barely able to hold back threatening tears.

"I need you to be strong, Brielle. To face this obstacle like you would stare down the most challenging student. I need you to find a husband. Quickly, ọmọ ọmọ. Let me see you marry, and then let me go."

Before I could reply, Mobo walked up with a man who could only be Chimnoya Sule.

"Your Majesty." Mobo bowed, as did Contender Number One. Great, Iris had me acting like this was a reality show. "Prince Chimnoya Sule of the Òkè tribe has come to pay his respects to Her Highness Princess Brielle Adebayo."

Prince Chimnoya's thin lips curved upward, and a shiver of foreboding slid down my spine. No way could I marry him. In addition to the gross difference in age, something about him made me want to guard my life.

His eyes squinted. "It is a pleasure, Your Majesty, Your Highness."

"Nice to meet you, Prince Chimnoya." I forced the words from my lips.

"The pleasure is all mine." He placed a hand on his heart. "Since the announcement at the parade, I have been praying for you, Princess. I am sure this is all so overwhelming, having to worry about ruling a country you are not familiar with instead of the joy of raising children to further the kingship. I am surprised the council approved a . . . female ruler." The prince arched an eyebrow.

My spine lengthened, and my chin popped up. "Do you question the council's decision?"

"Not at all, Your Highness. I merely express my surprise."

Yeah, okay. Pass! Instead of giving my thoughts free rein, I moved my mouth upward. Hopefully it looked like a smile of understanding instead of one conveying how I felt about his intelligence . . . or lack thereof. I squeezed Grandfather's arm.

"If you will excuse us, Prince Chimnoya." Grandfather smiled. "There are others I must introduce to the princess."

"Of course, my king." He bowed and walked away.

Apparently, when you were royalty, others made their exit, not you. Grandfather instructed Mobo to bring the next candidate. My stomach had loosened its grip now that I'd met one wannabe suitor. Mobo came back with the next gentleman, making another round of introductions, this time with Mr. Kambili Udo.

"Did you enjoy the festivities today, Your Highness?" he asked.

"I had a wonderful time." Pleasure filled me as I remembered everything. "The music, the parade, all of it, especially the food."

"Ah yes. The food vendors do a magnificent job every year," Grandfather said.

"They could do better," Mr. Udo said.

I froze. "How so?"

"Well, the seafood offering could have been better."

My paiis had been delicious. Although I'm sure that wasn't Mr. Udo's concern. "But the fishing industry has been hit hard the past few years."

His eyes widened, and for the first time, he looked into my face. I'd thought he was going to carry on an entire conversation with his gaze roaming my figure. "What do you know about that?"

I swallowed. Not much. I'd done a little digging after Chidi had brought it up, and I'd discussed the issue with Mobo when we delved into the concerns of Ọlọrans. But right now I didn't feel confident enough to go toe-to-toe with a resident who made his living fishing. "I know that you can't blame the food vendors for something they have no control over."

He scoffed. "If we allowed commercial fishing in Opolopo, then we could improve the industry."

"But then you'd have to build more structures and deforest the surrounding area. Is that what you want?" Surely he didn't want to see the beautiful lake without its abundance of trees.

Mr. Udo pursed his lips. "Maybe we can discuss the issue in the future."

I didn't want to. A very childish desire to throw a tantrum poked at me. I swallowed. "I'm sure I'll be in touch."

"Very well, Your Highness." He bowed. "Your Majesty."

Mr. Udo walked away, and I breathed a sigh of relief. "Grandfather, I don't have any warm fuzzies about these men."

"Nonsense. Look at the way you and Mr. Udo discussed the fishing industry. I told you he has a keen mind for politics."

Oh yes. Grandfather had cheerfully told me all about the contributions of these men to our political arena. With him, it was always about the kingdom. A way of thinking I hadn't yet transitioned to, especially when it came to linking my life to another for the remainder of my days.

"Prince Ekon Diallo, Your Majesty and Your Highness," Mobo stated.

The young man smiled, his teeth straight and white. I took a moment to study Prince Ekon. His skin reminded me of the smoothest milk chocolate, and his broad shoulders filled out his suit jacket well. He was the most handsome of the three, but I felt absolutely no spark. Not like I had with Tomori. *He's not a candidate.*

I huffed out a breath. Would I come to love the man of my choosing or only ever feel the same way I did when choosing vegetables—tolerating them just to get it over with?

"It is an honor to meet you, Your Highness. You are from America, right?"

"Yes, Prince Ekon. And you run a jewelry store with your father, correct?" That was what Dayo had said.

"I do." His bright white grin sparkled. "I am sure we have something that would match your beauty."

A charmer. "I'll have to visit one day."

"Please do. We would be honored." He paused. "What is it you did before coming here, Your Highness?"

"I was a middle school teacher."

"Impressive. Maybe running a country will be no different than keeping children in line."

I couldn't tell if he was being condescending or earnest or making a joke. His smile came effortlessly and didn't hold the smarm factor of Mr. Udo's or Prince Chimnoya's. Still, there was something about him I couldn't quite put my finger on.

Just then I caught sight of my mom and Iris. They were standing close, whispering about something upsetting judging from the twin frowns on their faces.

"If you'll excuse me, Prince Ekon."

"Certainly, Your Highness." He bowed and then left.

"What is wrong?" Grandfather asked.

"That's what I'm going to find out." I made my way through the crowd until I reached my mom and best friend. "What's wrong?" I lowered my voice so no one could hear.

"Uh . . ." Iris bit her lip.

"Mom?" I asked.

"Bri, we were . . ." She clenched the champagne glass in her hand. "We overheard some comments that concerned us."

"What?" I whispered.

"Some people think the king is making a mistake naming you heir and not Sijuwola."

My breath hitched. Knowing people were talking about me at the very ball meant to celebrate me was like a slap to the face. I struggled to school my features, but seeing the worry on Mom's and Iris's faces didn't help.

"I knew this could happen," I whispered. "Dayo and Digi have warned me. Plus, not too many people were clapping at Grandfather's announcement today."

"Still . . ." Iris leaned forward and gripped my hand. "I didn't want to say anything, didn't want to ruin today. So *don't* let them ruin it. God wants you here, and that's what matters the most."

"Right," I breathed. *Right, Lord? Please tell me I'm not making a big mistake.*

Because as I gazed around the ballroom and looked at the Who's Who of Ọlọrọ Ilé, inadequacies threatened to snuff out every certainty I had that I'd made the right decision.

TWENTY-SIX

I stared at my new Instagram account. The palace public relations team had created a royal profile, announcing me as heir to the throne of Ọlọrọ Ilé. They'd tagged my personal account, and my messages had filled with notes from so-called friends. They were people I'd met over the years and followed on social media, but we had no real contact outside of Instagram. They weren't the ones I called when I left New York, and they weren't on my list of people who could be patched through to me via Dayo's guardianship.

A photo of me in my gown had garnered various comments of well wishes. Some from people claiming to be from my school, and others from citizens congratulating me. I'd purposely ignored the hateful comments telling me I didn't belong. Well, after I read the first bad one.

Was this how my life would be going forward? Being center stage and on display for the world to see? I needed something that was just my own, but what? I didn't have any hobbies outside of reading. And after being introduced to the PR team, I figured they would probably try to publicize that.

I wanted to slow time, because if what Grandfather said was true, it ticked with no respect to life. I had to marry quickly. But to whom?

An image of Tomori filled my mind, and I sighed like a teenager with a crush. Hanging out with him during the Independence Day celebrations had been wonderful. A part of me wondered what it would have been like to dance around the ballroom in his arms, the scent of his cologne enveloping us and creating a cocoon that kept the prying eyes away.

Sometimes when we had our lessons, I wanted to ask him to rescue me from the path I was on. To whisk me away to some romantic destination. Actually, it could be to a fishing cabin for all I cared. I just wanted to be near him and rest in that calm he always brought with him.

A rap of knuckles interrupted my daydream. I straightened and called for entry.

Dayo opened the door and smiled. "Your Highness, Tomori is here for your lesson."

My ears burned. "Thank you, Dayo."

She shut the door behind her, but Tomori did not take his seat across from me like he normally did.

"E káàsán, Ọmọba Brielle Adebayo."

My lips quirked. "E káàsán, Tomori. Won't you sit?" I motioned to the chair.

"Actually, I thought today we would take our lesson out of this room."

Really? I rose. "What did you have in mind?"

"A couple of schools are doing tours today. The guide will only speak in Onina." He quirked a grin. "I want to see how much of it you can understand. We will only speak in Onina while we are doing the tour."

I bit my lip. "Won't they realize who I am?"

He held up the bag he'd been holding. "Nika gave me some items to help you go in disguise." He pulled out a ball cap, eyeglasses, and a jacket. "I know it looks like an odd selection, but we all know that eyeglasses alone make a good disguise."

I snorted. "I'm not Superman."

"But perhaps you are Wonder Woman. Now that I think about it, she goes around without a disguise."

"Her clothing is the camouflage."

He laughed, and my stomach dipped. "That is why I brought the jacket and ball cap. See? Oh, and . . ." He dug through the bag and removed a hair tie. "For the ball cap."

"All right. Let's do this." I put on the items, then peered up at Tomori. "Do I look ridiculous?"

"You could never."

My cheeks heated, and I wanted to envelop him in a hug. I cleared my throat. "Will Azuka or Merrick be shadowing us?"

"Yes. Security will also be watching the cameras."

"Okay."

Soon we stood behind a group of about a hundred children. They chattered happily, their teachers and chaperones asking for quiet periodically. I'd brought a notepad with me to take notes, hoping I could accurately relay what was being said.

Except I couldn't think. Every nerve was attuned to Tomori's movements. His languid stroll through the palace. The richness of his chuckle when the tour guide made a joke. How he ensured no kid was left behind when we moved from room to room. Everything about this man made me want to go deeper than a surface-level relationship.

I wanted a chance to be his. Would the council even consider someone like Tomori, or was his job as a palace runner an immediate disqualification? Who was I kidding? *I* was barely qualified. No way the royal council wanted *two* unsuitable monarchs.

When we got back to my office, I focused on the task at hand, ignoring my feelings. Unfortunately, there was so little I understood and so much that was beyond my grasp in the tour. Frustration coursed through me. How could I go to official functions without speaking the language? I'd have to hope they chose to speak in French or, better yet, English.

"What is wrong? You have been quiet all afternoon."

I met Tomori's gaze and shrugged.

"Do you want to talk? I am a good listener."

"The best." I grimaced inwardly. *Just tell him you have a crush on him, why don't you.* I shifted in my chair. "I mean, you've listened to me in the past, and I appreciate it."

He nodded. "But you do not wish to talk now? Is your burden that heavy?"

"No. Yes." I paused, trying not to drown in his eyes. "How am I going to marry someone I don't know?"

His Adam's apple bobbed. "I have been praying for you. Every day since I met you and twice a day since you told me of the council's order."

Could he be any sweeter? I popped my knuckles. "Thank you. I need every prayer I can get. Some days I'm confident I made the right choice, and other days I want to curl up in bed and wait for a new day." My lips twisted. "Some faith, huh?"

"Our faith is not without hardship. God did not promise easy, but He did promise to be with us."

"I don't know if I can lay my desires down for the good of the kingdom. Was I too hasty in deciding to become queen? Surely someone who was raised in the monarchy could do a better job than me."

Tomori tilted his head, his gaze assessing. "You know what? I think you are just the person for the job. You will work the hardest to ensure the people have someone on the throne who does not want to mess up. You will work the hardest to ensure that trust has not been blindly placed in your reign. Plus, your faith is an asset. You have Jesus on your side and His example of how to rule."

His example of how to rule. That phrase brought a hope and an understanding that surprised me. "Thank you, Tomori."

"It is my pleasure." He shifted in his seat. "Have you met the men the council suggested?"

"I have."

"What happens next?"

"I have to go on a date with each of them."

Something flashed across his face so quickly that I thought I imagined it. But for a brief second, I thought I saw jealousy. That was crazy, right? Tomori couldn't possibly feel the same way about me that I felt about him . . . right? He'd always been respectful and given me no hint he wanted more.

"Tomori . . ." My breath hitched as the desire to ask him how he felt surged through me.

"Yes?"

"Do you . . ." I licked my lips.

He leaned forward, brow furrowing. "What is it?"

I shook my head. "Never mind." I tried to paste a smile on my face and give him some kind of assurance I was fine. "Never mind."

"Are you sure . . . Brielle?"

My heart quickened at the use of my name. I hadn't heard it since before the Independence Day celebration. That one word was like a lifeline I wanted to grasp and never let go. But once I opened this line of questioning, I couldn't undo it. Knowing if Tomori thought of me romantically wouldn't help me on my dates with the council's choices.

"Yes. I'm sure. Everything is as it should be."

I would become queen, but Tomori had no place in my future. Once I could speak Onina passably, I doubted I would ever have a reason to speak to him again. The thought made my eyes well up, and I glanced away, willing the tears to leave and for my composure to stay.

"Brielle, if you ever need to talk, I will be here. Do not forget that, please."

I nodded, then dismissed him for the day.

TWENTY-SEVEN

The end of June signaled a royal council meeting and my first attendance as the future queen. The council gathered once a month to bring citizens' concerns to the table to be worked on for resolution. They had made an exception when they confirmed me as heir. Since Grandfather wouldn't transfer power to me pre-death, my presence wasn't required. However, I wanted to learn the inner workings and understand how the council settled problems before it was too late to gain Grandfather's wisdom, so he'd agreed to let me tag along.

The whole process was a little much for my brain to wrap around, but I couldn't let the overwhelmed feeling deter me. I desperately wanted to be a good queen, and I couldn't do that if I was afraid to learn. So I walked in behind Grandfather, presenting a façade of confidence and pushing my shoulders back. I would fake being a royal until it came naturally to me.

When we walked into the chamber, the four council members were convening at a round table. Grandfather and I took the open seats.

Jomi Oladele cleared his throat. "Let us proceed with today's agenda."

A secretary sat in the front corner of the room, scribbling on a pad of paper. I took my own notepad and favorite pen out of my tote. Grandfather wanted me to take notes for him to pass on to Mobo. I also planned to keep separate notes for myself. There would probably be a whole list of items I'd need to ask about in my lessons with Mobo.

"I, Jomi Oladele, alàgbà for the Etikun tribu and *alága* of the council, call to order the June meeting of the Ọlọrọ Ilé Royal Council. Ms. Lola Keita will relay the citizens' petitions."

"Thank you, Mr. Oladele. I have the list of issues here. All the ones brought through proper channels have been approved for the month. Those who did not contact their elders and request petition have been notified. We have twenty needs to address before the council will officially adjourn for June."

My eyes threatened to cross. Grandfather said the meetings could take days depending on the number of predicaments brought before us. I prayed that the requests were small and easily fixed, because twenty sounded like a lot to my untrained ear. Already my stomach was reminding me that I hadn't eaten a big breakfast due to nerves.

Ms. Keita started reading the complaints. There were problems addressing land disputes, trade within the country and its districts, exports with neighboring countries and the world beyond Africa. My mind dizzied as she droned on.

Still, I kept a steady hand, jotting down each issue and leaving enough space to make notes. Granted, I'd most likely have to use another page or two if council went longer than I expected.

Finally, Ms. Keita stopped talking. "That is it. Shall we address these in order?" She looked around the table at the other elders.

"Let us go by region," Mr. Ladipo said. His lips tilted in a smirk. "And not the Opolopo region. You always go first."

"I do no such thing."

"You do like to propose Opolopo each time," Mr. Ibrahim stated. "I say we begin taking turns and let one of the other districts go first."

"I object," Mr. Oladele stated. "We should discuss them as presented. It is more orderly that way."

I agreed but kept my mouth shut. Grandfather said we only spoke when a tie needed to be broken or a major decision needed to be overridden. Of course, we could contribute to the discussion if we had advice we wished the council to consider.

The elders took a vote and deemed going in order as the petitions were listed to be best.

"The first issue of the day is the land dispute," Ms. Keita stated. She described two neighboring men who lived in the cocoa hills. Each believed they owned a section of land, but delving into records had not cleared up the matter of ownership.

"It seems," Ms. Keita said, "that the records show each family to have owned that parcel of land. It has been equally shared, so their confusion is understood." She looked over her spectacles, making eye contact with each member. "How shall we vote?"

"Can the parcel be divided?" Mr. Oladele asked.

His deep voice was soothing, and I fought to keep my eyes open. I hadn't been getting much rest the past couple of days.

"It cannot," she said.

"Why not?" Mr. Ladipo asked.

She explained the land's position, the awkwardness of the division, and the impact on the crops.

"Why did this dispute come about?" Grandfather asked. "Were they no longer satisfied with sharing it?"

"It seems the father who had been farming passed, and his eldest son has taken over. He does not think sharing is beneficial and thinks it should be owned by one person."

I listened as they argued back and forth. Their voices began to rise as each tried to make a suggestion. I cleared my throat, and acid welled in my middle as five pairs of eyes swiveled toward me.

"Yes, Your Highness?" Mr. Oladele asked. He arched an eyebrow, impatience flowing through his hands as he tapped his pen against the table.

"Excuse me, alàgbà. Could you tell me how much that parcel is worth?"

Ms. Keita consulted her notes and named the figure.

"What's under that portion of land?" I asked.

Mr. Ladipo sneered. "*Soil*, Your Highness."

"Truly?" I pointed to the map that had been displayed on the projector. "Because it looks like it could run into the Fadaka River. If so, I bet the argument is over the water source and who controls it."

My Model UN group had had to argue about water sources last year. I was no stranger to water disputes.

Everyone turned, studying the map.

Grandfather squeezed my elbow, murmuring, "Good eye."

Ha! I wasn't as ignorant as they supposed. One by one, the council members faced each other. Silence descended, but I had no plans to break it. That was not my job as the princess.

"If that is the case," Mr. Ladipo stated slowly, "then the land should be owned by the council. They can rent its use."

"But that still leaves you with who gets to use it," I interrupted. After all, that was the issue before us.

"Your Highness, really. We can handle this." Mr. Ladipo's patronizing tone sent steel up my spine.

"That land needs to be farmed and cultivated, Mr. Ladipo." I stared at him, daring him to object. "Are you ready to put a renting process into effect? Ready to pay them their wages for farming the land? Reverting to the original agreement of having them both share the workload and receive equal profits would be the fairest, regardless of if they like it or not. If either man does not wish to accept the council's terms, then revert the property to the one who wishes to put in the work."

I folded my hands in my lap and waited for someone to speak. Grandfather was strangely quiet, and I couldn't decide if the waves of energy I felt were nerves pricking throughout my system, disapproval from my king, or the urge to give myself a clap on the back.

"You know, that actually could work." Mr. Oladele dipped his head toward me.

The nod was grudging, but I didn't care. If I could win over the council members, then hopefully any future transitions would be smooth.

"I do not oppose that," stated Ms. Keita.

"Nor I," said Mr. Ibrahim.

We all looked toward Mr. Ladipo. He shifted in his seat. "Fine," he snapped. "Issue resolved."

"Next is . . ." Ms. Keita presented the next petition.

I took notes as my heart drummed in my chest. I had done it. Solved an issue they had been arguing about. I wasn't sure if all the issues could be solved so quickly, but a little confidence now pulsed inside me. I could do this—learn how to be a queen and help the people in a very real and tangible way.

Two hours later, we adjourned for lunch. Grandfather and I walked toward our private dining room. As we sat down, I gathered my courage and studied him. He didn't seem overly exerted. No sweat beads, no coughing.

"How are you feeling, Bàbá àgbà?"

"I am fine." His lips curved. "And I am proud. You did well this morning."

Relief swept through me. I hadn't realized how much I'd needed him to say that. "Thank you. For a moment I thought I'd overstepped."

"No, you did not. They were beginning to bicker like children."

I stifled a laugh. "Do they often act that way?"

"Unfortunately."

Pitiful. "Grandfather, the council seats are for life, right? We can't give them term limits or add more seats?"

"Yes and no. The seats are for life and pass on to an elder voted in by the tribe. Each tribe has multiple elders who are given duties by the sitting council elder. We could write term limits into law if the whole council agreed. We could also add more seats if they wished to. Why? Do you think that needs to be done?"

"No. The question was more out of curiosity and thinking ahead into the future. It amazes me that only those four have power over the whole country." I paused to gather my words to make sure I wasn't being accusatory. "The other elders in the tribe, you say they answer to the council elder?"

"Yes."

"Do they have governing power?"

"Within their district they do. Like I said, they are given duties to perform, and if they neglect those, their power can be stripped."

I took a bite of my salad. Last week I had asked to be provided a light lunch. Eating heavily in the afternoon made me want to curl up in my bed and sleep the day away. The crab added a delicious flavor to the veggies but didn't weigh down my stomach.

"Brielle, make sure you observe and understand the people before you make changes."

My head shot up. "I'm not trying to make any waves. Truly, I was just asking for informational purposes."

"I understand and am not upset. But you *will* make changes. Every good leader does. They assess what did not work and how they can make it better. Or sometimes they have the ability to improve upon a matter. Do not fear that you will hurt my feelings if you make changes in the future. I expect it."

"Okay."

What else could be said? Grandfather was at peace with his illness and the consequence of a lifetime of smoking. He even seemed fine with me ruling one day. I wished I could be so at ease and have the fortitude of Esther to do what needed to be done. Perhaps I should spend more time in my Bible.

"Grandfather, could you take me to church Sunday?" I hadn't been since landing at the airport almost a month ago.

"I would love to. Now that you are acclimated to the time, you will be awake for the service. Remember, it is at eight."

Oh, that was early. "Couldn't we go to a later one?"

"The royals always go to the first service."

Eight o'clock it was.

Hopefully my mother and Iris would accompany me. I still felt a little uneasy going out in public as Princess Brielle Adebayo instead of Bri Bayo.

Lord God, I pray that I can get back on track with You. That I can tune out the noise that doesn't matter and pay attention to the things of the heart. Amen.

TWENTY-EIGHT

This is beautiful." Awe tinged my mom's words as she looked around the royal gardens we strolled through.

"And relaxing too," I said. "There are plenty of places to sit and unwind without someone walking past and bothering you." I loved the hideaway benches surrounded by hedges that offered quiet moments of privacy.

"I can only imagine." She inhaled deeply. "The air smells divine."

I laughed. "I didn't know you were a closet garden lover."

"Oh, I don't want to create my own, but I do appreciate the hard work of those who do."

"Same. There are some great men and women who keep this so picturesque."

"Have you met the groundskeepers?"

"No. They don't like to be disturbed. I try to come when I know they're almost done so I can say thank you but they can still leave without embarrassment."

"You're going to make a great queen, Bri."

"If I can find a husband." A thought I couldn't escape from.

"When do you have your first dinner?"

My stomach churned. "Tomorrow. I almost wish you could come and spare me the time alone with him."

She chuckled. "That would take awkward to a new level." She gestured to a pair of seats flanking a bistro table. "Want to sit a bit?"

"Sure."

"Have you already decided when to dine with the others?"

"Yes, but I don't remember the schedule. I let Dayo handle the appointments." I winced. "Or should I say dates?"

"Who is the first one with?"

"Prince Chimnoya." My mouth twisted. How could I truly choose someone so much older than I was?

"He's the oldest one, right?"

I nodded.

"I can't imagine you marrying someone so much older. He's in my age bracket."

"Way to make it worse, Mom." Yet for the good of the country, didn't I have a duty to sacrifice my wants?

"Do you truly have to date them all? You can't just cross him off the list as unacceptable?"

"No. Grandfather told me I'll have to explain why they're objectionable to the council. If I don't go on a date or two, the council may feel I'm letting personal reasons sway me instead of political ones."

"Do you have a list of questions you're going to ask them?"

I stared at her blankly. "What could I possibly put on there? I have no idea if I'm allowed small concessions that would make me happy or if it should all be about governing Ọlọrọ."

"Oh, sweetie. You need something to give you hope. Even if it's as small as sharing a hobby. It matters."

I nodded. That made sense. If I could share an interest in reading or something similar with my husband, maybe the years of loveless matrimony wouldn't be such a depressing thought.

"Thanks. I'll think of some questions tonight."

"Iris and I could help."

Iris would *love* to create a list of things to ask. However, she just wanted Prince Chimnoya off the list. She wasn't a fan of his after I relayed the comment he'd made about me raising children.

My thoughts froze as Tomori rounded the corner of the garden pathway. The pulse in my neck jump-started. He looked relaxed, wearing a black tunic with purple and white trim at the hem. His linen pants were of the same design.

I waved when he spotted me. My cheeks warmed, but more from the holes my mom was boring into the side of my face. I stood and motioned for him to come over.

"Who's that?" Mom whispered.

"Give me a sec, and I'll introduce you," I murmured.

Tomori bowed before me. "Ẹ káàsán, Your Highness." He turned toward my mother. "Mrs. Adebayo."

Her eyes widened. "Hello."

I feigned rubbing my nose to hide my smile. "Tomori, this is my mother, Marie. Mom, this is Tomori Eesuola. He's a runner here at the palace and has been giving me lessons in Onina."

"How nice of you. Does that mean you two spend a lot of time together?"

I narrowed my gaze at Mom. She had an overly innocent look on her face. I wanted to roll my eyes but instead diverted my attention to Tomori.

His full lips twitched. "I do not know if it counts as a lot, but I am her standing appointment in the afternoon. Unless she has days like today when she is in council meetings."

"He's been very helpful in preparing me for those as well," I added. "Knowing how to greet the council members. What words to say."

"She is a quick study."

"You're a good teacher." Our eyes locked, and my breath caught.

Why, oh why, couldn't I explore the feelings Tomori stirred within me? If I were Iris, I could easily give in to a summer romance and hope for a future filled with love. As things were now, seeing him, knowing he was out of reach, just chipped at my dead dreams.

I broke eye contact, studying the polish on my nails.

"Well, my lunch break is almost over. I will see you tomorrow, Your Highness," Tomori said, bending slightly at the waist.

My gaze shifted to his once more. "Good-bye, Tomori." I resumed my seat.

As soon as he was out of earshot, Mom asked, "*Who* is that? No, more importantly, *what* was that?" She studied me, mouth agape.

I blew out a breath. "I just told you. He's a palace runner and my tutor."

"Oh, honey, that boy is much more than your language instructor. The sparks between you two, whew." She shook her hand as if burned.

"*Nothing* is going on there." It couldn't, no matter what I wanted. My life was for Ọlọrọ now.

"Not from lack of chemistry. You two remind me of meeting your father for the first time."

"What?" How could we even compare?

"Oh yes. I met your father in the registration line. He stood behind me and struck up a conversation. Next thing I knew, he had changed some of his classes to match mine. He was that interested."

"That's not the same thing."

"I'm not saying it is. I'm talking about that instant chemistry. That boy is attracted to you, and I could tell by the look on your face that the feeling is mutual."

"It doesn't matter."

"Why not?"

"Are you serious?" I hissed, leaning forward. "I have to marry a council-approved man before Grandfather passes."

"What's wrong with . . . what's his first name again?"

"Mori. Tomori."

She arched an eyebrow. "You two are on nickname basis?"

"Mother." My face flushed. I'd never said his nickname out loud before and wasn't sure why it had slipped out this time. "I'm the princess and Mr. Eesuola is a palace runner. There's nothing improper going on. We've been appropriate at every meeting. For goodness' sake, Dayo sits right outside my office."

"Do you study with the door open?"

"No. I don't want to disturb her. Sometimes she takes phone calls."

"Then how does she know you're not kissing him?"

If my face got any hotter, I'd need my own personal fan. "I'm not. We're *not*. Besides, I speak Onina much better now. That's proof enough." Tomori still laughed at my American accent at times, but he said my pronunciation was improving.

Mom huffed. "You're the princess, and everything you do needs to be above reproach. If you're going to take lessons with a man you're attracted to—well, any man for that matter—keep your office door open. That way no one can accuse you of something that is untrue."

"But being princess affords me a certain level of privacy. When I become queen, I can't leave the door open when heads of state come to visit. That's ridiculous." I huffed. "I can't believe you'd insinuate something like that."

She rubbed her forehead. "I'm sorry, Bri. I just don't want you to go through some trumped-up harassment charge if it can be avoided. Because anyone with eyes could see there's more going on between you two than you want to admit."

"Mom, you don't know Tomori. He tells me all the time to remember who I am. He is very much aware of my station and where he fits within the kingdom. He would never dishonor his job or my title."

"If he's that noble, why isn't he on your list?" She raised an eyebrow to emphasize her point.

My heart hammered at the thought of Tomori being added to the list of potential husbands. I couldn't imagine the council ever agreeing to that, despite how much happiness the idea of him as a possibility brought me.

"He would never be approved by the council, and that's a major stipulation. Grandfather has no other recourse." I could just imagine Mr. Ladipo sneering with disdain that I'd suggested a palace runner to be my prince. He'd laugh me out of the council chambers.

"But you are the *princess*. Their future queen. Surely that means you can add whomever you want."

Instead of continuing to go back and forth, I smiled and suggested we walk back inside. I had about ten minutes before I had to listen to the rest of the council petitions. Hopefully we could finish the last fifteen before we broke for the day. If not, council duties would continue the next day.

Lord, grant me strength and help me not be so frustrated by my predicament. Please grant me wisdom on choosing a husband.

I parted ways with my mom, making plans to eat with her and Iris that evening. Iris was planning to show Mom Fort Battre and explore some leads on fabrics in that region. She was scheduled to leave next week. Her boss had given her a week's extension if she could bring back fabrics no one else had access to.

As I neared the council chambers, the guard snapped to attention. "I have a note for you, Your Highness."

I raised my eyebrows in surprise, taking the letter. "Thank you."

I opened it and halted.

You do not belong here. Make it better for everyone and leave.

My heart drummed out of my chest. I went back to the guard. "Excuse me, who delivered this letter?"

"A palace runner."

"Do you know which one?"

He relayed the name.

"Thank you."

I passed the letter to Grandfather as I sat. "The guard gave me this. A palace runner gave it to him."

Grandfather unfolded the letter. The lines in his forehead deepened as his mouth turned downward. "I will see that Mobo gives this to security."

"Should I be worried?"

"No, but keep an eye out."

I wanted to ask more questions, but Mr. Oladele resumed the meeting. *Lord, I pray that You help me focus and that the letter is of no consequence.*

But it felt like a chink in my armor. Another doubt on whether I was what was best for Ọlọrọ.

TWENTY-NINE

Dressing for a date you didn't want to go on made picking out clothes difficult. I liked looking pretty—what girl didn't?—but the thought of Chimnoya Sule finding me attractive made me want to pick out a hazmat suit.

I reached for an emerald-green jumpsuit with three-quarter sleeves. The color complemented my complexion. More importantly, it wasn't a skirt or a dress, so maybe Prince Chimnoya would get the memo that I was wholly uninterested.

"Bri?" a voice called. A rap on my door followed.

"Come in."

Iris's face entered the mirror above my dresser as I put in a gold hoop earring. "Hey, girl. You ready?"

I shook my head and slipped in the other earring. "I had a hard time picking an outfit."

"I bet. Can't look too cute," she quipped.

"You so get me." I smiled at her, and she grinned.

"So, hey, I wanted to run something by you," she said.

"Okay."

She began fidgeting with her hands.

"Do I need to sit down for this?"

"Um, maybe?" Wrinkles popped in the middle of her forehead as her shoulders rose.

"What's going on? Are you sick or something?" She'd seemed fine earlier in the day.

"No." She waved a hand. "Nothing like that. It's about staying in Ọlọrọ."

"O-kay," I drew out. "Just spill. The buildup is making me antsy."

"I want to stay, but I have to submit paperwork explaining my reasons and basically apply for a work visa."

I had no idea how that process worked. Dayo had filled out diplomatic paperwork for me, and after accepting my title and all the responsibilities that came with it, I'd had to give up my American citizenship and turn over my passport. Granted, I got a diplomatic one instead.

Everything about my American life had been neatly handled by my royal secretary or diplomatic staff. My belongings had been packed up and shipped over. The royal bank had paid to break my lease. The only thing I had done myself was inform my boss that I wouldn't be returning. After that, the staff had filled out the paperwork.

Which meant I knew nothing about what Iris had to go through if she wanted to stay longer. "Do you just want to extend your vacation? Wait, you said you have to get a work visa. Is it because you're working remotely?"

"Actually, I've been thinking about how I could make a difference here. I don't want to extend my vacation so much as move here."

"What?" I sat down. "Really? Why? I thought you loved your job."

"I do!" She wrung her hands. "But when your mom and I went back to Fort Battre, I talked with a woman selling dresses at a booth. She told me about all the hardship she's been through and how she's trying to feed five mouths. Bri, there's so much poverty in certain areas of Ọlọrọ, and no one seems to care."

My mouth dropped.

"I don't mean you." She held up a hand. "I'm just saying that no one seems to be doing anything to change it, but I want to. It hit me like a ton of bricks when doing my devotional. I have skills and experience that match their skills and very real need."

"What are you saying?"

"I want to help these women sell their products worldwide. They'd get the majority of the profits, hopefully eliminating their poverty status. Of course, that would mean the Oloran economy would improve overall. I've been in contact with a friend back home who did something similar in another African country."

"Wow. That sounds amazing. So besides applying for a visa, what else do you have to do?"

"I'd like to bring a petition before the council, but I'm not sure if I go through the Etikun tribe, since that's where I'm looking at starting the nonprofit, or if I could come to you and ask you to put it on the docket since I'm in Àlàáfíà. Plus, you guys only meet once a month, which means the petition wouldn't be heard until the end of July. Which *then* means I'd need approval to stay longer even before the work visa is approved."

"I'm sure that won't be a problem."

"Are you?" Her shoulders dropped. "I really wrestled with asking you. I don't want you thinking I'd use your status for any kind of pull."

I got up and gave her a big hug. "We're best friends. Of course I'll listen and help in any way I can. I'll make sure everything is done properly so you won't be accused of favoritism."

Hopefully, granting her a longer stay wouldn't be seen as nepotism. The idea of preferentialism if a person wasn't qualified made me uncomfortable, but I was sure Dayo could advise me on how to help Iris and keep it ethical.

"Thanks, Bri."

I stepped back. "I guess I should go to my date." I made a gagging motion.

Iris laughed. "I'm going to be honest, I cannot wait to hear the details. I'll have popcorn ready. We both know he's getting crossed off."

"Pray he makes it really easy for the council to agree with me." I paused. "Too bad I can't record it."

Iris's eyes practically popped out of their sockets. "I would love that! Please find a way to do so. I'm sure he'll be sitting perfectly straight in his chair with that condescending smile on his face. As if he's doing you a favor by allowing you to be in his presence."

"Truth. But I'm pretty sure no cameras are allowed in the private dining room."

"Boo."

I walked to the door. "Pray it goes quickly and that I don't lose my cool."

Iris scoffed. "If you can handle thirty kids in a classroom, you can handle one pompous prince."

I chuckled. "Thanks for that perspective." I waved and left my suite.

Navigating the palace had become second nature, and I quickly found myself seated in the dining room as I waited for Prince Chimnoya.

And waited.

And waited some more.

Thirty minutes later, I stood, ready to go back to my room and rejoice with Iris. Except the door opened, and Prince Chimnoya waltzed in. He eyed me and came to a stop behind the chair across from mine.

"Your Highness." He dipped, but not into a full bow.

When he straightened, I met his gaze. "You're late."

"It could not be helped." He sat, spreading the cloth napkin on his lap as if he didn't have a care in the world.

Heat flushed down my back, and I clamped my teeth hard. Willing myself to calm down, I took my seat once more. I motioned for the servers to bring out the food, which I'd had sent back to the kitchen after waiting ten minutes.

They came out with trays, placing them before us.

"Let us bow our heads," Prince Chimnoya said. "I will say grace."

"What if I want to?" I asked, genuinely curious about his answer.

He graced me with a patronizing smile. "Your Highness, I do

202

not disregard your status in our country. However, in a marriage, the husband is the head of the household and spiritual leader. Hence the reason *I* will pray."

"We are not married."

"It is only a matter of time."

Was he serious? I searched his stern features for any hint of a joke, but the impatient glare in his eye told me how much he believed that to be true.

"You do know you are not the only potential husband in Ọlọrọ, Prince Chimnoya?"

"Prince Ekon and Mr. Udo are not real contenders. They are still young and inexperienced in the ways that count. They cannot lead this country."

For once, the age difference didn't capture my attention. "Prince Chimnoya, *I* will be the one leading the country."

He huffed. "Please. You know nothing of our ways. It only makes sense that your husband will be the ruler."

"And how do you imagine that will happen? I will *not* sign over control to my husband."

He sputtered, and I sipped my ice water, waiting for him to compose himself.

"Surely the council will not condone this. They will not seriously let *you* lead our great kingdom."

"They will, as soon as I can find a suitable husband."

He popped his collar, and I was reminded of every rich frat boy who thought he could get by on looks and status.

"Prince Chimnoya, I must be honest with you. I agreed to this dinner out of respect for you, the king, and the council's wishes. After waiting for you for half an hour and then listening to your condescending remarks, I have no intention of dating you and will move on to the next man on my list as soon as this dinner concludes."

He reared back. "You dare speak to me in such manner?"

"You dare show up thirty minutes late to a meeting with your crown princess?" I didn't want to pull the rank card, but he needed to be put in his place. Bile filled my throat at the confrontation, but I held his gaze steady in mine.

"I will speak to the king about this."

"You will do *no* such thing unless you make an appointment with Mr. Owusu. But rest assured, I will be sure to let my *grandfather* know not to grant you such a meeting. He has better things to attend to than a petulant prince irritated that I didn't cave to his whims."

His chair screeched as he shoved away from the table and stalked out of the room.

When the door shut behind him, I sighed in relief. Thank goodness that was over.

"I did not like him for you."

I whirled around and gaped as Mobo Owusu walked forward.

"I told your grandfather he would not do, but he was determined to give the prince a fair chance." He lifted a shoulder. "Next."

I stifled a laugh. It was so odd to hear Mobo joke like that. He always had a stoic expression and a dry tone, never breaking protocol as the king's secretary. Even now, he sounded the same as when he taught me everything I needed to know about running Ọlọrọ.

"At least he saved me the trouble of having to eat with him."

"You definitely—how do they say it?—dodged a bullet." He winked, then pointed to the abandoned dinner plate as if he hadn't just made a joke. "Shall I have them remove this, or do you wish to continue your meal?"

"Actually, I think I'll take a plate back to my room. Maybe watch a movie with my mom and Iris."

"If you will allow me, I will see that a tray is brought to your suite for the three of you. Perhaps you may even want some ice cream?" He watched me patiently, waiting for my reply.

"Ice cream would be perfect."

He bowed. "You shall get it as swiftly as possible, Your Highness."

"Thank you. And please let the staff know I appreciate their efforts in keeping dinner warm." I paused. "Did the king eat yet?"

"No, Your Highness."

"Please prepare a plate for him and let him know I want him to eat."

The tiniest of smiles graced his lips. "I will tell him."

"Thank you, Mr. Owusu."

I hurried away, ready to grab a T-shirt, yoga pants, and a pint of ice cream. Prince Chimnoya Sule was officially off my list, and I had lived to tell the tale.

Now to continue my search for a prince.

THIRTY

A s much as I wanted to go to church, the thought of wrestling with interpretation the entire service made me want to stay at the palace. I wanted a blessed hour of worshipping and forgetting the role I'd stepped into. Which was kind of difficult, since I would be attending service in an official royal capacity.

Grandfather had asked me to wear something purple, so I chose a purple silk blouse with a blue-and-purple plaid pencil skirt. I completed the outfit with my purple amure. The sash hung from my left arm and swung with each step as I walked a half step behind Grandfather down the aisle to the front-row pew.

Whispers ran through the congregation the closer we drew to our reserved seating. This was only my second public appearance, and it made sense that the citizens would be curious about me. The local news had mentioned that the people wanted to get a clearer look at me. The PR team was already in negotiations for future one-on-one interviews.

Requests from African media outlets that wanted to find out about my upbringing and how I came to be in Ọlọrọ Ilé had poured in. Even the American and European reporters wanted to interview me. Grandfather thought it would be a good idea if I did one for TV, a popular magazine, and a news show. I didn't want to do any of them. The mere thought made me wish for anti-nausea medication.

I tried to ignore the whispers, hoping desperately that people wouldn't pull out their cell phones and record me or take pictures like they would in America. We *were* in church, after all.

Just when I thought the noise of the crowd would wipe away my joy at being in a house of worship, I spotted Tomori in a middle pew.

You can do this, he mouthed.

Tears stung at the offer of comfort. *Thank you,* I replied.

Soon I slid into the first row, making room for Grandfather to sit by the aisle. I placed my hands in my lap, pulse drumming in my throat. Grandfather patted my hand, and the flight of bees in my stomach settled to a dull buzz.

Earlier at breakfast, Grandfather had gone over the order of the church service. Before the service began, the congregants would acknowledge us, so we would stand and wave to the crowd. I'd have to concentrate on waving to everyone and not just locking eyes with Tomori.

"Are you all right, Brielle?"

"Yes," I murmured. I peered up at Grandfather, noting the fatigue in his eyes. "How are you feeling today?"

"Old, but thankful God has blessed me with another day. I am all too aware how fleeting time is."

He was a visual reminder to live each day like it could be my last. Still, I had to admit my ideas of death were different since the disease wasn't ravaging my body. In the time I'd been here, Grandfather had lost weight. I knew for a fact his clothes had needed altering, and his face had started to sink in, making his cheekbones all the more prominent. My heart hurt watching him shrink, but I could tell his spirit was just as strong as when I'd arrived a month ago. He wouldn't let death take his faith.

A pastor wearing a white robe entered the stage from a side entrance and made his way to the pulpit. I straightened as he greeted everyone, his voice booming from the microphone attached to the podium.

"Greetings, my brothers and sisters," he said in Onina. He said a few more words I didn't catch, and then I heard, "Let us welcome our king and our princess."

I stood with Grandfather, turning to face the crowd. With my palm in the air and a smile on my face, I waved to everyone. A quick peek showed Tomori looking proud. I focused and dropped my hand so Grandfather could have an extra moment.

My mind wandered once we sat back down. Did Tomori always attend the palace chapel, or had he come because I'd mentioned I would be here? I thought he went home on the weekends to escape the palace dormitories.

I remembered his sister's invitation to dine with them. Part of me still wanted to see what his family was like, only now that the world knew an Ọlọran princess existed, I couldn't roam the streets by myself. Sometimes the change in my life stifled me. I wanted just to *be*. The palace gardens and the private stretch of beach were the only places I could seek solitude now. Iris and my mom were constantly knocking to see if I wanted to hang out, so my suite wasn't even a sanctuary.

Not that I didn't value their love and support. I constantly apologized to Mom since I couldn't spend as much time with her as I'd hoped. I'd asked her to visit me and then had all but foisted her off on Iris to entertain. I sighed.

The pastor continued speaking, and my brain struggled to translate some of the words. Perhaps I should ask Tomori to give me a religious lesson in Onina. That way I could understand more when I visited the next time.

Soon the pastor called up some men and women to lead us in singing. I perked up. They would probably sing in Onina, but maybe I would hear the reverence and understand what they were saying. Two men started playing, one on the drums and the other on a keyboard.

I stood with Grandfather and swayed back and forth as the praise band began singing. The only word I could really catch was *hallelujah*, but the music settled something inside me, helping me cast my cares aside as I remembered the greatness of God.

The congregants behind me clapped and sang with the team as a woman led a call and response. I smiled at the enthusiastic worship. Song after song was played until I felt slightly winded from swaying to the music.

Grandfather had sat down after the first song, and I cast a surreptitious glance his way. Beads of sweat popped across his upper lip, and he looked paler than usual.

The song ended, and I sat, leaning toward him. "Should we leave? Do I need to get you some water?"

"Do not fret, Brielle. I will live a little bit longer."

An exasperated sigh filtered through me. "Bàbá àgbà," I said sternly.

"No, granddaughter. You cannot scold me in my native tongue. That is not fair."

"I don't want you to overexert yourself. We can go back to the palace."

"The Lord will sustain me through the service. He knows how badly I need the Word today."

What could I possibly say to that?

I faced forward, hands clenched in my lap. The pastor turned on a projector, and a Bible passage filled the screen. I discreetly looked to my left and noticed the congregants gazing intently at the screen. Then I looked over my shoulder before facing forward again.

"There are no Bibles?" I whispered.

"Many cannot afford them," Grandfather whispered back.

"Why have we not provided them for the people, then? Especially as this is the royal chapel?"

"We will discuss this later, Brielle. Listen."

I wanted to argue but couldn't deny that I needed to listen. Except I couldn't understand every word in front of me. I pulled out my cell and opened the Bible I'd downloaded to my phone. "What book is that, Grandfather?"

"Judges chapter six."

I read the chapter while the pastor talked. I could so relate to Gideon feeling less than, but as I read his story, the thing that jumped out at me was that God had come to him. Like the Lord had visited me in my dream. Did that mean I was in Ọlọrọ for some divine purpose that I couldn't see at the moment? I only knew that He had called me to step into my role. Yet I did so unwillingly at times.

I bowed my head, seeking forgiveness for my less-than-stellar attitude. For the times I doubted I could do any good in my father's home country. I had to let my heart and mind meet and have faith in God's calling. He would not leave me floundering. That wasn't who He was. But if I could stop looking at what I expected royal life to be like, maybe then I could hear God's still, small voice leading me.

Time passed as I read a few passages again and occasionally tuned in to the pastor's voice. As much as I enjoyed sitting in church, the desire to hear English overcame me. Maybe Grandfather would allow me to attend the other service as well. It might be inconvenient getting guards to attend, but I desperately wanted not to have to work so hard to understand.

The pastor called the service to its end, and Grandfather stood. I followed him as he walked down the aisle, waving good-bye to the people. I pasted a smile on my face and copied his manner. Some of the ladies returned my greeting, but a few of the men stared straight ahead and ignored me. It was like the silence at the Independence Day parade and the condemnation I'd received from the council.

My heart dipped, but I held on to the reminder that the Holy Spirit had given me during church. God put me here for a purpose, and I would let no one dissuade me from it.

THIRTY-ONE

o, switch the two words around," Tomori suggested.

I groaned but did as he said. Grandfather had urged me to draft a statement to the country that the PR team would disseminate to media outlets. Later on, I had a virtual interview with an American talk show host. Shade, the head of the palace's PR team, had gone over the questions with me. The host wasn't allowed to ask me any questions other than the ones supplied. I would have my makeup redone right before the meeting. Until then, I had to finish the statement.

"Your Highness—"

I glared at Tomori.

"Brielle . . . I can write the statement for you."

"That would negate my efforts in trying to learn the language."

He chuckled. "It is good that you have a stubborn streak. I am sure you will need it as princess."

"Are you calling me names?"

"What? No." Tomori's eyes widened.

I couldn't help it. I laughed at the look of horror on his face.

"You have a sense of humor, hmm?" he said dryly.

"I have to, or I'll go crazy." I put down my pen. "Can I ask you a question?"

"Anytime."

"Do the men in this country hate me?" I couldn't meet his gaze

211

as my words created a silence full of angst and probably awkwardness on his part. "You know what? Never mind. Forget I asked." I picked up my pen and proceeded to write the next word.

"Brielle, look at me, please."

I stared down at the paper in front of me, then lifted my eyes to find his ebony gaze focused solely on me. I swallowed.

"Your value as a princess is not dependent on whether or not the country likes you. Your value is in how you lead us, how you portray nobility, and how you care for us. If you do those things well—and I know you will—then the most hateful internet troll will have no choice but to see how wonderful you are."

My heart pounded in my chest. How I wished he were telling me how wonderful I was because he liked me as a woman and not his future monarch. Still, his words were a balm. "Thank you, Tomori. I feel like I have a constant battle in beating the doubts away."

"I can only imagine. Did church help?"

"Oh!" I perked up. "I need biblical lessons, because I didn't catch half of what was said. I read an English translation." I frowned, remembering the lack of Bibles. "Do you know why there are no Bibles at the church?"

"People cannot afford them."

"Yes, but don't the churches provide them?"

"They do not."

I tilted my head, studying him. "Do you own a Bible?"

"Yes. I got one for my sixteenth birthday."

"I'm going to buy some Bibles, then." I wasn't sure exactly how much money was in my royal account, but surely there was enough to outfit the palace church with Bibles. I would ask Dayo to get me the numbers for all the other Christian churches in Ọlọrọ.

"For church?" he asked.

"Yes."

"And that is why the country—all citizens—will fall in love with you."

I froze, eyes locked on the man who made my heart quiver with longing.

"I have to go out with Kambili," I blurted. I wanted to take the words back as soon as they left my lips, but obviously my brain had executed Self-Preservation Measure Number One. Tomori was not for me.

"I wish you well. And—"

A knock sounded.

"Come in."

Dayo entered and bowed. "Your Highness, makeup is here to prepare you for the interview."

My gaze flicked to Tomori, who had already risen. "I will see you tomorrow, Your Highness," he said.

"Thank you for your help."

He nodded and left the room. What had he been about to say? My thoughts churned as I tried to focus on my interview instead of the things left unspoken.

Soon a laptop and bright lights were set up to ensure I looked perfectly polished on camera.

On the screen, Kristina McGee's pink-lipstick grin widened. "Welcome, Your Highness. I'm so honored to have you on the show today."

"Thank you for inviting me. I've always enjoyed your show in the past."

She placed a hand on her heart. "I can't believe you're a New Yorker. It must have been mind-blowing to discover you were royalty. Tell me how it all came about."

The PR team had given me strict instructions to speak of Grandfather's illness in vague terms instead of the terminal sentence the doctor had given him. I repeated the talking points, hoping she wouldn't dig further.

"That's so sad. I'm sure we'll all keep him in our prayers." She paused a moment. "So how is it, being a princess?"

"It's a lot of work." I laughed. "I'm learning the language, the history, basically everything I need to know to give the country my best."

"Are you still considered an American citizen?"

"I'm not. I couldn't, since I shifted my allegiance to Ọlọrọ once I agreed to become a working royal."

213

"Does that mean you can't come back?"

"I can. Just as a diplomat visiting in the future."

"What do you miss from the States?"

"Halal carts."

Kristina laughed. "Spoken like a New Yorker. What's your favorite thing about Ọlọrọ?"

Tomori popped into my mind, and I swallowed. Instead, I told her about the paiis and the different flavors.

"Those sound amazing. Does Ọlọrọ have a lot of tourism?"

"We do." I talked about the beautiful beaches and my favorite spots I'd visited so far.

Our conversation was easy, though my pulse raced the entire time and my palms were damp. Thank goodness she couldn't see the number of times I wiped them on my slacks. I'd probably need to change outfits and put on more deodorant.

Finally, we ended the interview with Kristina wishing me well and thanking me for my time. I smiled until I was kicked into the virtual green screen. The producer thanked me once more, and I signed off.

I sank bank into my chair.

"Do you need anything, Your Highness?" Dayo asked.

"Maybe a glass of water?"

"Right away. Oh, and you have some correspondence." She handed me a stack of envelopes.

One thing I wasn't used to was knowing that security had probably read all of these. Since the letter I'd received at council meeting, Nonso, the head of security, thought it best if they received my mail before me. They would only let me read letters that passed their test and were deemed safe.

I opened the first envelope, which was from an elementary class. They congratulated me on becoming the first female heir. It had been written in English. I wondered if that was because they thought I wouldn't know Onina. I set it aside, making a note to thank them and write back in their native tongue.

The next two were more of the same, but the last one was different. It didn't have the palace address listed on the envelope like the others. It looked exactly like the note the palace runner had slipped to the guards. My brow furrowed as I opened it, pulling out another typed sheet.

To the American Princess,
    I confess I have no desire to greet you using your title. You are not one of us. You are an imposter and should abdicate the throne or sign it over to someone who has the knowledge and allegiance to this great country. Women were not meant to rule, so please step aside.

Sincerely,
A concerned loyalist

My mouth dropped. Had security let this through, or had someone slipped it into the stack in transit? The letter was longer than the other warning, so I didn't know what to think. Same person? Another person who didn't like me?

I rose to my feet and opened the door that separated me from my secretary. "Dayo?"

She walked into her office from the corridor with a glass in her hand. "Did you need something? I am sorry if I was slow. I was talking to Mr. Owusu in the hall."

I held up the letter. "Did you see this? Did you put this in the stack?"

She handed me the glass of water, and I extended the letter. I watched as she read each word and shock covered her features. "No, Your Highness. I assumed the letters had all come from security. I will see to this right away." She folded it back into the trifold.

"Actually, I'll handle it." I held my hand open.

"Do you not trust me?" Hurt darkened her gaze as her bottom lip quivered.

My heart softened. "Of course I do. But I want to follow this up on my own. Please don't be concerned."

"Naturally I am concerned, Your Highness. I told you there would be those opposed to you."

"I remember," I stated softly.

Dayo passed the letter back.

I thanked her and grabbed my purse. Since Mobo hadn't seen the last letter, I would seek his help for this. Hopefully Dayo wouldn't take offense.

THIRTY-TWO

Lush countryside streamed past my window as Azuka drove me to Opolopo. We were on the way to see Kambili Udo. Grandfather had urged me once more to ensure I put my best foot forward. He wasn't happy that I'd removed Prince Chimnoya so easily from the list and had urged me to remember that compromise often went hand in hand with a good marriage. Mr. Udo claimed he couldn't possibly leave his home, since he'd been to Àlàáfíà recently for the Independence Day celebration, so I'd compromised and had my guards take me to him. Still, I was annoyed I was picking the guy up for our date. Call me old-fashioned.

I was eager to see the lake once more, so that was a plus. Tomori always spoke about the area with such fondness. Granted, it could be his love for fishing that made him love Opolopo.

You told yourself not to think about him on your date. I sighed.

The guards were abnormally quiet. Azu had an intense focus going on, while Merrick's neck constantly rotated, keeping a vigilant alertness. The longer we drove, the lusher the trees became and the lower the temperature dropped.

Since no one spoke, I turned to prayer. *Lord God, please help me find a husband in time.* Every single time I saw Grandfather, I couldn't help but search for signs of failing health. I'd made friends with his doctor in order to get a realistic expectation of his condition. Dr. Falade had shared Grandfather's lab results—with the king's permission. So far, Grandfather was hanging in there even though his numbers had begun to dip into dangerous ranges. Dr. Falade believed Grandfather still had about five months to live.

I prayed it was true, because if the list of eligible men failed me, I'd have to go back to the drawing board. *Please don't let the throne revert to Uncle Sijuwola.*

My great-uncle had returned to family dinners, but the reception from him and his family was on the frigid side. Digi was the only one happy to see me. I wondered if Sijuwola was the one sending me notes. Security had no leads and no fingerprints other than of those we already knew had handled them.

Azuka turned down a dirt road, and thatched-roof homes popped up along the horizon. I smiled as children ran outside, playing with a soccer ball. Did Mr. Udo live in this village or in a different area?

I soon got my answer. After a few twists and turns, Azuka pulled up to a huge house. The thatched roof lent an air of romantic tropical getaway. The wood shone brightly in the sun, gleaming like mahogany. I was surprised not to see the same black wood used throughout the palace. Then again, the trees out here were different from the ones in Àlàáfíà.

Merrick scanned the premises, then left the car. I waited patiently, knowing he'd let me out when he deemed it safe. The door opened, and he offered a hand. I stepped onto the green grass and inhaled the fresh air. Opolopo seemed more humid than the capital. Hopefully my silk blouse and black slacks wouldn't wilt in the damp air. I never knew who would see me in public nowadays, and I'd learned always to look my best no matter how much I wanted to reach for lounge pants instead of the ones with a hidden button inside the waistband.

I swear that button was there to mock me if I gained even the tiniest bit of weight.

Azuka led me up the wooden steps and knocked on the door. We waited. And waited.

"Where is he?" Azuka muttered.

Just as a response formed on my lips, a scream rent the air.

I gasped, and Azuka broke through the door. A girl about three years old stood with her hands shaking in front of her, her mouth wide as she continued to scream. She stopped suddenly, pointing at a boy standing a few feet from her.

The older boy held a doll above his head while a toddler sat at his feet, mashing his food into the floor. Another girl sat curled up in the corner with a book, ignoring the mayhem.

"Mine!" the screaming child shouted in Onina.

"It's stupid," the boy countered.

"What in the world?" Azuka muttered.

"Are these *his* kids?" I asked. Had I failed to ask if any of the men had children?

"Mr. Udo has four, I believe," Azuka said.

"Four?" My face heated, and my knees went weak. "Is this what I have to look forward to? Life with four kids?"

"I have five," Azuka said. "They do not act like this."

I looked at him, shock coursing through me. "*Five?*"

He shrugged. "My wife is from a big family and wanted one of her own. My children are angels."

"Isn't that what parents say when their kids are the exact opposite?"

Azu laughed. "She is a teacher, and they are terrified of her teacher face. Their words, not mine."

I smiled, thinking of my students back home. Or rather, in New York. Àlàáfíà was home now. My heart turned over, but I shrugged off the sadness. Right now, my dilemma was wrangling four children—or at least figuring out where Kambili Udo was. We walked farther into the house, and Merrick closed the door. The kids jumped at the sound and faced us.

"Aren't you the princess?" the boy asked suspiciously, speaking in Onina.

"I am," I replied back.

His eyes widened. "You speak Onina."

"A little. I'm learning." I wanted to applaud at the perfect accent I applied.

"How many languages do you speak?" he asked in French.

219

"Three," I replied in English.

He grinned. "I know four." He switched to my native tongue as well.

"You're smart. What's the fourth language?" I asked in English.

"Spanish. I wanted to learn, and Bàbá said I could."

"Where is he?"

The boy rolled his eyes. "He is at Ledi's house."

"Who is that?"

He pointed to the girl in the corner. "Her màmá."

Oh. Did that mean the boy didn't share the same mom? "Does she live nearby?"

"Yes. She lives next door that way." He pointed to the right.

Say what now? I quickly schooled my face. My eyebrows had begun inching up in disbelief. I took a deep breath. "And your mom?" I asked cautiously.

"She lives next door the other way." His hand switched to the left.

Uh-oh. I pointed to the other two children. "And their moms?"

"Lulu's mom lives across the yard, and the baby's mom lives here. She is sick and cannot take care of him."

I tried to catch my breath at the absurdity of it all. They all had different moms within walking distance to Mr. Udo? Was I supposed to say *I do* and pop out another kid for his crew? What would other heads of state think of our situation?

My heart drummed in my chest, my breathing ragged. I needed to leave. "Let's go," I whispered.

Azuka placed a hand on my elbow and guided me out the way we came. Merrick stood with the car door open, scanning the area.

As soon as we were in the car, driving away from the house of crazy, I broke the silence. "We're going fishing now, right?"

I'd asked to fish before I left Opolopo. Grandfather had mentioned a royal dock in the area. He'd made plans to send someone ahead to prepare the place.

"Yes," Azuka responded. "The royal dock has already been secured."

Part of me wanted to apologize for making them do so much

work just so I could attempt to fish. I hoped whoever they'd sent ahead was an expert, because I didn't even know a fishing pole from . . . well, whatever else might be used.

We drove quietly, and soon my cares slowly eked out of my shoulders as I leaned against the back seat. The SUV went off-road and came to a stop behind the back of a hut.

"This is the royal fishing hut. I will go and clear it, and then you may enter," Merrick stated. He immediately got out, not waiting to see if I would follow orders.

"Are you going to teach me how to fish, Azu?" I asked.

He snorted. "I do not fish. I know we live on an island, but I cannot abide the smell or anything about the creatures."

I laughed. "Neither can I. But I do love other seafood. Just not fish."

"Exactly." He threw his hands up in the air. "Disgusting."

"Do you know who will teach me?"

"Tomori Eesuola."

My heart pounded and drowned out the rest of his words. Tomori was in Opolopo? He was just at the palace yesterday. Had they sent him officially as part of his palace runner duties? Or perhaps he lived in the area and they deemed him close enough to help?

Merrick appeared on the back deck of the hut and gave a signal to Azuka, who was already leaving the car to open my door. My palms dampened as I thought of what to say to Tomori. He'd been oddly reserved at our language lessons this past week. He no longer joked or called me anything but *Your Highness*. Each time, the words chipped at me. I missed our early friendship when I was simply Brielle.

Inside the hut, Azu pointed to the French doors leading to the dock. "Tomori is outside. We will keep our distance so you can have fun, Your Highness."

"Thank you." I made my way slowly through the room, admiring the gorgeous view of the lake from the little hillside. I stepped out the door and scanned the area for Tomori. Seeing no sign of him, I walked over a slight ridge and finally saw him. He stood near the lake, hands in his pockets.

"Tomori," I called softly. I didn't want to disturb him if he was in a contemplative mood.

He whipped his head around, his gaze intent. For a split second, my mind imagined me all in white and him waiting at an altar. I sighed, pushing the wish away. When I stopped a few feet from him, Tomori said nothing.

"What are you doing here?" I asked.

Slowly his lips curved into a smile. "I did promise to teach you how to fish, Brielle."

Brielle! I wanted to catch my heart from falling at his feet. "That you did." My voice came out huskier than I intended. Delight coursed through me that I was Brielle again, not *Your Highness*. "I guess you'll give it your best shot. I'll probably be a horrible fisherman."

"I do not believe that. You excel at everything you put your mind to."

Pleasure unfurled through me. How I'd missed this easy camaraderie between us.

"What happened to your date?" Tomori's voice sounded a bit stilted.

"His kids happened." I told him about the scene we'd walked in on and the close location of Udo's exes.

"I am not surprised."

"At least that's one less person I have to worry about. Prince Ekon is next."

Displeasure flashed across Tomori's face, then disappeared. I wanted to ask why he was bothered. If he wished *he* were on the list. But there was no point in torturing both of us. We could never be. Grandfather was adamant that I choose for political purposes, and the council had their own wishes. I needed to accept that and find someone acceptable before time ran out.

THIRTY-THREE

Tomori led the way to the end of the royal dock, where two lawn chairs reclined. There were also a couple of ice chests and some netting. I swallowed down my trepidation. If I actually caught a fish, would he expect me to touch it? My stomach revolted when I put a cooked piece of one in my mouth. What made him think I'd be able to touch one of the scaly things? Then again, Tomori hadn't been at the dinner when I'd humiliated myself by projectile spewing all over Uncle Sijuwola's face.

"Did I ever tell you I have an aversion to fish?" I asked.

Tomori paused, net in hand, and cocked his head toward me. "Then why do you want to learn how to catch them?"

I sighed. "I kind of don't, but I kind of do." I shook my head. "It's a chance to get away from the pressure of marriage. Plus, you told me fishing is fun."

More than anything, I want to experience something you like. But I couldn't say that. What kind of desperation would a phrase like that reveal?

Tomori's gaze roamed my features. I tried to keep my muscles relaxed under such scrutiny, but my cheeks burned with heat, and my heart thudded faster with each second that passed.

"All right, then. If you want to fish, I will teach you."

I bit my lip. "Do I have to touch them?"

"No, Brielle." His lips quirked. "I can do that for you."

223

My shoulders sagged. "Thank you."

"You are welcome." He held up a rope with a loop on the end. "I am going to show you how to net fish."

I looked around the dock once more, really taking in the items before me. "No poles?"

"No, ma'am. I always use a net. It is the best way to get a haul, in my opinion."

Oy. "Okay. Show me how it's done."

"*Arídunnú mi*, it would be my pleasure."

I loved hearing him speak Onina. "What does that mean?" I hadn't heard the phrase before, and the way he said it elicited goosebumps along my arms despite the warmth of the sunshine.

His eyes widened, and he coughed. "It is nothing." He placed the loop on his right wrist. "You do not want this loop too tight. It is there so you do not lose the rope when you throw the net. If you make it too tight and something happens, you may be dragged."

"Um . . ."

A soft chuckle fell from his lips, and I shivered. "I promise, Brielle, I will not let anything happen to you." He reached toward his right foot, pulling up his pant leg to reveal a knife. "Plus, I can cut the rope if needed."

Good. I wanted to avoid anything embarrassing happening in front of him. "Okay, so, rope on wrist."

"Yes. Then you coil the rope." He looped the rope around his hand as he spoke, making circle after circle, about a foot in diameter.

"Why is the rope so long?"

"It allows you to cast it farther than just at the dock."

"The net won't float?"

"No, it has weights on the end. We are aiming for catfish, so we will let the net sink pretty deep."

"How will you know if you've got something?"

He held up his wrist. "You will feel it."

Eek! "What if the weight is too much for me to handle?"

"I will be right here when you cast the net for the first time. For now, you will just get the hang of how to use it."

Tomori took his time showing me how to set up the net in order to throw it. After a few demonstrations, he cast the net in the water. I watched as it sank.

"That's amazing." I shifted on the lawn chair. I'd taken a seat at Tomori's insistence.

The sounds of the lake were different from the lull of the ocean. The lake seemed to bubble, and various insects added to the symphony of noise. The longer I sat, the more the tension seeped from my body. Watching Tomori's lean form as he held on to the rope relaxed me further.

"Did you know yesterday that you'd be out here?"

Tomori turned to look at me. "I did. I left the palace last night and stayed at the home of one of my sisters. She moved to Opolopo when she married. Whenever I visit, she offers me a place on her couch."

"Did you get to have a nice visit? Will you stay with her again?"

He grinned. "No. She has six children. It can be a tad on the noisy side."

I laughed. "Just a tad?"

He held up his forefinger and thumb. "That much. I may have been eager to leave this morning."

"Thank you for taking the time to teach me today, especially considering you're with your family."

"I do not mind. Truly."

I bit my lip and turned my gaze back to the water, ignoring the heat of his eyes on my profile.

"How did you come to dislike fish?" he asked.

My nose wrinkled. "Besides the smell?"

"I have seen you eat seafood."

"Every other seafood tastes delicious and smells nothing like fish."

He laughed. "There are some who would disagree with you."

"I'm sure." I rubbed my hands on my pants. "My mother likes to eat out for important events in our lives. We go to her favorite restaurant, and she delivers her news, usually when we're eating dessert." I gathered a breath. "One year, she told me the story of how she met my dad. I was eating salmon. She was about to tell me something special about him, but my salmon had a small bone left in it. I choked. Freaked out. My mother saved me, but I couldn't eat fish again after that."

What had she been about to tell me? I'd never thought about the start of my fish aversion that much, but now my brain spun like a cotton candy maker. Had she intended to tell me about his regal status? About *mine*?

Tomori called my name, interrupting my thoughts. "Brielle, watch as I pull the net in. See how I pull at the horn of the net? This creates a bag and keeps the fish from escaping."

He grunted as he tugged the net up and into an ice chest. My mouth dried watching him use the corded muscles in his arms to lift the net, and I redirected my thoughts and eyes to the ice chest. I didn't know what it held. The sound of the fish flapping greeted my ears as Tomori emptied the net, then checked the empty webbing. Whatever he was looking for, he was diligent in his search.

Finally, he lifted his gaze, and his obsidian eyes caught mine. "Your turn."

"Uh . . ."

He motioned me over. "Come. It is not scary. I promise."

"Right." I stood and joined him, inhaling the earthy scent I'd come to recognize as purely him.

"Let us put this on your wrist." He handed me the loop.

I did as instructed, then counted foot-length coils as he'd done earlier. "What next?"

"You must stand with half the net on your left and half on your right. That way when you gather the net to your hip, it will be evenly distributed."

Tomori guided me with each step until I had the net prepared to throw. I could feel the weight of it, but it seemed strangely light at the moment. "I just toss it?"

"Right. Throw with your right arm, then let the portion in your left go a second later."

I did so and frowned when the net hit the end of the dock. "What did I do wrong?"

"It takes practice."

After recoiling the net, I threw it again. This time, the net hit the water. "I did it!" The net tugged at my wrist as it sank. "You're sure I won't be pulled in?"

"Very." He slipped a hand around my elbow. "But I have you just in case."

My throat seized, and every nerve ending in my body responded to his touch. How easy would it be to turn into his arms and whisper his name? *Mori*. I would measure the closeness between us and melt into his arms.

But the time for my dreams had passed. I had to think of the greater good of my country and ignore the way my hormones spiked whenever Mori came around. Ekon Diallo was next on my list, and Tomori was not.

A tug on my wrist jolted me from my musings. "I think something's in the net."

"Oh yeah?" He plucked at the rope dangling from my arm. "It is tight. Do you want to pull it in now or wait to see if it gets heavier?"

"Heavier?" I squeaked.

He chuckled. "Now it is. Tug on that rope and pull it in."

"Okay." That sounded simple enough.

I pulled on the rope, using muscles that weren't often activated, since I spent the majority of my time in the office.

"Pull on the horn."

I did as he instructed. "I don't know if I'm going to be able to pull this in. It's getting heavy."

"Let me help."

His arms came around me, and soon we were both lifting the net above the ice chest and dumping the haul.

"Wow." I stared down at all the new fish, ignoring the tingles from Mori's touch. "That was kind of cool."

"See?" He snapped the lid closed. "That is all we will collect. The Opolopo region has strict regulations on how much we can keep. The council does not want to deplete the reservoir, especially during the summer and winter seasons."

"Why not? What happens?"

"It could mess up the life cycle of the fish and, in doing so, lower the amount available. That in turn affects the economy and consumption of your favorite food." He winked.

I chuckled. "Is this the cause Mr. Udo oversees?"

Mori nodded. "Yes. But he also wants to bring tourism here. He is trying to get others to turn Opolopo into a getaway retreat. Right now, there are a few fishing huts owned by elders and, of course, the king, as well as a small hotel. He wants a massive resort, though."

"What happens to the fish if more people come?"

"Obviously they will decline. Mr. Udo has suggested we simply import more."

I bit my lip. "Thank you for sharing."

"You are welcome. I will clean the fish and have them delivered to the palace."

"Should I help?"

"Do you think you are okay to? I do not want to compound your aversion."

"Maybe it's time I made a new memory," I replied.

"Then follow me."

Mori's movements were fluid as he cleaned the fish. Clearly, he'd done this many times before. While he cleaned and I watched, we talked. He shared memories of himself as a boy, raising a ruckus to torment his older siblings. I told him how I'd liked to imagine my father as an astronaut stuck on Mars, a man in witness protection, or a fisherman lost at sea—and oh, how close to the truth that was.

After he finished, Mori asked if I was hungry.

"A bit. Should we make something to eat?"

He arched an eyebrow. "You will cook? Or we will do it together?"

"I'd love to do it together—if you want, of course."

"That would be my pleasure."

We took stock of the fridge's contents and decided to make akara balls and seafood. Mori showed me how to form the bean balls and get the fried dough exterior. I showed him my favorite way to season and grill shrimp.

The entire time, I couldn't help but imagine us as a married couple. One who worked together, enjoyed being together, and lived happily ever after. It was on the tip of my tongue to ask if he'd consider marrying me. Surely Grandfather would want my happiness more than the country's, right?

Azuka stepped into the kitchen. "Your Highness, we need to leave soon. I believe you have another virtual interview this evening."

"Right." I'd forgotten about the French journalist.

"I will clean up," Tomori offered.

"Are you sure?"

"Yes," he murmured. "Go and delight the world."

All the way back to the palace, I wondered if I could go against expectations and marry for matters of the heart instead of the state.

THIRTY-FOUR

I was on a *date*.

That sounded weird, considering my meetings—or non-meetings—with Prince Chimnoya and Mr. Udo. However, this night with Prince Ekon Diallo was the epitome of a *real* date. He'd arranged for the guards to take us to a restaurant for dinner in Àlàáfíà, but he'd arrived at the palace first. He had shown up with a bouquet of flowers for me and a box of liqueur chocolates for Grandfather. He'd also insisted I call him by his first name.

From the moment he escorted me to the SUV—under the watchful eyes of Azuka and Merrick—he'd been attentive. And I didn't know how to react. Part of me wanted to relax, hoping my search was over. The other part remained wary. Oh, so wary. Where were his skeletons? Would one show up at the eatery in the form of a deranged ex? Or was Ekon just in it for the status?

Something had to be lurking around a corner. I prayed that the proverbial shoe would remain in the air—or wherever it was when not about to drop.

"You said you were a teacher, yes?" Ekon asked.

His voice wasn't as deep as Tomori's. Something I couldn't help but note. There was no bass to pebble my arms with awareness. Ekon didn't have a bad voice, but it wasn't Mori's.

"Your Highness?"

"Uh, yes." I met his gaze. "I taught middle school civics."

He looked nice in a black suit paired with a black collared shirt. He'd chosen to go tieless.

"Did you enjoy teaching, or are you thankful those days are over?" A dimple flashed with the quickness of his smile.

And still, no spark. What woman alive didn't love a dimpled smile?

I shook my head to make myself focus. "Most days, I loved it. I think it's like having kids of your own. You're overjoyed with them and their intelligence, but there are some challenging days. Those days that remind you why you wanted to be a teacher in the first place are the ones you hold close."

"I am not a parent, so I could not compare, but I believe I understand you."

Was the comparison that bad? I stifled the thought and searched for a question to ask Ekon. I couldn't let him do all the talking. I had to make sure he was worth another look if this date wasn't a disaster.

"How do you enjoy the jewelry business?"

"My family is responsible for the mining of Ọlọran agate. There are other gemstones and minerals our business mines, but the agate is our number one export. We also have a division that works on designing jewelry for sale."

"What do you do on a daily basis? I assume you don't mine yourself?"

He erupted in laughter. "You are very funny."

I wasn't trying to be. "I'm sorry. I meant to ask what kind of degree you hold." Surely that was a safer question.

"I have a business degree. Father requires it even though I will inherit the operations."

"Do you have other siblings?"

"No. I am an only child. Are *you* an only child?"

"I am."

He flashed his dimples. "Maybe that is why I feel a sense of connection with you."

Was it too early in the date for me to ask how? I offered a smile, hoping I didn't look as annoyed as I felt, considering my jaw had started ticking. Why wasn't I moved by his declaration of a connection?

I steadied myself. I was looking too deeply at things. "People with brothers and sisters don't understand the only-child thing, do they?"

"How can they? They are constantly surrounded by someone. It is hard to understand the dynamic of an only child."

"Well, I have a best friend who's like a sister. Did you meet her at the ball?"

Ekon nodded. "Yes. But having a best friend is not the same. The required love is not there."

Uh, spidey-sense tingling. "Required?"

"You know. You *have* to love someone because they are related to you."

"I'd like to think love is always a choice."

He scoffed. "Do you love every Adebayo?"

Uncle Sijuwola came to mind. "Well, I don't *know* every Adebayo, which makes a difference. Growing up with someone lends a level of understanding that can't be manufactured."

What kind of conversation was this for a date? Granted, we were trying to see if we could marry for life, so maybe unusual questions were warranted. Still, something about the whole conversation felt off. I just couldn't pinpoint what.

"Hmm. I am glad I am an only child. I think I would have made a terrible brother."

Should this be Spidey-Sense Number Two, or were we still on the same thread that alerted Number One? "Why?"

"I am a little selfish." He shrugged. "Perhaps I like a little too much attention."

I didn't want to fault him for his honesty, but I totally did. "What makes you a little and not a lot?"

"My father." A bemused expression covered his face. "He would not abide me being a waste of resources to the family or the nation."

What am I supposed to do with that *information?* I had somehow lost track of my simple bullets of things to ask. No way would I have guessed the conversation would turn into this. I glanced at the rearview mirror and caught Azuka's gaze. I raised an eyebrow, trying to communicate silently. Azuka's shoulders lifted discreetly. Even he didn't know what to think.

I guess I'll continue on with the date. Maybe ending the other dates early and escaping their presence had turned me into a flight risk. Already I tired of hearing Ekon talk. Still, Grandfather would want an honest report, and I couldn't really say that he deserved to be crossed off. Who wasn't selfish at times?

"What do you like to do for fun, Ekon?"

"I hang out with my friends when I am not working."

"Yeah, but what do you *do*?"

He looked at me from the corner of his eye, mouth tilted in a smirk. "We usually do an outdoor activity. Rafting, hiking, things like that."

"Do you fish?"

"No. I cannot abide the smell. Nothing from the sea should touch my plate."

"Not even crab?" I so loved crustaceans.

Distaste curled his lip. "Do you eat that?"

"I like it." *A lot.* My stomach did a happy dance, thinking of all the delicious seafood dishes I'd tasted in Ọlọrọ.

"If you eat some tonight, do not fear. I carry mints with me at all times."

Why? Did he have bad breath? Expect to go around kissing girls? *Chill, Bri. You wouldn't suspect every answer on a normal date.* But speed dating to save my place as heir *wasn't* normal.

I focused. "Is mint your favorite flavor?"

"Not when it comes to food, but I do like the fresh feeling."

The conversation fell to a lull. Thankfully, a few minutes later we arrived at the restaurant. As Azuka parked at the back of the restaurant, Merrick bolted from the car.

"Your Highness," Azuka said, "we have already talked to the restaurant and sent men early to ensure your safety. Two are still inside and will meet Merrick at the back door. When he gives the signal, we can enter the building."

"Thank you, Azuka."

"My pleasure, Your Highness."

After Azuka saw us inside with Merrick leading the way, the owners greeted me with a low bow.

"Such a pleasure to serve you today, Your Highness," the woman said.

"Thank you for accommodating my security."

"*Bien sûr, Votre Altesse*. This way, this way." The woman directed us to a table for two.

Merrick and another gentleman sat behind the table, and Azuka and the other took the one in front of us. The male owner pulled out my chair as Ekon seated himself.

"Ẹ seun." I gave him my palace grin, one I'd been practicing that I hoped looked regal and grateful at the same time.

"No thanks necessary," he said. Then they disappeared.

Ekon looked at me. "You do a lot of thanking."

I froze, napkin in midair. "Am I not supposed to thank people?" This was certainly not a flaw I'd been chastised about before. Not that his tone held censure. I really was overly sensitive tonight.

"It is all right. It is the American in you."

Come again? "I've heard people in Ọlọrọ express gratitude as well."

"Not like you Americans."

My stomach knotted. "Do you have a problem with Americans?"

Ekon smiled. "Of course not. It is a great country. A little noisy in some areas, but one I don't mind visiting."

Okay, it was official. I was losing my mind. I couldn't let the past dates curdle my opinion of this one. Ekon had done everything right so far. Maybe I just needed to relax and enjoy myself.

Out of politeness, I didn't order any seafood. Instead, I placed a request for the same rice and meat dish Ekon asked for.

"You will love the food. They have the best kabobs here."

"Sounds good."

He grinned, flashing his straight white teeth. "Tell me, Your Highness, how have the other dates been?"

I paused. "Less than ideal."

He chuckled. "I can imagine. I have interacted with those men before. I hope I am doing better than they did."

"Do you want to?" Besides being married to the future queen, how would marrying me benefit him?

"I do. I believe in doing my duty for the good of the country."

"As do I."

"I would hope so."

And I would overlook that somewhat snide tone. "How do you feel about marriage?"

"I have always imagined I'd marry someday." He shrugged. "I know my duties to family and country."

Did I want to be with someone who saw marriage merely as a duty? Yes, I had to do what was required of me for the good of Ọlọrọ, but I still wanted the possibility of love. Surely feelings could develop past a marriage of convenience. *Right, Lord?*

I sipped my ice water. "Tell me, Ekon, what do you think about love?"

"What is love?" he scoffed. "Sometimes I think of it like Christmas. Manufactured to suit certain businesses. Our jewelry business promotes love because that brings us more francs. Outside of that, I am not sure it exists."

My heart sank to my toes. "Are you saying you don't believe in love?"

"No." He leaned forward. "But I do believe that two people can live a life of mutual respect and affection. Love is for children and pets. Just like Santa."

How could I marry someone who didn't believe in love? Would adhering to the council's edict shrivel my heart in the process? I wasn't asking Ekon to love me now, but I so badly wanted the hope that romance could develop in the future. If I chose him out of duty and the fact that he had not repulsed me tonight, would I be left with respect and affection only? Or could I show him love was real?

Ugh, he makes my brain hurt.

The rest of the night was more of the same. We carried on a cordial conversation and enjoyed a good meal, but there were no sparks. No heart racing with just one glance from him. Ekon wasn't a bad man, but I didn't know if he was my prince either.

THIRTY-FIVE

I knocked on Iris's door, praying she hadn't fallen asleep. I really needed to talk to her about my date with Ekon before getting Mom's opinion.

Shuffling feet sounded before the doorknob turned. Iris greeted me wearing a satin shorts pajama set. "Hey, girl. Another bad date?"

"Actually . . . no." I walked past her and sank into the chair nearest her bed.

Iris crawled onto her bed, legs folded up beneath her. "Then why do you look so upset?"

That was the question of the hour. "I have no idea. Everything was going well, even though I spazzed out about how well it was going." I pulled at my fingers. "Ekon was a gentleman. He brought me flowers and chocolates for Grandfather. Opened my door and kept the conversation flowing." I stopped and met Iris's gaze. "I really thought the date would end with me thinking he was perfect."

"But he's not?" she asked cautiously. She worried her lip, brows furrowed.

"He doesn't believe love exists."

Her face flushed a dull red before her mouth dropped open. "Seriously?"

"Right? What am I supposed to do with that?" I groaned, flopping back against the chair. "I mean, I know this is all about convenience right now. I have to have a husband, and he—whoever *he* ends up being—will elevate in status, maybe even gain a title. But in the back of my mind, I want to fall in love with whomever I marry. You know?"

"He doesn't believe in love at all?" Iris repeated, her voice rising.

"He believes in mutual respect and affection. He says love was manufactured for commercial businesses."

"I don't even know what to say to that." Iris looked like someone had told her silk was no longer in fashion. Finally, someone who understood my dilemma.

"What do I do? Should I just ignore his ideas? I mean, that was literally his only flaw tonight." Besides not being Tomori. I shoved that thought away.

"But you have to marry." She stared off into space, then met my gaze. "Can anyone else be added to the list? Then you could find someone you're attracted to who believes in love." She shook her head. "How does he *not* believe in love?"

"I have no idea. As to your other question, I can't just choose someone because he makes my knees weak." If I could, I'd have picked Tomori and called it a day.

"Well, no. You have to make sure he's compatible in other ways. What do you want in a husband? What do you need in a prince? Then look at the list of guys. You've already crossed the first two off. Will Ekon fit those needs, or do you need to keep looking?"

"That sounds perfectly logical, but it makes me want ice cream."

Iris chuckled. "I know you don't want to be logical about this. I certainly want to root for love and for you to find the perfect guy. But you're a princess now," she said softly.

"I know," I whispered.

"Okay, let's set aside logic for a moment."

"All right."

"What do you want in a dream man?"

"For him to love God, love me, and any children we may have." That alone would cross Ekon off the list.

"What else? Any hobbies you want him to have? Any specific personality traits?"

I thought of Tomori. The patience he always exhibited. The kindness he showed everyone. "I want someone steady and dependable. Someone who will respect me and those I interact with regardless of whatever issues we may have. I want to enjoy spending time with him, even if I don't like the particular activity he chooses." Although, net fishing had been kind of fun. Mori had made it seem so effortless.

"Who are you thinking of?" Iris asked. "You're smiling."

I waved a hand. "It doesn't matter. But you're right. I think it's best to keep searching. Or should I go on another date with Ekon to see if something develops there?" Maybe I could fall in love with him, but did I want to live a life of unrequited love?

"It sounds like someone else was sparking your mind, though. *Not* Ekon."

"What's wrong with Ekon?"

"Nothing." She threw up her hands. "But he's not making you blush. Someone else is." She narrowed her eyes, studying my face, and then her eyes popped wide. She gasped. "It's Tomori, isn't it? You two are always together. All those language lessons. You like him, don't you?" The more she talked, the more animated she became.

I slumped forward, resting my elbows on my knees and my head in my hands. "That doesn't matter. It wouldn't work."

"Why not?"

"He's a palace runner, Iris."

"Oh my goodness! You're a snob!"

I rolled my eyes and straightened. "*I* don't care about that. I'm telling you what everyone else's reaction will be. Grandfather wants someone who understands politics inside and out. The council wants someone more important than me. Probably because they believe the *man* will run the country and I'll be home popping out babies."

Iris giggled. "Prince Chimnoya definitely was that type, and Mr. Udo already has kids."

"I still shudder thinking about all of his baby mamas in close contact. How do they live like that?"

"I don't know." Iris ruffled the end of her curls. Her mane flowed wild and free. "What are you going to do? Ekon or Tomori?"

"Do you seriously think they would give Tomori a chance?"

Iris shrugged. "Maybe with the king's backing and the power of your station. If you fight for it hard enough, why not?"

What would Grandfather say if I told him I wanted to choose Tomori? Would he stand by me? Would the council yield?

I stood. "I think I need to go pray."

"Of course." Iris hugged me. "I'll say a prayer for wisdom." She pulled back. "But honestly, if Tomori is who you choose, then I think you'll be happy."

"Why? Because you've seen me blush a time or two?" I studied her dark eyes, praying she had some insight I lacked.

"Because I see the way he looks at you when you're not looking."

My breath hitched. "Really?"

Iris nodded. "He's interested, Bri. But only he and God know if he could handle the limelight of your life."

"You're right. Thanks, Iris."

"It's why I'm here." She smiled and nudged me toward the door. "Now leave. I have more paperwork to finish before the next council meeting. It seems my visa has been extended."

I grinned. "I may have called in a favor."

"You shouldn't have, but I'd be lying if I said I wasn't grateful. I'm so excited about this, Bri."

"I can't wait to hear what you come up with."

She beamed. "You'll love it. I promise."

"I believe you. I'll talk to you tomorrow."

She nodded, and I slipped through our adjoining door and into my suite.

I went through my nighttime routine, then pulled out my journal, searching for the words to write. What did I want to say to God? What emotions had muddied my mind and created the swirling mass of confusion I'd been stuck in?

239

Dear Lord,

Today has been one of those days. The tug of being at a crossroads has me almost at a breaking point. Somehow my future has me choosing between Ekon and Tomori. I could probably go on more dates with Ekon and even begin to like him, but I fear that denying the feelings Tomori evokes every single time I'm with him would cost me. The weight of my duty feels too heavy, Lord. I don't know if choosing Tomori is selfish and would put the country at harm. I can't see the future, and the unknown has me in such a knot. How do I choose? If I pick Ekon, am I denying love? Couldn't a marriage of convenience turn into more, if it's Your will, regardless of how Ekon feels about love?

Your Word calls a wife to respect and love her husband. Could I do that with Ekon? If he thinks love is manufactured, what does he believe about You?

My heart clenched at the thought. I hadn't asked any of the men what they thought about God. It had been first on my list when Iris asked about my ideal man. I knew Tomori loved God, as we'd spoken about Him many times. But Ekon?

If I'm honest, my heart wants the opportunity to see what could happen if I dated Mori. My head says my heart is leading in this entire matter and to stop thinking emotionally. But, Lord, Tomori and I click. When I'm with him, I feel calmer. I feel a hint of something that could be amazing. Until I remember I have to run an entire country when Grandfather passes. Then the tasks before me seem too impossible.

I know with You nothing is impossible. I know You've placed me here for a reason. And that You always provide. So maybe, just maybe, one of these two men is part of that provision. And if that's true, Lord, then I can't help but think Tomori would be the answer.

I'd be a better person because of him. Dare I suggest a better queen as well?

I tapped the pen against my chin as an idea took hold, righting the pieces inside that didn't seem to fit.

> *I trust You, Lord, and know You'll provide the answers in the right timing. I pray for the wisdom to choose wisely and in Your will. I pray for ears to hear, eyes to see, and a heart of faith.*
> *In Your Son's mighty name. Amen.*
>
> *Bri Bayo*

Seeing my old name, the name of my youth and early adulthood, brought tears to my eyes. I erased my last name, thankful I always carried erasable pens, and rewrote it.

Bri Adebayo.

I knew the whole of who I was now. I was no longer simply Bri Bayo but Tiwa Adebayo's granddaughter. Naade and Marie Bayo's daughter. Princess Brielle Adebayo. And the sum of those parts would help me make my decision.

THIRTY-SIX

Nausea had me popping a Dramamine as I waited for Tomori to show up for language lessons. The ginger soda I'd requested had done nothing to settle my nerves. After a few days of intense prayer and seeking my mother's advice, I had my answer—an overwhelming sense to ask Tomori if he would be my prince. I hadn't brought up the idea to Grandfather because I wanted to know Mori's thoughts first.

I drank soda after soda and stared at the clock as if the timepiece would suddenly move to the time I waited for.

When the knock finally sounded, I jumped, almost sloshing the contents of my glass.

"Come in," I croaked. I cleared my throat to repeat myself, but Dayo had already opened the door to usher Tomori inside.

I stood, sliding my hands against my pencil skirt. I wouldn't shake his hand. Mine were so clammy that they would surely make him run the other direction.

"Thank you, Dayo."

"My pleasure, Your Highness." She dipped her head, then closed the door with the barest of clicks.

Tomori's brow furrowed. "Are you sick, Your Highness?"

"No. I'm fine." *But I might die of embarrassment if you turn me down.* "Have a seat." I studied the wood grain of my desk, trying to breathe in and out before I made myself look foolish.

"Your—*Brielle*, what is wrong?"

I could hear the uncertainty in his voice. I couldn't prolong this. The bandage needed to be ripped off. I lifted my head and met his gaze. "I have something I want to say, and I need you to listen until I'm finished. Okay?"

"Yes. Please. Whatever it is, I want to help."

I almost laughed, the kind that bordered on hysteria. I swallowed down a ball of stress and began. "You know I've been crossing council-approved men off my list."

"Yes." His brow crinkled, and he lurched forward. "Did Prince Ekon do something improper?" His hands gripped the edge of my desk.

"No! No," I said, calmer. "No, he was a perfect gentleman."

The fierce frown that had drawn Tomori's jaw tight eased. His hands flattened on the desk as he exhaled. "Good."

"I'm not in trouble or anything, Tomori."

"But something *is* bothering you."

"Sort of. It's more nerves than anything else."

His eyebrows rose. "What are you nervous about?"

The time was now or never. I let the words fly free before I could lose my resolve. "Because I want to ask if I could add your name to the list."

"Are you asking me to marry you?" His voice rose in pitch.

But in disgust, interest, or somewhere in between, I couldn't tell.

I didn't want to confirm his question, because I'd always dreamt of being proposed to one day, not the other way around. Though I'd never imagined I'd rule a country either.

"I'm asking if you'd be willing to be presented to the royal council as a potential husband. I won't say anything to them until I know how you feel about it."

His Adam's apple bobbed, his gaze locked on mine. "That is a serious question."

"It is." Why wasn't his face giving me clues to his thoughts?

Instead, a hundred unspoken thoughts flitted through his gaze. "I would need to pray first, Brielle."

"Of course. I completely understand that. I've been doing the same." *But give me an idea if you're leaning toward yes!* I wanted to wring my hands like the ladies in classic movies.

His brow dipped in confusion. "I am flattered—"

Ugh. That wasn't good.

"—but I am not sure why you would ask me. I could never be what you deserve, Brielle, or what this country needs."

"Tomori," I breathed. "Don't you know how amazing you are? You've been so patient and kind to me. You treat every person you meet with the utmost respect. The country would be blessed to have a man with such integrity at its helm, and I would be *honored* to call you my husband." I licked my lips, my heart running faster than if I'd drunk a shot of espresso.

"That is what you see when you look at me?"

"You don't?" How could he not?

"You do not understand how it is in my family. I know I have been vague about their attitudes toward me, but maybe you need to know the entirety. It is only fair to know what you would be stepping into. The things you see in me, the Eesuolas do not see the same. As the youngest, I am known as the one who does not contribute to anything, the one who is not serious."

Heartache burned my chest at the quiet acceptance in his voice. "You've got to be kidding. That's not you at all."

Mori reached forward, then stopped, placing his hand back on the desk. "You see a man I could only pray to be. I do not know if I am the one for you, Brielle Adebayo."

I could understand his reticence, but my time in prayer had reminded me that God viewed us through a different lens. "Mori, please pray before you say no," I murmured.

His black eyes softened. "I will. If things were different—" He stopped, gaze lowering as his jaw ticked. I kept silent, heart raging in my chest, as he fought for composure. Finally, he looked at me. "This is my last shift this week. I will be back Tuesday with an answer."

Four days without seeing him? Wow, I really did have it bad. "All right. I pray we both have peace with your answer."

A small smile lifted his cheeks. "You are a good woman. A good princess. I am honored that you would even ask. Whatever happens, I know you will find the right prince."

"I think I have." I gave him a pointed look.

Two days later, my office phone rang. I frowned at the number. It wasn't one I recognized, and unfortunately, Ọlọrọ didn't have caller ID. I picked up the receiver, knowing Dayo would be on the line to properly transfer the call.

"Please hold for Her Highness Princess Brielle Adebayo. Your Highness, you have Tomori Eesuola on the line."

Oh. "Thank you, Dayo." I listened for the click that said she had successfully hung up. "Tomori, I wasn't expecting you to call."

"Yes. I can imagine. Um, is that okay?"

"Totally." I slapped a hand to my forehead. I sounded so juvenile. "What's up?" That didn't sound much better.

Soft chuckles greeted my ear and eased my fears. "I was wondering if you would join me tonight to meet my family. My mother would love to have you over."

"You told her?"

"I told her I worked for you and saw you often for language lessons. I think she is—how do you say it in America?—calling my bluff."

I laughed. "I need to double-check with security, but I don't think it will be a problem."

"I called them first. They are fine with it and will be expecting your call."

"Why would I call if you already did?"

He sighed. "You are still the princess. Do not take my word."

"Okay. I will call them and see you at . . ."

"Is seven good? My mother does not cook early."

"That's perfect." Plenty of time to completely melt down about my wardrobe and being introduced to his family.

"Then I will see you later, Brielle Adebayo."

"Good-bye."

I grinned. This had to be a good thing, right? A guy introducing a girl to his mother? Did that mean God was leading him to say yes? Or was he merely testing the waters to see how I would interact with his family? *Eek!* My brain spiraled, and I reached for my cell, fingers flying across the screen as I typed out an SOS to Iris and my mother. Hopefully we could find something for me to wear that would impress his mother but also knock Mori's socks off. Oh, and still appear regal.

Really, getting dressed these days was so much more complicated than it used to be.

Before I could look at their replies, the office phone rang again.

"Please hold for Her Highness Princess Brielle Adebayo. Your Highness, Azuka Kalu is on the line."

"I was just about to call you, Azu."

"Was it regarding the request from Tomori Eesuola? I wanted to verify that the request is valid, so we know if a team needs to be dispensed."

"Yes, it's valid." I tried to focus on the conversation instead of the crazy ping of notifications from my cell phone, making me wonder what Iris and my mom were typing.

"Then we will dispatch a team, Your Highness. What time are you scheduled to arrive?"

"Seven."

"Please be ready by six so we can be there on time."

"You know where he lives?"

"He gave me the address."

Something I'd forgotten to ask. "Thank you, Azu."

"It is my pleasure, Your Highness. We will see you later."

I traded one phone for the other.

Iris

What time should I clear my schedule for?

Mom

Oh, I'm so excited for you. Do you think he decided to say yes?

Iris

He better. I'll be mad if she gets all beautified only for him to turn her down.

My stomach lurched. I hadn't even thought of that possibility.

Mom

He won't. I've seen the way he looks at her.

Iris

Right? I said the same thing to Bri!

This was why I should have texted them separately.

Me

Sorry. Was on the phone with security. Can't believe you two are ganging up on me in a text.

Mom

You need it, sweetie.

Iris

Just a tad. What are you going to wear?

Me

I have no idea.

Mom

Something blue. It does wonders for your complexion.

Iris

Or ivory. Subliminal message of being a bride one day. OMG! Can I design your wedding gown?

I smiled.

> **Me**
> Cart before the horse. Slow down, girl. Get me dressed for tonight first.

> **Iris**
> I'm calling it. It's a done deal.

> **Mom**
> I agree.

> **Me**
> I have to leave at six, so let's meet in a couple of hours to get me dolled up.

> **Mom**
> I'll be there.

> **Iris**
> So will I.

I set down the phone and exhaled. *Lord, please let this be a step in the right direction and a blessing from You. I pray that I will get along with his family. Whatever reservations he still has, please answer them for him. Amen.*

THIRTY-SEVEN

The view before me filled me with ease. Lush greenery filled the yard of Tomori's childhood home, and flowers hugged the sidewalk. I peered out of the car window as I waited for Merrick to give the all clear.

I saw movement in my peripheral vision, and I turned. My breath caught.

Mori walked out of the house, confidently strolling down the sidewalk. With the sunlight behind him, the moment was reminiscent of a scene from a Jane Austen movie—the hero walking on-screen to declare his love. My heart did an extra patter at the smile he lobbed my way.

Would he really have me come all this way just to say, *No, thank you, find the next man*? I didn't want to entertain the possibility, but I couldn't deny the thread of fear of his refusal. I wanted a future with this man.

Tomori opened the door at Merrick's nod and lent me a hand. How long could I rest my palm against his before it was considered hand-holding and not an assist?

"Hi," I said, feeling ridiculously shy. As if I hadn't seen him a few days ago.

Granted, asking someone to marry you—even in a roundabout way—kind of erased any easy camaraderie that had once existed between you.

"Hello." His lips curved into a smile. "My mother will die from shock when you walk into the house."

I stepped back. "I thought you told her I was coming?"

"I did." He shrugged. "She does not believe me."

"Uh-oh."

He chuckled. "She will bounce back once the surprise of it passes."

"I hope so."

He placed a hand on the small of my back and led me forward. I concentrated on every step, hoping the nerves pinging in excitement at his touch wouldn't cause me to swoon and make a fool of myself.

"Brielle?"

"Yes?" Would I ever stop shivering at the way he said my name?

"I hope you won't be shocked by dinner."

"Why would I?" I paused on the steps leading to his family home. Anxiety swirled in my stomach as dozens of scenarios flitted through my mind.

"I have a big family, and they do not always behave. I am hoping they will once they see you, but . . ." His voice trailed off, and a single shoulder lifted once more in a shrug.

I'd come to recognize his way of deflecting. Though his body displayed nonchalance, his eyes held a host of storms I didn't even understand.

"I'll be fine, Mori. Promise."

"Say that again," he said, his voice low.

"Promise."

"No." He shook his head. "My name."

Warmth filled me. "Mori."

A wide grin popped across his face, defining his cheekbones. My heart fluttered at his handsomeness. "Thank you for coming to dinner, Bri," he murmured.

I nodded, too overcome to do anything else.

"Come. Let us go inside." He twisted the knob and guided me through the door. "Màmá, my guest is here," he called out in Onina.

A hearty chuckle rang through the house. Footsteps sounded, and an older woman came from another room, presumably the kitchen. She stopped dead in her tracks as she spied me. Her eyes flew to Tomori.

"What are you thinking? She is the *princess*!" Her rapid-fire Onina was almost too much for me to follow.

"I told you she was coming," Mori replied.

"But she is the *real* princess."

I smothered a laugh and dipped my head in acknowledgment. "Ẹ kúròlé, *Arábibrin* Mope *Aya* Eesuola. It is a pleasure to meet you."

She gasped. "You speak Onina?"

"Yes. Tomori has been teaching me," I continued in her tongue. My hands shook as I struggled to remember the phrases I'd worked on since Tomori invited me to dinner.

Mrs. Eesuola peered at Tomori. "You really *do* know the princess? You really have been teaching her?"

"Yes, Màmá."

"Oh, my boy," she shrieked in English before wrapping him in a hug. "So clever you are. I knew you had it in you." She let him go and turned to me in a deep bow. "It is an honor to have you and your guards here, Your Highness."

I looked over my shoulder, surprised to see Merrick and Azuka filling the room. I still hadn't gotten used to my permanent shadows.

"Thank you so much for having me." I wanted to thank her for switching to English, too, but I remained silent.

"Oh, that was all Mori." She looked sheepish. "I admit we thought he was pulling our legs. He is a scoundrel, this one. The reason I have no more children." She laughed as if this was a known fact—and a jovial one at that.

Acid filled the back of my throat. Was this something Tomori heard often? Did she treat all of her children like this or just him? I wanted to slide my hand in his and offer a squeeze of reassurance, but we'd never touched in that manner. Would he think me presumptuous?

I gave him a surreptitious glance out of the corner of my eye. A lazy smile covered his features, but his eyes were vacant.

251

I turned to Mrs. Eesuola, trying to think of my next move. "Whatever you're cooking smells delicious."

"Oh, thank you, Your Highness. I admit I did not want to make crab tonight, but Tomori insisted, so I gave in. Who am I to say you would not show? Even my daughter, Nika, insisted Tomori knew you. She is why I prepared the meal. If she believed his tale, perhaps there was a thread of truth to his claims." She shook her pointer finger at him. "You still surprise me. What more could you do? Please, have a seat, Your Highness. I must check on the meal."

Tomori showed me to the maroon loveseat.

"Azu? Merrick? Come sit, please." Tomori gestured toward the other seating.

Merrick shook his head from his station near the door. "We are on duty, Tomori, but thank you for the offer."

"We would not say no to a dinner plate later, though," Azuka added.

I chuckled. "I'm glad to know dinner trumps all."

Azuka's face flushed. "No, Your Highness. We meant no disrespect."

"I'm joking. Truly. I expect you to eat."

Azuka nodded, relief flashing across his face.

Tomori sat beside me, and I grinned at him. "So you *actually* know the princess?"

A huff of laughter escaped him. "I do."

"I take it you still haven't told her about my request?"

"No. I thought about talking to Nika about your . . . situation, since she has a strong head on her shoulders. Then I thought perhaps she would be too shocked to think soundly."

"Is there anyone in your family you *can* talk to?"

"No. I told you. They do not see me like you see me."

"That's a shame." I thought about the impossible situation I'd put him in. "Would talking to my grandfather help?"

His eyes widened. "No."

I laughed at his insistence. "Sorry. I thought getting another man's perspective would help."

"*Not* the king."

"I'm praying for you. I know I put you in this predicament, but I am praying."

His gaze searched mine. "I know."

A knock sounded on the door. "Who locked the door?" came a shout.

Merrick turned and coolly cracked the door. "State your name and your business."

"Nika Eesuola. Family dinner."

He held the door open, and Nika stepped inside. She looked the same as when I saw her at the parade. Her eyes scanned the room, stopping on Tomori and me.

"Your Highness, you came." She walked over to us, bowing before me. "I am so excited."

"Me too." I grinned. "Tomori was just telling me how wise you are."

She laughed. "It sounds like he is laying groundwork to ask for a favor."

"No. I was sincere."

"Well, wait until you meet Abbey, Your Highness. She is the oldest and definitely the smartest of us all."

Tomori huffed.

"How many of you come to family dinners?" I asked.

"At least five at a time. Màmá doesn't have the biggest dining table, but we make it work. Tonight, I think only three others are coming. No one believed Tomori." She grimaced. "I did try, Mori."

"It is fine. Maybe they will have a chance to meet her in the future."

I turned to him. Did that mean he was going to say yes? I wanted to touch his hand, seek some assurance that an answer was coming, but I stopped myself. I wasn't sure how much Nika would catch, and I didn't want to find out in front of his family. The decision was private and had such powerful ramifications that it needed to be kept that way.

"Your Highness, tell me about New York. I have always wanted to visit."

I smiled at Nika, but then another knock sounded at the door. "Sorry. The guys have this thing about security."

Nika chuckled. "I was so confused when I tried to walk in. Even though I saw the car out front and knew you were here, I did not think about the security aspect." She spoke English quickly, as her accent wasn't as pronounced as Tomori's. She was almost his opposite in every way. Except they had the same kind eyes.

A woman with a crown of braids walked in, a little girl on her hip and a young boy walking in front of her. She halted, shock widening her features as she watched us. She pointed, her mouth opening and closing.

"That is Abbey," Nika said. "The oldest."

"Your Highness." She set her daughter down, then bowed before me. "Oh my goodness," she whispered out the side of her mouth to Nika.

"Nice to meet you," I said.

She took a spot on the couch with Nika. "I cannot believe my eyes. Tomori truly knows you?"

"He's been teaching me Onina. He's incredibly intelligent." I smiled up at him, and my heart fluttered as the corners of his mouth quirked. He wanted to smile, but for whatever reason, he seemed hesitant around his family.

"Dinner is ready, Your Highness," his mother called as she walked into the room. "Oh, Abbey, you are here." She hugged her daughter. "Nika, hello."

"Hello, Màmá."

"Who else is coming?" Mrs. Eesuola asked.

"Yinka and Wale," Nika replied. "The others are busy."

"They are not. They just did not believe Tomori." Mrs. Eesuola shook her head. "I am still shocked. Come, let us eat."

Tomori laid a hand on my arm, and I froze as tingles erupted.

"Brielle," he murmured, "you can back out. I will not hold you to anything you said in our last meeting."

I stared into his obsidian eyes. "The ball is no longer in my court. The decision is no longer up to me. I don't need to take anything back because I regret nothing."

His gaze took my measure, searched and assessed. I prayed he could see the sincerity of my heart.

"Okay, then."

THIRTY-EIGHT

Dinner had a rhythm that awed me. Tomori's brother, Yinka, prayed over the meal first. As soon as he finished, everyone reached for a dish from the center of the table. They filled their plates before passing the serving platter to the person next to them. I sat stunned by the symphony of movement.

Tomori nudged me gently with his elbow. "Do you want some of this?" he asked, motioning to the dish in his hand.

"I'll take a little bit of everything."

"That makes it easy," he chuckled, scooping a spoonful of rice onto my plate.

"Tomori?"

"Too much?"

I stared at him, bemused. "I can serve myself."

"You are the guest. It is a rule my father made up a long time ago."

"Where is he?" I whispered.

Tomori looked away. "He moved out when I was ten. You will have to meet him another time."

"Okay."

His shoulders sagged at my simple acceptance.

I took a bite of my food. The shrimp was a little spicy. I was still getting used to the spices and peppers a lot of Olorans cooked with, but I couldn't deny how good the meal tasted.

Laughter flowed around the table as the others told jokes, shared how their weeks had been, and looked forward to the joy of the weekend.

The one thing I noted was the lack of interaction with Tomori. Was that because of me? Were they afraid to include him in the little things for fear of what I would think?

"Your Highness," Mrs. Eesuola said, interrupting my musings, "how do you like Ọlọrọ Ilé? Is our island very different from New York? That is where you are from, yes?"

"Yes. I was born and raised in the city. There are always crowds rushing to their destination. There's no place like it." I sighed. "It's been bittersweet, knowing I won't live there again, but Ọlọrọ is where I want to be."

Especially with Grandfather's declining health. He'd looked terrible this morning. I'd checked on him because the night before, when I was reading to him, he'd had a coughing fit that couldn't be stopped. Dr. Falade had been paged and had given Grandfather a swift-acting shot of medication. This morning, he still seemed out of breath. Dr. Falade felt that Grandfather needed to be put on oxygen, but Grandfather didn't want the treatment. He worried what kind of impression an oxygen tank and tubes would leave on the people, the council, and the watching world. I'd finally managed to convince him to use the oxygen when in his room. No prying eyes had access, and he could get the treatment needed to better perform his duties.

"How is the king?" Yinka asked. He was the second child and the oldest boy.

I pasted on an artificial smile. "He is doing well. Every night we read together, and it's been a blessing getting to know him." I cut myself off, unsure of how much I could or even wanted to say.

"We are praying for him in my Bible study group," Nika said. "And for you."

"Thank you so much." Gratitude overwhelmed me as I stared at my plate, hoping tears would not fall.

Tomori squeezed my elbow. I gave him a smile of thanks.

"You are an only child?" Mrs. Eesuola asked.

"I am. Although, my best friend came to Ọlọrọ with me. She designed my dress for the Independence Day parade."

"Oh, it was so lovely," Nika said. "Will she design any future clothes for you?"

"I hope so. She's very gifted." *And chomping at the bit to make me a royal wedding dress.*

"I love fashion."

"That is Nika," Mrs. Eesuola said. "All my children have been gifted with a passion." She stared at Tomori. "But I am not sure about Mori. He likes to go with the flow. He is never in a hurry. Always fishing." She paused. "I suppose fishing could count as a passion."

The others laughed, and I fought the desire to frown. What was wrong with his mother? How could she not see the cuts her words carved?

I stood up, and the laughter stopped. "Excuse me. I need some air." I stalked out of the living room. Right now, I didn't care what they thought of me. I couldn't bear sitting there another moment while they made snide remarks disguised as humor.

Merrick saw me coming and got up from the couch, placing his plate on the end table. "Are we leaving, Your Highness?"

"I need air," I stated.

Azu popped up and opened the door before I reached it.

"Brielle, wait."

I paused, glancing over my shoulder as Tomori exited the dining room. I motioned for him to follow me and walked outside. I dragged in a breath and exhaled as I tried to push all the thoughts out of my head, including my wish to shake some sense into Mrs. Eesuola.

"Are you okay?" Tomori asked quietly. He spared a glance at Azu, who stood on the steps, scanning the premises for any signs of danger.

"I'm . . . frustrated."

"With?" Mori gently prodded.

"Your mother isn't funny." I frowned, peering into his eyes. "I know that sounds awful. I'm sorry. It's just that . . ." I bit my lip, trying to gather my thoughts. "How do you put up with the way she treats you?"

"I am used to it."

"Don't you find it offensive?"

He sighed. "I try not to let it get to me anymore." He rubbed his beard. "My mother blames me for my father leaving us. It is why she has no more kids, because he left when I was two. Came back and left again. He did this until I was ten, when they finally divorced."

"Why?" And what had that done to his family?

"My mom says I was not supposed to be born. That my father wanted to stop at seven kids, so he did not want to stick around to deal with eight."

I gasped. "Is that true? How could she *say* that?"

"It is her truth."

"Does your father have a different version of events?"

Tomori nodded. "He does not believe I am his, but he does not want to do a paternity test."

My mind stilled, focusing on this new detail. "Can you have one done without his consent?"

"I have considered asking one of my brothers or sisters to give me their DNA. The results would show if we have the same mother and father." He sighed. "But I do not want to damage their relationship with him. They still see him and talk to him. They do not know his doubts about me."

My heart broke for Mori. "And how do you see him?"

"He is all I know, but he does not want to be my dad. I take care to avoid him or decline an invitation from my brothers or sisters if he will be there."

"No one thinks that's weird?"

"They think I am ungrateful and hold a grudge for his abandonment."

"Tomori . . ." I sighed, frustrated the words wouldn't come. Really, though, what could I say?

"Do you see now? Do you see why I had to pray? You are asking me to be your husband. To join our families together. My background is so inferior to yours."

"How do you figure? My mother is American. She can't trace her history like the Adebayos can. Trust me, the council sees that as inferior. At least you are all Olóran."

"That will not matter to the council."

I hoped it would be a plus. We would need all we could to stand up to them. I paused, threading my fingers together. "Is your parentage the only objection you have?" *Or do you object to me?*

He stepped forward. "I invited you here to see if meeting my family would change your mind. I had to be honest and show you who I truly am."

I cautiously took one of his hands in mine, trying to ignore the skittering of my pulse. "Your family does not define you. You are a man of God. One who has encouraged me so much since I've come here. You've helped me find my own strength in being a princess and in holding on to the parts that feel strictly like Bri. Just like my family does not put me in a box, yours doesn't either. I told you, Mori, the decision is yours."

His black eyes drank me in, and I prayed with my whole heart that he would not fear.

"I see who God created," I said.

"Brielle," he murmured, cupping my face.

I leaned into his hand, loving the warmth and the gentleness that enveloped me. Too soon, he dropped his hand, then slid it into his pocket.

Before I could react to the loss of his touch, Mori dropped to one knee and pulled out a pearl ring. My breath hitched as he slid his palm along my left hand.

"Brielle Eden Adebayo, I am nowhere near half the man you deserve, and I do not know what you see in me. But the moment I saw you, my heart felt whole. You have brought me the most peace I have had in years. The only hesitation I have had was knowing I could not measure up. Then God reminded me that His measurement is different from man's, something you have reiterated. I believe He wants us together." Tomori took a measured breath. "Brielle, would you do me the highest honor of becoming my wife and joining the rest of your days with mine?"

Tears I hadn't known were there surprised me as they slid past my mouth. "Yes, I will, and the honor is all mine."

Tomori slipped the braided pearl ring onto my finger. "I gave this to my grandmother when I was thirteen. She loved watching me fish, and when I found a pearl one day, I knew it was hers. I had it set into this ring. Before she passed, she told me to save it for my future wife." He squeezed my hand. "I know the king will want you to wear something more fitting, but it is yours now."

"Thank you so much. I'll wear it every day."

He brushed my hair behind my ears. "Thank you for asking me."

"But did I really? Seems like you were the one down on bended knee." I quirked my lips into a teasing grin.

Tomori threw his head back and laughed. "Well played, Brielle."

I grinned and cautiously threaded my arms around his waist, sighing as he enveloped me into the warmest hug I'd ever known. "Thank you, Mori," I whispered.

His arms squeezed me tighter, and we stayed that way, soaking in the moment of a *yes*.

THIRTY-NINE

"You want to marry Tomori Eesuola?" Grandfather rasped. My heart pounded in my throat as I sat next to his bed, his hand clasped in mine. When I arrived home from dinner with Tomori's family, I'd immediately come to check on Grandfather. I'd been surprised to find him still awake, sure that he'd be resting. Instead, he'd chosen to stay up and wait for our nightly reading session. "Yes, I do." I bit my lip. "Do you object?"

Grandfather heaved a deep sigh, and I remained quiet, waiting for him to process. Was he thinking as a king right now or as my grandfather?

"Brielle, I do not know if the council will like this."

But what do you think? He hadn't called me ómọ ọmọ, so perhaps he had his mental crown on. "Grandfather, the council *did* say I could choose my own husband. Plus, it's not like I picked someone who isn't Ọlọran."

"Yes, I know this, but Tomori may not be who they desire either."

Didn't being a hereditary monarchy mean I didn't have to care if the council liked my choice? My skin prickled. If Mr. Ladipo hadn't found that decree, would they have forced the issue? On the other hand, would I have had to give up my crown down the road if I hadn't been married when crowned queen?

"Bàbá àgbà, I've prayed about this. Tomori has prayed about this. Both of us feel that this is what God wants. I promise, I didn't make this decision lightly." How could I, when I knew the uphill battle I'd face? I remembered all those agonizing moments when I'd refused to look at Mori as an option.

Silence reigned between us—well, that and the sound of oxygen pumping through the nostril mask on his face.

"Why Tomori, ómo omo?"

Could I tell Grandfather that Mori made my heart race and made me believe I had a real chance at love? My face heated at the idea of sharing something so personal.

I relayed some of the same reasons I'd given Tomori, including facets of his personality, and mentioned how my own confidence had grown with his encouragement.

Grandfather nodded, a thoughtful look on his face. "You are coming along in your language studies. It is obvious he is a good teacher. But can he make a good monarch?"

"If I can learn, so can he."

He rubbed his chin.

"Please, Bàbá àgbà," I said, my voice low. "I can't go forward without your blessing. Surely the council will not balk if you support my choice."

"Oh, Brielle." He cupped my face. "I want your happiness, but I want the prosperity of the kingdom too."

"As do I. Tomori too."

His rheumy eyes flitted back and forth. "I will back your decision and lend my vote if the council draws to a tie."

"Will they allow you to vote?"

"It is about my succession, so they have no choice. But we will not worry about that right now. We need to prepare Tomori to stand before them, and we need to alert them that you have made your decision."

I nodded.

"You need to find out if your fiancé has an outfit acceptable to wear before the council or if we need to buy him something."

"I will call him and ask."

"Please alert Iris to begin making your wedding dress. The sooner you marry, the better for us all."

How soon? I bit my lip. "Are you feeling poorly tonight?"

He sighed, squeezing my hand. "I am not leaving you yet, Brielle. Yet I do not wish for you to put off the wedding until December either."

My heart turned over. Would Grandfather still be here for Christmas?

"Come. You must smile. Tears are for after."

I dared not blink in case that caused the waterworks to start. "All right." I forced my lips into the biggest grin I could manage with my bottom lip quivering.

"There you go." He patted my hand. "I am tired. Perhaps we can read tomorrow at breakfast."

"Of course." I stood, brushing a kiss across his forehead. "Get some rest."

"You as well. Tomorrow will be busy."

I bid him good night and walked back to my guest suite, although my room wouldn't be in this corridor much longer. Dayo had informed me that Grandmother's room—now mine—would be ready tomorrow.

After changing into pajamas, I checked the sitting room for Mom and Iris.

Iris looked up and smiled. "Hey, you just missed your mom. I think she was going to sleep."

"Oh, but I need to tell her something." I hurried over to the adjoining door and knocked. It amazed me that all three rooms connected to the sitting room.

Mom cracked her door open, her hair wrapped in a head scarf. "Brielle, you're back." She opened the door wider. "Do you have news?"

"Yes. Come, and I'll tell you both at once."

They gathered around me, and I leaned forward, left hand extended.

Iris squealed. Mom teared up.

"I'm so happy for you," Iris said. "How did he do it?"

I recounted the proposal.

"Aww." Iris placed her hands over her heart. "That is so romantic."

"I think you made the right decision, Bri," Mom said.

"You think so?" I asked.

"Yes!"

"Absolutely." Mom's voice echoed Iris's emphatic statement.

I sighed in relief. "Grandfather said he'll stand by my choice."

"Good." Mom squeezed my hand. "And you feel settled about it all?"

"I'm still nervous. The royal council is the next obstacle."

"Does Tomori need any clothes before meeting them? Can I make him something too?" Iris bounced.

I chuckled. "I'll find out and let you know."

"And your wedding dress?" she pressed.

"Grandfather says go for it."

"Yes! Yes! Yes!" She pumped her fists in the air and wiggled in her seat.

Mom laughed outright. "I guess I should have brought bridal magazines with me."

"Oh no, Ms. Marie. I have a secret Pinterest board I've been pinning ideas to," Iris said.

"Really?" I leaned forward. "Can you send me an invite?"

"Sure." Her fingers flew across the screen of her phone, and then I heard a notification ping on my own device.

I accepted the invitation, then scrolled through the pictures. A mixture of American-inspired gowns with white veils and long trains along with African-inspired wedding dresses with amures and headdresses filled my screen.

"I have no idea what style or theme the wedding will be. I should have asked Grandfather."

"Maybe ask Dayo?" Mom offered.

"I can do that tomorrow. You'll definitely need that information, Iris."

"Okay. I'll wait and see what's what before I let my brain go wild. Looking at the pins, do any of the designs appeal to you?"

I bit my lip as I scrolled through them once more. "Some of these gold dresses are gorgeous. I never thought I'd like something other than white, but . . ." They were just so pretty. Or maybe the model made the gowns look so breathtaking.

Mom scooted close to me, staring at the pictures on my phone. I slowed my scrolling so she could view them all.

"I think you would look magnificent in a rose-gold wedding dress," Iris said.

"But it seems so bold." And I was anything but.

"What about the dresses that fuse the traditional white with tribal colors?" Mom asked.

"I don't know. I'm not sure what the Ọlọran people would think about such a thing."

"Hmm, good point," she muttered.

"Maybe two ceremonies are an option?" Iris asked. "You could wear the traditional American wedding gown to one and pick a traditional Ọlọran dress for the other?"

"That's certainly an idea. Then I would get the best of both worlds." And see Tomori in a tux. *Gee, it's warm in here.*

Iris cackled. "You just got a look on your face like you saw your knight in shining armor on his trusty steed."

I cracked a grin. "I was thinking of my fiancé—wow, that's wild to hear—in a tux."

"Oh, he would make a striking figure. His lean lines were made for that."

We continued talking and looking at different dresses. After an hour, Mom bid us good night. Shortly afterward, I said good night to Iris.

In the middle of saying my prayers for the night, someone pounded on my door. I hustled over to answer the summons.

Dayo stood there, wringing her hands. "Your Highness, you need to go to the king's suite right now."

My heart dropped to my toes. "Do I need to change?"

She shook her head. "Grab a robe."

I did as instructed, and we sped down the hall. I practically ran in my slippered feet. The door to Grandfather's room stood ajar. Mobo stood in the bedroom, concern etched into his features like stone.

"Is he still alive?" I whispered.

Dr. Falade spared me a brief glance. "Yes." He then ignored me as he continued listening to Grandfather's heart via the stethoscope hanging from his ears.

I walked over to Mobo. "What happened?"

"He began coughing and could not stop. Then his body seized."

Oh no. My heart raced. *Lord God, please do not take him. Please, I'm not ready to say good-bye.* Yet how selfish was that? Grandfather was in a lot of pain. Didn't he deserve rest?

But what would happen to Ọlọrọ? I wasn't married yet, and the council had been clear on their instructions.

"Your Highness," Mobo said, "please sit." He gestured to a chair he must have brought over when I was deep in thought.

"Thank you, Mobo."

He nodded and returned to his post in the corner. I continued praying until Dr. Falade spoke.

"He will be fine now. My staff will bring in machines to better monitor his vitals."

"Dr. Falade, how much longer do you think he has?" I asked. I didn't want the answer, but I needed to know. "Will he make it five more months?" More like four now. A month and a half had already passed.

The physician heaved a sigh and removed his glasses, rubbing at his face. "I am afraid not. After examining him tonight, I would estimate a month more. I am sorry, Your Highness."

I had a vague notion of nodding, but the shock of his pronouncement was too much for anything more. I had a month left with my grandfather.

Lord, what am I going to do?

FORTY

The council had agreed to see me and let me present my choice of husband. To say I was nervous would be a gross disservice to the word and my emotions. I couldn't eat, hadn't slept, and had done nothing but pray since they granted my request. I knew Iris and my mother were also praying without ceasing.

I put the finishing touches on my subdued makeup. My hair had been softly curled and fell across my shoulders. My black pencil skirt, cream silk blouse, and purple amure completed the regal look. My earrings even matched my sash. All I had to do was wait for Tomori to arrive. Mobo had sent guards to retrieve him and bring him straight to my personal sitting room, the one that now adjoined Grandfather's.

Grandfather claimed he would be at the council meeting, presiding as king, despite his episode a few nights earlier. Dr. Falade and I had argued against his attending the meeting. Grandfather had stressed the importance and informed both of us that he would *not* attend the meeting as an invalid and stir unrest. So Dr. Falade agreed to remove Grandfather's oxygen at the last possible moment. I prayed he would be fine and that the council wouldn't drag out their inquisition.

I jumped at the knock on the door, then let my fiancé—*wow*—into the room.

"Tomori." A smile curved my lips before I could filter my reaction through the thumping of my pulse. He wore a suit, an actual suit. The navy color looked wonderful on him.

"Good morning, Brielle."

Mobo gestured for my attention. "You have a few minutes, Your Highness, then you must present yourself to the council."

"Thank you, Mr. Owusu." I shut the door and turned to Tomori. "Are you ready? Nervous? Wondering why you asked me to marry you?"

His slow chuckle settled my insides. "You asked first."

"No, sir, Mr. Eesuola. I recall you on bended knee."

"That is true." He stepped forward and took my hands in his. "I am ready. You will do fine. I will not disappoint you. It is the last thing I wish."

"I'm not worried *about* you but *for* you."

"We will not worry, Brielle. We have prayed, and now the rest is up to God."

"You're right." I exhaled. *Sorry, Lord. Please steady my mind and give us the words.*

"Shall we?" Mori asked.

I nodded and slipped my arm through his. Warmth filled my middle as we stood close in the elevator. At the council chamber, the guard's eyes widened when he saw Tomori, but he said nothing. Just dipped his head, then slipped into the council room. Tomori squeezed my hand, then stepped to the side to remain out of sight until the council allowed him entry.

The double doors opened, and I walked straight to the center of the room. Now that I was officially the princess, I did not have to bow before the alàgbà tribu members, just the king. I executed the maneuver before Grandfather with utmost respect, keeping a calm façade instead of the concern I wanted to show at his wan pallor.

"Ẹ káàárò, Your Majesty. Alàgbà tribu." My voice was strong and steady.

"Ẹ káàárò, Princess Brielle Adebayo," Mr. Oladele said. "The council acknowledges your presence on this day. You are here to request acceptance of your choice of husband, the future prince of Ọlọrọ Ilé. Is this correct?"

"Yes, Mr. Oladele. I have considered the choices the council presented at my request to succeed King Tiwa Jimoh Adebayo. After much prayer and deliberation, and with the blessing of my king, I have come to request that my husband be Tomori Debare Eesuola." My lips tingled as I said his full name.

"Should that name ring a bell?" Mr. Oladele asked. The other council members whispered amongst themselves.

"I make no assumptions of your knowledge of him, Mr. Oladele. Before asking for my hand in marriage, Mr. Eesuola worked as a palace runner."

"Are you serious?" Mr. Ladipo shouted.

"Peace, Yemi," Ms. Keita said. "It is not your turn to speak."

"We cannot let her make a mockery of our institution." Mr. Ladipo gestured toward me, disgust curling his upper lip.

Although his words pierced me, I stood still, waiting for them to give me the chance to speak. I peeked at Grandfather, glad to see him still holding on. *Lord, breathe for Grandfather, please.*

Mr. Oladele held up a hand until the grumblings quieted. "Your Highness, please state your objections to the men presented to you by the council. They were the finest picks of Ọlọrọ."

"Oh yes," Mr. Ladipo inserted. "Their sins must have been unpardonable for you to choose a *palace runner.*"

Once more, Mr. Oladele held up a hand.

I drew in a breath. This was a question Grandfather and I had practiced yesterday. Yet, staring at the council face-to-face, my stomach dived toward my toes faster than a peregrine falcon. *Lord, please give me the words. Please ease my fears.*

"I first met with Prince Chimnoya Sule." I stopped to look each council member in the eye. "I found his misogynistic attitude offensive. I am the royal princess of Ọlọrọ Ilé, yet he arrived thirty minutes late for our dinner, then prayed for me to relinquish my duties to someone more fitting—him."

Mr. Ladipo stroked his beard and looked around the council table. The members shared pointed looks and murmured amongst themselves.

"This is your objection?" Mr. Oladele asked.

"I would hate to see how you handle a heads of state meeting when certain rulers refuse to acknowledge your presence," Mr. Ladipo said.

"Mr. Ladipo." I gave him a pointed gaze. "You accepted me as princess. If that is so, and as I have now been introduced to the country as such, then their allegiance is to me and the throne regardless of how they feel about my gender. To have a prospective husband disregard me as if I were gum on his shoe tells me how he'd handle my reign when I become queen. So yes, I object to him. As for heads of state who do not believe in a woman ruler, I do not care. They did not pledge their allegiance to me or this country."

Mr. Oladele looked around the table. Ms. Keita nodded, as did Mr. Ibrahim. Mr. Oladele spoke. "We accept your objection to Prince Chimnoya. Please move on to the next candidate."

"Thank you, alàgbà." I steadied myself. "My next meeting was with Elder Kambili Udo. He, too, did not treat me with respect. He made me drive out to Opolopo, where my guards and I came upon a scene of mayhem. His children were screaming at one another, and Mr. Udo was searching for one of their mothers. All of the mothers live near him in an almost harem-like commune." I stifled a shudder. "I can't see Mr. Udo being able to divide his time from his current responsibilities in order to see to the needs of the entire nation. I didn't even meet with him, as I left him to get his life in order."

Ms. Keita's lips twitched as she stared down at her notepad. At least someone enjoyed my list of objections. I didn't want to paint the men in such a negative light, but I needed the council to accept Tomori. All I had left was to explain my objection to Ekon.

There was more murmuring as the council conferred. Finally, Mr. Oladele acknowledged my objection and encouraged me to move on to the final candidate.

Here we go. "I last saw Prince Ekon Diallo, who was a perfect gentleman. He arrived at the palace with flowers, took me to a nice restaurant, and kept the conversation moving."

"This does not sound like an objection," Mr. Ladipo grumbled.

"Probably because I haven't finished speaking," I stated, meeting his gaze.

His lips flattened. "My *apologies*, Your Highness."

"Received." I stared at Mr. Oladele, preferring to ignore the grump at the end of the table. "The reason I didn't choose Prince Ekon is because he doesn't believe that love is real. As a person who very much believes in the emotion, the acts, and the command to love, I found we were at a fundamental impasse. One I simply couldn't overlook. His disbelief prompted me to question his allegiance to God, whom the Bible declares *is* love, and wonder if he could pledge loyalty to a country if he does not believe in love. For how can anyone *not* love Ọlọrọ?"

Mr. Oladele raised an eyebrow but said nothing. We stared at one another for a few more moments, and then he broke eye contact, whispering with the other council members.

While they conferred, I studied Grandfather, noting the sweat beads on his upper lip. I willed him to look at me and give me a sign he was okay. Instead, he watched the council.

Finally, Mr. Oladele straightened. "The council accepts your objection to Prince Ekon Diallo."

Relief flooded me, and my knees threatened to buckle. Did that mean they would accept Tomori?

"We grant permission to bring in Mr. Eesuola so we may question him. You may be seated and are not permitted to speak for him. Do you understand, Your Highness?"

"I do, Mr. Oladele." I sat in the chair a guard provided.

The double doors opened, and Tomori strolled through. He looked calm and collected, while my mind whirled. *Please give him the words, Father. Please let him handle the darts the council throws his way.*

Mobo had coached Tomori all day yesterday, but I hadn't been privy to those lessons because Grandfather had a hunch I wouldn't be able to speak up today. Considering I'd just been sidelined, he'd been correct.

Tomori bowed and greeted the king before moving on to each council member. His voice sounded melodic in Onina. I could happily listen to him all day, except the council agreed to speak in English for my sake. I wanted to shrink in my chair, but Tomori needed me to be brave and fearless.

My gaze remained locked on the spectacle before me. I watched in fascination and horror as the council asked about Tomori's family, how he was raised, and his current employment. A couple of the council members looked surprised to hear about the other palace jobs he'd held in the past. I clasped my hands over my crossed knees, trying to be a picture of ease despite the litany of *please help him* going through my head.

"Mr. Eesuola," Mr. Ladipo sneered, "what makes you think that a mere *palace runner* could ever be a worthy prince?"

Tomori turned and met my gaze, a soft smile curving his full lips, then studied Mr. Ladipo. "I admit, I had the same reaction when the princess first spoke to me regarding the arrangement."

"What? *She* asked *you* to marry her?"

Mori's dark eyes twinkled. "No, alàgbà. *I* asked her to marry me. However, she did ask if I thought I could be the next prince of Ọlọrọ Ilé. After much prayer, I realized it is man who puts stipulations on what we can and cannot do. The princess saw something in me that she thought would benefit the country and herself as a ruler and a wife. Perhaps the reason nothing in my life before now seemed like it came together was because God was preparing me for this very moment. To be available during these circumstances. I am not a man who would argue with God."

"God is your answer?" Mr. Ladipo scoffed.

"A man's religion is vital," Mr. Ibrahim spoke up. "If he does not follow the God he claims to profess, his word means nothing."

I wanted to cheer. Mr. Ibrahim rarely spoke at meetings, but the conviction in his voice could not be denied. I gave mental fist pumps.

"She is not fit to rule," Mr. Ladipo accused.

"We already determined she is at a prior council, Yemi," Ms. Keita countered. "We cannot go back because you find fault in her choice of husband."

"Make her pick another prince," Mr. Ladipo cried. "Our country needs knowledgeable people at the helm."

"Enough, Yemi," Grandfather countered. He stared him down, then speared Mr. Oladele with his gaze, making a *wrap it up* motion.

I waited for the council to respond.

"Your Highness, Mr. Eesuola," Mr. Oladele said, "please leave the room while the council confers."

As soon as the doors closed behind us, I reached for Tomori's hand. "You were perfect. Absolutely perfect," I murmured.

"I think I may lose my breakfast."

I laughed. "I skipped breakfast. Too nervous to eat."

"That would have been wise. I did not want to pass out, so I ate. I should have picked your route."

I peered up his tall frame. "I think the meeting went well, don't you?"

"I do not know, but I do not think I was too shabby."

"You were great. Not shabby at all."

"Then we wait and see." He laced his fingers through mine as we stood side by side, waiting for the guard to let us back in.

After what seemed like forever, we returned to council chambers.

"Your Highness, Mr. Eesuola. The council has deliberated and come to a final decision. Your Highness, the Olọrọ Ilé Royal Council accepts your choice of Tomori Debare Eesuola as your husband. Upon the end of the engagement ceremony, he will be known as Prince Tomori Eesuola. Upon marriage, he will be known as Prince Tomori Debare Eesuola é Adebayo. If you fail to wed before the prescribed time, then his title will be stripped, and the council will reconvene. Is all understood?"

We'd done it. I was stunned, but a squeeze of Tomori's hand brought me to my senses. "Yes. We understand."

"Council is dismissed."

FORTY-ONE

After the council meeting, Mobo escorted Mori and me to Grandfather's chambers. We sat on the couch, waiting for the king to appear. I wasn't sure what he wanted to meet with us about. Hopefully just to talk about the engagement ceremony and wedding.

After a few minutes, Grandfather shuffled in. Tomori started to rise, but Grandfather waved him back down. I could feel the coiled tension in Mori's figure as he hunched forward, prepared to jump if assistance was needed.

"Thank you for meeting with me in here versus my office," Grandfather said. "I am about ready to retire for the day."

"Of course, Your Majesty," Tomori said. "Is there anything you need? Anything we can get you to make you feel more comfortable?"

A small smile graced Grandfather's lips. "No, thank you. I want to talk about your next steps." He motioned between the two of us.

"Something other than the engagement ceremony and wedding?" I asked.

"Yes." He stared at Mori. "Tomori, you will need to begin studies with Mobo. He will empower you with all the historical facts you need to know now that you will be the prince for our nation. He will work you through similar lessons to those Brielle

275

has already received. It is imperative that the future monarchs of Ọlọrọ Ilé be equipped to handle their duties."

Mori dipped his head. "Yes, my king."

"In private, you may call me Tiwa," Grandfather said softly.

"Oh no, Your Majesty." Tomori's eyes widened. "I could *never.*"

I stifled a chuckle at the horrified look on his face.

"Son, we will be family soon. I promise, you will not lose your head for calling me by my first name. I look forward to getting to know you better, now that you will be taking care of my granddaughter."

Grandfather sighed, and I wanted to ask him to wear his oxygen mask. But perhaps he wasn't ready for Tomori to know such things.

"Iris is prepared to design the wedding clothes," I stated. "She just needs to know the traditions of an Ọlọran wedding."

"Yes. Make sure you have a conversation with Dayo and have her invite Mrs. Eesuola to join you. Wedding preparations are a joint effort between the families, but because of our station, you, as princess, get final say."

"Okay."

He turned to Tomori. "Please invite your father and your eldest brother to meet with me. Mobo will put you on the books so you can officially request Brielle's hand in marriage."

"Uh," Tomori interjected, "my king, I do not know if my father will be in attendance."

Grandfather straightened. "He would dare be absent?"

Tomori looked at me, a question in his eyes. I nodded, knowing Grandfather would keep the information confidential.

"Sir, my father does not believe I am of his paternity. It is why he divorced my mother."

Grandfather rubbed his chin. "I see. Do you have doubts?"

"Only the ones born from his absence."

"Understandable." Grandfather paused for a beat, then continued. "Please ask him to come anyway. I will be very shocked if he says no. But if he does, please contact Mobo and ask your oldest relative to stand in his place."

"Yes, Your Majesty."

Grandfather raised his eyebrows.

"T-T-Tiwa."

I reached over and squeezed Tomori's hand, and he returned the grip. Grandfather's gaze did not miss a thing. Did I notice a glimmer of pleasure?

"After the wedding ceremony, you will have an official residence here, Tomori. If you wish to move in beforehand, we can prepare a room for you in the guest wing of the palace. That way your lessons can start first thing in the morning."

"I would be honored."

"Then Mobo will make the arrangements before the day is over." Grandfather turned to me. "Brielle, you have moved into your grandmother's old chamber?"

"Yes."

"Good." He rubbed his eyes.

"Is that all, Grandfather? We should let you rest."

"There is one other thing, but I wish to speak to you alone."

Tomori rose. "I will wait in the hall."

"Hold on. Mobo," Grandfather called.

His chamber door opened, and Mr. Owusu walked through. "Yes, Your Majesty?"

"Please see that Tomori gets a room in the guest wing and begins his lessons."

"Right away, Your Majesty."

They both left, and silence descended. I licked my lips, stomach churning in the quiet.

"Are you prepared to share a room with him after the wedding ceremony?" Grandfather finally asked.

My face flushed. "I, uh, actually hadn't given that part much thought."

"Palace staff talk, and they will note if you do not share a room. Perhaps you should have a private conversation about the wedding night expectations."

"Grandfather," I whispered.

He chuckled softly. "I do not mean to embarrass you. Only to prepare you."

"Duly noted. I will have a *private* conversation with Tomori."

"Good. I would suggest that when you sit down with Dayo, Iris, and his mother, you schedule the wedding for as soon as possible."

"Do you think a month is too far away?" I asked quietly, wanting some kind of hope.

"Yes." His blunt tone echoed in the room.

My breath shuddered. "Okay. I will schedule the ceremony for as soon as possible."

"Thank you." He sighed. "I would like to rest now. Could you help me to my room?"

"Of course." I lent him an arm as he heaved himself off the sofa.

We walked slowly into his chambers, and a nurse, who'd been sitting quietly in the corner, began hooking Grandfather up to the machinery. His heart beat a steady rhythm marked by the heart monitor. She placed the oxygen in his nostrils, and I exhaled. Knowing he was getting the proper medical care eased my nerves. Now I needed to plan a royal wedding as soon as humanly possible.

I could only hope Iris would have enough time to design the clothes and get everything sewn. I had no idea how much time was needed for that kind of endeavor. And if a month was too far away, how far in advance could I schedule it before it was considered too soon? What would the people think? Would the media speculate about the rushed ceremony and possible reasons for it?

The elevator doors opened, and I halted. "Uncle."

"Is it true?"

Since he wasn't coming out of the elevator, I stepped into it and pressed 2. "Is what true?"

"You are marrying a palace runner?"

Who spread that news so fast? "I am marrying Tomori Eesuola."

"You tell my brother I will not stand for this."

"Uncle, the council approved both me and Tomori. Do you question their judgment?"

"Yes!" he shouted. "You do not know our ways and obviously have no respect for our traditions. Marrying someone without a title—bah!"

"Did your wife have a title?"

He reared back. The elevator chimed, and I let out a breath. "Have a good day, Uncle Sijuwola."

"I will have a good day when you are on a flight back to the States."

I ignored the comment. When I arrived at my office, I motioned for Dayo to follow me.

She poised a pen above her notepad. "How did the council meeting go? I do not remember what you said it was for."

"To present my choice of husband."

Dayo's head flew up. "How did it go? What did they say?"

"They agreed with my choice, and Tomori will be my husband."

"What!"

I stared at her, momentarily stunned by her outburst.

She composed herself. "I am so sorry, Your Highness. I am just . . . surprised. I thought they would insist on one of the men on the list."

"They asked for my objections and, after hearing my answers, agreed with my concerns."

"You objected to them all? Even Prince Ekon?"

I nodded. "Yes."

Her mouth opened, then closed. I'd never seen her so flustered.

"Are you sure you're fine?" I asked. Maybe she agreed with Uncle Sijuwola about Tomori's suitability.

She nodded but didn't meet my eyes.

"Okay. Please invite Mrs. Eesuola to the palace as soon as possible."

"Yes, Your Highness," she said flatly.

O-kay. "Once Mrs. Eesuola is able to meet with me, my mother, and Iris, we will schedule the engagement and wedding ceremony."

"Yes, Your Highness."

A knock sounded, Dayo rose to answer it, and Iris and my mom walked in.

"Good news?" Mom asked.

I nodded.

"Yay!" Iris squealed.

"Except I just learned I've asked you to come prematurely."

279

I'd stopped a passing palace runner to get them on the way to Grandfather's chambers. "I need Mrs. Eesuola here before we can make any preparations."

"What about the dress? I need to get started on that ASAP," Iris said.

"We need a gown for a traditional engagement ceremony and one for the wedding ceremony. Grandfather said the colors and all of that have to be decided with Mrs. Eesuola."

Iris poked out her bottom lip. "Okay. I'll draw up a bunch of sketches with different silhouettes, and then we can talk about color when she arrives."

"When will the ceremonies be?" Mom asked.

I bit my lip. "Grandfather wants them scheduled as soon as possible."

Silence descended.

Dayo cleared her throat. "You will need a master of ceremonies for the engagement ceremony. This person is usually a friend or can be a relative. I know you have Iris here, but perhaps consider someone in Tomori's family or even Fade Adebayo." She explained that the emcee would lead the attendants in prayer and narrate the ceremony for all.

My nose wrinkled. I could not imagine Uncle Sijuwola's daughter-in-law as master of ceremonies. "What about Digi?" I asked. We texted regularly, and she genuinely felt like family, unlike her parents and Uncle Sijuwola.

"She is not yet eighteen. It is traditionally an adult."

I sighed. "I would like to ask Tomori's sister Nika, then. If you could add her to your list to come with Tomori's mother."

Dayo scribbled on her paper. "Is that all, Your Highness?"

"Yes, Dayo. Thank you."

She nodded and left the room, closing the door softly behind her.

"What's wrong with her?" Iris asked.

"I have no idea."

And no time to be overly concerned. I had a wedding to plan.

FORTY-TWO

Mrs. Eesuola had no words.

She appeared part fish, part sloth, as she blinked with a dazed look on her face and her mouth open.

Nika glanced cautiously at her mother. "Màmá, are you okay?"

"I do not think so. My son, a prince?"

"Yes, Màmá, that is what they said. We need to set a date for their wedding."

"My baby boy, a prince?" she wailed, throwing a hand up in the air. Mrs. Eesuola seemed to come out of her stupor as she thanked God for the blessing, but then I could no longer translate as she switched to rapid-fire Onina.

She got up and wrapped Tomori in her arms, sobbing against his shirt. He patted her on her back and looked at Nika and me helplessly. I passed him some tissues.

"Please, do not cry, Màmá," he murmured.

"But I thought you did not care about life. Always you just go with the flow. Now my son, my baby boy, will be a prince of Olọrọ Ilé and married to the future queen."

I didn't think her cries could possibly get any louder, but I was very wrong. Nika covered her face, embarrassed by the display.

Mrs. Eesuola's hiccups and boisterous nose-blowing made me grimace.

After a few more minutes, her tears slowed, and her thanks to God fell to quiet mutterings. I blew out a breath and looked at Tomori, who'd returned to his spot next to me on the velvet chaise in my sitting room.

"Mrs. Eesuola, do you have a date in mind?" I asked.

"Oh, there is much to prepare, much. How about December?"

Tomori and I shared a glance, and he silently passed me the reins.

"Mrs. Eesuola, the king is not well, so the sooner we have the wedding, the better."

She blinked at me, then Tomori. "Mori? What does she mean?"

"We must get married as soon as possible or the council will not approve of Brielle as the future queen."

She gasped, clutching her heart. "Who would dare go against the king's wishes? Lord have mercy on their souls." She shook her head. "I will call the family for help. We will ensure everything gets done in one week, Your Highness." She pulled a calendar out of her purse. "Next Friday we will do the engagement ceremony and Saturday the wedding ceremony. This is good?"

I peered up at Tomori to get his take. Although, what was there really to ask? Grandfather had said as soon as possible.

Mori squeezed my hand. "Yes, that is fine."

"Ah. We have much to do, so much to do," his mother muttered.

"My friend Iris will make the dresses." I looked at Tomori's sister. "And I would love it if you would be the emcee at the engagement ceremony."

She beamed. "I would be honored, Your Highness."

Thank goodness. Already a headache was forming, a pounding at the base of my skull. "Thank you, Nika. Please—when we are alone, you can call me Bri."

Her grin widened, and she clasped her hands together.

"We must begin planning right away," Mrs. Eesuola suggested.

"I will have my mother and Iris join us, then. That is, if you are ready to plan now?" I asked.

"Yes. We will honor the king and do this quickly."

I picked up the phone and asked Dayo to send my mother and Iris to my office.

Tomori squeezed my hand, then stood. "I have a meeting with the king. Father should be here in a few minutes."

Mrs. Eesuola froze. "He dares arrive?"

"Màmá, he was invited by the king."

A myriad of emotions crossed her face. I could only imagine what she must be thinking. Wanting to object because of all the hurt her ex-husband had caused, yet not wanting to go against her king. Her lips flattened, and she nodded her understanding.

Tomori kissed her forehead, then left.

I wanted to call him back and ask if he would be okay with his father here. Since our engagement, we hadn't had much time to be alone and talk. He was busy learning from Mobo, and now we were adding wedding planning to the mix. Hopefully, once the ceremonies were behind us, we could pause and get to know each other even better.

I still hadn't brought up the sleeping arrangements.

"Your Highness, Ms. Blakely and your mother are here," Dayo said, sticking her head through the cracked doorway.

I motioned for her to let them in.

"Where do we start?" Mom asked Mrs. Eesuola once introductions were complete.

Mrs. Eesuola asked Dayo to take notes, then proceeded to plan the entirety of the engagement and wedding festivities. Not once did she stop talking. I'm not even sure she took a breath. If it weren't for the rumble of her stomach two hours later, she would still have been talking.

I peeked at my watch. We'd missed lunch.

"I'll see lunch is prepared in the family room. Is that okay, Your Highness?" Dayo asked me.

"That sounds wonderful. Thank you."

"Of course."

"Ladies, we can leave all the notes here and return after lunch," I said.

"That sounds easiest, Your Highness," Mrs. Eesuola said.

"Please call me Bri."

Hesitation crossed her face. Was she thinking the same way as Mori when Grandfather had told him to use his first name?

We made it to the third floor for lunch, but I stopped short after crossing the threshold of the family dining room. Grandfather, Tomori, a scowling gentleman, and Yinka were gathered around the dining room table. Yinka rubbed the bridge of his nose as if the conversation was a difficult one.

What had I interrupted?

"Ah, Brielle, did you just now remember lunch?" Grandfather asked, a calm look on his face.

Tomori, Yinka, and the other gentleman jumped to their feet. The older gentleman had to be Tomori's father.

"Please, remain seated." I cleared my throat. "Grandfather, we didn't mean to disturb you. The ladies and I only now became aware of the time."

"Come in, come in. You are all welcome. Did Dayo call the kitchen with your request?"

"Yes." I motioned for the ladies to come in.

Tomori's mother gasped, saying a prayer under her breath.

"Bàbá," Nika cried, moving around her mother to hug her father.

I followed her, unsure what I should do. I wanted to offer comfort to Tomori's mother but needed to meet my future father-in-law.

"Bàbá," Tomori said, "this is Princess Brielle Adebayo, my fiancée."

"Ẹ káàsán, Your Highness." He bowed. "It is a pleasure meeting you."

"It's nice to meet you as well, *Ògbéni* Eesuola."

"No, no," he said, waving his hand. "You may call me Sino." A thin smile spread across his face. "We will be family soon."

Something told me Sino lacked trust in his own statement.

"Sit, Brielle," Grandfather said, motioning to an open spot near him.

Tomori moved his place setting over so I could have my regular spot next to Grandfather. Mori held the chair out for me, and I caught a huge grin on Grandfather's face.

"Mrs. Eesuola," Grandfather directed, "Tomori says the wedding will be next week. You will have full access to our caterer and whatever else you need."

"No, Your Majesty. Please, let us provide the food. It is the least we can do. It is not every day you become family with royalty," she simpered.

He stroked his chin. I had done an internet search and knew the bride's family usually shouldered most of the financial aspects of an Ọlọran wedding, but I could understand Mrs. Eesuola wanting to be part of the event.

"I thank you for your hospitality," Grandfather said. "But there will be many people at the wedding. Perhaps you can cater the engagement ceremony?"

"Certainly, Your Majesty. It is our pleasure. We will look after the princess once . . ." She paused, and silence fell.

Once the king has passed. How could I look at my impending marriage as a joyous occasion when its necessity was due to Grandfather's upcoming death? It didn't help that I wasn't in love with Tomori. I liked him and could admit my attraction, but love? I didn't *know* him enough to love him.

Although, the Bible didn't say we had to know a person to love them. The commandment was quite firm, but my mind wrestled with the notion of *falling* in love and celebrating that happiness with all my friends and family on my wedding day. Nothing about this followed the norm.

At least Mom, Iris, and Grandfather would be in attendance—oh, and the rest of the country. Thankfully, the engagement portion was strictly for family. The public relations team had already informed me that the wedding would be televised. Also, multiple media outlets had reached out, requesting one-on-one interviews with me and Tomori. The PR team had made statements from my official accounts and new ones they'd created for Tomori, as well, to announce our engagement.

I was staring at my plate, trying to slow my speeding thoughts, when a hand slid under the tablecloth and gripped mine. I wrapped both of my hands around Tomori's, thankful for his presence. Despite all my turmoil around my feelings for him, I did count him as a friend.

That thought loosened the bands squeezing my chest and slowed my spinning thoughts.

"Thank you," I whispered.

"Anytime," he replied.

Later that evening, my fiancé, Mom, Iris, and I gathered in the guest sitting room. Dinner had been delivered so we could relax. Mobo had assured me that if anything happened with Grandfather, I'd be the first notified.

"So what does Mobo teach you in these lessons?" Mom asked Tomori.

"Everything."

I laughed. "It's true. He doesn't care if your head is going to burst open with facts as long as those facts are recited correctly."

Mori's deep chuckle filled the air. "That is the exact impression I get. It is obvious he is very knowledgeable. I cannot imagine how long he has been working for the king."

"Twenty years," I replied. "I asked."

"How *old* is he?" Iris cried. "I thought he was in his late thirties."

I paused, forkful of rice frozen in midair. "I don't know. I thought he was in his fifties."

"No, no, no." Mom waved her hands back and forth. "He's definitely around my age."

"How do you know?" Iris, Mori, and I asked simultaneously.

Mom blushed. *Blushed.* "Some things you just know."

Iris and I exchanged a look.

"Tomori, how many siblings do you have?" Mom asked.

I ate, listening to the conversation around me. It was so nice to relax and not have to worry about what everyone thought of my upcoming nuptials. Shondra and Tami had been shocked by the announcement of both my royalty and my impending marriage, and I'd had to call both of them to put out the fires. I hadn't intentionally left them out. Everything had moved so quickly that the world knew before they did.

Mom had extended her leave and would stay until after the wedding. She'd fly out that Monday and return to her New York life . . . without me. I hoped I could handle the change. Now that we'd made up, I'd miss her terribly when she returned.

"Oh, I can tell you *all* the stories about Bri as a child," she was saying.

My ears perked. "Mom! Please don't."

She grinned wickedly. "Parent's prerogative, sweetheart. I'll be sure to find some pictures of when you were young and mail them to you."

"Please, Mrs. Bayo," Tomori said. "That would be wonderful."

"Oh no. Call me Marie."

A slow grin filled Tomori's face. "Thank you, Marie."

After sharing some embarrassing stories—well, not too humiliating—Mom called it a night, and Iris followed suit. Tomori offered to walk me back to my room.

As we came to a stop in front of my door, I bit my lip, then wrapped my arms around his waist. His scent enveloped me as the warmth of the hug filled my heart.

"Today was a long day," I mumbled against his chest.

"The longest." He nestled his chin on top of my head.

"Everything okay with your father?"

He shrugged. "We will see."

"Thank you again, Mori. For doing this. I know it was a lot to ask of you."

He squeezed me. "Do not thank me, arídunnú mi. It is my pleasure." He stepped back. "I will see you at breakfast?"

I nodded and watched him walk away.

FORTY-THREE

I wanted to throw up. I pressed my hand against my churning stomach, concentrating on breathing slowly. The stars behind my eyes receded, and bit by bit, the noise around me filtered back in.

"Ten minutes and they will announce your arrival," Dayo stated.

"She'll be ready by then," Iris answered as she concentrated on placing the amure over my shoulder. It was the same one I'd used at the Independence Day celebration. "Hold still, please," she said around the safety pin in her mouth, which she used to secure the amure to my shoulder.

"Iris," I whispered.

"Hmm?" She slipped the pin through the fabric.

"I'm kind of freaking out." My gaze flicked around the dressing room as Nika and the other women donned their headdresses for the engagement ceremony.

Iris squeezed my arm. "I know," she murmured. "But I've been praying since the council told you to marry. I know this isn't how you wanted life to go or how you wanted your marriage to be, but I'm convinced that God is up to something good and that twenty years from now you'll marvel at all you've accomplished. So breathe, hold your head high when you walk out there, and show the families that you and Tomori are the right choice for this country."

I closed my eyes, soaking in her words as she continued to ensure my dress was perfect.

Father, I don't know why I feel so petrified. I don't know if it's because tomorrow I'll be a married woman or because this is one step closer to me being a future queen. Or if it's because I'm just having a lack-of-faith moment and a complete meltdown!

Okay, so I was panicking a little. I exhaled.

Sorry for the mental shouting, Lord. Please forgive my doubt. Please bless this engagement party. I pray that my family and Tomori's will get along and develop a relationship that will bless us. And most of all, may we glorify You and encourage the people of Ọlọrọ. In Jesus's name, amen.

"Okay," I said. "I think I'm ready."

"I know you are." Iris smiled and stepped back. "Okay, you can look."

I turned and peered in the floor-length mirror. My dress was perfect. Iris had stuck to the color scheme of purple, blue, and white. My royal purple gown fell to the floor in A-line fashion. It had a boatneck top and a cinched-in waist. The bell sleeves were purple, blue, and white and puffed to give dimension and a noble air. The look went perfectly with my jeweled headdress—a moss agate dangling in the middle of my forehead.

"I love it, Iris."

She beamed. "So do I. I can't wait to see what everyone else thinks."

Dayo walked into the dressing room. "Five minutes. Ladies, please line up so we can do the procession."

The royal dressing room was a couple of doors down from the palace ballroom. Tomori's sisters lined up at the door, along with Digi and Iris. Nika and Abbey had been very happy to stand up with me as bridesmaids. Iris's amazing skills had clothed them all in royal purple and matching headwraps.

I walked behind Iris, trying to think regal thoughts instead of picturing myself running back to my room and never coming out. Hopefully my nerves would settle once I saw Mori. Then again, knowing I would be his wife tomorrow added a whole other host of nerves I wasn't ready to unpack. And that pesky conversation on where to sleep still hadn't come up.

After the wedding, once Tomori and I were settled into marriage, Grandfather wanted to throw a party and invite dignitaries and heads of state from neighboring countries and allies. I would be the first future queen in the African Kings Alliance. The other monarchs only passed their reign to their sons. Mom kept calling me a trailblazer, but all I could do was pray that I wouldn't fail those who looked up to me as a public figure.

Nika smiled in preparation as we waited outside the ballroom. Dayo handed her a microphone, and Nika went through the double doors. I could hear her acknowledging the guests and welcoming them to the engagement ceremony. She called for some music, and soon a drumbeat pulsed in the air. Abbey automatically started swaying and snapping her fingers. Iris copied her motions. Soon all the ladies were swinging on beat. Nika called them forward, dancing to the music as well.

"Family and friends, please welcome Princess Brielle Eden Adebayo."

I started walking, staring down at my feet as instructed. The bride was to appear demure and humbly come before the groom's relatives so they would officially welcome her to the family. Then Tomori would come forth, and we would make the walk to the other side of the ballroom filled with Adebayos.

I stopped before Mr. and Mrs. Eesuola. They rose to their feet, and I kneeled before them, acknowledging their place as my elders and Tomori's parents. Wale, Mori's brother, helped me back up.

Nika translated the words her father spoke to English. "The Eesuolas welcome you to our family. We pray blessings over you as you unite with our son Tomori. We pledge to support your marriage and to love you as our own daughter."

Mrs. Eesuola gently cupped my chin and peered into my face, speaking rapid Onina. "We pray many years of fertility—"

My face flamed at Nika's translation.

"—to bless our son with children. Boys who will grow into the Eesuola strength. Girls who will mature into women of abiding faith. We pray for future princes and princesses to bless and honor our country."

Someone had forgotten to tell me about the prayers. One by one, the elders of the Eesuola family prayed a blessing over me, with Nika translating for all to hear. And I do mean *all*. How was I supposed to talk to people casually after this? So many of the Eesuola women prayed that I would have many children. Yes, Tomori came from a big family, but did they honestly expect me to have eight children as well? I would need to have a child or two to continue the Adebayo line, but not eight. *Right, Lord?*

Finally, the last family member ended her prayer and escorted me back to Tomori's parents. His mother beamed when Tomori walked forward. He looked handsome in his engagement clothes. He had on a white long-sleeved undershirt and matching pants. His top was reminiscent of a poncho and stopped at his knees. Down the center was a white strip, and the rest was dark purple. The edges of his hem, collar, and sleeves were in the same checkered pattern as my sleeves. The traditional Ọlọran cap, which reminded me of a military officer's hat, completed his ensemble.

Sino laid a hand on Tomori's shoulder, then placed the other on mine. Mrs. Eesuola took each of our hands and laid mine on top of Tomori's.

Nika narrated. "The Eesuola family accepts the engagement of Tomori Debare Eesuola and Princess Brielle Eden Adebayo. They promise to perform their royal duty to support the couple for many blessed years of marriage."

Mori tucked my arm in his, and we walked to the other side of the ballroom and bowed before Grandfather. Relief washed through me. He sat in a chair and looked much better than the other day, when he'd had to get a steroid injection to keep his lungs from spasming.

Tomori spoke to Grandfather, asking permission to marry me and care for me the rest of his days. My heart pounded at the sincerity in his voice.

Mori was such an honorable man. Even though this marriage

was a necessity, I was glad that he was by my side. I had faith that somehow, someway, we would come to an understanding and have a marriage that at least held affection and respect for each other.

Thank You for that, Lord.

FORTY-FOUR

I needed ice cream.

Everyone was sleeping, so sneaking into the kitchen was easy. I padded quietly past the island and opened the stainless-steel freezer door. Surely the palace staff stocked ice cream. Didn't they know it was my cure for insomnia and loud thoughts? Like the ones telling me I would be married tomorrow.

I rifled through the freezer, finally spotting a few cartons behind packs of meat. The rectangular containers were labeled . . . in Onina. *Okay.* I could do this, decipher the different flavors. Tomori had taught me food vocabulary, after all.

The first one was . . . mango coconut. Nope. I could put that one back. A big scoop of chocolate ice cream was in order. I peered at the clear containers and lifted two whose contents were brown. One had bits of nuts, and the other had a dark brown ribbon. Nuts for the win. A quick cabinet search procured a bowl, and spoons were in the drawer below.

"So you like ice cream?"

I froze at the deep voice, then slowly turned to face Tomori. "Hi."

"Hi."

"Do you want some?" I bit my lip and held up the ice cream.

"What kind is it?"

"Chocolate with nuts."

"Yes, please."

I grabbed another bowl, ignoring my shaking hands. I put three scoops into my bowl and four in Tomori's, all the while wondering what he was doing in here.

"You could not sleep?" he asked as I handed him his treat.

"Not at all." I glanced at him. "You?"

He shook his head.

I looked around the kitchen to ensure we were truly alone before fixing my gaze on his once more. The low light above the island cast a warm glow across his face, lending an intimacy that made me nervous. Tomorrow we'd be husband and wife.

Eek! Breathe, Bri. "Um, about tomorrow . . ."

His spoon paused in midair. "Yes?"

"Well, um, you'll be moving into my room. Grandfather said the staff would talk if we maintained separate quarters." Thank goodness I was eating ice cream. If my face heated any more, I would melt the treat.

"Oh."

There was so much weight in the word that my eyes automatically flew to his. Silence wrapped around us as we stared at each other for a minute. Two. Honestly, I don't know how long we gazed into each other's eyes. But when Tomori finally spoke, my heart beat so furiously that I felt light-headed.

"I would never do anything you were uncomfortable with. I hope you know that."

"I do." I *did*. I'd picked him for a reason, but still, we hadn't declared any feelings that would make tomorrow easier.

"Brielle, I care about you. You are a remarkable woman. I promise, you never have to worry about anything from me. If at any time you are not sure about something, please talk to me. I know this is all very . . . awkward, but I hope you are comfortable enough to talk with me."

"Thank you." I tucked my hair behind my ear. "I admit thinking of you as my husband has made me anxious. I didn't know how to bring up the sleeping arrangements without feeling like I would pass out."

He chuckled nervously. "We will not share the bed. I am sure your room is big enough for a pallet on the floor."

"What?" I could feel my eyes bugging out. "You can't sleep on the floor, Mori." We were adults. Surely we could share a bed and respect each other's boundaries.

"I can if that will provide you with the most comfort. Tomorrow, when we say our vows, I cease thinking of only myself. When you asked me to be your husband, I took that request seriously. Prayed about all it entailed. You will be the best part of me, which means you get the bed." He winked and swallowed a spoonful of ice cream.

I stared into my bowl, blinking back tears. He was such a good man, and I couldn't be more grateful that he'd said yes and the council had approved him.

"Thank you." I swallowed, thinking about what he'd said. "If we're going to do this right, you can sleep next to me. I trust you not to do anything until . . ."

Until what? Until we thought we knew each other well enough? Until we magically fell in love? I smothered a groan and took a bite of my ice cream instead.

"Until we are ready."

My face heated, and I nodded so he'd know I'd heard him. But I couldn't look at him, knowing that eventually, somewhere down the line, we'd consummate the marriage and produce an heir.

"Okay," I croaked.

"All right. Let us talk about tomorrow. Are you nervous?"

"I'm terrified." I chuckled, meeting his gaze once more. "What if I pass out in front of everyone?" I wasn't marrying for myself but for my country.

Our ceremony would take place at the palace chapel, and afterward we would drive the parade route to where Tomori and I would exit the car as husband and wife to sit on the thrones. There would be music, dancing, and other performances to celebrate our union.

"You will not. I will not let you."

I arched an eyebrow. "How can you stop me?"

"I will hold your hand, and you will know you are safe with me."

My lips twitched. "You're very confident."

"You did choose me for a reason."

I laughed. "Touché, Mr. Eesuola."

Tomori reached across the island, touching the engagement ring on my left hand. The one he'd given me. "You are still wearing it."

"I told you I always would."

"Yes, but the king does not want you to wear that for your wedding ring."

I rolled my eyes. Grandfather would not budge on that issue. "I know. He sat me down to tell me the people's expectations and that you'd picked a ring from the royal accessories."

Mori nodded, looking contemplative. "I hope you will like it. How will you wear this after tomorrow?"

"My mom bought me a gold chain so I can wear it around my neck." I studied him. "Is that okay?"

"Yes." He squeezed my hand, then picked up his spoon. "Thank you for wanting to wear it."

We ate the rest of our ice cream in silence, then Tomori took our bowls to the kitchen sink to wash them.

"How do you like living here?" I asked.

"It is strange. People bowing before me, calling me *prince*, using palace runners when I need something." He shook his head in bemusement.

"Right? It blows my mind."

"Oh yes. Mine too."

I laughed. "How do you like Mobo?" I'd been thinking that Tomori could keep him as an advisor after Grandfather . . .

"He is very knowledgeable and respectful. Why?"

"Well, when Grandfather passes"—I cleared my throat—"we will have to decide if we wish to continue having him work for us. Or he may want to retire."

"I say we leave it up to him."

"Okay."

Tomori paused, dishrag in hand. "Okay?"

"Yes. It's a good idea."

"And just like that"—he snapped his fingers—"you will take my advice?"

"Yes." I cocked my head. "Did you think I wouldn't listen?"

"Well, you have before. I guess now, knowing I will be your husband, it seemed more significant."

"You're right. It does." I bumped his shoulder. "I can argue with you if you'd like."

"Ha. No. I have seen that with my sister and brother-in-law. I will pass."

I laughed. "I can't wait to see who Nika ends up with. She's a pistol."

He arched an eyebrow in question.

"Firecracker? Strong-willed?"

"Ah yes. She is. She will need an even stronger man."

"He's out there somewhere."

Tomori dried his hands, all the while watching me. Did I have something on my face?

"What?"

"I just had a thought. Tomorrow we will be married in the chapel. Our families, the tribal elders, and everyone else who can squeeze into the church will be there."

There went the butterflies in my stomach, trying a full-blown migration all at once. "Right." What was he getting at?

"Do you want our first kiss to be in the presence of most of the country?"

"Uh . . ." My pulse raced. "I completely forgot about that part." I stared down at my slippered feet. "What do you propose?"

"I would like to walk you to your room and kiss you good night. But only if you are comfortable with the idea. Or if you wish, we can skip the kiss tomorrow."

I shook my head. "Then everyone would speculate something we don't want them to." *Oy, could I have said that in a more convoluted way?*

"Then you are okay with my kissing you tonight?"

"Yes." My answer came out on a breath as flutters took flight in my chest. Kissing Mori had definitely crossed my mind a time or two. Okay, I'd lost count.

Tomori held out his hand, and I laid my palm against his. Affection filled me as we walked down the hall. We remained quiet as we traveled through the palace corridors. Finally, we stopped in front of my room.

"Maybe we should go in the sitting room?" I suggested. "I'm not sure who roams the halls at night."

"That is true."

I opened the door, then closed it behind him. My heart pounded in my throat. "I'm nervous."

"So am I."

"Really? Why?"

He stepped forward, cupping my face. "Because this matters."

"Very much so," I breathed.

His other hand slid along my cheek. "I will be careful with your heart, Brielle."

My heart melted, and I gripped his wrist. "As will I."

He inched closer, his breath fanning against mine, and my eyes fluttered closed. The faintest brush of his mouth caressed my lips, and I inhaled sharply as the nerve endings woke with anticipation. He feathered his lips once more before placing them firmly against mine. I sighed, curling my fingers against the fabric of his shirt.

Then he was gone. Cool air greeted me, and my eyes opened to find Tomori standing a few feet away. I touched my lips, captivated by the sensation he'd left behind.

"Good night, Brielle." His Adam's apple bobbed.

"Good night, Tomori."

Then he slipped out of my room and into the night.

FORTY-FIVE

M y precious girl, I can't believe this day is here." Mom
gripped my shoulders as she peered into my face. "Are
you ready?"

"I am." I'd woken up this morning feeling calmer than I had
in a long while.

"Are you sure? Are you really sure, Bri? Marriage is for life."
Her eyes held a sadness and regret.

"I'm sure, Mom. Tomori is the right choice." Just remembering
last night's kiss affirmed that. "Marrying for the sake of Ọlọrọ
might not be how I imagined my love story would go, but I think
there is enough respect between us that love can grow."

The care Mori had shown last night gave me hope I could fall
in love with him. Our situation just changed the order of things a
little—marriage, then love. *Please, let it be so, Lord.*

"If you're sure this is the right thing to do, then I'm happy for
you." Mom gave me a hug. "*Proud* of you."

"Thank you," I whispered. "I love you. Thank you so much
for being here."

"There's nowhere else I'd rather be. I love you *so* much, my
darling Bri." She squeezed me tight.

I blinked back tears as I rested my head on her shoulder. Thank
goodness I hadn't done my makeup yet. Any moment, Iris or Dayo

would storm in and demand I finish getting ready. Until then, I soaked up this moment with my mother.

We broke apart.

Mom wiped the tears from her face. "Are you nervous about anything?" she asked hesitantly.

"No. I had a good talk with Tomori last night."

"Good. I'm praying for you, Bri."

"Thank you."

A knock sounded at the sitting room door, and Mom moved to open it. "Do you think it's Dayo or Iris?"

"Iris," I said.

Mom twisted the knob, and Iris came hurtling in.

"I can't believe you're getting married today. Wait until you see the dress. It's perfection! You'll love it. Tomori will love it. The *country* will love it."

"How many cups of coffee have you had already?" I asked, laughing.

Iris halted her mad pacing and looked up at the ceiling. "One after I woke up, one after checking to make sure your dress was as I left it and hadn't been destroyed in some weird attempt to prevent your marriage, one as I checked on the bridesmaids' dresses, and . . ." She stared at the travel mug in her hand. "I think this is the fourth cup."

"Girl, you're going to crash."

Iris bobbed her head up and down. "But not until this evening when it no longer matters."

I chuckled. "Time to get ready?"

"Yes. Dayo is escorting the hairstylist and makeup artist to the dressing room. I'm in charge of making sure everyone looks good in their gowns. Dayo will keep us on schedule so that you arrive at the church on time." She blew out a breath. "Are you ready?"

The question on everyone's mind, apparently. I shared a look with my mom. "I am."

"Good. Ms. Marie, go get changed. You'll be going with us to get hair and face done."

"Yes, ma'am." My mom snapped her fingers and jogged to her room.

As soon as her door closed, I whirled and faced Iris. "He kissed me."

She squealed, then clapped a hand over her mouth. "Oh my word," she mumbled behind her fingers.

"He didn't want our first kiss to be in public in front of the world."

"Aww." Iris placed a hand on her heart. "That is the *sweetest*. Did it give you all the feels?"

"So many feels."

She squealed again. "I love it. I love you guys. I'm so happy for you." She wrapped me in a hug, squeezing me as she swayed us back and forth.

"Thank you for all you've done," I said. "I'm so glad you came with me."

"Every heroine needs a sidekick." She stepped back. "We need to get you ready for the royal wedding. *Your* royal wedding. Ack! I love it." She clapped her hands together.

"Maybe you should switch to water."

We chuckled, and Iris grabbed a bottled water out of the mini fridge.

The stylist did wonders. She transformed each bridesmaid's hair into a braided crown, then she scooped my long mane into a curled updo to show off my princess tiara.

The delicate piece sat on a velvet cushion, shining with three green agate stones at the crest. A gold-and-diamond leaf pattern made up the rest of the tiara. The stylist slid the piece carefully into my hair.

I gaped as I took in my reflection. With the jeweled tones of my makeup—shimmering gold eye shadow and a rose lip gloss—I looked . . . *regal*.

"Now for the dress," Dayo called over my shoulder.

I stood and made my way to the dressing area, where Iris and Mori's sisters sat in their lilac chiffon gowns. Mom wore a beautiful navy mother-of-the-bride gown.

"Okay," Iris said, closing the screens around the dais so no one could see us as I changed. "Let's get you dressed."

Anticipation hummed through me as Iris went to uncover the dress.

"Close your eyes," she said.

"Seriously?"

"Yes."

I humored her and waited for her to bark out more instructions. The rustle of the gown reached my ears a moment before Iris asked me to step into it. She guided my hand to her shoulder, and I lifted my foot. The material caressed my skin as I lowered my foot back to the dais. Was it tulle?

Iris began zipping the gown.

"Can I open my eyes?"

"Almost," she muttered.

I waited as she tugged here and there to adjust the gown's fit.

"All right. You're ready."

I opened my eyes and stared at the floor-length mirror. White tulle flowed from my waist in ball-gown fashion, making a beautiful contrast to my top. The sweetheart bodice had elbow-length sleeves and had been embroidered with purple, blue, and white beads. The pattern resembled an orchid and had been overlaid by see-through lace. It was two cultures married into one. A nod to every American girl's dream of wearing white on her wedding day and a nod to my Ọlọrọ roots, showcasing the colors of the country I would rule one day.

My eyes filled with tears. "Oh, Iris. I love it." I touched the bodice in awe.

"Oh, thank goodness. You were quiet for so long."

I laughed. "Stunned silent, but in a very good way." I smoothed my hands down the tulle, loving the feel of it. "Let's go to the chapel."

"Yes! She's ready!" Iris yelled.

Cheers erupted as Iris opened the screen and I turned to face my friends and family. Mom dabbed her eyes. Nika smiled, as did Abbey.

Mrs. Eesuola walked right up to me. "You look magnificent, Your Highness."

"Thank you, Mrs. Eesuola. But please remember, it's Brielle."

"And you can call me Màmá."

My emotions couldn't handle any more sweetness if I didn't want to ruin my makeup. "Thank you, Màmá."

The morning had seemed to move slowly as we did hair and makeup, but now that I was dressed and ready, a flurry of activity hit us. Dayo quickly whisked us to the cars waiting to take us to the chapel. The moms went in one car, the bridesmaids in another, and I had a limo all to myself.

If I'd known how my mother's news at the restaurant that day would affect me, I don't know if I'd have had the courage even to show up to the lunch date. But in spite of the hurt, the chaos, the international travel, and all the council had put me through, I'd found my purpose.

My head cocked to the side as I saw a familiar white envelope lying on the seat next to me. Really? I reached for the paper and unfolded it.

Your wedding won't solve your inferiority. There is still plenty of time to right the wrongs of the royal council.

My hands clenched around my white orchid bouquet. I didn't have the headspace to devote to this. I passed the note to Merrick, asking him to hold it for safekeeping. I didn't want them to know it was another note. Not right before my wedding.

Azuka pulled up in front of the walkway leading to the chapel. I could see local media and news outlets from other countries and continents lined up in the press walkway across from the chapel.

"Merrick will open the door, Your Highness."

"Thank you, Azuka."

"My pleasure."

Merrick soon offered his hand, which I accepted, inhaling and exhaling as gently as possible. With the cameras focused on me, my nerves wanted to be front and center. I pushed them back, recalling the assurance of God's desire for me to be here. With a lift of my chin I walked slowly down the walkway, letting people admire my dress, the tiara, everything. When I reached the door of the chapel, Grandfather rose from the back pew and offered me his arm.

We walked down the aisle together, the affair quiet, as there was no wedding march or any other song played for an Ọlọran wedding. I didn't need music, not when Tomori's intense gaze pierced me with every step that drew me closer to him.

My breath caught. Nothing could have prepared me for Mori in a tux or Mori without his beard. Why had he shaved? Had Grandfather required it of him? Yet I couldn't be upset, because the effect devastated me. I wanted to throw my arms around him and kiss his smooth cheek.

Grandfather squeezed my hand, then took a seat in the pew beside Mom. I joined hands with Tomori as the pastor spoke of the solemn affair and the sovereignty of the kingdom and our marriage. How our marriage would not just be two souls uniting as one but also a symbol of our sacred duty to govern the people God saw fit to bless us with.

Through it all, my gaze never wavered from Tomori's, and his never wavered from mine. Through the repeating of vows, the exchange of rings—*wowzers,* the pearl-shaped moss agate surrounded by diamonds stunned me—and the pronouncement that I was now Princess Brielle Eden Eesuola Adebayo.

"You may now kiss your bride."

Tomori framed my face, hiding us from the crowd, and kissed me until my heart dropped to my feet.

I couldn't believe we were now husband and wife, but with Mori by my side, my future held a hope I'd cling to.

FORTY-SIX

Finally, the day was over. Silence enveloped me as I stepped into my bedroom suite. The celebrations had seemed to go on forever. I couldn't even remember if I'd eaten. I glanced over my shoulder as Tomori shut the door to my—*our*—room.

Awareness strummed along my nerve endings. "Now what?" I asked.

"I am not sure." He studied me, sliding his hands into his tux pockets.

If he didn't know and I didn't know, what were we supposed to do? We'd already decided against a honeymoon. Staying near Grandfather was of the utmost importance right now. Instead, we had tomorrow and Monday to relax and ignore our royal responsibilities.

"I guess, first things first, we change," he said. Mobo had moved all of Tomori's belongings into my room earlier. My suite had two walk-in closets, so giving him one had been easy.

"Sounds good."

Tomori nodded and walked to the left. I headed for the right, then stopped. My gown had a zipper. I reached behind my back. *Nope.*

"Uh, Mori . . ."

"Yes?"

I turned to face him. "Um, could you unzip my dress?" My

face heated, and my eyes looked everywhere but at my husband. *My husband!*

"Uh . . . yes, I can do that."

He walked to me, and I turned my back to him. My heart heaved up then down as his fingers brushed my neck and slid my zipper down to the sway of my lower back. I grabbed the top of the material, hoping he didn't have a view that would lead to something neither of us was ready for.

"Thank you," I croaked.

"Uh . . . yes. Right. I am going." His footfalls raced across the floor.

I hurried to my closet and shut the door. I hung up the dress, thankful Iris would be able to preserve it for me. Then again, it might end up in a museum instead of on the shelves of my closet for years to come.

I tugged my pajama drawer open and stared at the choices before me. *No, can't wear just an extra-long shirt.* I moved to the next pile. *Those shorts are too short.* I exhaled, hands shaking as I flipped through stacks of nightwear. Why didn't I own any pajama pants? Shame on me for getting rid of all my winter clothing when palace staff hired someone to pack and mail my items from New York. *Big mistake. Huge!* I could have been walking around in flannel, guarded against the illustrious *wedding night*, if I'd been a forward-thinker.

A knock sounded on the door. "Brielle, are you okay?"

"Yes. Sorry. I'll be right out." I grabbed a silk button top and matching shorts. They would have to do.

I was a big girl, a grown-up, a *married* woman. I could sleep next to my husband without having a conniption. Right?

When I exited the closet, Tomori waited in a chair beside the bed, elbows braced on his knees, hands clasped in prayer. I stared at his still form. Was he actually praying or just resting? Was he afraid to get in the bed before me? Did he feel just as ridiculous for being nervous about something that had been happening between men and women around the world for centuries?

Lord, please take this awkwardness away. Please help me de-

velop a relationship with my husband so we can laugh about this moment sometime in the future.

My face heated once more. It felt odd to talk to God about this, but He already knew. Still, it didn't make it easier.

"Brielle?"

I blinked and focused on Mori. "Yes?"

"We can do this. We will just walk up to it"—he pointed to the bed—"like it is our own regular one and lie down and sleep."

I raised an eyebrow. "Have you ever slept with anyone before?"

His face flushed. "Yes." His Adam's apple bobbed. "I am not proud of it, but I have."

Uh, totally not what I meant. My mind stumbled over the knowledge. "Oh." I searched for the right words. I didn't want him to think I was judging him, but my brain had temporarily short-circuited. "Thank you for your honesty, but I was being literal."

A rusty laugh fell from his lips. "Oh, *sleep* sleep."

"Yeah."

"You may have noticed how small my mother's house is. I shared a bed with my brothers."

"Sleepovers were the closest I came to it, and we always made a pallet on the floor. I haven't shared a bed in any way, shape, or form."

He nodded slowly. "I see." He gestured toward the king-sized bed. "I will stay on the right side, and you can take the left. Or do you normally sleep on the right?"

"I like the middle." I shrugged. "I don't have a preference."

"If you do not mind, I would like this side."

"All right." *Ugh!* This was maddening. The newness of it all was so awkward.

Regardless, I went to the left as he requested, pulling the covers back before slipping beneath the sheet. I froze as Tomori watched me. "What did I do?"

"Nothing. I just . . ." He ran a hand over his bare chin. "This is surreal."

"Completely."

"I am tempted to pinch myself."

"Go for it."

He did.

I chuckled. "Did that hurt?"

"Yes. I guess that means we really are married." He sat on top of the covers.

I pinched my arm as well. "Yep. It hurt."

"See? You really are my wife."

I lay back on my pillows. "And you're my husband."

"And tonight is our wedding night."

"And it's filled with the awkward rambles of two people who don't know how to be quiet."

His laughter filled the air, and then he brushed his fingers against mine. We threaded our hands together and lay there.

"Brielle?"

"Tomori?"

"That cake was the most disgusting thing I have ever tasted."

Laughter burst free, and soon I was wiping tears from my eyes, remembering the chocolate monstrosity we'd eaten. "What was that?"

"God only knows. We need to ensure we never use that baker again."

"Did you see Nika's face when she took a bite?"

"Ha! I almost choked on a piece, trying not to laugh at her expression."

We fell silent once more, only this time the silence was cozy. We'd shared a laugh, we were holding hands, and nothing bad had happened.

"I'm not tired," I said.

"Neither am I. My brain keeps thinking over everything."

"Same. At least we don't have to show up at church tomorrow. I can sleep in for the first time since I came here."

"You do not want to go to church?"

My face burned in the night. "Grandfather said that since we're newlyweds, we won't be expected to show. If we do, people could think there is trouble in our marriage."

"Oh. Then sleeping in it is."

I stared at the ceiling, wondering if I should say anything else or will my brain to sleep instead.

"Brielle?"

"Yes?"

"I have a nighttime ritual. I like to read from my Bible, then pray over anything that comes to mind." He exhaled audibly. "Would you like to do that with me?"

"I would." I smiled. "Where are you in the Bible?"

"The Psalms."

Tomori pulled his hand away, flicking on the lamp on the nightstand. He pulled open the top drawer and grabbed my Bible, then flipped pages. I fluffed my pillows behind my back and leaned toward him so I could read along.

His deep voice read Psalm 8, and I listened, smiling as the words from the third stanza sank deep into my heart.

> "'When I consider Your heavens, the work of Your fingers,
> The moon and the stars, which You have ordained,
> What is man that You are mindful of him,
> And the son of man that You visit him?'"

I thought of my dream, my visit from God. The psalmist was right. Who was I that God would come to me in a dream and show me His will?

> "'For You have made him a little lower than the angels,
> And You have crowned him with glory and honor.'"

Tomori finished reading and closed his Bible. "We are blessed. Blessed that God loves us enough that He wants a relationship with us."

"I agree." I settled into my pillows. "He takes care of us. Everything in the world has a purpose and works together for His good."

"Mm. Yes. It is humbling to think we can be a part of His grand plan, yes?"

"Agreed." I reached for his hand this time, smiling as he took it in his. I told him about my dream, the real sense that I would lead. "And to think, marrying you enables me to do that. You are a part of His plan for this country just as much as I am."

"I am honored," he said.

"Me too."

"Should we pray to stay humble? After all, you are a princess and now I am a prince. I imagine that could mess with our identity. Make us think more of ourselves than we should, yes?"

"Yes."

I listened as Tomori prayed for our hearts, protection against pride, and a desire to remain servants of the Lord. It was a beautiful prayer, and after we both said amen, a peaceful quiet descended.

I fell asleep holding my husband's hand.

FORTY-SEVEN

The sun shone brightly as Mori and I lay on lounges out on the palace's private portion of the beach. We'd had breakfast delivered to our suite this morning, then agreed to relax by the ocean.

I took a sip of my coconut smoothie and uttered a contented sigh. "Can we just stay out here?"

"That would be nice." Mori folded his arms behind his head. "We could just lie out here until they demand we work."

"Exactly. Sounds like a perfect way to have a staycation honeymoon."

He chuckled. If I could bottle up his laugh, I would. The melodious undertones always gave me goosebumps.

"You know what else would be fun?" I asked.

"Hmm?"

"Let's find a TV show to binge-watch this afternoon. We'll fill the sitting room with snacks and just relax."

"Or we could watch movies. Maybe a *Lord of the Rings* marathon?"

I smiled. "Did you read the books or just watch the movies?"

"Just the movies, but I did read *The Hobbit*."

"Same." I watched the waves, the sun glittering off the surface. "I'm sure there are movies we could watch."

"We will make a list? Is that fair?"

"Yes. Maybe I'll add one I love and watch all the time, and you can do the same."

Mori nodded slowly. "Let me guess. Yours is *Pride and Prejudice?*"

"No. I've seen it, but the movie I watch over and over is *Return to Me.*"

The blank expression on his face was comical.

I grabbed my chest as if wounded. "You haven't seen it? A woman needs a heart transplant and gets the hero's deceased wife's heart."

"And this is romantic?" His brow furrowed.

"So romantic. I bawl every time I watch it." At his confused expression, I explained, "It makes me cry, but they're good tears. Whenever I need a good cry, I watch it."

"Why would you need to cry?" The wrinkles on his brow deepened.

"Sometimes it's the safest way for me to let my emotions out."

He threaded his fingers through mine. "I hope I will be a safe place for you to feel, Brielle."

I couldn't have stopped my smile or my racing pulse if I'd wanted to. "Do you think we'll be a hundred percent comfortable with each other one day?"

"I hope not."

My mouth dropped.

He held up a hand, then rubbed his chin. Already his face held stubble. "What I mean is that I do not want to get in a position where I take you for granted. Yes, I want to be at ease with you, but not so comfortable that I forget what a gift you are."

"Mori," I breathed.

He kissed the back of my hand.

I couldn't find the words, so I squeezed his fingers.

We sat in silence for a couple of hours, listening to the gentle laps of the waves. When we decided we were hungry, we made our way inside for lunch. I marveled at the way my hand fit in his as we walked. Somehow, I managed to ignore our guards following at a discreet pace.

Once in the privacy of our room, Mori ordered lunch while I took the bathroom first to wash off the sand and change from my bathing suit to loungewear.

When I came out, he was sitting in a chair, cell phone in hand.

"Looking at social media?" I asked.

"I was curious what they were saying about the wedding."

"And?"

"America loves you. They are enamored with your beauty and the fact that you were born there."

"What about the rest of the world?"

"There are some countries who feel you should turn the reign over to me."

"African countries?"

Mori nodded, and I sighed. Probably the other monarchies.

"Do not let it worry you, though." He rose, coming to stand before me. He slid a finger across my cheek. My breath hitched as my nerve endings came alive, heat traveling in the wake of his touch. Mori cupped my face with both hands, his dark gaze captivating me. "Brielle?"

"Yes?" I gripped his wrists, loving the close contact.

"May I kiss you?"

I bit my lip, then let go as his eyes tracked my every movement. I nodded.

He kissed me swiftly, firmly, and so fully that all I could do was slide my arms around his neck. A quiet murmur escaped when his hands gripped my waist to pull me closer. My body exploded with feeling as his kisses warmed me through and through.

He pulled back, gently laying his forehead against mine. "I have been wanting to do that all day."

"You can kiss me anytime you like . . . *husband*."

Mori groaned and kissed me again. "I find I like kissing my wife."

And I liked receiving them. My fingers trailed featherlight touches on the back of his neck. "We did kiss yesterday."

"With everyone watching." He groaned again. "Besides, that was not a kiss, just two lips touching."

313

I snorted. "The very definition of a kiss."

He shook his head and kissed my cheek, then the pulse thrumming at my neck, trailing kisses all the way up before I pulled him back to my lips.

A while later we broke apart, breaths heaving in unison. "*That* was a kiss," he said. He stepped back, then took another step backward.

"Where are you going?"

"To shower before I do something we are not ready for."

Heat pooled in my middle. "Are you sure we're not ready?" I asked breathlessly.

His eyes darkened, glistening with desire. His Adam's apple bobbed, and he nodded slowly. "We have only been married a day."

True. Part of me wanted to be able to say I loved him before we took our relationship to such an intimate level. The other could only think of how his kisses made me feel.

"Okay," I said.

By the time he finished in the bathroom, our lunch had arrived. I patted the spot next to me on the sofa. Mori picked a Nollywood—Nigerian Hollywood—movie to watch. I hadn't even known the category existed on our streaming app.

Once more I was thankful that I had asked Tomori to be my husband, that he had felt led to propose. I couldn't imagine that the ease I felt with him would have been possible with the other candidates. Prince Chimnoya would probably have shut me up in my room and told everyone I was indisposed while he made a power play for the kingdom.

Or worse, what if one of them wanted me out of the way and poisoned me like in some Grimms' fairy tale?

"Oh, I forgot to tell you," Mori said. "The king requests our presence at dinner tomorrow. Mobo asked if we would accept the invitation."

I peered up at him. "When did you talk to him?"

"When I requested lunch."

"Oh. Right. Did you say yes?"

He nodded. "I could not say no to the king."

314

"Are you going to call him Tiwa at dinner?"

Mori sputtered bits of his food everywhere.

I fell over laughing. "He's not scary. I promise."

"Sure he is not."

"Did Mobo say if anyone else will be there?"

"Yes. It is the family dinner."

I groaned. "Uncle Sijuwola will probably make snide remarks the whole time." Should I bring up the note? I'd forgotten about it until now. I wondered if Merrick still had it. Part of me thought Uncle was the one sending them.

"I will not let him disrespect my wife."

I kissed Mori's cheek, glad he had pulled me from spiraling thoughts. "It's okay." I lifted a shoulder. "I know I'm not people's first choice. Honestly, I wouldn't be surprised if the men on the council's list only wanted to marry me in order to kill me for the throne." I watched Tomori's face for his reaction.

But all he did was blink and blink some more. "Come again?"

"I mean, don't you think it's plausible they had some deal with Mr. Ladipo to marry me, then dispose of me? Take the crown and let their family rule?"

He shook his head. "That seems so . . ."

"TV drama? Streaming-only movie plot?" I pointed to the TV.

He chuckled. "Yes. All of the above. I do not even want to know why your mind went that direction."

"We're royalty, Mori. Wouldn't it make sense for people to plot against us?"

"I think you have been reading very strange books or watching too much law drama."

True. Was it any wonder *Law & Order* had so many seasons? "You're right. Maybe I need to read something else."

"A romance?" he suggested in a deep rumble.

My face heated. "One with a happily-ever-after ending and the couple falling madly in love with each other," I countered, trying not to blush.

"Why 'madly'?"

"Isn't that how it works?"

315

He shook his head, rubbing my cheek.

"Then how?"

Tomori leaned forward. "Love is the click of two hearts becoming one. Knowing that no matter what you believe of your plans, that person must fit into them, even if it seems impossible. Because once you have found them, you would do anything to make them happy. Their dreams become yours."

My heart thumped furiously. Was he saying he . . . *loved* me? "Tomori?"

He kissed me, silencing my questions. I returned his fervor, pouring in every emotion filling my heart to the brim. With a groan, he deepened the kiss, clutching me closer.

Then just as suddenly as the kissed started, it stopped.

I whimpered. "Tomori . . ."

He placed his forehead against mine. "When I think you are ready to hear the words. Until then . . ." He kissed my forehead.

"You're right."

Somehow, we continued to watch the movie. Well, he did. I couldn't focus. All I could wonder was when I would be ready to hear those three words or say them myself.

FORTY-EIGHT

Silence shrouded the dining table. We'd all filled our plates, Grandfather had asked Mori to say grace, and now . . . nothing. There was no happy chatter or joy like eating at the Eesuola home. Just cold silence and glares from Uncle Sijuwola and his son, Maseso.

Fade occasionally cast glances my way, but the animosity I expected was missing. It was like she didn't understand what she saw. I wasn't sure if it was my marriage that gave her pause or myself. I wanted to clear my throat and break the quiet, but what would I say?

"Is *no one* going to talk?" Digi asked.

Grandfather smiled. "It seems you are blessing us with your voice, Digiola."

"Because everyone else is acting like we are at a funeral."

Fade gasped, clutching her pearls. I stifled a laugh.

"Quiet, Ola," Maseso censured.

"But really, Bàbá. The king is still alive, and Bri has married. This should be a celebration. Break out the cake!" Her nose wrinkled. "Wait, you do not have cake from the reception left over, do you? If so, I will take some other dessert."

"Hear, hear," Lanre added.

I laughed, and Digi winked at me. She loved getting a rise out of everyone else. It was one reason she got along so well with Iris.

"I agree with Digi," Mori said. "This is definitely a celebration." He squeezed my hand.

Our palms had been pressed together since we'd sat down. I literally couldn't get enough of holding my husband's hand. His quiet affection unfurled something in my heart each time. I wanted to ask if he loved me but needed to ensure I could say it back when he did declare his feelings.

"I quite agree, ómọ ọmọ."

Tears filled my eyes. I loved that Grandfather thought of Mori as his grandchild as well. Mori tightened his fingers around mine.

Grandfather turned to Uncle Sijuwola. "Brother, let us celebrate our family and the new couple. Would you like to make a toast?"

I stared at my uncle, wondering what his response would be. He'd made it quite clear there was no love lost between us.

He tugged at the collar of his shirt. "Very well. I will toast."

Grandfather pointed a finger in the air, and champagne glasses were set before us. We took hold of the stems, raising them in the air.

Sijuwola cleared his throat. "Tomori, we welcome you to the Adebayo clan. We bless you with prosperity. May you and my . . . *niece* have a joyful marriage."

"Amen," Grandfather said.

"Amen," we repeated.

I nodded thanks to my uncle, but he avoided my gaze. Fortunately, the rest of the family had no problem filling the silence with conversation after that. It was like Uncle's toast had signaled to his son and daughter-in-law that all was well and he held no grudges. But the coldness in his eyes said otherwise.

As soon as Mori and I walked into our room after dinner, I turned to him. "We survived."

"We did."

He led me out onto the balcony. Yesterday he'd requested a chair big enough for both of us to sit on together, and an hour later, we had one. I leaned into his touch and let the cool breeze from the ocean caress my skin as I stared out into the night. I could barely make out the waves on the beach, but I could hear them. My other ear listened to Mori's steady heartbeat.

"I had a dream last night."

"What was it about?" I asked.

He tensed, and my nerve endings went on alert. "You were pregnant."

My mouth dropped. In the back of my mind, I knew kids were expected, even desired. No one who'd ever watched a royal couple through news articles and grocery magazines could escape that expectation. I recalled all the fertility prayers from the engagement party. Did Tomori expect us to have a child right away?

I gulped. "What happened?"

"We lost the baby." He blew out a breath as if he'd been holding in the tension all day.

Shock coursed through me, along with surprise at the sorrow that quickly followed. "Oh." I could hear the smallness in my voice.

Tomori pulled me closer. "I woke up with tears on my face."

"That's why you were up before me?"

"Mm-hmm."

"Why didn't you wake me? Talk to me about it?"

"I did not want you to think I was being odd, crying over a dream."

"Maybe I would have cried with you."

He stilled. "You do not think my dream strange? It saddens you too?"

I nodded but spoke even though he could feel my movement against his chest. "If I was to become pregnant, I know how much love I would have for our baby. I mean, obviously I don't know from experience, but I've heard the stories of that instant love women experience. I can only imagine the heartbreak of such a loss."

"Yes. That is what it felt like. Heartbreak . . . and regret."

I pulled away, studying his profile in the dark. I could make out the faint line of his eyelashes. "Why regret?"

"Because I realized I had refrained from telling you something important. Maybe if I had, it would have made things different in my dream."

"What haven't you said?"

He turned to me, his hands warming my face. Something he did often when he wanted to tell me something of worth. I looked into his eyes, waiting patiently for my husband to say whatever was troubling him.

"Brielle . . ."

I waited as his breath fanned against my face.

"Brielle, I love you."

My heart skipped a beat, then set a pace more suited for a marathon runner.

"I do not expect you to say it back. I know you may not be ready to hear this, but I cannot deny my feelings any longer. I do not want to. Not if being honest could keep us together, unlike in my dream." He sighed. "From the moment I saw you waiting before the plane, my heart recognized something in you. And every day I have known you, the feelings have only grown. Now I finally have the courage to voice what they are. Love." He slid a finger down my cheek. "I love everything about you, and I want to love you for years to come."

"Oh, Mori." I didn't say the words back, unsure if what I felt truly *was* love. Instead I pressed my lips to his, and a sort of desperation tinged his kiss.

He gentled his lips, then laid his forehead against mine. "Maybe we should wait to have kids?"

"Why? What happened in your dream after we lost the baby?" I murmured.

"We drifted apart until we resided in separate bedrooms. We never had another child. It was so . . . so . . . cold." His mouth turned downward.

"I don't want that," I whispered.

"Neither do I."

I studied his features. Could I say I loved him? There was no doubt that I had feelings for him. Was I ready to believe it was love, or was it merely guideposts toward the final destination? Was love why I hadn't been able to stop thinking about him when I was focused on the council's choices for a husband? Was love why my heart had pounded furiously when he'd proposed? Was love why I could lie in his arms at night and feel I was home?

What was love but a melding of two hearts into one? Or as Mori had phrased it, two becoming one.

"You know what?"

He pulled me closer. "What?"

I cupped his face, guiding it closer to mine. "I *do* love you, Tomori Eesuola."

"You are sure? I did not coerce you? These are not feelings of pity because of my dream?"

"Pity is not a feeling I've ever felt around you."

"How do you know? We are having a moment. Perhaps it has made you believe something that is not real."

"Mori," I breathed. "You are perfectly amazing. Every time I'm around you, I feel like I'm home."

Relief flooded his eyes, and his hands squeezed my waist. "I cannot believe how victorious I feel right now."

I chuckled. "I think we've both won."

"Definitely." He paused. "Promise me something."

"What's that?" I ran my hand against his beard, which was quickly growing back in. The roughness against my palm elicited shivers in my middle.

"That we will always talk to each other. Share a meal at the end of the day. Not let duty make us drift apart."

"That sounds doable."

"Yes, but I would not be surprised at how easy it will be to skip a day and justify the absence."

I sighed. "You're probably right. I promise."

"Now we must seal it."

"With a kiss?"

"Listen to you. Always thinking with your lips."

I chuckled. "Don't you love it?" Now that I felt the freedom of loving him in return, I wanted to see how many times I could mention it.

"Of course." He kissed me. "But something that will be our little thing. Like a secret."

"Something like a pinky promise?"

"No." He huffed. "I am a man. How about something better?"

"Then it should be a kiss. What's better?"

"How will this kiss be different from the others?"

I laughed. This conversation was ridiculous, but I hadn't felt this light since stepping foot on Ọlọrọ Ilé. "Maybe when we make a promise, we'll just look into each other's eyes and know that our yes means yes and our no means no, and a promise is just that."

"I like the way you think."

"Not love?"

He chuckled and looked deeply into my eyes. "Yes, love. I love you, Brielle Eesuola."

I loved hearing my name next to his. "I love you, Mr. Eesuola." I slid my arms around his neck and showed him just how much. Our kisses quickly heated. I pulled away, trailing kisses across his face. "Make me your wife, Mori."

He pulled back, his gaze searching mine. His eyes darkened, and he crushed me to him.

Neither one of us said a word for a very, *very* long time.

FORTY-NINE

Two weeks had passed since our wedding. Mori and I had settled into a new routine. We had breakfast together, went off to our individual royal duties, then made sure to have dinner together. Occasionally, I ate with Iris, and of course, there was the weekly family dinner.

Nothing compared to spending the evening with Mori. We could relax and be our true selves. We'd moved from the Psalms to Proverbs, continuing to pray together each night.

It was in the midst of our prayers that a knock sounded one evening.

I raised an eyebrow at Tomori, then motioned for him to stay seated. I threw on a silk robe and shuffled through the sitting room to the outer door. I opened it and froze.

The look on Mobo's face pierced me. Sorrow etched every feature, aging him in a way I'd never seen.

"No," I choked. "No, Mobo, please tell me it's not so."

"Your Majesty—"

A sob erupted, and I slapped a hand over my mouth.

Grandfather was dead.

I wasn't sure how I made it to his room or stood staring down at his still form. I had a vague recollection of Mori holding me up, of whispered condolences. The ache in my throat was so intense that my eyes pricked with tears from the pain. I gripped the edge of Grandfather's bedsheet. How could he really be gone?

"When?" I croaked.

"He passed five minutes ago," Dr. Falade answered in calm, measured tones. "I had Mr. Owusu call you as I tried to revive him."

I wanted to rail. Tell him to put some emotion into his voice. The king was dead. My grandfather was no longer with me. There was so much we hadn't done. So much we hadn't said. We hadn't even finished reading *The Lion, the Witch, and the Wardrobe.*

Tears spilled down my cheeks. "What now?"

"With your permission, we will move him to the morgue and begin preparing for his burial."

A sob rose up in my throat. "After that?" I couldn't look at the doctor. Couldn't tear my gaze from Grandfather's sleeping—*dead*—form.

"We will enter the mourning period, Your Majesty," Mobo answered.

I jolted at the title, eyes flying to his. Twice he'd called me that. It made me want to crawl out of my skin.

I shook my head. "Don't. I'm not . . ."

Mobo's brow furrowed. "Your Majesty, I know you are in shock, and I know it has not been ordained by the royal council, but you are now the ruler of Ọlọrọ Ilé. You need to have the PR team issue a statement. You need to alert the council so they can schedule your coronation after the mourning period as well as make a motion to assign you as interim ruler until your crowning. I promise I will help you every step of the way, Your Majesty."

I stared at him, too shocked to say anything.

"Please put all of those things into motion, Mr. Owusu," Tomori said. "Let me know if I can do anything to help as well." He moved to my side and curved an arm around my back.

I tensed. In the back of my mind, where reason existed, I recognized Mori was only trying to help, but the shattered part of me wanted everyone gone. I needed to be alone, to say good-bye without everyone waiting for me to step into a position I wasn't ready for.

"Please go," I whispered.

Tomori bent down. "All of us? Or . . ."

But I was already nodding.

"Gentlemen, let us continue this conversation in the sitting room."

My shoulders sagged in relief as the nurse, doctor, *everyone* left. The door clicked shut, and I let the first sob go free as I cried against my grandfather's chest. *Lord, why now? Why couldn't You have given me more time?*

Tear after tear fell until my eyes swelled and the waterworks stopped. My heart cracked wide with grief. Grandfather had tried to prepare me. I hadn't known how much I would love him and value his presence in my life. I straightened and dabbed at my face to wipe away the gritty feeling, but it was no use. My eyes began watering once more.

"Just why, God? Why?"

But even I knew that Grandfather had been tired of fighting. He'd told me repeatedly that he was ready. He wanted to see me married and know the country would be in good hands. My time with him was spent.

"I love you, Grandfather. I'm so very glad you reached out and called me, even if it took a death sentence for you to do so." I paused. "I pray I make you proud."

At the wedding reception, Grandfather had assured me he was already proud. However, I couldn't help but worry about how he would view me as a queen. Getting to know my grandfather had been a twofold blessing—a chance to learn who my father was and an opportunity to love the man who had a hand in both of our lives. I couldn't trust the rest of the Adebayos to share that level of love. Uncle Sijuwola probably hated my guts.

I squeezed my eyes shut. How would he react? Would he demand another meeting with the council and ask for the seat of power? *Lord, how am I going to get through this? How can I lead without Grandfather showing me the ropes?*

Unfortunately, I had no choice. Not that I didn't want to rule. I'd accepted my role and knew it was God's will. But today the task seemed too much to ask of me. How could I tell the people that the king was dead and take up his mantle?

I'm not worthy, Lord. I cannot fill his shoes, so I ask for grace. I ask for mercy as I find my way and try to rule these people You have placed in my life. Please give me the wisdom I need and the strength to walk out of this room.

Dr. Falade—and, most likely, Mori—wouldn't let me hole up in Grandfather's room all day. I didn't remember all the rules of mourning, but I knew getting the burial ready and allowing the black flag of death to fly was necessary.

Did I own any black clothing? I shook my head at the thought.

"Grandfather, I don't want to say good-bye." I swallowed around the ache in my throat. "So instead, I'll say 'see you when the trumpet sounds.'"

I twisted away and fled from his still form before I broke down and sobbed all over again, hindering my ability to walk away with dignity. I opened the sitting room door, and the occupants jumped up at my arrival.

Tomori stepped forward, his gaze roaming my face. He reached for my hands. "Are you all right?"

I shrugged. I didn't want to answer only to have the waterworks start up again. "What's the plan?" My voice cracked, the ache in my throat intensifying.

"Mobo wrote a statement from us as the royal family. I viewed it, and then he sent it to the PR team. The extended family has been notified. A palace runner is seeing to the black flag." Tomori sighed. "I had someone tell Iris. She is waiting for you in our room."

I nodded.

"Do you want me to call your mom?"

"Yes." My bottom lip trembled, and I slid my arms around him, pressing my face into his shirt as tears fell once more. Tomori rubbed his hands up and down my back, murmuring nonsense that was nonetheless soothing. I sank into his arms, thankful I didn't have to be strong right now.

"Let us go to our room, okay?"

I nodded, then stilled myself, pulling back. He placed a handkerchief in my hand, and I stared at it in surprise. "Where did this come from?"

"My mother made them as a wedding gift. I have been carrying them so that when she asks me if I am using them, I can say they are always with me." He shrugged. "I would use my sleeve if I needed something, but that does not seem princely."

I choked out a laugh. "It doesn't, does it?"

He ran a thumb down my cheek. "Wipe your face," he murmured.

"All right." I did as he suggested and followed him out of Grandfather's quarters.

We held hands as we walked to our room, and I squeezed his fingers like my life depended on the strength he had to offer.

When we walked through our sitting room, Iris rushed toward me and enveloped me in her arms. The tears flowed freely, and I didn't even bother to stop them as we swayed.

Death's sting wasn't a fleeting poke to the heart, but a scar that left an imprint on the soul. I would never be the same again, and if that meant I would hold on to the memories I'd made with my grandfather all the tighter, then so be it.

FIFTY

I sat in Grandfather's old council seat as Ms. Keita went over the order of business and the petitions the people had brought to their tribal elders. My face remained neutral as memories of the funeral pushed against my present, beckoning me to remember the somber quiet that had filled the chapel. How the pastor had lamented Grandfather's passing, extolling his accomplishments and the blessing of his rule. How I'd stared straight ahead, eyes locked on the pastor so they wouldn't drift to the open casket as I gripped one of Tomori's handkerchiefs in my palm while the other hand rested in his.

My whole family had been there—not just the Adebayo clan, but Mom and my in-laws as well. The city had filled with citizens from other parts of the country as they came to mourn the loss of a great king. Even the drums had beat a somber rhythm as the casket paraded down the streets to the royal cemetery. Hundreds of people followed, all wearing the kingdom's colors.

At the end of the procession, Tomori and I had stood by Grandfather's grave until the workers placed the last scoop of dirt onto his casket. When they'd finally left, bowing as they went, I'd let my tears break free in the arms of my husband. He'd been a saint, dealing with my crying jags. More than that, he'd been a comfort. His love made the loss of Grandfather and the expectations of being interim ruler bearable.

The council had voted unanimously for me to be interim ruler and scheduled my coronation for after the mourning period. Now I sat in Grandfather's seat, wondering how I'd ever fill the throne and rule as he had.

I tried to focus as Ms. Keita got to Iris's request to come before the council and explain what she wanted to do for the people of Ọlọrọ, specifically the women from impoverished areas. Iris had toured the entire island to see if only one district dealt with poverty or if others could benefit from her ideas.

After Ms. Keita finished reading the list, she proposed we start with the Opolopo region. Mr. Ladipo objected as usual, and Mr. Oladele kept a cool head. Mr. Ibrahim proposed we start with Iris, knowing her request was the most extensive and would require a lot of back and forth.

The guard opened the doors, and my friend strolled in. She wore a printed V-neck dress that stopped below her knee. The golds and reds in her dress made her skin glow, and her hair hung down with all her curls out in full glory. She exuded confidence, and I prayed she felt capable as well.

"Ms. Blakely, please explain to us why you are here," Mr. Oladele requested. Her nationality meant she warranted an audience with the council, since she didn't belong to any of the districts.

"I'm Iris Blakely, and I came to Ọlọrọ Ilé in June with Her Majesty Brielle Adebayo." Her eyes darted to mine then back to Mr. Oladele. "During one of our outings, I fell in love with the beautiful beadwork and different wares the women sold. When the princess's bodyguard explained the plight of some of the poorer citizens in the area, it got me thinking."

She paused, and I sent up a prayer that the council would hear her and believe in what she wanted to do. Iris hadn't told me much, wanting to work on her own and not stand on my name. Still, anything that could help the country was a good thing, right?

"After much prayer, I was inspired to establish an organization that would help the impoverished citizens of Ọlọrọ start their own businesses. I modeled the idea after other nonprofits on the mainland. The company will enable Ọlọrans to bring in funds to provide for themselves and their families. The organization would also benefit the country, as Ọlọrọ Ilé would gain an opportunity to trade with the rest of the world. My research has shown you only trade with France and other African countries. You have some of the best textiles, which the rest of the world would love to have access to. I'm petitioning a request to start up this organization and help the less fortunate of Ọlọrọ Ilé."

"Do you have a business plan, Ms. Blakely?" Mr. Ladipo smirked.

Seriously, could he speak without condescension dripping from his words?

"Yes, sir." She presented a pack of papers bound together with a clear overlay.

Mr. Oladele motioned, and a palace worker moved forward from the shadows, retrieved the paperwork, then placed it before Mr. Ladipo. He peered down, a stunned look on his face. When had Iris prepared that? I wanted to cheer her for effectively shutting him up.

"Ms. Blakely," said Mr. Oladele, "the council will review your business plan, then let you know its decision once it has been made."

"Thank you for your consideration." She bowed and left.

I wanted to clap and yell *well done*, but I remained mute. As soon as the council doors closed, Mr. Ladipo began talking.

"This business plan is actually pretty good," he said grudgingly. He turned to me. "Did you assist Ms. Blakely, Your Majesty?"

I hid a wince at the title. "I didn't, Mr. Ladipo. I had no idea she'd made one until you asked it of her."

He nodded, his eyes appraising me as if searching for the truth.

"Did you read it all, Yemi?" Ms. Keita asked him.

"Of course not. I merely skimmed through the document. She has a business name, a proposal if we wish the business to be nonprofit, and a proposal if we wish for the organization to be an individual business. I am . . . surprised."

So was I, but I hated having anything in common with Mr. Ladipo.

"Pass it along, please," Ms. Keita said.

Mr. Ladipo handed her the proposal. "Your Majesty, what do you think of her endeavor?"

I stared at him, barely concealing my shock. He actually wanted my opinion? Was this some trick? Maybe in a strange way he was grieving Grandfather's death, and this was how he handled it.

"I think it would be wonderful for the people and country as a whole. I know other countries have similar avenues in place for nonprofit organizations. It helps ensure those funds go straight to those who seek help. Running it as a business has its benefits to the country, but I'd have to read her proposal to see if the women still get most of the profits."

Grandfather would have loved this idea. I sniffed back tears.

"Do you need a tissue, Your Majesty?" Mr. Ibrahim asked.

I shook my head. "No, thank you." I lifted my gaze and caught a concerned expression on Mr. Ladipo's face. Was he truly worried?

"I cannot disagree that a worldwide trade in textiles would be a boon to our economy," Ms. Keita said.

"I agree," Mr. Oladele said. "Do you think Ms. Blakely wants to be the owner of the company if we choose to make it a business?"

I hesitated. "She is American. Wouldn't there be a conflict of interest, especially considering she works in the textile business there?"

"Hmm." Mr. Oladele stared off in thought. "That is something we need to consider."

"What if Ms. Blakely is a consultant and in charge of the hiring process?" Ms. Keita asked. "We could put someone else at the helm. Surely we could also locate a building that can be used for the venture. The women will sell their wares and get paid accordingly."

That was something to think about. Still, I wasn't sure how Iris would feel about their suggestion. Was her concern strictly to help the ladies, or did she want to run the business? I really needed to view the proposal.

"Your Majesty, what do you think?" Jomi Oladele asked.

"I think this is an issue that we need to table until we've all had a chance to read the business proposal and discuss how it could or could not benefit Ọlọrọ. We can go through the rest of the items on docket until then," I stated.

"All agreed?" Mr. Oladele asked.

Each council member held up a hand.

"We will table the conversation until we have all read the business plans." Mr. Oladele motioned for a runner. "Please see that a copy is made for each council member."

"Right away, alàgbà tribu." The runner took the business plan and left the room.

Before breaking for the day, we managed to get through half of the list. We adjourned, planning to reconvene tomorrow. I took the day's paperwork and left the council chambers for my suite. My stomach growled as my heels clicked along the marble tiles.

My chambers were empty, and the quiet beckoned me like a warm afghan. I slipped off my heels, then picked them up and padded across the floor toward the closet. I stopped abruptly. The balcony doors were open. Hadn't they been closed this morning? I'd been the last to leave the bedroom, and shutting them was usually my last action. Maybe Mori had come back during lunch or something and forgotten to close them again. That was probably it.

I closed the French doors, then placed the photocopy of Iris's plan on my nightstand. An envelope lay there, waiting for me. It couldn't be another. . . .

I tore it open, unfolding the paper.

It is time for you to declare your incompetence. Someone more capable, worthier, can be declared ruler.

Who was this? Maybe I should talk to my uncle face-to-face and demand answers. First, I needed to contact security.

I peered down at my bare feet, remembering I hadn't put my heels away. I opened the door to my walk-in closet and shrieked.

Clothes were strewn about, and some had even been cut up. My breath came in short bursts. A commotion sounded in the other room.

"Your Majesty!"

"In my closet, Azu." I placed a hand on my heart, backing out slowly.

Azuka appeared at my side, his gun drawn. "What happened? Did you see a rodent? A bug?"

I shook my head. "Someone's been in my closet." I moved out of the way.

He stepped forward, then froze, muttering what sounded like a curse under his breath. He met my gaze. "I need to clear the room."

"Of course."

I eyed the gun in his hand. Had he carried one each time he'd been on duty? Handguns were illegal for everyday Olọran citizens, but Azu *was* security, so that made sense.

I stayed out of his way as he cleared the closets and bathroom then came to me. "Is anything else amiss?" he asked.

"The balcony doors were open, and another note was waiting for me."

He held out a hand, and I passed the envelope and its contents over. His eyes went back and forth like a typewriter, his lips flattening.

He pressed the Bluetooth in his ear. "Princess Brielle's closet was ransacked and a note left. No . . . okay . . . will do. Yes, sir." He straightened to his full height. "Your Majesty, I need to take you somewhere else. Merrick is grabbing the prince and alerting the appropriate staff members of the issue. We will take you to a safe room."

A safe room? I stood there, stunned, until Azuka motioned for me to follow him. I let him lead me to safety, too numb to question anything.

FIFTY-ONE

I'd gotten complacent. When I'd first received a note, I'd been nervous, a little wary, but Grandfather and security had assured me that my safety was their highest concern. Add to that the fact that the letters hadn't threatened bodily harm, and I had adopted a blasé attitude.

How wrong and *stupid* I'd been to think that.

Now I sat in a safe room in the palace. *Alone.*

Azuka said having Tomori with me would go against safety protocols, which, logically, I understood. You couldn't have two members of the royal family shelter together, because what if the room were breached? But alone, my mind had nothing to do but spin other possibilities.

Who wanted me gone?

Uncle Sijuwola was an obvious suspect. He'd hated me on sight. Should I add cousin Maseso to the list? He barely spoke two words to me, but he mimicked his father's actions. Which meant he could be the instigator if Uncle had put him up to it.

I sighed. What if it was someone else? Who else could be named king or queen? I bit my lip. Mobo had taught me about throne succession, and only family could inherit. Was I missing some obscure decree that enabled someone else to take the throne? If so, my money was on Yemi Ladipo, the one council member who'd made my life miserable. If someone wanted me to declare myself unfit, then he and Uncle Sijuwola were the obvious choices. I needed to ensure security looked into Mr. Ladipo's whereabouts or find out if a palace runner was being paid to do his dirty work.

I groaned and rubbed my forehead. Azu hadn't allowed me to bring my cell phone—afraid someone could track my location—and now I had no way to keep track of the time. All that was left for me to do was agonize over every single *what-if* I could think of.

Lord, what's going on out there? What do I do? Is this personal or merely political?

Enough, Bri! Going down the *what-if* buffet line wouldn't reveal any clues. I stood and paced the small room, wishing there were *something* in here to occupy my time. Why didn't they store any games? I needed a way to waste time and keep myself from following every rabbit trail. Why wasn't one of the guards in here? Then again, maybe they were outside to prevent entry. Wait, that made no sense because my location was supposed to be secret.

Maybe the guards were in on it. Whatever *it* was.

"Ahhh," I whisper-screamed. "What is going on?"

The door opened, and I jumped.

Azuka entered. "Your Majesty, the palace has been cleared. It does not appear that anyone has entered or left who does not have authorized access."

Okay, that told me absolutely nothing. I stared at him, waiting for him to continue.

"Your office and other places you visit have been searched." He stopped, eyes looking everywhere but at me.

"And? What did you find?"

He swallowed. "Just a note in your office. Security has it."

I didn't want to know what it said. "Is that all?"

"The head of security plans to interview all palace staff."

"What about council members or . . ." I took a deep breath. "Or Sijuwola and his family?"

Azu studied my face. "Nonso believes it is an inside job and will be working tirelessly to find out who exactly is behind it."

"But he has no clue right now?"

Azu shook his head.

I studied my bodyguard. I liked to think we'd developed a good working relationship. That this was more than a job to him, and that this meant he'd be honest with me. "Azu, should I be worried? Do you think my life is in danger?"

"You should be vigilant, Your Majesty."

Was that his genuine answer or a pat response? I sighed. "Where's my husband?"

"The prince is being debriefed by his guard. We are waiting for the all clear from security before you can return to your chambers."

Ugh. I flopped onto the only chair in the safe room. "Who am I supposed to trust?" I muttered into my hands.

"God."

I snorted. "That I can agree with." I frowned and looked up at Azu. "Not you?"

He rolled his eyes. "I figured I was a given. Think of all the long drives I have taken you on. If I wanted to hurt you or take part in some master plan, I had plenty of opportunity. Besides, my honor cannot be bought."

The sentiment was admirable, but caution told me not to jump up and hug him for his self-proclaimed loyalty. I would trust God and pray He showed me who my enemy was.

Another half hour passed until finally, Azu let me out of the box. I could return to my suite. We strolled down the hall, Azu maintaining a brisk pace. Perhaps for safety's sake?

"Brielle!"

I whirled at the panic in Tomori's voice. He ran down the hall, leaving his guards scrambling to catch up. The earnestness in his expression coupled with the very real fear I'd heard in his voice had me sprinting toward him. We met in the middle, and he crushed me to him.

"You are okay?" he whispered.

I nodded against his chest, thankful that I didn't have to let go of him. "Are you?"

"I am now."

My grip tightened around his waist.

336

"Your Majesty, Your Highness, let us continue to your room," Azu interrupted.

I wanted to tell him to go away, but instead I held on to Mori's waist and walked alongside him. He matched my step so we could walk in tandem.

Azu cleared the room once more, then paused on the way out. "Please make sure you two remain vigilant until security deems the threat eradicated."

My mouth dried. *Threat?* Just hearing the word made everything that much more real.

"A guard will be with you at all times. We will not come into your bedchamber or en suite unless we hear a noise that makes us think you are in peril. Otherwise, one or two guards will be outside your room as usual. You will be escorted everywhere, even within the palace."

I wasn't sure how Azu could become more of a shadow than he already was, but I nodded. Tomori thanked him.

Then we were alone. I sagged against Tomori. "Longest day ever," I groused.

Mori scooped me up and settled me on his lap as he sank onto the sofa. "I agree. It was torture being without you for so long. Not to mention that safe room was not meant for a man over six feet tall."

I chuckled. "Or someone over five feet. Seriously, they need to add board games or something."

"A deck of cards for solitaire?"

I laughed. "Peanuts to snack on and a notepad to make a list of things to do once you escape."

"A walkie-talkie to find out how everyone else fares in their safe rooms."

"Yes!"

"Does that mean I win?"

I laughed outright and peered into his face. "I didn't realize this was a contest."

"I just wanted to hear you laugh." He ran a finger down my cheek. "Are you sure you are all right?"

I shrugged. "I don't know what clothes are ruined. I'm sure I'll cry if any favorites are beyond repair." A shudder went up my spine. "They told you about the notes, the one in my office too?"

"Yes." He frowned. "Who do you believe is behind this?"

"It has to be a family member, right?" I ran a hand down his shirt. "Did you ever hear anything when you were a runner? Did someone ever complain about me?"

"No. Some staff were surprised a woman had been named heir, but not to the point of this."

"Maybe someone's a good actor," I muttered.

"The guards will figure this out. God will show them the way."

"I hope so."

"We will pray so."

I sighed and laid my head on his chest. "Thank you."

"It is what I am here for."

Certainly a blessing and silver lining. I stayed in his arms until I slowly drifted off to sleep.

FIFTY-TWO

Azu had asked for me and Tomori not to say a word about the incident, and I assumed he'd had the same talk with the cleaning staff. We agreed to keep mute, which was why I said nothing as Lola Keita read the list of items up for deliberation on the second day of the council session.

Last night, I'd shown Iris's business proposal to Tomori, and he'd agreed to read it. I valued his opinion on what we should do, although the council might not need my input if it reached a decision. Hopefully the other members hadn't finished reviewing the proposal, because I hadn't. Business proposals were not light reading, and I'd been preoccupied with all that had unfurled.

Iris offered to make me a new wardrobe and replace the items that had been ruined. I'd made the decision not to inform my mother. She couldn't do much back in New York.

I tuned back in when Ms. Keita asked me a question.

The council members discussed issue after issue, took a break for lunch, then reconvened once more. Finally, Mr. Oladele concluded the day after Ms. Keita reminded us of the items left for review tomorrow. One more day to read Iris's full proposal.

I needed a crash course in business and African nonprofits. Perhaps Mobo could point me in the right direction. *Wait a minute.* He'd mentioned that Grandfather kept binders full of information in his office. I was still using my old office while I waited for the mourning period to end before switching to Grandfather's. I did a U-turn in the hall, the guards keeping up with my movements in silence.

The black door stood resolute at the end of the hallway. My breathing shallowed as I neared. After staring at the doorknob for far longer than necessary, I twisted it open. A hint of leather and musk greeted me, and tears sprang to my eyes. I leaned against the doorjamb, staring at Grandfather's empty chair. How was he really not here with me?

Even after a month, there were days I couldn't believe he'd been buried. Couldn't stop myself from knocking on his bedroom door to read the next chapter of *The Lion, the Witch, and the Wardrobe*. From making a note to tell him a joke, only to remember he wasn't here. I couldn't even sit in his chair at the family dining table and had completely rearranged the seating so that no one would.

Eventually, I'd have to clear his office, his bedroom, and other places where he'd left his mark. For now, I just couldn't. I cleared my throat and rushed over to the bookshelf, scanning the spines. I knew enough Oninan words to figure out which binder would be the most helpful. I might need Tomori to read the contents if I couldn't muddle my way through or use an online translator.

After I grabbed the necessary binders, the guards escorted me to the royal corridor. Azu entered my room to clear it. After a few minutes, he came out looking disgruntled.

"Please don't tell me the rest of my clothes have been shredded." Or maybe there was simply another note.

Azu shook his head. "No, Your Majesty. Your bedding has been slashed."

I gaped at him.

"Was there another note?" Merrick asked.

Azu held up a slip of paper. "It simply says 'Imposter.'"

"This is ridiculous. Why doesn't Nonso have any leads yet?" I paced back and forth, not expecting anyone to answer. I halted at the sound of running footsteps.

"What happened?" Tomori asked, out of breath.

Judging by the guards jogging behind him, he'd sprinted down the hall. He tugged me to him, eyes roaming my face.

Azu cleared his throat. "I was just telling Her Majesty that someone . . . um . . . ripped your linen."

"You cannot be serious," Tomori said. "Who keeps gaining access to our room? I thought everyone who entered would be escorted by a guard."

"That is what Nonso assured," Azu replied.

"Then is someone paying the guards to look the other way?" Tomori asked.

I straightened, watching Azu's and Merrick's faces. Azuka looked troubled, and Merrick was clearly irritated.

"We made a pledge to the crown. How could you suggest one of us could be crooked?" Merrick asked.

Tomori scoffed. "As if there is no such thing."

I placed a hand on Mori's chest, feeling his heart pump. "It will be fine, Mori," I said. But I needed to address his concerns. "Merrick, I'm sure you can understand how we feel. You put measures in place to keep our chambers secure only for someone to walk in like they have carte blanche. If everyone who enters our room is being escorted by a guard, what conclusions are we supposed to draw? We're not accusing you personally, unless you can be in more than one place."

Merrick's chest heaved, and he rubbed his chin. "I apologize, Your Majesty. Your Highness." He nodded at Tomori.

"Apology accepted," Tomori said.

I sighed. "Can someone check if my old guestroom is able to be used? I'd like to relax before dinner, and I have a bunch of reading to do tonight."

One of Tomori's guards accepted the assignment. Azu stepped aside to talk to Nonso via his Bluetooth.

"Can they check the cameras?" I asked Merrick.

"Yes, Azu is probably having them do so now."

There were no cameras inside our suite, but they'd installed cameras in this hall late yesterday. Hopefully the perpetrator didn't know that, but at this point, it seemed he was one step ahead of us.

Tomori and I waited in the hall for someone to tell us what we could do next as all the guards worked on different assignments.

Merrick stepped up to us. "Your Majesty, perhaps the two of you should pack clothes and whatever you will need."

"All right." Tomori threaded his fingers with mine and led me into our room. "Do not look at the bed," he murmured.

But my gaze had already turned to the torn comforter. Pillow stuffing littered the bed and the floor. How could I return to this room after the staff cleaned up the vandalism?

I went straight into my closet and pulled down a suitcase to fill with the few business outfits I had remaining. Pajamas and other essential items went next. Item after item got tossed in.

"Brielle, are you done?"

"Yes." I zipped up my luggage. "You?"

He held up his suitcase as if it were filled with bubble wrap. "I am." Who knew my husband was so strong? Heat filled my cheeks, and a knowing look entered his eyes. He leaned forward, placing a kiss softly on my lips. "Keep that thought for later."

I smiled. "I will."

"Good." He winked. "Let us go."

Azu and Merrick bookended Tomori and me as we went to the guest corridor. Tomori's guards waited outside the room I'd stayed in upon arrival. They confirmed no one had entered since they'd cleared the room.

As soon as we were alone, I kicked off my shoes and sat on the edge of the bed.

The mattress dipped, and Mori reached for my hand. "Want to talk about it?"

"Not really. Do you?"

"No." He threaded his fingers through mine. "I am glad you were not alone."

"The shadows won't let me be."

He squeezed my hand. "Promise me you will follow your guards' directions. That you will stick by their side."

I tilted my head to gaze into my husband's eyes. "What has you so worried?"

"The fact that no one saw the guy who did this on camera." His brow furrowed. "That they were able to do this even after security was increased. I do not like it, Brielle. This person holds a lot of rage. Who knows how it will erupt."

I hated the truth of his words. "I promise. I'll follow their instructions." I tucked myself into the crook of his arm. My tension drained as his unique scent enveloped my senses. I nuzzled my face into the curve of his neck.

"You're the best part of the day," I whispered.

He stilled, then turned, scooping me closer. "And I thought your ice cream raids were your favorite."

"You know, I do believe I love you more than ice cream."

"I am honored." His voice rumbled with amusement. "Shall we stay like this a little while longer or head to the dining room?"

"I just want to be Mori and Bri. Is that okay?"

Tomori kissed the top of my head. "For a bit."

FIFTY-THREE

A nonprofit would be the best," Mr. Ibrahim argued, using his index finger to emphasize his statement. "It would keep the mission free from corruption and help our people."

I wanted to applaud his impassioned plea. He'd never spoken so much at a council meeting.

"You dare suggest that a business would be corrupt?" Mr. Ladipo sneered.

Now I wanted to give myself a round of applause for not rolling my eyes at Mr. Ladipo's typical derision.

"I did not say that," Mr. Ibrahim said. "However, you have to admit things can become corrupt in the wrong hands."

Mr. Ladipo gasped. "Wrong hands—"

"Cool it, Yemi," Mr. Oladele interrupted. "You know what Jamal means. Nonprofits have a way of keeping their focus without becoming politicized."

"Yes, but greed still exists in the nonprofit circles," Ms. Keita tacked on.

"Of course. You cannot escape greed as long as man wishes to part from God's will," Mr. Oladele stated. "Though that is neither here nor there. We must decide what course of action to take. Ms. Blakely is the only one who remains on our docket." He rubbed his face. "I miss my wife."

"Please. You go home and see her every night," Mr. Ladipo groused.

"Just to sleep in my bed after the drive," Mr. Oladele countered.

"I believe I have a suggestion, if you are open to hearing it," I interrupted smoothly.

"Please, Your Majesty," Mr. Ibrahim offered.

"Why not approve it as a business?" Mori and I had decided that was the better idea in the late hours of the night. "Ms. Blakely can oversee the company—if you wish—hire the women to create the merchandise, and then those goods can be exported. Since her company would be an Olóran business, it would be subject to the country's taxes and hiring laws. Jobs will be created, poverty will diminish in the target areas, and our government will get a piece of the pie, so everyone will be happy. Not to mention the business laws that keep companies in check."

Did Iris actually want to run a business as opposed to a non-profit? I hadn't talked to her about it, knowing the council was reviewing this. She understood, so we kept our conversations to the whodunit variety. Iris thought Maseso was behind the notes to get in Sijuwola's good graces. The idea had merit.

Silence descended as the elders ruminated over my suggestion. I waited for them to spout objections or bicker as they generally did, but not a single person opened their mouth. Tomori and I had pored over the binders from Grandfather's office. I'd tried to read them but eventually gave up and let him translate. There'd been so much information, and my Onina was nowhere near fluent.

"Mr. Oladele, your thoughts?" I asked.

"Well, Your Majesty," he started slowly, "I am thinking of any loopholes or issues this could cause. Yet I cannot find one."

"Surely you can," Mr. Ladipo jumped in. "We cannot allow *her* friend to run a business here and then do who knows *what* back in the States."

"We can certainly make a stipulation upon granting Ms. Blakely's request," Ms. Keita stated. "If we do not want her working for anyone in the States or running a business back there, we will make that a condition of approval. We could even require that at least one Oloran sit on the board of the business. This is not an issue, Yemi."

The others nodded in thought.

"I think this situation reeks of Her Majesty's influence," Mr. Ladipo suggested.

I held my tongue, waiting to see what everyone else would say before I put him in his place.

Ms. Keita huffed. "Think logically, Yemi."

"I have no objections, and I am favorable to the condition," Mr. Ibrahim said. "It only makes sense."

"Then we will grant her a yearly work visa?" Mr. Oladele asked.

"Come now," Mr. Ladipo cajoled. "Your Majesty, you would have us believe that you did not give *any* advice to your friend? Your *best* friend who flew all this way to aid you?"

I raised an eyebrow. "That's correct, *Mr.* Ladipo. While Iris was writing up this plan, *I* was planning a wedding, mourning my grandfather, then running a country. You know, everyday things that leave me *no* time to write a business plan of this magnitude. I barely finished reading it last night." I snapped my jaw shut. I hadn't meant to admit that out loud.

Ms. Keita laughed. "I guess that answers your question, Yemi."

He rolled his eyes.

"A vote then," Mr. Oladele suggested. "All in favor of granting Ms. Blakely the ability to start a business in Oloro as outlined in her proposal, say aye."

Mr. Oladele, Mr. Ibrahim, and Ms. Keita chorused *aye*. They turned to look at Mr. Ladipo. "Aye," he snarled.

"All in favor of granting her a yearly visa to conduct said business?"

They all said *aye*.

"And all those in favor of the condition to ensure she does not operate a business in the States that would conflict with this one as long as she runs it?"

Once more, they all moved in favor. I squealed inwardly, excited that Iris would be staying in Oloro. That is, if she agreed to the council's terms.

Mr. Oladele called for a runner to let Ms. Blakely into the council chambers so we could inform her of the decision. Soon she walked through the double doors and stopped before the council table. I kept my hands in my lap so I wouldn't give anything away. I really wanted to stand and applaud her, but I would exercise all royal decorum.

"Ms. Iris Blakely, the council has reviewed your request, and after much deliberation, we have denied your request to create a nonprofit."

Her shoulders dropped, and I wanted to roll my eyes at Mr. Oladele's dramatics. Although, I did understand the need to go in order for the stenographer's notes.

"However," he continued, "we are open to your proposal to create a business."

Iris's eyes widened.

"Ms. Keita, please inform Ms. Blakely of her choices."

"Ms. Blakely, if you so choose, the council will grant you leave to start a business in Ọlọrọ and hire men and women who wish to participate in your textile business, exporting Ọlọran goods to the world. You will be granted a yearly visa as long as you live here and oversee the business. However, there is a condition. You will not be allowed to work for or run a business in the United States or any other country that would be in direct competition with the Ọlọran business. We also require that an Ọlọran sit on the board of your business. You may state your choice now or notify the council within two business days of your acceptance or refusal."

"Yes!" she shrieked.

I bit back a laugh, staring down at my hands to hold my amusement in.

"My apologies," Iris said more calmly. "Yes. I would love to start a business here, and I agree to the conditions."

"Very well, Ms. Blakely," Mr. Oladele said. "We will ensure paperwork for your visa gets to the office. We will also have a secretary draw up the rest of the files you will need and submit them to you. And if I may . . ."

"Yes?"

"It might be time to get yourself your own place."

I stared at Mr. Oladele, who winked at me.

"You are dismissed, Ms. Blakely," Ms. Keita said.

"Thank you."

She walked out, and I let out a pent-up breath. We would have a lot to discuss later. That is, if another surprise did not await me in my own chambers.

Mr. Oladele adjourned the meeting, and I raced to Iris's room, Azu barking at me to slow down every few steps. But I paid no heed and knocked on Iris's door. She opened it and promptly threw her arms around me.

"I can't believe it. My own business!" She pulled away, wincing as she saw my face. "I didn't mean to shriek."

"Huh?" I cupped my ear, exaggerating my deafness. My ear was hearing a high-pitched ring.

She laughed. "I can't believe it. I'm so excited. I have so many questions. I need to find a location. I need to find staff. I can't wait to hire people!" She sank into a chair, her eyes widening. "Oh my goodness, how can I run a business? I can't run a business. What was I thinking? James is going to *flip* when I turn in my notice."

"Breathe, girl. You run his business, so of course you can run your own."

She grinned. "You're *so* right. Why was I even worried?"

"I don't know, but I think it's my turn to tell you 'one step at a time.'"

"Ha!"

We grinned at one another.

"Will you go with me to look at commercial properties?" she asked.

"If I can. I'll check my schedule and see if I can pencil in free time to go with you."

She rubbed her hands together. "Yes! So awesome."

"You get to stay!" I cheered.

"I know. That's the reason I didn't even hesitate." She bit her lip. "Am I being impulsive? Should I have taken the time to think about the council's stipulations?"

I studied Iris. She'd let her hair down and thrown on leggings and a tank top. "I assume you prayed a lot before you even requested petition before the council."

"I did! I just couldn't shake those poor women and the lack of help they seem to get."

"And did you think maybe this was what God was preparing you for? You did mention He'd been working on your heart."

Her head bobbed up and down.

"Then I think you know the answer."

She grinned. "Thanks, girl." She paused. "Do I need a new place to live?" she asked hesitantly.

"There's no rush."

She rolled her eyes. "It's not like we see each other much in this place anyway. Well, not since you tied the knot."

My face heated as I remembered lying in Mori's arms last night.

"I don't even want to know." She waved a hand in the air.

I laughed and settled into a chair as we caught up and enjoyed our girl time.

FIFTY-FOUR

Dayo escorted Uncle Sijuwola into my office, and I stood to greet him.

"Thank you for coming."

"Yes, well, you did say it was important." He sat down, crossing his ankle over his knee.

I settled into my own chair. "It is. I promise."

"Well, what is it?"

Lord, please give me the words. Grant me patience and remind me to be respectful. Amen. I cleared my throat. "Uncle, have you been sending me notes?"

"What?" He squinted, his eyes like black beads.

"I've been receiving letters of a . . . threatening nature. They question the legitimacy of my rule and urge me to declare myself unfit."

Sijuwola's mouth dropped. "And what, you think I am the one?"

"You've made it quite clear how you feel about me."

He sputtered, and a torrent of Onina fell from his lips. His speech flew fast, and my ears couldn't keep up. I had no idea what he said.

I held up a hand. "English, please."

"I cannot believe you would think this of me. No, I did not agree with Tiwa's decision, but I would *never* threaten you. You are my grandniece, after all."

Funny how he wanted to claim familial ties now. Still, he seemed sincere, as far as I could tell. I wasn't an expert in detecting lies, but my gut was silent and, dare I say, my spirit?

"If not you, who? Would Maseso do this?"

Uncle laughed, slapping at his knee. "Maseso would not hurt a fly."

"Then would he hire someone to be a flyswatter?"

His head tilted, and his face grew grim.

My stomach tightened. He knew something. I could feel it with every alert nerve ending. "What is it? *Who* is it?"

He rubbed his chin. "Fade has always expected the reign to pass to Maseso. Maybe this is her way of ensuring it happens? Get you to go back to the States?" He shrugged as if he couldn't yet decide if this was a viable option.

"Digi's mom?" I gripped my desk, thinking over every interaction with her. "She doesn't seem malicious, just a little . . ." What? Fade snubbed me at every turn yet still let Digi hang out with me. So she couldn't be that bad, could she?

"Do you want me to talk to her?" Uncle asked.

"No, please don't. I'll reach out to her."

Sijuwola rose to his feet. He studied me, then cleared his throat. "How long have you been receiving them?"

"Since the council approved me as princess."

A look I couldn't quite decipher filled his face. If I didn't know better, I'd think it was regret.

"*Ẹ má bínú sí mi.*"

I blinked. He was sorry?

Taking my silence as answer enough, he opened the door.

I shot to my feet. "Uncle, I forgive you."

"Thank you."

He left, and I popped my knuckles as I walked around my office. Sijuwola had been sincere, which meant I couldn't keep him on my list of suspects. I had never thought that Fade might be an issue. Should I add Digi or some other Adebayo to the list?

No. Digi had been wonderful since I'd met her. She was a sweetheart, and I couldn't see her stooping to this. She'd been so happy to see a woman rise to power. Maybe I should just talk to Fade and see if all of this could be resolved.

A rap of knuckles interrupted my thoughts.

"Come in." I whirled to face the door and smiled when Dayo stepped through it. "Do I have another appointment?"

Most of the journalist interviews had been rescheduled to account for our mourning period, and Tomori had been moved off my schedule now that we could study Onina whenever we wished. I'd contemplated leaving him as my standing afternoon appointment just so I could see him before dinner, but Mobo had him on a strict schedule.

"No, you do not, Your Majesty." Dayo's gaze flitted to mine. "I wish to talk to you."

"Oh, of course." I motioned toward the chairs before my desk. "Is everything okay?"

Dayo clasped her hands together, resting them on her knee. "No."

"Are you ill?" My heart pounded. I wondered if that would always be my first thought.

"Not in the physical sense." She placed a hand over her chest. "I am sick at heart."

"What is it?"

She scrutinized me. "You should not be our next ruler."

I blinked. "I thought you were happy for me."

"Happy?" She scoffed. "I have been eating antacids every day just to fake this so-called 'happiness.' You *sicken* me."

My mouth parted as everything slid into place. "It was you. You left the notes." When she told me that people weren't happy I was here, I'd never imagined *she* was the unhappy one.

"Yes!" She leaned forward, a fierceness entering her features and wiping away every trace of warmth.

From day one, I'd thought Dayo had my back and would help me navigate the royal waters. My brain couldn't comprehend just how wrong I'd been.

"All of them?"

"Every single one." She pointed an accusing finger my way. "I could not believe it when Jomi told me you existed."

"Wait, what?" Why would the head of the royal council tell Dayo anything?

"We see each other privately."

"He's married."

She rolled her eyes. "Women in my family have been comforting men in power for generations. It is not something to be ashamed of. I can help him in ways his wife cannot."

"Dayo . . ." I whispered.

"He told me about you, and my heart broke. And when *he* approved you, saw you fit to rule a country, after years of promising to promote me in politics, I could not believe it. Even threatening to tell his wife did not gain me what was rightfully mine."

"So you thought, what, I would just say there's a better person for the job and leave?"

"Exactly. But no, you thought you could make some changes. Donating Bibles to the churches. Having food delivered to the poorer areas. None of that makes you fit to be queen."

"Then what does?" I sat back. I wished there were a panic button under my desk to alert Nonso and the rest of security.

"Blood!" She stabbed a finger at her chest. "Royal blood. And yours has been tainted by that American woman who saw to Tayo's death."

My heart wrenched.

"How the king ever found you satisfactory is beyond me."

"So because I'm half-American, I'm not royal enough?"

"Clearly. Not when there is a better option right here in Ọlọrọ."

"Who, Dayo? Surely you don't believe Sijuwola would have done a better job than me or Grandfather?"

She sneered. "That sniveling man could never be king. I am talking about me." She threw her arms wide. "Right here. I have been waiting and waiting to be seen, but he refused."

What? What was she saying?

I stared deep into her eyes, past the pain, past the anger, trying to see to her beginnings. "Who are you?"

"Dayo Layeni, daughter to Iyanu Layeni and"—her lips curved with pleasure—"Tiwa Jimoh Adebayo, king of Ọlọrọ Ilé Ijọba."

FIFTY-FIVE

No," I whispered. "That can't be true." Shock stunned my system.

"Oh yes. I am the illegitimate daughter of the king."

How was this real? How could Dayo be claiming to be my aunt? "What? How?" I sputtered, searching for understanding.

"There was a time when the king and the queen had separate bedchambers. Rumors abounded. Some believed it was because she did not bring forth an heir and the king found her lacking. Others believed her grief over a barren womb kept her to her quarters. Regardless, my mother sought to comfort the king during this trial."

My lunch churned in my stomach. How could Grandfather cheat? Every word out of Dayo's mouth tore down the foundation of my beliefs. Were they merely carefully constructed lies, or had I not known Grandfather as well as I'd assumed?

"Màmá was there until he decided he no longer needed her. He forced her to retire and bought her a house in Etikun. How easy it was for him not to think two more thoughts of her. A year later, the queen gave birth to Tayo, but I was born two months earlier."

"No," I rasped. "No. You're lying."

"I have no reason to lie."

"Did Grandfather know? Did he know about you?" Oh, how I hated to ask, but I needed to know.

"He had to."

I straightened. "You're not sure?" Then she had to be lying. This was all a ruse to find her way to the throne.

"He *had* to. I look like him. Màmá said he was my father."

I did not see Grandfather in her facial features, but we all saw what we wanted to see. More important was the validity of her mother's accusation. "Did your mom ever do a DNA test?"

Her eyes narrowed. "Are you insinuating something?"

"No." *Yes!* Of course I was. I couldn't just take Dayo's word for it. There had to be some kind of protocol in place for this, right? "Please, Dayo. Was there a DNA test?"

"No. You cannot just take a piece of hair from the king and ship it to a DNA site." She stared at me as if I had just claimed the sky was pink.

I sighed. "Is that why you've come to me? You want me to prove you're his daughter?"

"And step down and turn over succession to me. You have not been coronated. There is still time left. Otherwise, I am afraid my brother will have to take drastic measures."

"There are *two* of you?" I shouted. "I thought you were an only child."

"He is a half sibling. We have the same mother but *not* the same father."

"And you have him on speed dial to, what, kill me?"

"No, Bri Bayo. My brother will end the days of the prince if you do not cooperate."

My blood ran cold. Surely Mori's guards would not let him come to harm. "Tomori is safe. He is in the palace."

"And one call from my brother will ensure he leaves through the palace runner tunnels and gets to my brother unseen and unguarded."

"Why would Tomori do that?"

"Because if you do not do as I ask, my brother will claim to be holding you hostage."

No, no, *no!*

"Who is your brother?"

"Ekon Diallo."

Her words rang loud in the depth of my silence.

My stomach dipped. "Gross. Are you telling me I went on a date with my uncle?"

"He is not related to you at all." Dayo rolled her eyes. "I would not do something so vile."

Still, knowing Dayo was my aunt and that I'd dated her brother was some kind of twisted.

"I wanted to ensure my rise to power as legitimately as possible. If you had chosen Ekon as your prince, he would have willingly signed over power to me."

"But Ọlọrọ is a hereditary monarchy. You could have simply gone to the council with your allegations."

"I did not think they would let someone as common as me rule." She pursed her lips. "Hence the reason I was sleeping with Jomi. But he failed me. I thought surely my brother would not. I am the one who told Ladipo about the decree, told him Ekon would make the perfect prince if the rest of the council did not vote against you."

"Did he know your aim?"

"Of course not. Only Jomi knew how much I wanted a better lot in life. I wanted a spot on the council if I could not have the throne."

"Does he know who your . . . father is?" I swallowed the acid rising up my throat.

She shook her head, resting her hands on her knee once more. "That is my ace, and I have guarded it quite closely."

"What exactly do you want me to do?"

"Abdicate." She leaned forward, a determined look in her eyes. "There is a decree that states you can abdicate and name your successor. I would have to get council approval, but if they approved *you*, surely they will approve me. I have Jomi already on my side. And I know Ladipo would do cartwheels to see you return to the States."

I rubbed my forehead and said a prayer for wisdom.

"I can draw up the official paperwork and deliver it to Jomi myself." She smiled as if it were all settled.

"I don't understand something. What was Ekon's part in all this?"

"He was supposed to get you to choose him. Imagine my disgust when you chose Tomori. I should have steered you away from those language lessons."

"And Jomi told you council secrets."

"I am a very, very good companion."

I resisted the urge to look at her with all the judgment rolling around in my head. "Did you have any other help?"

"Just Nonso. He made sure to pause the camera feed when I needed to go into your room."

"Why would he do that?"

Her smile was full of secrets, the same one she used when talking about her relationship with Jomi. Did she use all of her relationships for her benefit?

"What about Azu and Merrick?"

"I did not get anyone else's help."

I wanted to believe Dayo, but this whole situation proved too much for my brain to comprehend. The head of security. A royal council member. Ekon. There were too many people she had used, and they would all have to be held accountable.

"How about this?" I offered. "If a DNA test proves you are Grandfather's daughter, then I will sign your papers."

Her head shook vehemently. "No. I want them signed now."

Ugh. Why did she have to be so difficult? "The council will want your claims verified. Having the test result will only go in your favor. I could ask Dr. Falade to perform the task discreetly."

Because I had yet to clean out Grandfather's room, there was bound to be some hair or DNA in there. If not, couldn't they figure it out by testing my DNA against hers?

"Sign them now!" she shouted.

"No," I snapped back.

"Have it your way." She pulled her cell out of her pocket.

I scrambled around the desk and lunged for it. We both gripped the phone, each of us trying to wrench it away from the other. I would have to make Dayo's height a disadvantage. I clung to her mobile, then dropped my weight, praying she'd loosen her grip.

Instead, she toppled over me. Furious, she slapped me. "Let go!" she screamed.

There was a scuffle, and then my door banged against the wall and all at once, Dayo was lifted off me. She kicked, screaming for Azu and Merrick to unhand her. I sat there, too stunned to make any movement as they hauled her out of the office.

Azu barked orders into his Bluetooth, and soon another guard appeared, offering to help me up from the floor. I dusted off my slacks.

"Are you hurt, Your Majesty?"

"No," I murmured, ignoring the sting in my cheek. "Has the prince been notified?"

"Let me check." He took a few steps away, then came back. "He has now."

"Thank you."

"Please sit, Your Majesty."

"Brielle?" Mori called, and the guard waved him in.

Mori wrapped his arms around me. "Are you okay, arídunnú mi?"

I peered into his eyes as he smoothed the hair away from my face. "You've said that before. What does it mean?"

"Loosely translated, 'the one who makes my heart happy.'"

"Oh, Tomori," I sighed. "You make my heart happy too."

He bent to press his forehead against mine. "Are you fine?"

"I am now."

FIFTY-SIX

Life had returned to normal. Well, almost. Dayo was currently in jail, awaiting trial. I'd had Dr. Falade send off samples for a DNA test, trusting his discretion. Jomi and Ekon were on house arrest as they waited to hear if they would be punished for their involvement in Dayo's scheme. Nonso had been fired from his position as head of security and would be punished by the council instead of the courts.

Meanwhile, Iris and I were out looking at commercial properties. I peeked at my watch. "Lunchtime," I whispered to her.

"Oh, I lost track of the time." She turned to the agent who had been showing us around. "Could we continue after lunch? Maybe meet back at your office in an hour?"

"Sure, Ms. Blakely," the gentleman said. He bowed before me. "Your Majesty."

I nodded in acknowledgment. We left the building, arm in arm, and Iris let out a puff of air.

"Worried?" I asked.

"More impatient than anything." She laughed. "I so wanted to find the perfect place on the first try. I guess that was a pipe dream."

Considering we'd viewed five already, definitely. "You'll find a place," I said instead. "I have faith." I thanked Merrick as he held open the SUV car door.

He'd been extra courteous since the whole Dayo fiasco. He felt awful that he hadn't taken the insider threat seriously enough. He'd worked hard this past week to assure me of his loyalty to his job and to the crown. Azu had been promoted to head of security. He'd tried to turn the offer down and remain on my detail, but I needed someone I could trust at the top. Which meant Merrick now drove me everywhere and had a new sidekick.

Traveling to Etikun this time was very different from the first time Iris and I had visited. Back then I'd been able to walk about freely. I now had a second car full of security detail following me—Mori and Azu had insisted. Not that I had anything to worry about. Uncle Sijuwola had been quite cordial at the last family dinner.

Iris couldn't believe the whodunit. And she'd been oddly subdued about Ekon's connection. If I didn't know any better, I'd think she had a crush on him. At this point, it seemed rude to ask.

The new guard brought our food, passing it to the back seat. I said grace, then bit into the paii. It was just as delicious as I remembered. "I need to ask the chef to add these to the palace menu."

Iris laughed. "You'd blow up eating these every day."

Not a bad way to gain weight, in my opinion.

Iris's phone pinged, and she gasped. "The flat I really want just became available." She squealed. "Let's go look."

"Okay."

I was sad at the idea of Iris moving out of the palace but took heart that she'd still be in the country. We'd already agreed to make a standard lunch date and girls' night.

We arrived at the flats in record time. They were situated in the heart of Etikun. A sage- and emerald-green building rose a few stories in the air.

"Is that it?" I asked.

"Mm-hmm." Iris smiled. "They're brand-new and had a wait list." She held up her cell. "I got an email saying I could come look and see if I wanted to enter into a rental agreement."

"How many bedrooms are you looking at?"

"Two. Just in case my parents ever want to visit. They're disappointed I don't plan to move back."

"Understandable. You've been near them your entire life."

Iris rolled her eyes. "My brother called me and said thanks a lot. Now they'll be all up in his business."

I laughed. "He's a bit dramatic."

"Just a little."

"Your Majesty," Merrick said as he put the car in park, "wait until the new guy checks the premises."

"Merrick, by now I know not to jump out of the car."

He shook his head. "I apologize, Your Majesty."

I sighed. He'd lost some of his joy, and it broke my heart. I leaned forward. "You have to stop with the *ho-hum* act. I'm fine. You helped saved the day. Please go back to your old self. Pretty please." I held up my hands and widened my eyes, going for the adorable wide-eyed routine.

Merrick shook his head. "It should not have happened."

"Well, now we know to install a panic button or some other device so you can burst through the door like a superhero," I said.

"We will do that, and I will find a time to joke when I am not insanely worried about your safety."

"Fair enough."

I sat back just as the new guy came back to the car. "We are good to go."

We got out, and Iris practically bounced up the walkway.

"I have a good feeling about this," she said.

"So do I." The property was nice, and the sun practically gleamed on the new windows.

We stopped at the office to meet the agent, who led us up to the vacant apartment—uh, flat—on the third floor. So much light filtered into the space. I commented on it to Iris, who quickly agreed. After we finished looking, we walked back to the leasing office, where the agent gave us time to discuss.

"What are you going to do?" I asked Iris.

She bit her lip. "I want it. I love it. But my fear is, what if the business location falls through?"

"I understand the worry, but isn't Etikun where you wanted to help first anyway? It makes sense that your apartment would be here too."

"That's the other thing," she said as if I hadn't offered advice. "Should I be living in something so new? Something so . . . rich?"

I laughed. "You're asking the woman who lives in a palace?"

"True." Iris sighed. "I think I'll take it. And continue praying that the commercial contract will be approved."

"Good idea."

When we got back to the palace, I had a note from my new secretary to contact Dr. Falade. My stomach dropped. Was I ready for the results? I texted Mori.

> **Me**
> The results are in. Are you able to be here when I call Dr. F?

> **Mori**
> Give me five minutes. Where are you?

> **Me**
> My office, but I'll head to our room.

> **Mori**
> K

I rushed to my room, and a couple of minutes later, Mori waltzed in behind me. He wrapped his arms around me, and I leaned back into his embrace.

"I'm nervous."

"Whatever the results, we will handle it together."

"You're right."

"Come. Call him."

He led me to the balcony. I curled up next to him in our big chair and waited for Dr. Falade to answer the phone.

"Hello, Your Majesty."

"Ẹ káàsán, Dr. Falade."

"I have the results."

"I'm ready."

Mori wrapped his arm around me.

"The king was not her father."

A breath whooshed out of me, and tears of relief sprang to my eyes. "Are you positive?"

"Yes. However, it looks like Lanre is."

"What?" I sat up.

"Yes, Your Majesty. Lanre is her father. Ms. Layeni's mother must have gotten it wrong."

"Thank you. Could you please send a copy to me?"

I didn't know what I would do with the information. Dayo had shared that her mother passed a few years back. Did I just tell Dayo? Let her tell Lanre? Confront him myself? I wasn't sure.

"Yes, Your Majesty."

"Thank you."

"My pleasure."

"The king was not her father?" Mori asked.

I shook my head. "Lanre is."

"I did not see that coming."

"Neither did I."

"You will tell her?"

I nodded. "But not today. Maybe after the coronation."

Mori brushed his lips over my temple once, twice. I turned, wrapping my arms around him. My heart filled with love and happiness. The worries of tomorrow would remain, but at least in this moment, life was kind to me.

FIFTY-SEVEN

I stared at my reflection in the mirror. The gold dress fit my frame perfectly. The bodice cinched in at my waist, which was covered in swirly ornamentation that matched the embellishment on the gold cape that fell against my back. Iris had done an amazing job picking out the fabric for my coronation dress. But despite looking and feeling regal, my hands still shook. I couldn't believe the day had come for me to be crowned queen.

So much had happened since I'd first stepped foot on Ọlọrọ Ilé. There was a surreal aspect to knowing coronation day had finally arrived. I desperately wanted to ask Grandfather for advice, but memories and the personal journals I'd found in his office would have to see me through the years. Mobo had chosen not to retire and to remain as Mori's royal secretary. Thankfully, we'd have his wisdom and advice in the years to come. Plus, each night Tomori had prayed that God would bless us, especially me, with wisdom upon this day.

Now I just waited for the signal to make my entrance into the throne room. I would be crowned queen and Mori king. Afterward, I would take the oath as ruling monarch and be presented to the onlookers as reigning queen and ruler. Mobo had gone over the order of the ceremony so many times I could recite the procession in my sleep. In fact, I'd had many dreams about the ceremony.

"Brielle, you ready?" Iris called through the door. She'd given me a moment just to sit and be. My time was up.

I cleared my throat. "Yes." This was it. The path that God had prepared before me.

The door opened, and Iris stepped into the royal dressing room. "You okay?"

I shrugged. There was no way I could put into words all that I was feeling.

"I know you're probably scared, but I also know that God's got you." She sighed. "I don't mean that as a platitude. Nor to diminish any of what you're feeling. Simply as a reassurance that no matter what you *are* feeling, God will see you through. He's brought you so far, Bri. If you look back at where you were and your journey to now, you'd know it. You'd see His handiwork."

"I do. I really do." I hugged Iris. "What would I ever do without your friendship?"

"Luckily I'll be around." She giggled, joy making her cheeks rosy. "Let's pray before you go out there."

"Good idea."

"Heavenly Father, today we come before You, asking that assurance and peace fill Bri's heart. That she remember You have placed her here and will continue to guide her. I know that Bri seeks You first in all things, but I pray she remembers always to do so. Help her know that if she makes mistakes as a queen, nothing will be wasted. You work all things for good because she believes and trusts in You. Please refresh her with a spirit of confidence as she walks into her purpose that You have crafted specifically for her. We pray that You would guide Tomori in his new role and that the people will feel blessed to have them as their king and queen."

She paused, and I continued to feel the warmth that had flooded my heart halfway through her prayer.

"Lord," I spoke, "thank You for blessing me with the best friend I could ever ask for. Please bless her for blessing me with such a beautiful prayer. Please prepare her way for her new business venture as she seeks to be the hands and feet of Jesus. May we both give You the glory in all that we do. In Your Son's precious name."

"Amen," we chimed.

Iris squeezed my hand, then snuck out so she could join the onlookers in the throne room. I took in a steady breath, held it for a few seconds, and blew the air out slowly. I practiced the measured breaths, repeating some of the words of Iris's prayer as I hoped for a supernatural confidence to overcome me. I didn't want to appear nervous before the people. Didn't want anyone to doubt Grandfather's choice to make me his successor. Didn't want to fail him either.

Even though I still felt so very inadequate.

My strength is made perfect in weakness.

My eyes watered as understanding flooded me. How could I forget that feeling inadequate wasn't something to fear but a moment for me to come before the Lord, laying my troubles at His feet? He was fully capable of solving them all and blessing me with talents and skills I hadn't thought I was capable of before.

"Thank You, Lord. Thank You for the sweet reminder."

Lightness sealed my heart. I didn't have to be a perfect queen. I didn't have to know everything. I'd been provided with a royal council who knew the ins and outs. Grandfather had left his wisdom behind in his journals, Mobo gifted Tomori and me with his vast knowledge. I had my best friend to encourage me and a husband to love me through whatever came our way.

I was inordinately blessed. God had indeed provided me with all that I needed.

The door opened, and a royal guard bowed. "They are ready for you, Your Majesty."

I'd missed the calling of my name. No matter. I walked through the door, hands gently folded before me, and strolled down the purple carpet leading to the formal thrones. I could hear camera shutters snapping. Other than that, silence blanketed the room as I stopped before the raised dais holding the chairs of the king and queen.

Mobo had already told me that I would sit in Grandfather's throne, the one marked for a king. Since I would be ruling and not Tomori, my husband would take the chair marked for the spouse.

366

"People of Ọlọrọ Ilé, we are gathered here today to see the crowning of Princess Brielle Eden Eesuola Adebayo," Mr. Ladipo intoned. "The Ọlọrọ Ilé Royal Council has recognized her as the successor of our late and beloved King Tiwa Jimoh Adebayo. We accept her as our ruler and will now crown her as such."

His steady voice rang out in the throne room despite the number of people gathered to watch. I waited as a palace runner dressed in royal garb brought a crown on a purple velvet pillow. The gold crown was a lot taller than my tiara, showing the country's native agate surrounded by diamonds.

Mr. Ladipo took it from the pillow and stepped down the dais. I knelt on the cushioned pad that had been placed before me for this purpose.

"I, Adeyemi Ladipo, alàgbà tribu of the Òkè tribe, crown you Royal Queen Brielle Eden Eesuola Adebayo of Ọlọrọ Ilé." He placed the crown on my head, then backed away.

He led me in the oath, my right hand raised throughout its entirety. I was so thankful I'd taken the time to memorize it even though it was a call and repeat. Cheers filled the room as I uttered the final words.

A runner came, offering me his arm as I rose.

Mr. Ladipo gestured to the monarch's throne. "Please take your seat as our queen."

I walked up the stairs, swung my cape to the right, and sat. Applause and cheers filled the room. I caught my mom's eye as she dabbed at the tears running down her face. She'd flown back for the ceremony and would return to the States tomorrow. Iris gave me a thumbs-up, and I sent her a grin before facing the people once more.

After a few minutes, Mr. Ladipo held up his hand. "Now we seek to crown the prince and husband to our great queen. Please bring forth the prince."

The crowd quieted once more as the door across from the chamber I'd been waiting in opened. My pulse picked up as Tomori strolled down the purple carpet, confidence pouring from him. My heart burst with pride as he stopped in front of the dais. He looked perfectly handsome in a white tunic edged in gold, with gold pants underneath. His outfit complemented mine perfectly.

"People of Ọlọrọ Ilé, we are gathered here today to see the crowning of Prince Tomori Debare Eesuola é Adebayo. The Ọlọrọ Ilé Royal Council has recognized him as the rightful prince of our queen and a suitable husband and father to the future line of the Adebayo heirs. We will now elevate him to king."

Tomori knelt on the pillow, and Mr. Ladipo lifted the crown that had been commissioned for him to wear. I was still amazed someone had taken the time and had the skills to create the crowns for us. They were stunning. Tomori's crown did not have the same height as mine but was still more regal than his princely crown.

"I, Adeyemi Ladipo, alàgbà tribu of the Òkè tribe, crown you King Tomori Debare Eesuola é Adebayo of Ọlọrọ Ilé."

Tomori made his way up the dais and sat next to me. Cheers erupted as the people applauded him. I looked to the side where his family stood, and his mom was hunched over, most likely bawling her eyes out, judging from the look on Nika's face as she discreetly tried to pass a handkerchief.

"I now present to you the queen and king of Ọlọrọ Ilé Ijọba of Africa."

I didn't know what the future held, but God had been with me every step of the way. Through the trenches filled with hardship and heartache, through crests of love and triumphant accomplishment. I didn't know what Ọlọrans would say of my reign, but one thing I knew—they would say I loved God, loved my country, and loved my husband.

Dictionary

Àlàáfià—peace
alága—chairman
alàgbà—elder (male)
akara—bean bread balls
amure—sash
Arábìbrin [first name] Aya [last name]—Mrs.
arídunnú mi—the one who makes my heart happy
bàbá—father
bàbá àgbà—grandfather
bẹẹni—yes
ẹ káàárò—morning greeting
ẹ k'aabọ—welcome
ẹ káàsán—afternoon greeting
ẹ káalé—night greeting
ẹ ku idaji—early morning greeting
ẹ kúròlé—evening greeting
ẹ má bínú sí mi—don't be annoyed with me / I'm sorry
ẹ seun—thank you
gèlè—headwrap

ilé—house
kò tópé—you're welcome (it's not worthy of thanks)
màmá—mom
mo dúpẹ—I'm grateful
ó dàbọ—good-bye
ó dàárò—good night
oba—king
Ògbéni—Mr.
Omidan—Miss
ómọ ómọ—grandchild
ọmọba—prince/princess
paii—pie
rárá—no

Author's Note

Dear Reader,

I want first to thank you for taking the time to read *In Search of a Prince*. This story held my heart from beginning to end. I pray you enjoyed Brielle's journey to becoming the queen of Ọlọrọ Ilé, Africa. I wanted to write this note to make clear the parts of the story that were fictionalized and the parts that were based on truth.

Ọlọrọ Ilé is very much a fictional location dreamed up in my imagination. I wanted this book to have an African setting, but I also wanted to ensure I didn't get any details of location, people, and culture incorrect. Since I've never had the privilege to visit the vast continent of Africa and I wrote this book during a global pandemic, I didn't have the opportunity to research the beauty of Africa in person. Instead, I elicited the expertise of a sensitivity reader from Nigeria to ensure I portrayed certain parts of the culture as realistically as possible while allowing me the freedom to fictionalize some things for the sake of a contemporary romance novel.

The Onina language spoken by the characters in this book actually features many words from the language of Yoruba spoken in Nigeria. Onina is not a real language, but Yoruba is spoken by millions of people. I changed the name of the language to go along with the history of the island country I made up. I also took license to use certain words for names and places in Ọlọrọ, so not all words may have been used as originally intended.

In creating Ọlọrọ Ilé, I researched several islands off the western coast of Africa and certain tribes of Nigeria to help create a different world in Ọlọrọ Ilé but lend authenticity as well.

I pray you forgive me for anything that rang false or untrue within these pages. Truly, my heartfelt goal was to take you on a journey to a new place while avoiding the pitfalls of inaccuracy. Thank you again for reading *In Search of a Prince*.

Blessings,
Toni

Acknowledgments

Ack! I can't believe the end is here. There have been so many people who have helped me, from the conception of this story idea all the way to publication. I have so many of y'all to thank, and I'll do so in no particular order.

Thank you, Rachel McMillian, for taking a chance on me and representing me. I appreciate all you've done and your encouragement in the process. You rock!

To my awesome critique partners Andrea Boyd, Jaycee Weaver, and Sarah Monzon. You ladies are like family, and I am so glad I get to journey with you. Thank you for your insights, suggestions, and prayers! Love you all!

A special thank you to my two alpha readers, Carrie Schmidt and Ebos Aifuobhokhan. Carrie, your kind words fueled me to the end! Thank you for all the support. Ebos, what can I say but a huge thanks. Thank you for answering all my questions about the region and showing me where I needed to be more realistic, sensitive, or could let my imagination run wild. I appreciate you.

Thanks to Benjamin Worlund for answering all my fishing questions, to Katie Ganshert for answering my nonprofit questions, and to Ochegba Adejo for spelling questions about Yoruba.

I'd love to thank the entire Bethany House Publishers team. From the interest from Raela, to the edits, cover designs, etc. I've been in awe during the entire process. Thank you so much for making my dream come true.

Last but not least, I'd like to thank my husband and kids. Glenn, thank you for listening to me talk about my "princess story" over and over. I'm sure I made your eyes glaze over a time or two. To my boys, thanks for putting up with me going around the house yelling "Bethany House" at random times. I love y'all!

Toni Shiloh is a wife, mom, and multipublished Christian contemporary romance author. She writes to bring God glory and to learn more about His goodness. Her novel *Grace Restored* was a 2019 Holt Medallion finalist, and *Risking Love* is a 2020 Selah Award finalist. A member of the American Christian Fiction Writers (ACFW), the Virginia Chapter, Toni seeks to help readers find authors. She loves connecting with readers and authors alike via social media. You can learn more about her writing at www.tonishiloh.com.

Sign Up for Toni's Newsletter

Keep up to date with Toni's news on book releases and events by signing up for her email list at tonishiloh.com.

You May Also Like . . .

After moving cross-country with her son and accepting a filmmaker's mentorship, Val Locklier is caught between her insecurities and new possibilities. Miles McKenzie returns home to find a new tenant is living upstairs and he's been banished to a ministry on life support. As sparks fly, they discover that authentic love and sacrifice must go hand in hand.

All That It Takes by Nicole Deese
nicoledeese.com

◊ BETHANYHOUSE

 Stay up to date on your favorite books and authors with our free e-newsletters. Sign up today at bethanyhouse.com.

 facebook.com/bethanyhousepublishers   @bethanyhousefiction

OB Free exclusive resources for your book group at bethanyhouseopenbook.com

More Captivating Fiction

When pediatric heart surgeon Sebastian Grant meets Leah Montgomery, his fast-spinning world comes to a sudden stop. And when Leah receives surprising news while assembling a family tree, he helps her comb through old hospital records to learn more. But will attaining their deepest desires require more sacrifices than they imagined?

Let It Be Me by Becky Wade
A MISTY RIVER ROMANCE
beckywade.com

After hitting rock bottom, January decides she has nothing to lose in working at her aunt's church—while hiding a lack of faith. A minor deception until she meets the church's guitarist and sparks fly. Can she avoid disaster—especially when a handsome landscape architect has an annoying ability to push her to deal with feelings she'd rather keep buried?

Love and a Little White Lie by Tammy L. Gray
STATE OF GRACE
tammylgray.com

More than a century apart, two women search for the lost. Despite her father's Confederate leanings, Clara is determined to help an enslaved woman reunite with her daughter; Alice can't stop wondering what happened to her mother in the aftermath of Hurricane Katrina. Faced with the unknown, both women will have to dig deep to let their courage bloom.

Where the Last Rose Blooms by Ashley Clark
HEIRLOOM SECRETS
ashleyclarkbooks.com

❖ BETHANYHOUSE

More from Bethany House

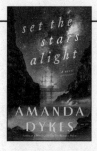

Reeling from the loss of her parents, Lucy Claremont discovers an artifact under the floorboards of their London flat, leading her to an old seaside estate. Aided by her childhood friend Dashel, a renowned forensic astronomer, she starts to unravel a history of heartbreak, sacrifice, and love begun 200 years prior—one that may offer the healing each of them seeks.

Set the Stars Alight by Amanda Dykes
amandadykes.com

After an abusive relationship derails her plans, Adri Rivera struggles to regain her independence and achieve her dream of becoming an MMA fighter. She gets a second chance, but the man who offers it to her is Max Lyons, her former training partner, whom she left heartbroken years before. As she fights for her future, will she be able to confront her past?

After She Falls by Carmen Schober
carmenschober.com

Tally Smucker's quiet world is shaken when her neighbor Danielle—who grew up Plain but joined the Army—returns in need of a friend. Tally invites Danielle to join her quilting circle, and they are both inspired by a story told of a WWI soldier. But when disaster hits Tally's family and Danielle's PTSD becomes unmanageable, can they find the hope they need?

Threads of Hope by Leslie Gould
PLAIN PATTERNS #3
lesliegould.com

⬧BETHANYHOUSE